GUARDIANS SAGA VOLUME ONE

MYSTGATE

SANDRA SALAS

ISBN: 979-8-9927713-0-5

To Jason.
Without you by my side I would be adrift in this world.
I am who I am today because of your endless encourage-
ment, support, and sense of humor that can make me
laugh even in the darkest hour.
Thank you for being my rock in the storm.

Mystgate is a nonstop action fantasy adventure set deep in the Appalachian Mountains, beyond normal human sight.

It is a story about the brave Warriors of the Citadel Alliance who fight day in and day out to protect the Earth's realm. A new threat disrupts our hard-fought peace and stability of this land, and the reality as we know it hangs in the balance.

This adventure includes elements of war, battle, hand-to-hand combat, blood, intense violence, brutal injuries, death, graphic language, and sexual situations.

Please take note and prepare to immerse yourselves in the Guardians who protect this realm.

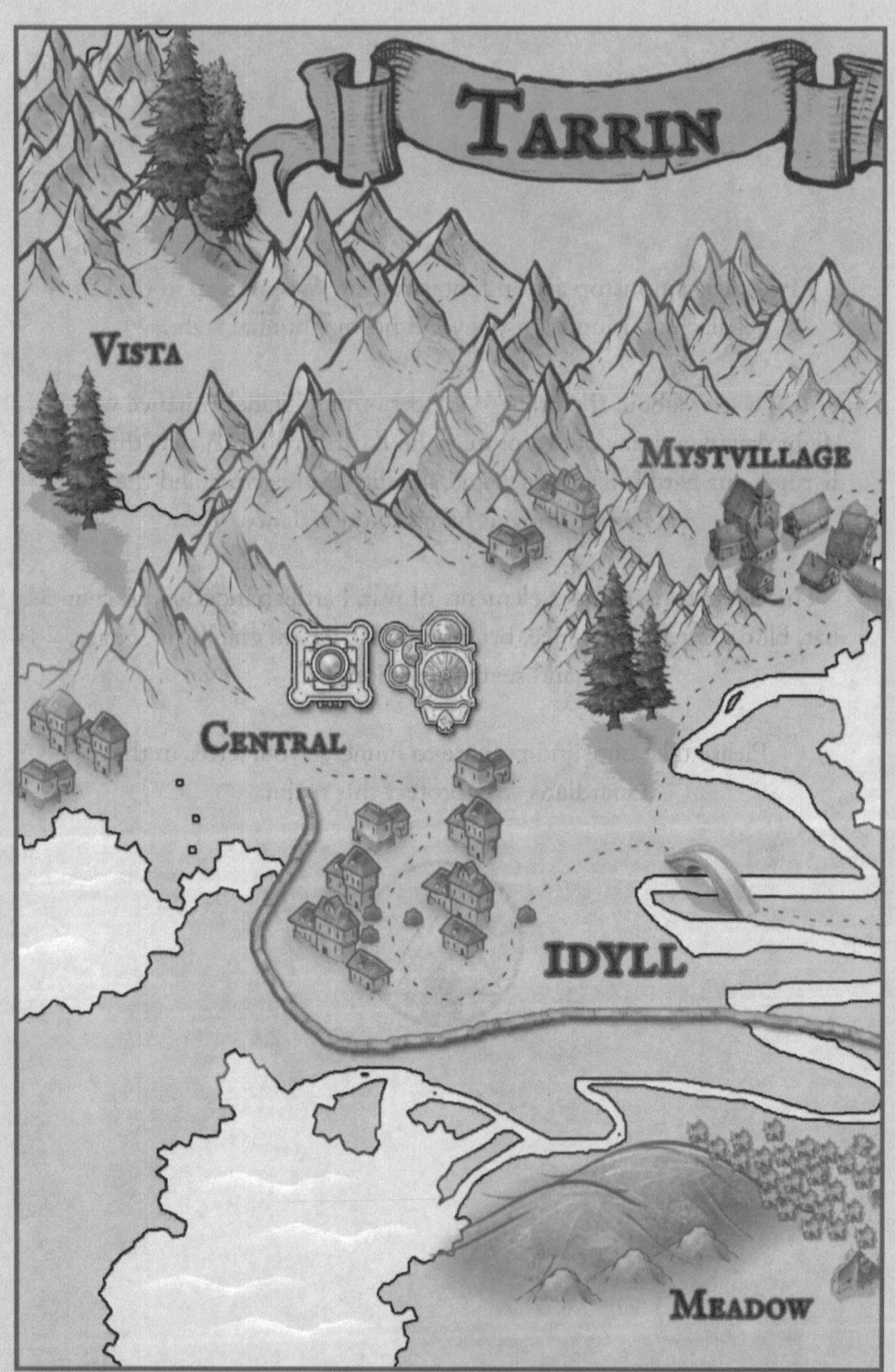

THE CHEROKEE CALLED THESE MOUNTAINS
"SHACONAGE" (SHA-KON-O-HEY), WHICH MEANS
"LAND OF BLUE SMOKE."

PROLOGUE

ate-afternoon sunlight filters through the dense canopy of the forest. Despite the shady afternoon, sweat trickles down my brow as my focus stays unwavering. We are close, closing in on our target. Months of tracking and strategic planning have led us to this grove. This specific time.

I look to my right and see Aden and Keenan in formation. Five years ago, I started my service at Vista Command with those two remarkable soldiers. Beyond Aden and Keenan, I see Kyle, one of our newest soldiers on the team. Kyle arrived a year ago, breathing new life back into our squad. He brought with him a drive and determination that had slowly leaked away from our team over the years. He is the reason we got the tip and are moving forward today. I pause, evaluating how close we are to the edge of the cliff. Through the coms, I say, "Standby."

I hear the response from the team. "Roger that, Garrett."

I look down at my screen strapped to my chest and see the cliff about two hundred yards straight ahead of us, the lake spreading out beyond the cliff.

I look at my watch—we still have time. Our intel, just received an hour ago, suggests a faction member meeting will take place at the edge of the lake at approximately 5 p.m. My watch reads 4:30, and we need to get into position.

I look through the canopy of trees toward the team, peering through the dense foliage. Autumn has lit the forest in a fiery display of color. Sugar maple and yellow birch trees create a kaleidoscope of reds, yellows, and oranges. I look at Kyle, Aden, and Keenan through the landscape and motion with my hands to keep moving forward.

We all feel the weight of being one step behind our targets. There is no room for error this time. Days of tracking our targets turned to weeks; weeks turned to months. Every time the intel suggests a meeting, the meeting location is empty. Every time we are closing in on a faction member's identity, they slip through our fingers. Meanwhile, the creatures are attacking, seemingly helped by these faction members, their motive still unknown.

One more delay could cause more lives to be lost. One more delay could result in another outpost being destroyed. One more delay could mean this is the time the monsters escape beyond the wards into the defenseless territory. Tarrin soldiers are the last line of protection against nightmares that, somehow, are slithering through the barrier. A barrier that has been held for a thousand years.

We move as one unit. Our training makes it muscle reflex, our loyalty to each other instinctual. Bonds formed that ordinary people have a tough time grasping. We rely on each other, especially when things are at their worst, through thick and thin. Mutual experiences cutting deep into our souls, leaving wounds that never fully heal. We have grown together by enduring these hardships.

The brutal fight is endless. Daily reports of wounded comrades, reports of dark creature hordes multiplying at alarming rates. The outpost that fell to a horde last year devastated our forces.

I see the ridge up ahead. We spread out silently. Ten feet apart, steadily moving forward. Aden updates his position, "Ten meters out."

Kyle thrums through the coms as the team moves forward. "Oscar Mike." There is a pause and a moment of radio silence.

Then I hear Keenan reply, "In position."

I sweep my Mark 6 binoculars down the ridge, focusing on the shoreline of the lake. I radio back, "Confirmed, in position." I begin to latch my harness and attach it to the tree's heavy exposed roots for our even-tual descent down the back side of the cliff.

We are on a peninsula, camouflaged by the dense foliage on the out-ermost point. On our left is the intended target's meeting location. The cliff tapers off to the forest floor approximately two hundred yards down, where we suspect our targets will be utilizing transport for the creatures.

I peer over the edge of the cliff. We have a good advantage from our position and should be able to get down the back side of the mountain undetected. I sweep my binoculars from left to right, following the gravel road that encompasses the perimeter of the lake. The water spreads out in front of us, sparkling in the late-day sun.

Keenan's voice filters over the coms. "I got eyes on the target." Inter-rupting the peaceful scene, tires crunch on the dirt road, and finally an engine roars to a stop. Zooming in on my binoculars, I see a blacked-out van. Until this point, we have only grainy surveillance footage from a drone to base the faction members' activity on. This is the first time we have laid eyes on the faction members in person.

As the van stops, two faction members get out. Dressed in an all-black ensemble, cargo pants tucked into shit kickers, long sleeves, cap over the head, and gators covering the lower part of their faces, they're indistinguishable, no identifying markers I can see. I check to make sure I am still recording the footage back to command.

I radio in, "You guys getting this?"

A moment later, I hear Manus's quick response from the pit, "Loud and clear, Garrett." The pit, how we lovingly refer to our surveillance department, is the eyes and ears of our Vista Command. Manus, the heart and soul of our surveillance and reconnaissance team, provides crucial information from the command center to the field. I check the screen strapped to my chest as I hear Manus over the coms.

"Two faction members seen getting out of the van, one lone faction member headed toward them from the forest, two creatures in tow. No other activity in the immediate vicinity."

I close the screen and go back to the binoculars. The two faction members scan their surroundings and head to the back of the van. They open the blacked-out doors and quickly unload two crates as the third member emerges from the forest. The newest member has two creatures in tow behind him, heading to the van and crates.

There is a collective intake of breath over the coms. These two creatures held captive today simultaneously let out a loud screech, disgusted at confinement. Wrapped around both necks are metal harnesses, a tether attached to the one member's hand. Black scales cover the faces and necks of these creatures, ending in their razor-sharp beaks. Their talons glint in the sunlight as they unfurl their wings covered in leathery hide. Standing about the height of a man with a wingspan twice that.

"Time to move." The starting command in our ears has our team propelled into movement. In unison, we each grab our rappelling cables, latch into the harnesses, and descend backward down the cliff, out of view of the beach.

I am closest to the peninsula. If I swing toward the edge, I can view the corner of the van. Halfway down, I pause, sitting back in the harness, ropes groaning slightly under my weight. In slow motion, I see the faction member who came out of the forest. He pivots, turning to stare upward, straight toward where we were sitting on the side of the cliff. I see a wicked smile light up his sinister eyes. Somehow, he knew we would be there.

That thought races through my mind as I radio on the mic, "We're blown. They know we are here." I pause for breath. "He knew we would be here."

With no hint of emotion, the faction member flicks his wrist, and I see a detonator in his hand. I hear on the radio from Manus in the command center, "Garrett, possible explosive!" I look up and scan the cliff. Obscured, set into a deep crevasse, I see a blinking red light of the devices set into the stone.

I shout, "Retreat!"

All four of us release the rigging and slide down the ropes, knowing we only have seconds to spare. A moment later, the bomb explodes above our heads, and the entire front of the peninsula implodes. The cliff above us dissolved, cascading down, obliterating our anchor to the trees. The earth starts to crumble, and I realize we are in the middle of a massive avalanche. The trees, rocks, and debris all come sliding down in one giant sheet of land, our team in the middle, as big as matchsticks compared to the trees around us. As the land slides, the sky and the ground start to tumble over and under me until I land in a heap at the base of the cliff in a cloud of debris.

I lift my head. Through red-rimmed eyes, I see the taillights of the van. I cough and choke on the dust still settling, a fine layer coating every inch of me. I hear the crunch of boots on the ground, doors slam, and an engine roar away. I drag myself from the wreckage, thankful for the helmet that kept my head in one piece. As I stare at the retreating lights, my rage boils to the surface, and I know we had failed our mission. Again.

I stumble toward the last-known location of my brothers and see Keenan in the distance pulling himself upright. I see Aden pushing up out of large rocks twenty feet away. My panic rises as I scan the perimeter. No, no, no... Where is Kyle? The sun beats down on my battered, bleeding face, and I see out of the corner of my eye a boot in the rubble.

I wave my arms and yell for help, the sound muffled, as if I were hearing myself through water. My voice horse, throat scratchy, hearing gone from the explosion. I see Keenan and Aden jumping over boulders and sliding down hills to get to us. I start digging, pulling cobblestones and rubble away from Kyle, tears streaming down my face, all the while fearing it is too late.

Finally uncovering Kyle's legs, I see a huge boulder sitting on his chest. His face untouched, it looks like he could be sleeping. I shift debris, cradling his head in my lap. I pulled his hand into mine. His runestone ring shimmered in the sunlight. His helmet falls to the side, as I catch a glimpse of the smiling faces of his wife, grown son, and young daughter in the still photo inside his helmet.

My bellow seemed to echo on forever.

ONE

Sophia—Museum

I sit in a stream of afternoon sunshine, relishing its warmth on my face, allowing a moment of peace to steal my soul. I push a stray lock of honey-colored hair that has come out of my low bun back from my forehead, enjoying the moment of quiet solitude. The museum doors just closed, and my real job is beginning. I have been posing as Sophia Evens for the last week, working as a curator for the Boston Natural History Museum. My role in presenting the Knoxville Museum of Natural History Native Art collection disguises my true objective. I will swap out the relic I am pursuing before the night shift starts tonight. Timing is everything.

"Oh, Ms. Evens, do you need anything before we close up for the day?" asks the normally very perky middle-aged museum director as she heads toward me in a rush. Her fizzled white-blonde hair has escaped her bun that started the day with every strand in place. Her harried expression tells me that my diversion tactic in the back warehouse has worked.

I smile at her neutrally. "No thank you, Ms. Williams. You have been so hospitable the past week. I am so grateful for your help." I am laying it on a bit thick, enjoying her squirming more than I should. "Today's my last day, and I will let my superiors know back in Boston how wonderful you have been."

"Yes, yes, of course," she replies distractedly. "If you don't mind, I have something to deal with in the back. If you could drop your set of keys off with Earl on your way out, I would appreciate it."

I murmur, "Sure, no problem."

With one final wave, she says, "Good night and safe travels!" Her perkiness is an innate personality trait that holds true despite the stress. She hurriedly turns to make her way back to the employees-only section of the museum.

I cover my small smile as I sweep my eyes downward toward the papers on the desk in front of me. Misplacing a new exhibition of sixteen oil paintings, on loan from a neighboring museum, is a surefire way to keep her busy. Once I am out of the museum, I will lift the glamor, and they will find the exhibition tucked behind the old statues in the back of the warehouse. I only wish I could be there to see their faces. Grinning to myself, I realize I am taking a little too much pleasure in creating chaos in the back room.

I tap my perfectly manicured red fingertips on the beautiful wooden desk as I wrap up my pretend paperwork. As soon as Ms. Williams is out of sight, I unwind from the desk. My glamor hides my true height and distinguishing hair color. My black Louboutins click on the marble floors, a flowing cream silk blouse tucked into a form-fitting black pencil skirt. I have a tall, lean frame with curves in all the right places.

As I walk, my hips sway, and I feed a tiny bit of energy into the camera to my right and the camera in the far corner, blurring the lens enough to seem like something flew in front of the cameras.

I walk toward the display in the back, one that has been there for a while. I look at the ancient collection of Native American artifacts, appraising the remnants for the specific object I found earlier this week. Right there, between a display of Native American garb on a headless mannequin and a beautiful ornately painted vase, is the object I am after. In a red velvet box, hanging on the wall amongst three other spears, is the Fae relic I found earlier this week.

Occasionally, Fae artifacts end up in human hands. The humans believe them to be of their own ancient civilization's, Native American descent in this specific region due to the age and recovery location. These artifacts in human hands can be dangerous. Only a Fae can control these relics, which harbor an innate magic.

Terrible things tend to happen when humans manage relics. Thankfully, when placed in a museum, they typically sit on a wall or shelf and collect dust. My task is to retrieve these items and bring them back to our command sector. Certain Fae may consider this a menial task, but I have been fully enjoying myself. Oh, how I love rare and sparkly things.

I slip the replacement spear that has been sitting on my back hidden from normal human view with the same glamor that alters my appearance. I glance around and swiftly insert the key, given to me upon arrival a week ago. I slip open the display case and swap out the exact replica of the spear for the real one. I slide the Fae relic back in the holster at my back, situating the hilt at the base of my neck. One final glance around the museum, and I am satisfied I have touched every object and know the rest are normal human treasures.

I walk toward the front of the museum, unclouding the cameras as I go, along with the glamor holding the poor paintings hostage in the back. I stroll down the long hallway toward the front, a little extra sway to my hips as I whistle a little tune. Snagging rare and valuable objects puts me in such a good mood.

As I get close to the front, I see out of the corner of my eye the middle-aged guard on duty. I put the key on the counter and send him a friendly wave. "Goodnight, Earl!"

He has been friendly to me this past week, ever the gentleman. "G'night, ma'am," he replies with a touch of his hat. I give him one last smile as I head out of the museum and into the late-afternoon sun.

Autumn is here, and I am fully embracing its languishing warmth, knowing winter is coming. These last drops of golden light remind me of Tarrin, my homeland, and I pause before getting into the vehicle. As I look at the changing color of leaves in the parking lot, a deep sadness trickles through the warmth of the afternoon. Tarrin is beautiful at this time of year, breathtakingly stunning in its deep reds and golds. I am a little homesick. I remember the smell of the forest, the curving river, nestled in the towering cove of hardwood forests. Autumn turns these valleys into sunbursts of color, the canopy of trees memorizing.

It has been a year since I was in Tarrin, and I can finally say my broken heart, although not healed, has had time to mend. The peace and quiet of my life outside of Tarrin allowed me to regroup unlike any other balm. This peaceful slice of the world is a temporary refuge. I know I am on borrowed time, and the peace has an expiration date.

Brenen would call this past year running from my problems. Maybe he is right.

This small slice of time has given me a glimpse of what my life could have been under different circumstances, different choices. Choices I look back on now and know deep down, even with how devastating the outcome was, I would never change. For as long as I could remember, my driving force was to serve and protect, until the day I could not protect the one person I cared about most.

Images of my sister Leona filter through my mind. We were twins, connected at the most basic level. Her absence has been a hole in my psyche, a missing piece of my soul that I will never get back. She died in my arms in the middle of Mirwood Forest with the same red, gold, and orange colors swaying overhead that I see in front of me now.

Leona and I were out on patrol. Upon returning, we found our remote outpost demolished, overran with dark creatures. It was unheard of, creatures forming a group to work together. They are solitary creatures by nature, this behavior a year ago like a puppeteer controlled them. The hunters became the hunted.

As we showed up on the scene, we fought off the creatures that were picking off comrades in the rubble of the facility. I turned after cutting down the last creature in my view, looking for Leona. I called out to her and heard a faint reply. I held her hand as the light went out of her eyes.

I blink and refocus, shrugging off these memories. I have discovered that the hurt never really goes away—you learn to live with it.

Annoyed with where my thoughts wandered, I focus on my surroundings. My head snaps up, and I have a nagging feeling that someone is watching me, due to years of experience, rather than any special talent. I scan the perimeter, seeing nothing out of the ordinary. I squint into the afternoon sun, shade my eyes, and think I catch a glimpse of a shadow that does not belong. There one second and gone the next.

A sound behind me distracts me from the shadow, and I see the tour guide coming out of the museum heading for the parking lot. I weigh my options. If someone is there, this is not the place to have a confrontation.

I approach my vehicle and hit the button to unlock it. I tuck the spear and my black Prada handbag in the backseat right next to the already packed matching set of luggage. I already had plans to get out of town.

My Fae heritage has a deep connection to the nature around us. Being stuck in this concrete prison for the last week makes my skin itch, the itch becoming an irritation I cannot push off anymore. I need to get out of town. I need to breathe fresh air. I need to feel the earth beneath my feet.

I wonder briefly if this itch is part of the unease that has been weighing on my chest for the last few days.

My family cabin is outside the Great Smoky Mountains, about an hour drive from Knoxville straight into the woods. The cabin has been our family retreat for hundreds of years, and this is where I went to mend my broken heart. Nestled outside the entrance to Tarrin, the Great Smoky Mountains have been the home to our race for a thousand years.

This is where we live and die to protect our families.

To the casual observer, the Jeep Grand Cherokee is my rental car while I am in town traveling to different museums. As I open the front door and wrap myself in the velvety interior, greeted with the aroma of new leather, the dash lights up. The glamor ripples and the true nature of the vehicle is a sight to fully enjoy.

I settle back into the luxury seats and heave a sigh of pure joy. I have a weakness for shiny objects—what can I say? I rev the engine of my Lamborghini Urus and enjoy the lovely tremble of the engine. My glamor fades on the inside of the vehicle as my hair turns from golden blonde to the deep midnight it normally is. Red streaks peek through in the bright afternoon sunlight, and I relish the moment.

As I press the pedal down with my five-inch heels, I peel out of the parking lot. I can see Earl in the window, a slightly confused expression on his face. The sound does not match the view.

No matter. I will not be back.

I let a true smile shine and enjoy the rumble under my feet.

TWO

Caleb—Memorial Park; Knoxville, TN.

The afternoon sun is warmer than it should be in late autumn in Tennessee. The sun illuminates the gravesite of my fallen friend Kyle Armstrong. Rhea sits in the front row with her grown son Evan and fourteen-year-old daughter Grace, grief etched in the lines on her face that were not there the last time I saw her. I stand behind the four rows of folding chairs, allowing the family members to sit in their sorrow.

The seats are full of Kyle's family, survived by his mother and four siblings, all with children of their own taking up the bulk of the rows. Standing next to me in the back are more military comrades than I expected. Despite their plain clothes, I can tell by their stances, their sharp eyes taking in every detail, that they are all cut from the same cloth.

Like recognizes like.

It has been a while since I worked with Kyle. I did not realize he had grown so close to his new unit. I counted twelve military men in attendance, aside from myself.

Kyle and I were close outside of work. We had been friends since we worked on our first undercover operation together ten years ago. We formed a bond, his life in my hands, my life in his. We continued to work together up until a year ago when Kyle was finally recruited for a specialized unit, one that if he told you, then he would have to kill you.

Before Kyle ever met Rhea, she was already working for this unit. I remember Kyle's excitement when he received confirmation of the new job last year. Rhea pushed for a promotion on her side, a promotion I am sure she is regretting now.

Still, Kyle would invite me over for dinner with Rhea and the kids or to the various birthday parties. Such bittersweet memories today. As I take in the standing men, I realize I did not know much about what Kyle was doing in his new unit. He was always vague when talking about his work.

My current role as criminal investigator for the southeastern division means I never pushed him for any details I knew he could not give me.

My eyes, drawn to two men at the back, notice them whispering to each other, low enough to not reach my ears, their facial expressions grim and determined. The two men are both large males, one over six feet tall with black hair and piercing blue eyes. The second is even taller than the first, traditional Nordic blond, blue-eye ancestry. My eyes sweep the rest of the scene, sensing something is off. Kyle's military comrades are all grim faced. I can almost feel the anger brewing under the calm surface.

Another pair of soldiers are standing about five feet to the left. One whispers to his friend, and I see grief etched in his face. His friend squeezes his shoulder and whispers something in his ear.

This reaction from his team tells me something bad happened to Kyle, not a run of the mill incident. I was only told that Kyle died in the line of duty, no further details provided. As I set my jaw, my teeth grind together. I silently send up a prayer to Kyle and vow to unravel the mystery of his death.

I shift my weight and scan the perimeter as the service continues, not seeing any new members arrive. Finally, the memorial ends. Roses are handed out, and a line forms to the side of the casket. I rouse myself from my musings and maneuver into the back of the line.

As I turn, a lock of deep-brown hair falls over my brow. My Italian-American heritage is on display today. Dark eyes, square jaw, and olive skin set against the white collar and black suit I pulled out of the back of the closet this morning.

As I pass over the casket, I place my single red rose on the top, amongst the other roses paying tribute and a final goodbye to my fallen friend. Something glints in the sunlight, catching my attention. I lean closer and see a coin. Tilting my head, I peer down, trying to identify the origin. It looks like a challenge coin. I have two similar coins at home from other squads and from when I graduated from the academy.

I stare at the insignia on the coin. I have never seen one like that before. There are three clearly defined mountain peaks with a half dome sitting in the foreground, which looks like a gate. Rays of light shine over the mountains. My brow furrows as I try to imprint the insignia into memory to research later.

Grace interrupts my deep contemplation by tapping me on my shoulder. "Hi, Uncle Caleb."

Rhea and Grace are standing slightly behind me. I turn and say, "Hey, sweet girl." I wrap her in a bear hug,. "I'm so sorry."

She nods and wraps her long blonde hair behind one ear and looks up at me with bright green eyes, the same shade as her mother's. "Are you coming over to the house?" she asks.

"Yea, give me a few minutes, okay?"

She gives me a watery smile and glances over my shoulder. "OK, see you." She turns away, walking toward her aunt.

I turned my attention to Rhea, her mother, beautiful even in her grief. Blonde hair pulled up in a chignon, green eyes red rimmed. I start, "If you need anything..." I stop myself. No matter what I could offer, it would not be enough.

I see her somber eyes appraise me, and catching me off guard, she says, "There might be something you can help me...and Kyle with."

She turns to look at the casket and then back at me. "When you get to the house, I have something in his study I want to show you." She leans in and hugs me tight, whispering in my ear, "You know he loved you." One last squeeze of my shoulder and she turns back to her family.

I glance up and see one of Kyle's comrades, one who was whispering in the back during the service, staring straight at us. His eyes bore into the back of Rhea's head as she walks away. My radar goes off, and I know something is not right.

He turns those piercing blue eyes on me, appraising me. His posture suggests brawn honed with lethal intentions. His look was calculating and assessing. He nods at me as if making up his mind. He turns to the friend he came with, the second huge male, and says something. Together, they turn and walk toward their vehicle.

I stare at their retreating backs until they are out of sight.

Whatever caused Kyle's death, it's still happening. It is clear his death was not a routine accident in the field. I set my lips in a grim line. In my experience, this meant it could only be classified as murder.

Kyle's old unit was itching for answers. So was I.

THRee

Sophia—Calling

I push my dark hair out of my eyes and let out a low groan when I see the gas light pop on. I was in the middle of having a mental debate about my state of paranoia when the ding interrupted me. My mind was whirling, and I wondered again if someone watched me leave the museum.

I tap my red fingernails on the wheel, a habit of mine, and bite my lower lip. It has been a year since I left Tarrin, and I have had only three visitors. My brother, Brenen Beaumont, Ian Cadell, my old mentor, and Alex Chambers, my best friend. Other than that, it has been radio silence. Why would someone come looking for me now?

Sitting at a stoplight, I pinch the bridge of my nose and debate the inner workings of my intuition. One of my latent powers has always bordered on precognition. A fancy word for me having a gut feeling and that gut feeling typically becoming reality.

For the past few days, I have felt an unease under my skin, a nagging feeling that my life was about to turn topsy-turvy. I have learned to listen to this gut feeling, as it usually turns out to be correct. The heavy weight that has been hanging around my chest tightens, and for the hundredth time I am at a loss for what is making its way toward me.

The little yellow light dings again, my annoyance exemplified. What timing. To the left, I see a strip mall attached to a shopping center and gas station. I pull into the gas station, disgruntled and annoyed at having to stop for gas in my impatience to get on the road. As I get out of the car, I push my dark hair away from my face and go through the motions. As the gas meter starts ticking, I stand next to the gas pump and wait, lost in thought. In my messy brain, that nagging intuition keeps building past the point of discomfort. I pause, my hand automatically going to my chest as though I can ease the ache externally.

Then it happens. Fate steps in and releases my gifts.

I see a mother and girl about fourteen years old. My vision doubles, what is happening now and what is to be appearing side by side. I see the tragedy unfolding in front of my eyes, the exact moment two lives are extinguished. Alongside this tragedy, I see in my double vision the mother and daughter walking on the asphalt heading obliviously for their demise.

Instinctively, I pull on the deep part of myself, the part I have not used in a year. Like using a long dormant muscle, it stretches and groans. I throw my hands up, and the world around me stills. The whole gas station within sight is at a standstill. The man at the next pump squeegeeing his window and the cashier inside the convenience store are frozen. At the busy intersection in front of me, cars are stopped mid turn.

In my mind's eye, I still see the blurred point of impact, a big ugly green Nova that has seen better days swinging around the parking lot. The driver doesn't notice he is heading directly toward the pedestrians.

Using the speed I naturally possess but have not used in a while, I pluck the two lives and move them ten feet to the edge of the curb. Those ten feet change the trajectory enough to avoid the devastating heartbreak of two lost lives.

In the space of a moment, I am back at my vehicle, rattled, and slightly confused. I wave, releasing the time warp. Unnerved, I look down at my shaking fingers.

I believed this gift was all but dried up and forgotten. These moments of calling, as my mentor calls them, are always pivotal moments that need changing, and fate decided I was the one to change them.

The question was, why would fate be stepping in now, and what was the purpose of saving those lives?

I look at the mother and daughter, memorizing their faces.

I feel the weight of someone's stare, look up, and connect with a particular shade of color exactly like mine. A deep-sapphire blue.

My brother is watching from the parking spaces by the entrance. He must have been the shadow I thought I tracked back at the museum. His strong, chiseled jaw, midnight-black hair, and blue eyes are a perfect likeness to mine. I can tell his attention was on the scene playing out in front of us, until the moment he realized what I had done.

His expression shifts from concern for the family to concern for me. I blow out a slightly shaking breath and shake my head to let him know I was fine. I get into the vehicle knowing Brenen is on his way toward me. Sure enough, he slips into the passenger seat.

I start the car and turn the air vents toward me, blasting warm air. I need warmth, not only from the chill in the air but also for my shaking hands.

The silence stretches between us. It has been months since I have seen Brenen. The last time we spoke, we fought over me returning to Idyll.

Finally, I glance over at him. He is staring out the front window. I see the object of his attention, the little family walking from the convenience store. The girl with a soda in her hands. The mom's eyes locked on to the taillights of the Nova now in the back of the lot. I can see her puzzling over the events that transpired.

Brenen breaks the silence. "Do you know her?" he asks.

I glance over. "No, but she must be important if I was called to save her."

He looks at me grimly. "Her name is Rhea Armstrong. She is the widow of one of the human soldiers who was killed last week." He pauses, looks down. "She is the new Fae collective member, elected six months ago. Two children, one Warlock in the program, and the fourteen-year-old girl who was with her tonight." He motions forward toward the two figures standing on the sidewalk. "They live in Idyll, but her husband's family is from Knoxville, and they have a second home here."

Seems my mental state of paranoia was spot on, as usual.

"How do you know that, and what are you doing here, Bren? If you are here to drag me back, honestly, I am not ready." I take a deep breath. "I am just not ready."

He looks at me, his eyes piercing in the close confines of the vehicle. "You are stronger than you think, Soph. Don't discount what you are capable of." I look away. He has more faith in me than I do.

Undeterred, he continues, "Ian told me you were working for him retrieving artifacts and suggested that I stop in and check on you. I came by the museum after the Armstrong funeral." I look at him a little confused. "Kyle Armstrong was a soldier in Vista Command. That's why I was at the funeral." He shrugs.

I sigh as I contemplate the connection between the females I saved and the soldier who died in the line of duty. "Sorry, Bren, I know how hard it is to lose a team member." I collect my thoughts. A slight frown creases my forehead. "Were you following me?"

He looks at me and says, "I got to the museum right when there was company. Didn't want to spook you in front of the humans."

I nod and relax back into the seat. There is a moment of silence as we sit in the quiet vehicle.

I turn and look him straight in the eyes. "Every time I have been called to use my gift before, there was always a connection, always an underlying reason, that I could not see at the time." I smile sadly and recite the old saying, "You can fight fate, but you can't escape it."

Bren smiles back. "You always had a way with words."

I shrug. "Doesn't change the fact that it's true."

His face sobers. "I know you are resentful of your gifts, especially this past year, but they have always led to the greater good."

That's like a strike to the heart. A tear leaks out of the corner of my eye. Because I know his grief at the loss of our sister runs as deep as mine, I reach for his hand, his palm warm and comforting.

I reply, "The greater good has not been good for Beaumonts this year."

He shakes his head. "No, but it is time for you to come back. We need you."

I look at him and implore, "Why now?"

He stares out the window, sighs heavily, and pinches the bridge of his nose, a habit we share.

"Kyle's death is the latest of three that have taken place in Mirwood in the past six months."

My brow furrows. "That's high but not unusual, given all the beasts that have been trickling through in recent years."

He looks at me. "These are not normal deaths caused by the creatures. We think there is a faction commanding the dark creature hordes, herding and using them against our own warriors."

I stare at him slack jawed. "Commanding the dark creatures?"

Bren looks at me. "We suspected something amiss with the first two murders. They were attacked by the creatures in broad daylight, in heavily trafficked areas. The second murder was close to the city." He pauses. "You know these creatures. They are secretive and stick to the underpopulated areas of the forest. What would draw them into the city? The first two deaths were individual Fae on patrol, no witnesses, and they did not have any tech on them."

I know that. Especially the older Fae do not particularly like the modern technology invented by humans. Solitary hunters by nature, they prefer to work alone.

I jump ahead, something that drives Bren crazy. "So because Kyle was on a human squad, there was witnesses and video?"

He grunts, "Yes, and now we know for sure these faction members are not killing the creatures. Instead, they are trapping and transporting them. We believe that the first two Fae crossed the smugglers, wrong place at the wrong time. The creatures were released to kill them when they interfered."

I sat there in stunned silence. "What on Earth are they doing capturing them?"

Bren grumbles, "That's what we are going to find out."

I mentally weigh all that he has told me. It was not a coincidence I had a call to save the widow of the fallen soldier. It was not a coincidence I felt this weight around my neck, growing in intensity. It is not a coincidence that Bren shows up at this exact moment asking for my help with the murders in Tarrin, inexplicably tied to Leona's death.

The wheels of fate have started to turn. We are never privy to when it might stop or how our lives will feel its effect in the end.

I groan at Bren, who holds up his hands in defeat and says, "I am sorry I dumped this all on you at once. There is one more thing Ian wanted me to mention." I gave him a look that speaks volumes. He shrugs and continues, "There is a young girl he wanted you to mentor when you got back as well. I am not sure why. He wanted me to mention it so you aren't blindsided."

I give him a slow nod of acceptance. Fate is propelling me back into Tarrin and the politics that go with it. I lean my head back on the headrest and look at the ceiling.

The silence stretches until Bren breaks it. "You headed to the cabin?" I nod, and he says, "Okay, why don't I pick up something for breakfast and meet you there?" He leans forward and kisses my cheek. "I love you, Soph. You are doing the right thing."

I can still feel the breath on my cheek when he disappears into mist right before my eyes. I sigh heavily and scoff. Bren and his dramatic exits.

"Show off," I mutter to the empty vehicle.

FOUR

Caleb—Betrayal

As I pull up to Kyle's family's house after the funeral, my heart is heavy. I am half tempted to keep driving and avoid the sadness all together. My promise to Grace plasters itself to the front of my mind. I sigh and get out of the truck.

The house is overflowing with people. The smell of coffee and perfume engulfs me as I enter. I wind through the rooms, headed to the back of the house where the kitchen is. As I suspected, Grace is sitting in the little breakfast nook that overlooks the sprawling backyard. Still in her black dress and Mary Jane's, she looks so young. I sit next to her and hold her hand. Grace lays her head on my shoulder, and we sit there for a while, letting the noise of the wake wash over us.

Rhea finds us like that a little while later. I wake to her gently shaking my shoulder as I rouse from sleep. Rhea asks Grace, "Can I steal Uncle Caleb for a minute?"

Grace sits up, stretches, and yawns. "Sure, I'm going to head up to my room to lie down."

Rhea nods. "Okay, I will check on you in a little bit." She squeezes Grace's shoulder as she passes and leaves up the backstairs. Her face turns somber as she focuses on me. "Let's go into Kyle's office. I have the box of paperwork I want to show you."

She turns, and I follow, realizing Grace and I must have spent longer than I thought sitting in the nook. The rest of the people have departed, only a handful sticking behind to clean up.

We enter the study and face the desk I have seen Kyle at on occasion. There is a box of paperwork, all neatly filed and labeled. I run my fingers over the well-organized labels and smile a little.

"Of course this is Kyle's. Not a paper out of place."

Rhea returns my smile and sits down on a small sofa against the far wall, slips off her shoes, and wraps her feet under herself.

"Yes, Kyle was beyond organized, used to drive me crazy." A small smile plays on her lips.

"What did you want to talk to me about?" I ask as I pace the room, feeling like I am intruding in Kyle's domain.

Rhea motions toward the chair. "Have a seat."

I pause in my pacing, sit, and lean forward on my knees. "What's wrong, Rhea?"

She looks at me with an expression I have never seen before. She speaks clearly and very matter-of-factly, "I want your help to catch Kyle's murderer."

I nod, unsurprised. "This was about a case he was working on?" I point to the box of paperwork.

She replies, "Yes. He was killed in the middle of a mission tracking down a ring of dangerous smugglers." She looks down. "We suspect there was an inside leak of intel leading to his target getting the jump on him."

My eyes narrow. That means betrayal by one of their own.

Rhea continues, "I want to bring you into the unit to investigate Kyle's murder. Will you do that?"

I reply, "Without hesitation. I would be honored to. He was my brother, and I know he would do the same for me."

Rhea smiles. "I hoped you would say that." She stands up. "There are a few particulars I need to brief you on before you commit one hundred percent to the case." She steps closer to me. "Can we meet tomorrow? We can drive out to our command center."

"Sure," I reply. "Before the funeral, I cleared my schedule for a few days."

"Great, if you want to meet me here, say around 9 a.m., we will head out."

"I will be there."

FIVE

Sophia—Wheels of Fate

pull the car into gear and head out of town. Finally.

I am not enjoying the open road as I usually do. Stepping on the gas, I give the engine the fuel it craves, and the road opens in front of me. My mind is turbulent, thoughts turning over and over like a great whirlpool of blackness. Fate and that unrelenting gift that I thought was dormant loom over me like a shadow. I scream at the dark road in front of me, letting out the emotion bottled up inside, finally bursting at the seams.

Tears fall in massive streams as I release the frustration. I have found myself tossed right back to where I so desperately escaped a year ago.

My heart rate slows. I take deep inhales of breath. I clutch the steering wheel as if it is my last lifeline. The resolve starts in the back of my mind, calming me. I know I have put off my calling long enough. I know I must go back to Tarrin.

It is twilight as my SUV's headlights sweep across the two-lane, heavily wooded forest road. The busy city noise fades away, transitioning into wooded rustling leaves. The sound of the early evening forest reaches my ears, the trickling of a stream, the early hoot of an owl and other creatures starting their night. My enhanced senses take it all in, this delicate balance of the ecosystem. My connection to the Earth intensifies, and I finally feel calm.

This close to the edge of the Great Smokey Mountains, the symphony of creation is what draws Fae to this magical piece of land. It renews and replenishes our spirit. As I pull up to the quiet cabin that has been in our family retreat for hundreds of years, my tears dry. My lights sweep the dark driveway and illuminate the front of the cabin.

Home.

On the porch waits Bren with a small black overnight bag and a brown sack that looks like groceries.

I get out of the car to his smart-ass comment. "Took you long enough."

I simply raise an eyebrow at him, cock my hip, and give him my perfect sister look. "Not everyone can get around in a blink of an eye."

He scoffs, "At least you get around in style." He appraises my new ride.

"No doubt." I smirk. "If you want to drive with me to Idyll in the morning, I wouldn't mind the company." Bren's ability to teleport himself and objects at will was a coveted gift. Though very annoying when we were younger, it has proven to be an especially useful tool in the field.

I grab the spear out of the back of the vehicle, leaving one of the bags and grabbing the other with essentials for the night. I toss the bag over my shoulder and head to the front door, which swings open with a thought. Still in my curator museum garb, I slip off the shoes at the door and pad barefoot past the large pile of various war paraphernalia on the left side of the door.

Various weaponry, spears, swords, and helmets by the dozen, with an occasional trinket here and there, was visible. I discard the spear and keep going to the kitchen, bent on a stiff drink. I pull a bottle of bourbon from the cupboard above the refrigerator, turn, and glance over my shoulder. My brother stops in his tracks to admire the loot.

He lets out an appreciative whistle. "Wow, Soph. How long have you been tracking down artifacts for Ian?"

I cross my arms under my chest. "He came to me about six months after Leona died and told me grief was doing me no good and that I needed to get out of this cabin." Bren picks up a particularly beautiful sword with precious gems inlaid in the hilt. "Ian said that and more relics are ending up in museums. We needed to get them back in case anything was particularly powerful."

I push off the counter I was leaning on, pull two short glasses out of the cupboard, and set them on the wooden island in the middle of the kitchen. "He knew I needed something constructive to do, and going back to Idyll was not an option."

I pause. "I've been traveling to each natural history museum between Tennessee and Boston, even as far south as Tampa, retrieving artifacts."

Bren finally closes the front door, makes his way to the island, picks up the bottle, and pours the liquid gold into two glasses. He asks with a raised eyebrow, "Have you found anything particularly powerful?"

I mentally catalog the items, tilting my head slightly. There are powerful objects, but nothing that stands out. "No," I say and then add quickly, "not yet."

Bren leans across the island from me, his broad shoulders taking up half the room. Holding his glass, he swirls the amber liquid. He raises it toward me and says, "To Leona."

We clink our glasses together, and before I take a sip, I whisper, "To Leona."

SIX

Gael—Selection Day

T he bright blue sky above filters in and out of view as the leaves sway in the wind. The view vanishes behind a blurred shape of a female figure, blonde hair splayed out in a golden halo. I cannot make out her features and only know she is beautiful beyond anyone or anything I have ever seen.

I reach toward her and see a single drop of golden light come from her fingertip. This drop of light suspends in the air as if held by magic until it slowly lowers to my chest. It hovers over me, wrapping me in golden light, until it slowly sinks into the very fabric of my being. The warmth spreads through me as the light disappears. I can feel the power course through my body. I am reborn.

Bang, bang, bang. I crack my eyelids open, promptly roll over, and pull the pillow over my head. The unrelenting pounding coming through the solid oak door is as familiar as the brightly painted walls and smells coming from the kitchen. My father is pounding on the door, his way of getting me out of bed. He is my adoptive father, but I rarely think of him as anything other than my dad.

"Gael, get up!" barked Bennett. "Breakfast in ten!"

That voice could wake the dead. I peek my head out from under the pillow, roll to my back, and stare at the ceiling. Those dreams always leave me with a profound sense of warmth. And lingering confusion. I shake off the recurring dream I have had ever since I could remember. Then it hits me.

Today's the day!

I throw my blankets off and am in the shower in seconds. My sluggishness immediately vanishes as I hurry through the necessities. Today is Selection Day, and I have been working toward getting into the Citadel Warrior Alliance program for four years. Once I pass Selection Day, I will begin my six-month qualifications training, or Q Training as the warriors call it.

Being the daughter of Bennett Monroe, one of the elder council members, has certain benefits. He has been training and preparing me for Selection Day for four years. Selection day is an annual event when young, aspiring Fae can try out for the Citadel Warrior Alliance. The requirements state you must be at least twenty years of age and must pass three tests to enter the program. Only two-thirds of the recruits make it past Selection Day.

This has been my calling ever since I can remember. I do not think I ever had a chance to want anything else. When I was six, Bennett gave me a wooden sword and had me practice swordplay with my sister. When I turned sixteen, he created an obstacle course behind our house in the woods for me to practice. This year, I turned twenty, the official age of all new recruits, and relished my opportunity. I am not going to squander it.

I am out of the shower and dressed in minutes. I plaited my long golden hair tight against my scalp, wrapping it intricately, starting at the crown of my head and ending at the base of my neck, encircling the woven strands to wrap around my head. Not a strand of hair out of place, I glance in the mirror and see my bright-blue eyes stare back at me. I am ready to meet the challenges of the day.

I will get into the Citadel Warrior Program. I whisper it, my mantra running through my mind. The same mantra that I have been reciting for weeks.

I give myself one final nod in the mirror as a little self-encouragement and slip out of my room, head down the stairs, and trot to the kitchen, where the smell of bacon and eggs greets me. I grab a plate from the cabinet and start to pile on the food, knowing I will need fuel today. Spirits are high in the Monroe house this morning. My mom, Gwyneth, is at the stove, turning off the fire. My sister Kay, short for Kathrine, is already at the table. Bennett is already finishing his first helping of bacon.

Kay is two years older than me and already lives in the dormitories at the Witch Academy. She is studying to be a ward smith, a part of the elite group of witches that replenish and strengthen the wards surrounding each of the gates. A high achievement for a second-year student.

I sit down next to Kay and ask, "Shouldn't you be in class?"

She nudges me with her elbow. "Remember, no school on Selection Day." She pauses and looks at me. "I came to wish my little sister luck on her big day, not that you need it. You've been kicking my butt since you were fourteen."

I swallow the eggs I'm shoveling in my mouth. Suddenly, my excitement turns to apprehension, and the familiar sensation of butterflies invades my stomach. I feel my face go a little green.

Kay sees my expression, her grin fades, and she envelops me in a hug. "Sorry, I was trying to lighten the mood."

I gulp down my juice. "I know. It's a big day, and I don't want to mess it up."

A grunt comes from the other side of the room. Bennett scoffs, "You are more prepared than any other candidate. I can promise you that." He gets up, strolls across the kitchen, and ruffles my hair as he ambles into the living room. Gwyneth comes and sits down next to me, her long blonde hair is lighter than mine, loose and flowing down her back.

She smiles and says, "You will do great. You are a natural." I nod and hope she is right. Gwyneth has a natural calming effect on everyone, and immediately I feel more at ease.

That is until Bennett barks from the living room, "Time to go." Kay rolls her eyes, and I smile into my drink. Typical Bennett.

We say our goodbyes to Gwyneth and Kay, who will be in the stands with the rest of the spectators this afternoon. While the main event will not start until late morning, all recruits must check in well before the event.

In the early morning light, we leave the house and head up the wide street toward the Capital Center. We reach the front of the massive glass building, walk up the steps, and head toward a specified entrance for recruits. There is a check-in table staffed by two administrative Fae. I see other recruits already standing in line. I check my watch and see the cutoff entry time is in approximately five minutes.

I glance over and see the entrance designated for council members and other elites of our society, currently roped off. I am sure later in the day it will be swarming with council members, advisors, trainers, teachers, and a variety of other support staff for the Warrior Alliance along with the upper crust of Idyll.

Bennett pulls me to the side presumably to give me his version of a pep talk.

He is a large man, his guff exterior a deterrent for anyone wanting to challenge him. Well over six feet tall, he cuts his light-brown curls tight to his scalp. His golden-brown eyes and tan skin give an overall impression of a lion, if his hair ever grew too long. He looks to be about a healthy thirty-year-old in his prime, even though I know he is an elder of our race, already alive before the gates closed a thousand years ago.

His always intense expression softens slightly as he looks down at me. "I know you are ready for these challenges. Don't be nervous." He sighs. "When you are nervous, you make mistakes. Remember, clear your mind and focus on the task at hand. During the physical and magic tests, do not look left, do not look right, look straight ahead, and finish the task."

I nod as these familiar words wash over me. They help clear my foggy mind as my nerves jump around inside my head. I anxiously rub my palms on my pants as he continues, "When you are in the arena, you must broaden your focus. Be aware of your teammates but do not focus on the spectators or me. I want your mind to be one hundred percent on the task at hand. If you do that, I know you will succeed."

My mind racing, I am not focusing on his familiar speech but rather obsessing over the one area I was the weakest.

I look up at him and ask the question that has been hanging in my mind these past weeks leading up to the Selection. I wring my hands, asking, "Can I still make the magic presentation we've been working on?"

Bennett has been helping me with the magic presentation for weeks. It weighs a third of each recruit's total score and highlights their magical abilities. As far as the world is concerned, my only power that ever emerged is a latent air-wielding power that barely holds any weight. It will certainly be a shock once my secret gets out.

Bennett reaches down and shifts my shoulders, so I am looking square up into his stern face. He asks, "Are you having second thoughts?"

I ponder that question for what felt like the hundredth time. Prior to registering for Selection, Bennett set me down and told me I had a choice. Either hide my gifts for the rest of my life or use them for the greater good. I made the choice not to hide anymore, even if that meant I would be thrust into the limelight. I shake my head, no second thoughts.

My latent power of air wielding is fickle and temperamental. It allows my peers to underestimate me. While my pride took a hit these past four years, it was worth it. I did not want to be singled out while at school or, worse, ripped away from my family and "recruited" early. So when my powers began to emerge, my true dominant power was kept a secret between our immediate family.

Bennet says reassuringly, "Don't worry about the magic section. The elders know of your fire ability. It was on your application. You may have a bigger audience at testing, but since you are going into the program, you are already complying with their mandate."

The mandate he is referring to requires Fae who have a dominant offensive magical ability to register with the Warrior Alliance. Most who have such an ability will register as soon as it manifests. There was a boy, Bane, who I was friends with who manifested telekinesis and voluntarily registered when he turned sixteen. He was taken to one of the far-reaching gates to train with another gifted teacher with similar abilities. I never saw him again.

I shiver remembering Bane. I don't regret keeping my secret for the past four years, but it is satisfying to finally be open about my gifts. If I'm honest, it will be truly enjoyable to wipe the grins off those who thought me weak for the past four years.

Bennet looks away and says, "I pulled strings and got Ari on your team, so you have a friendly face. I know how brutal the competition is, and I wanted someone there who had your back." He seems a little sheepish, like he thinks he may have overstepped.

I reach up on my toes and give him a kiss on the cheek and a wide smile. "Thanks, Dad." He squeezes my shoulders as he releases me from his bear hug. "Once you get through the Selection, I have arranged for someone to help you with your magic during your Qualifications Training. I think she can really help you."

He pauses as though in deep thought. He shakes his head slightly, and I wonder what the shadow over his eyes meant.

He refocuses on me, giving me a wide grin. "You will do great. Remember that I love you no matter what."

I give him a watery smile. "Courage, Honor, Strength." I recite the warrior motto and heave a heavy sigh. He smiles and ushers me over to the check-in area.

I feel Bennett squeeze my shoulder briefly, and then he is gone, heading through the roped-off area to the right.

I look around, realizing I am on my own.

SEVEN

Sophia—Surprise Encounters

I wake to the comfort of the cabin. Memories of the happy times roll over me. I stare out the window at the forest that has been our home away from home for so many years. I know today I face my grief. Today, I am returning to where I thought I could never step foot again. Bren filled me in on the comings and goings at the various command centers. Soldiers killed on watch, the crack in the barrier releasing continuously more creatures than seen before. Faction members profiting from chaos. Unacceptable.

I shower and dress in record time. Soft brown leggings tucked into warm ankle boots and a long-sleeve tunic complete my ensemble. I sheath the daggers in the slots specifically made to hold them, on the insides of my boots. I braid my freshly washed hair, ending at my low back. I glance in the mirror and red highlights gleam in the sunshine.

Ready, I head to the kitchen for much-needed coffee. Bren is leaning against the counter, cup in hand. As he sees me, he hands me the steaming cup and goes to get a new one out of the cupboard. What a saint my brother is. Double cream and double sugar. I wrap my lips around heaven.

Out of the corner of my eye, I glance at the living room. The pile of artifacts... Gone. My eyes budge. I swing toward Bren. "What did you do?"

He looks at me in confusion. "The artifacts?"

"Yes, the artifacts, where are they?" I growl between clenched teeth.

He shrugs. "I teleported them to central command. I gave them to Ian. I thought that was what you were doing with them eventually."

I look down at my steaming cup and take a breath. It is not Bren's fault that I did not grab what I wanted earlier. I wasn't expecting this trip to Idyll before last night.

I take a sip of my coffee and reluctantly admit, "Yes, but there were a few items I wanted to keep."

I had my eye on a particular trinket, a stunningly beautiful necklace inlaid with rubies. Why put it away in a vault somewhere when it was made to be worn?

Bren gives me a self-satisfied smile. "What one did you want to keep?"

I glare at him over my cup. "Oh, never mind."

I fume silently, and some—maybe Bren—would say it was pouting. Maybe he would be right.

Bren with his cocky swagger slides up next to me. He holds out a finger, and dangling from it is the ruby neckless I was completely obsessed with.

"Oh!" I squeak and jump away from the counter to throw my arms around him.

He chuckles, "Come on, Soph. I know you would never willingly give up something so pretty and shiny."

"Consider yourself forgiven, and thank you for this beauty. I will find a place to wear it soon."

He looks at me with an arched brow. "You know Selection Day is today, and the ball is tonight."

I release him and rock back on my heels. With all the drama over the past year, Selection Day was the farthest thing from my mind. I look back over at Bren. "Since I'm jumping in feet first, I might as well look good doing it." I turn from him, slipping the necklace in my pocket, my smile radiant. How I love shiny things.

Bren puts his coffee cup in the sink. "Soph, we've got to hit the road. I need to be at Selection by—"

Bren is cut off by a piercing screech of the alarm Ian gave me when I started staying at the cabin after Leona died. Ian put in added security. I tap the brightly lit face twice, and the alarm stops. Bren looks over at me, and our eyes meet.

I say, "It's the alarm Ian gave me. Something triggered the sensors in the backwoods."

In perfect sync, one moment we are in the cozy kitchen, and the next Bren wraps his arms around me and transports us to the clearing in the back section of our cabin. I rise out of a crouch, daggers in hand as I scan the perimeter. Back-to-back, we turn in a slow circle, analyzing, spreading out our senses to the deep woods and beyond.

The quiet is deafening, not a creature rustling in the bush, not a bird singing in the trees. The only sound is a quiet breeze, until my sensitive ears make out a slight humming coming from a far distance. I glance over at Brenen, and we start our hunt through the forest, silently in a way only Fae can move.

Bren gestures toward the back of the clearing, signaling he will proceed from the other side. I give him a single nod, and he vanishes. I start forward on silent feet. I peer into a small clearing where the low noise is coming from. Twenty feet wide, the foliage densely encircles the space. I can hear the humming sound that drew us to this spot, interrupted by short bursts of muttering.

Light is spilling out through the dense vines. I squint through the cracks and make out a figure darting to and fro so quickly I only catch glimpses. Short, male, and certainly of magical nature, he clearly seems riled up about something. I glance around the den he has created, and the light seeping out of the clearing is the reflection of hundreds of gold and silver objects lining the entire space. The creature, darting amongst his treasures, only has a small trail of dirt to move about on, the rest of the area completely covered in trinkets of every imaginable size. Coins, precious gems, goblets, and statues are all piled on top of each other, spilling out of containers, tucked into every single space available.

The humming abruptly quiets. I finally see the figure still, his back toward me. His head tilts, and then Bren emerges from the other side of the clearing.

He calls, "This is our family's land. You are trespassing."

The figure turns and gently places a box right in the center of his worktable, as if the box was his most prized possession. A surprisingly deep voice says, "Beaumont?"

Bren give a slow nod. "What business do you have with us?"

The trespasser's face becomes clear in the golden light, a handsome male, light hair brushing his collar, an intense expression on his face. My eyes fixate on the box in the middle of the table. Unlike the rest of the golden surroundings, this box is made of stone, a blue glow illuminating the elaborate etchings in the lid. My eyes snap back to the intruder as he begins to speak.

"Beaumont, huh? Trespassing you say?" He lets out a snort of indignation. "The land belongs to no creature, human, witch..." He looks pointedly at Bren. "Or Fae."

Brenen's lips tighten. "This piece of land has been in our family since the gates closed. You are trespassing. What are you doing here?"

The trespasser lets out another loud snort. "Worry not, Beaumont. I found what I was looking for, even though it keeps jumping around." He looks toward the box on the table and says to himself, "It was not what I expected." My eyes narrow, wondering what that means. He turns toward me, as if he can see me through the vines and says, "I will be out of your woods soon enough."

I step forward, feeling the thorns shredding my skin, minor aches that will be gone in moments. As I emerge into the clearing, I see the treasure trove is utterly amazing and cannot help but look around at the golden surroundings in awe.

"What exactly did you find in our woods?" I tilt my head, noticing his height is equal to my shoulders. "Tomte? I have not seen one of your kind with my own two eyes. The history books tell us you were all trapped on the other side."

The trespasser's face twists into a scowl. "Humph, that was exactly what you were supposed to think, *Fae*," he says with distaste. "Our kind wanted nothing to do with you after the wall. Your great queen stranded us here in this awful place, no magic, no family." He turns and starts to pace in the small space, agitated.

I work my way close to the table and have a clear view of the box. Uniquely beautiful, it is unlike any other magical relic I had ever seen. I raise my eyes to the creature and see him pause in his pacing, intensely peering at me from across the room.

I ask, "So what is in the box?"

"Ah, my dear, that is the cue to take my leave."

In a flurry of motion, too quick for me to even react to, he disappears into a whirlwind that has me kneeling on the ground. I shield my eyes and peer up into the vortex created by his power, and then as suddenly as it started, the storm winds are gone and silence stretches over the clearing.

I rise to my feet and notice the trees are now empty of any gold or jewels. Bright sunlight spills into the clearing as I spin in a slow circle. The Tomte and his treasure vanished into thin air.

I look over at Brenen and ask, "What the hell was that?"

He grimaces. "I'm not sure. Whatever that object was, it was powerful." He rests his hand on my shoulder. "There's not much we can do now. I will report it to Ian when we get back. We really need to get going. I have to be back for opening remarks, and introductions at nine."

I look at my watch, 7:30, and reply, "Okay, I'm pretty much ready. My bags were packed yesterday."

We head back to the cabin and finish our makeshift breakfast, small pastries and fruit Bren picked up last night. As we jump into the Urus, I lovingly glance back at the cabin, taking in the sight for a moment before pressing the start button. The engine roars to life, and we leave the cabin and its memories in the rearview mirror.

We are near the entrance of Tarrin. Only a couple of miles take us to the closest runestone. I see the rocky outlet at mile marker forty-three and pull off the road. The runestones surround Tarrin with a vast network of drop points totaling one hundred and twenty markers. The drop points are spaced seven miles apart in a diamond-shape pattern that wraps around the entirety of Tarrin.

The runestones allow any owner of a talisman, like Bren's ring, and mine currently tucked down deep in my luggage next to the precious ruby necklace, to move within the perimeter. The owner of each talisman needs only to press their ring to the stone and touch the drop point location that appears. Each drop point is strategically arranged, specified by command center region and number. This allows transport for each talisman owner through the ruins to each location instantaneously. This is how the soldiers move around on patrols, set up meeting points, and transport supplies to each outpost.

The runestones also keep Tarrin concealed, remaining hidden for a thousand years from human eyes. The witches continually replenish and strengthen the wards surrounding Tarrin, monitoring it for any unwanted intruders. If a human happens to wander too close to the wards, they might hear birds flying above and water trickling. But if they followed the sounds, all they would see is a dried-up pit of mud with no animals or blue waters in sight.

I see Bren pull the talisman from around his neck and place it in his palm. The front of the ring is flat and oval shaped with the crest of Tarrin. The intricate scrollwork etched into the base of the ring tapers down the sides. Each ring, specifically made for each soldier by our Witch Academy, is a highly coveted asset.

As Bren places his talisman against the stone, a shimmer of light illuminates the etched rune marks in a brilliant display of power. The illusion of the Great Smokey Mountains fades, revealing the true nature of Tarrin. From this vista viewpoint, you can see the vastness of the mountains, aglow in the early morning sunlight.

Displayed center stage is Emerald Lake, gleaming in the sun above Idyll. The waterfall runs, feeding the Aurora River that winds through the city, the crown jewel of Tarrin. Mirwood Forest spreads to the right, catching the sun in a fiery kaleidoscope of reds, golds, and oranges. The dense canopy of trees rarely allow sunlight to penetrate the forest floor.

With a heavy heart, I left a year ago, and now I feel it swelling with homecoming. Grinning, I go back to the Urus, the roads switch-backing with sheer drop-offs on one side and steep cliffs on the other.

Descending into Tarrin, I have a sense I am exactly where I am supposed to be.

EIGHT

Caleb—Revelations

pull up to the Armstrong family home at nine the next morning. My eyes are red rimmed and feel like sandpaper. I did not sleep well last night. Images of Kyle meeting his untimely demise run through my head in a constant loop, various outcomes that may or may not be true. I should have taken the box of paperwork with me so I could have at least done something constructive at 3 a.m. Instead, I stared at the ceiling imagining all the ways Kyle could have died.

I heave myself out of my black GMC Sierra 2500 Denali. Not knowing what the day would bring, I wore my standard weekend garb, jeans, work boots, and a black T-shirt that pulled tight against my biceps. A light jacket covers my shoulder holster and the 9mm I never leave home without. I ring the bell, and Rhea opens the door, looking ready for the morning. She is wearing a long cream sweater, jeans, hiking boots, and a puffer vest. She motions me inside, and I walk along the familiar path, sitting on a stool in the bright kitchen.

"Want some coffee for the road?" Rhea asks. When I nod, she pours a travel mug full of steaming coffee. "Grace is still sleeping. I think she needs the extra rest today."

I'm anxious to get on the road. I see Amber, Kyle's sister, as she walks into the kitchen. She smiles as she passes by. "Morning." After getting coffee, she glances over at Rhea and me. "I'm going to watch over Grace for the next week or so, until we can get life back to a new normal."

I reply, "I'm glad Grace has all of you to look over her. Kyle would be happy to see that."

She says, "You should get on the road. I've got it covered here."

Rhea motions toward the front door, and I stand to leave. As we walk toward the door, I ask, "Do you want to drive?"

She looks up at me. "Why don't you drive? I may stay at the compound for a while after our meeting, I have some work to catch up on that can't wait. I can get a ride home from a coworker later tonight."

I shrug. "Okay, but you have to give me directions."

Rhea pulls herself into the cab. "Head straight out 441 toward the Smokies. Our command center is located out in the forest."

"That's a strange place for a command center."

She glances sideways at me. "We needed privacy."

My internal alarm goes off. I purse my lips in silent contemplation and put the truck into gear. I will get to the bottom of this.

It is a quiet drive; we do not have a lot to say in the aftermath of yesterday's emotional roller coaster. Kyle's death, his funeral, and cryptic details of his murderer revealed last night are still playing through my mind.

As we get close to the top of the mountains, Rhea sits up. "Mile marker forty-three is coming up. Go ahead and pull onto the turn off."

I follow the directions and pull off to the side of the road at a vista viewpoint.

Under different circumstances, I may have enjoyed the view. Tree covered mountains spread out in front of us in an endless view of fall colors. I turn the truck off. "What's going on, Rhea? Why are we stopped here in the middle of nowhere?"

She sighs. "Caleb, you know I have been working for a specialized unit, one that is on a need-to-know basis, for the better part of twenty years. There are some truths you need to hear before agreeing to jump in and help with Kyle's investigation. They may be hard to hear."

My eyes narrow and reply, "Okay, let's hear them." I spread my arms wide, indicating to get the show on the road.

She puts her hand on the door handle. "Come with me." She climbs out of the truck, walking toward the forest line. I run my hands through my dark hair in frustration, get out, and follow her. My annoyance is growing. What is the big secret she can't come out and tell me?

She heads over to a large granite rock that sticks up from the ground. Strange, as there are no other rocks like that surrounding it. She pulls a necklace from inside her shirt. Dangling from the end is a large ring, flat on top, oval shaped. It looks like an old-fashioned wax seal molded into a ring. She places the ring on the stone. A light filters out of the stone and seems to ripple the air around us. Strange markings appear on the stone. A slight wind brushes my face and then settles as if nothing had happened.

I turn and look at her, asking, "What on Earth was that?"

She gazes out at the horizon. "I wanted to show you Tarrin, my home."

I see a vastly different horizon than what I was looking at before. My jaw goes slack as I take in the new vista. An enormous lake takes center stage in the distance, nestled in the center of a large valley. There is a wide gap of stones at the edge of the lake. Water is falling between these rocks into a massive waterfall. To the right is a dense forest that looks like no light would ever reach the ground, and to the left is a beautiful river forming at the base of the waterfall, winding through a city that was not there a moment ago.

"What is this place?" I ask. "Give it to me straight. What is going on?"

She nods sharply and folds her hands in front of her. She begins as if it was a well-rehearsed speech she has given many, many times before. "The reality you know of Earth is limited. There are other beings in this world that did not originate here." She lets that marinate in my brain and then looks back down at her hands.

"There is a parallel universe, my parents' homeland, that I have never seen with my own two eyes, nor stepped foot on, nor breathed in the sweet air." My attention is focused on every detail of her posture. She is calm, no indication of nervousness or that she is lying or pulling my leg. She is looking down at her hands as if this is a difficult confession.

45

Her eyes come back up to meet mine then look out at the vista in front of us. "For a thousand years, the gateways to my Fae heritage have been closed, barricaded by our Great Queen Morrigan."

Rhea takes a deep breath. "One thousand years ago, there was a great war between light and dark creatures, and the queen saw the tides turning. She foresaw, with her gift, that we could not defeat the darkness. Endeavoring to save her people, she chose to instead try and trap it, containing its darkness in our homeland. Many of our kind died during this war."

I analyze her movements, looking for any indication of deceit. All I get is sadness and resolve in her body language.

"At that time, Earth had many gateways. My people, the Fae, were able to come and go as we pleased. Morrigan evacuated as many as she could through the gateways in those final days to find refuge on Earth. Once she was satisfied that she had saved as many as she could, she went to work on closing the barriers across the globe. She used every drop of her magic until her essence was completely absorbed in the fabric of the barriers, each one closed, trapping the darkness in Faerie. And by extension trapping the Fae on Earth, never to have access to our homeland again."

Rhea walks toward the ledge of the vista outlook. "These barriers have held strong for one thousand years. We have lived here on Earth, adapted, raised our families, intermingled with humans. Many of the Fae fell in love with humans, and over the years offspring resulted in what you would call witches or warlocks."

"Early on in our lives here on Earth, we determined it was best to keep our heritage a secret due to the destructive results anytime our secret came to light. Any of the human-Fae relationships were held to strict secrecy. For a long time, the Fae lived in peace, usually congregating close to the old gates where we can still feel the magic of our queen pulsing and alive."

I stared at her in disbelief. What she was talking about was so far-fetched. If she did not seem so sad, I would have scoffed in disbelief. Her melancholy in reciting the tale wrapped around me, and I found myself waiting to hear the end of her story.

She's unaffected by my slack jaw and disbelieving eyes. "The Fae can live for thousands of years, while the witches have a much shorter life-span of a few hundred years. There are many Fae who still remember Faerie and still hold hope of returning someday."

She turns and looks at me. "About three hundred years ago, we felt a crack in the energy around the gates. As we went to investigate, we encountered dark creatures that started to slip through the cracks. We would encounter one or two here and there and eliminate the threat. Then it became obvious that we needed a greater force to combat the incoming flow. We had our military units, of course, hundreds of Fae at each of the gates. Occasionally, the creatures would escape beyond our reach, and the humans became aware."

"This was when the Collective was established. Three parts to a whole. The Fae, the humans, and the witches working together to keep our secret, and to keep the creatures contained."

She continues, "Witches have magic of the Fae coursing through their blood, along with a connection to this earthly realm. This combination allows witches to wield a different kind of magic than any normal Fae. Through their magic, the witches have created wards to protect Tarrin and our city, Idyll." She motions toward the city in front of us. "The witches maintain the wards to this day."

"This rock you see in front of you is one of one hundred and twenty runestones scattered throughout Tarrin, covering over 840 square miles or 537,600 acres. Each of these runestones are connected to the talismans that each of our soldiers are issued." She holds the necklace with the ring up to the light. "The runestones offer camouflage of the true nature of our city to human eyes, along with providing a protective barrier the creatures cannot cross and roam free. This vast network of interconnected runestones allow the soldiers to transport from one stone to the other via the talismans.

"The Fae recruits the strongest and most magically talented of our kind. The Citadel Warrior Alliance patrols Tarrin and keeps our people safe. Each year, there is a selection, an appraisal of talents and physical attributes. It is the highest honor for a Fae to be chosen to continue the long line of warriors who have defended this land.

"The humans formed units, and they patrol these areas with the Fae. They also run interference within the human government, hiding data when necessary, routing monetary funds, technology, or manpower when needed. We have many Fae, human, and witches scattered throughout the various governments worldwide.

"This collective has been in place for three hundred years. We have worked together to keep our families safe, to keep the creatures at bay, and to protect our beloved cities close to the gates."

She makes a sweeping motion with her hand toward the golden city before us. "This is Idyll, where I grew up."

Rhea grows silent. I needed it to entertain the idea that what she told me may be the truth.

I turn from her and walk to the edge of the vista. I stare out at the landscape that had changed before my eyes.

After a few moments, I turn and look back at her. "I need to see everything."

A slight smile plays on her lips, and she nods and speaks in the same way she did last night. "I was hoping you would say that."

NINE

Gael—Warrior Alliance

walk up to the desk. The other recruits have already checked in, and the desk is empty except for the clerk, who asks without looking up, "Name?"

"Gael Monroe."

He glances up at me, his only reaction to my surname. His eyes go back to his list, he marks my name off, and he says without looking up again. "Straight through the double doors and then take a right. Uniforms are handed out at the locker rooms located three doors down."

I've never been to the capitol building. I walk forward through an expansive convention hall, looking at the tables and chairs set up. Plush red carpets under my feet give way to marble floors as I walk through a massive set of double arched doors. Immediately, I look up at the brightness of sunlight streaming in. The roof above sprawls out in a massive glass atrium that reaches from the front steps to the back entrance, at least three hundred yards long and one hundred yards in width.

The glass planes form a huge dome over the entire open hallway, giving the atrium a feeling of being outside. Through the glass roof, I can see heavy ancient trees arch and bend overhead, a brilliant display of golden reds, oranges, and yellows.

Right in the center of the atrium, there is a large curving planter em-bedded with curving benches where people have decided to sit and enjoy the garden along its path. Inside the planter is a variety of orna-mental trees, some so large they brush the very top of the glass roof. Flowering bushes and vines fill the lower space with greenery and give a sweet aroma that permeates the air.

On the outside edge of the glass atrium, massive marble columns hold up the structure. In between the columns that line the long corridor are arched windows intersected with doorways, such as the one I came through. These lead to various ballrooms, conference rooms, and offices.

I turned right as the clerk had instructed and walked down the long hallway in awe of its beauty. A set of arched double doorways comes into view, "Lockers" written on the nameplate above the door. I reach another check-in desk, where another clerk is seated. I give them my name, and they hand me my uniform.

I turn from the beauty of the capital atrium, shake my head to clear it, and change in the locker rooms, forcing my focus to return to the task at hand.

Good advice from my father, indeed.

I button up the recruit's uniform, black cotton under shirt, black canvas long-sleeve jacket, black canvas pants tucked into shit kickers, as my father so lovingly describes them. The only color on the uniform is found on the front breast panel, the Tarrin logo in red stitching.

A circle, with three mountain peaks, the gate shining in the foreground.

Being one of the last members to arrive, the locker room is empty. I close my locker and head to the front. I make my way to the adjoining double doors that swing freely both ways and find myself in a huge gymnasium. About a hundred and fifty recruits are standing or sitting on the bleachers, all in the same uniform. The instructors are clustered in front speaking to each other in low voices. Standing off to the side, I scan the gym for my friend Ari, full name Adriana, but I don't see her. I find a nice spot against the side wall and plant my feet. The in-structions are about to begin.

The six Fae instructors, four male, two female, break from their con-versation and move to stand in front of the recruits. I recognize a few of them, having seen them with Bennett over the years. One male Fae steps forward with a commanding presence, wavy light-blond hair about shoulder length tied back with a leather strap. Piercing light-blue eyes, tall and broad as most Fae are. He begins the introductions in a booming voice.

"Good morning." There is a pause as some of the recruits who were not paying attention quiet. "For those of you who do not know us, we are the six commanders for the six sectors of Tarrin. If you are lucky enough to pass today's selection, you will be split amongst these six sectors for your ongoing training."

"My name is Damaris Allard, Commander of Central Sector. I will introduce each of our commanders in order, starting from my left. Ava O'Hara, Meadow Sector." She steps forward. Porcelain skin offsets her fiery-red hair braided down her back.

"Angus Brando, Grove Sector." He steps forward, light-brown hair cut short. Tall, broad shoulders, light-brown eyes.

"Gabriella Ventura, Mystgate Sector." She steps forward, Latin heritage is predominant in her dark eyes and skin, wavy, thick dark hair is pulled back in a slick ponytail, the locks falling down her back.

"Ethen Graham, Domain Sector." He joins the others. Tall, broad shoulders, olive skin, dark eyes, dark hair slightly long and falling over his brow.

Damaris continues, "Lastly, Brenen Beaumont, Vista Sector." Of similar statue to the others, he waves, his midnight-black hair and piercing blue eyes getting all the attention.

"We expect today to be a challenge for many of you. On average, only two-thirds of recruits pass the beginning day Selection. Please know, we appreciate all who come to compete and value your dedication to the Warrior Alliance. There are many roles that need to be filled in the organization, and not all of them are in the field. If you are not successful in today's Warrior Selection, we invite you to apply for the many other roles that are available within the alliance."

I shift my weight and look at the floor. I refuse to acknowledge any other outcome than making it through the selection process.

Allard's eyes sweep the crowd. "At this time, I would like to invite Gabriella Ventura forward to go over the schedule of events for today."

I feel eyes on me and look up to see Liam. Sure enough, directly behind him, I see Max, Archer, and Nova, the only female in the group. I let out a breath as I glance away. Liam's father is also an elder council member. We all went to the same academy. Until our powers manifested, we were comrades, equals. When it became apparent my power was the weakest in the class, Liam made sure to highlight my failures at every turn. The mocking and ridicule were expected, but what hurt the most was I thought we were friends.

Ventura has the same stoic demeanor as Allard. She projects from a handheld device up on the wall of the gym, placing it on the podium that was set up for that purpose. "Good morning, recruits. Our selection process is separated into three segments. First, to evaluate your strength, agility and alertness." I smile, knowing I've been training for the physical tests nonstop. "Second, to evaluate your magical abilities."

My smile fades. This is the section I am least confident in. I see Liam and Archer nudge each other and laugh as they see my expression. I square my jaw and try my best to ignore them.

"Third, to evaluate how you work in a team environment. Recruits will be separated into groups of five. Your group will rotate to each of the three tests at your designated times. You will all begin with the strength, agility, and alertness test, if you do not pass the first test, you will not be able to continue to the rest of the tests today. If your group loses more than two members, we will reassign groups on an as needed basis.

"The attached schedule has been sent to your phones." She pointedly looks around. "If you are late to your tests, you will be disqualified." She glares to make sure everyone knows how seriously she takes punctuality. It makes me think of Bennett, and I smile slightly.

"Lunch is scheduled for all recruits from 12:30-1:00 p.m. in the dining hall. Our final announcement of candidates moving forward in the warrior alliance will be at our rally at the end of the day, 4 p.m. in the arena. If you are chosen, you are invited to the opening ball hosted in your honor. The festivities will begin at 6 p.m. for dinner in the main ballroom here in the Capital Centre, dancing to follow at 8 p.m."

Ventura's gaze sweeps the group of recruits one last time, her sharp eyes missing nothing. "Good luck to you all. Remember, courage, honor, strength."

The commanders leave the front of the gymnasium through the far door. I look down at my phone and see the same schedule on the wall pop up on my phone. I scan the schedule and see I am in Group 12. We are scheduled for strength, agility and alertness at 11 a.m., magic after lunch at 1:00 p.m., and our group event at 2 p.m. I look down at the list and see my teammates: Caden Emery, Gavin Pierce, Logan Barlowe, Gael Monroe, Adriana Blane. I am so excited to see that Adriana is on my team, although I should never have doubted Bennett. I was also excited I was not with any members of Liam's crew.

I let out a sigh, two hours left before our first test. I look around and gauge how everyone else is feeling. Some look overly confident, others slightly worried. I see some start to stretch to loosen up, while others pace back and forth nervously. Finally, I see Ari heading toward me, and I rush to give her a hug.

"Oh, I'm so glad I found you," she says, her voice a little higher than normal. She pushes her dark bangs out of her eyes, her long, dark hair in a ponytail. Her big blue eyes are fringed by beautiful long lashes that I would kill for.

I say, "Me too."

Ari looks at me intently. "We are both going to do great. Bennett has been putting us through the wringer for months. We got this dialed in, *blindfolded.*"

I smile. "Yes, we've got this." I say, but it sounds flat even to me. Ari and I have been friends since we were little. Her dad was a friend of Bennett's, and we practically grew up at each other's houses. I give her hand a squeeze to reassure her we are going to be fine. "We have a few hours before our first test."

I look around. In the span of time while we were catching up, organizers have been busy arranging the gymnasium for what looks to be the magic testing location. They have sectioned off half of the space, and I see runestones being set up. I recognize these stones. Bennett has been training me in the magic portion of the test in off hours.

The stones are designed to insulate and control magical powers that are not fully developed. While we are learning to control our powers, very often those powers can rage out of control. Bennett told me during our first practice that these stones were created when one of the warriors with Air Wielding Magic destroyed half the room during the selection process. Better to be safe than sorry.

Allard steps forward. "Recruits, the gymnasium will be off limits to anyone not testing in their time slots. Please wait either in the atrium or the cafeteria until your time arrives."

I look at Ari and roll my eyes. "So much for scoping out the competition." She smiles, and we turn and head to the atrium.

There are worse places we could wait, I suppose. It is so beautiful that my eyes kept dart to the left and to the right trying to take it all in. We settle onto a small section of the huge curving bench that wraps around the entire center of the atrium. I hear songbirds singing their favorite tune, perched high in the trees in the center of the island. The peacefulness of the atrium surrounds us, at odds with my current energy. My foot taps the ground in anticipation. I notice my nervous twitch and push down on my knees as I try to soak that peacefulness into my soul.

Ari puts her hand on mine. "Stop. It's going to be fine. You freaking out is going to make me freak out!"

I smile and squeeze her hand. "Sorry, I have wanted this for so long and don't know what I will do if I don't get in."

"Breathe and focus that energy on the tests."

We sit like that for a moment. I stand up and pace between a set of beautifully arched windows, chewing on the side of my fingernail. Then I head back to the bench to sit back down.

Ari kicks her legs out in front of her and cringes at my display of anxiety before taking out her phone. I glance over and see candy gems on the screen and hear the rhythmic music. *Are you kidding me?* I jump up from my seat like it is on fire. Games? I can't believe it.

I am up and pacing again. I have never understood how Ari goes through life in such a nonchalant state, and I'm sure she can't fathom my level of anxiety. I guess that's why we complement each other so well.

Before I realize it, she looks at her watch. I glance up at the large clock on the atrium wall I've been watching creep at a snail's pace. Two hours lost to my relentless pacing.

Ari reaches up high over her head in a long stretch, yawns, and says,

"Should we get going?" I stamp down my irritation at her calm demeanor.

"Sure, let's go," I reply, and we head out the rear doors.

TEN

Caleb—Rhea's History

Rhea and I go back into the truck and start the descent into the sprawling, shimmering city below, a hidden gem that was obscured from my view before today. Thoughts are tumbling and rolling around in my head as I try and re-assimilate my view of the world.

I glance at her. "So, while we drive, can you give me some background on you, Kyle, and the kids?"

I can see her slight smile out of the corner of my eye. "Of course," she begins. "You know, Kyle and I met about twenty-three years ago. I was working for the Warrior Alliance at the time and had switched to a new role. In the Human Sector, we typically rotate our positions every twenty to twenty-five years to avoid suspicion as to why we are not aging. We rotate locations where we will not run into anyone from our old lives. Some move to Tarrin, and others we will relocate to different cities. Transfers occur all the time.

"Anyway, I had started as the south-central division controller, responsible for overseeing human recruitment to the alliance. I was posing as a college student at the time. Kyle was one of the recruits."

My brow furrows and I ask, "If you were sent to recruit him, why didn't you?"

Rhea glances out the window. "Kyle and I hit it off at once. It was a whirlwind, a wonderful, beautiful romance that resulted in pregnancy early in our relationship." A tear tracks down her cheek. "I had not yet told him about any of this. It is normally very difficult to conceive as a Fae, so it was a shock when we found out."

She clears her throat. "Once I got pregnant, I told him about Tarrin, about my heritage, about the assignment that I was set to recruit him for. Kyle had grown up without a father and was determined to be in the picture long term. He worried about taking such a high-risk job, concerned he could leave his child fatherless like he was."

I reach over and squeeze her hand, giving her what little comfort I can.

She shakes her head slightly. "Kyle agreed to be an agent in the human career path he was on. Agents are scattered throughout the world in a variety of normal human roles and help the alliance in times of need. Agents are essential to keeping security tight, stopping any leaks of information, and they do this by effortlessly blending into society. That is what he did for most of his career."

Rhea paused for so long I thought she might not continue. The silence stretched and became like a weight in the truck. She visibly shook herself out of the memory.

"Two years ago, it was brought to my attention there was a heightened number of creatures filtering through the cracks in the gate. Some of the sector commanders recognized the unusual behavior. Typically, dark creatures will shy away from populated areas, being lone hunters, and will not come out during the day. We found attacks close to town, one in the middle of the day. At that time, all I had was a theory. When I brought it to the elders, they dismissed the unusual behavior as a coincidence."

I ask, "Who are the elders?"

Rhea explains, "The council is made up of elders, Fae members who were alive before the gates closed a thousand years ago. They work in an advisory capacity and collaborate between Mystgates and other elders around the world on global issues. When there is an overarching problem, the Collective will bring it to the council for review."

I arch my brow. "The Collective?"

She gives me a rueful glance. "I am one of six Collective members from Tarrin. We are nominated and elected by our own races, two from Fae, witch, and human sectors in each territory. We work on behalf of constituents to negotiate trade agreements, perform oversight of rules and regulations, and resolve issues that are brought to us. The dark creature's abnormal behavior was brought to me by a sector commander. I escalated it to the elders and got shot down."

I nod, contemplative, and can feel her eyes on me.

She continues, "I knew something was not right and continued to work on it at home. I traced the dark creature movements and found evidence of them being corralled, held in hordes in remote areas of Tarrin. The remnants of where the dark creatures were confined popped up in each sector. It seemed like the horde kept moving or that there were multiple hordes in play.

"I personally met with each of the sector leaders and told them of my findings, to alert them to this new danger. Unfortunately, the warning came too late for one of the outposts. One horde rampaged a remote sector, overrunning the compound. There were fifteen dead and over twenty severely wounded in the attack."

Rhea looked down at her hands, and then back out the window. "Kyle saw my research while I was working at home and wanted to get involved. That was what he was great at, after all, infiltrating the impenetrable, finding the needle in the haystack. He convinced me to recommend him to be put on duty, and he was assigned to a squad in Tarrin."

I glanced over at her and see tears streaming down her face.

She looks at me and says, "It's my fault Kyle was in Tarrin, my fault he's dead."

I squeeze her hand again. "Do you know what Kyle was working on right before he died?"

"I have his notes in the backseat. I was also briefed by his surviving team members. Kyle was approached by an informant a few months back, someone who was feeding him information about the faction members who were moving the creatures through Tarrin. Every time he got intel that there was going to be a move, no one would show. The informant swore he was telling the truth, and Kyle seemed to trust this individual, but the meeting would get switched at the last minute, almost like they were warned.

"The last meeting was the day of the ambush. He found out about it at the last minute and pounced on it. He mobilized the team, and they headed out immediately. One of the surviving teammates says that he was sure the faction members knew in advance they would be there, set explosives into the cliffside, and set them off when they got into position. He thinks someone from our team betrayed them."

I let out a long breath I did not know I was holding in. I sure had my work cut out for me.

ELEVEN

Sophia—I'm Back

Bren stays with me until we are parked in the underground parking garage next to the Central Sector Headquarters. After a kiss on the cheek, Bren teleports to the capitol building where the Selection Day's beginning speeches should be starting any minute. I grab my bags out of the backseat along with the extra-long weapons carrier I added to my luggage ensemble once I knew I was coming back to Tarrin.

I head up the stairs leading to the Central Sector main entryway. Most of the buildings in Idyll blend seamlessly into our environment. This is no exception. The building sides are made entirely of glass, creating an illusion of sitting in the middle of a gigantic tree house. From the main entrance, I can see all the glass hallways leading through the compound. Three branches of the building spread out to form the three areas of the sector: operations, intelligence, and the dormitories.

I take the steps two at a time and place my ring on the stone standing by the large arched-glass front doorway. This normally allows me access, but since I've been gone a year, I have a moment of panic. "Come on, work. Come on. *Come on,*" I mutter under my breath.

Relieved, I hear the door click open and let the air out of my lungs in a slow trickle. I did not want to have to track down my brother or Ian for access. On this first trip back to the Central Sector, I want a moment to re-acclimate myself without prying eyes.

The roof above me as I enter is made of exposed wooden beams crisscrossing, blending with the outside trees that can be seen by the walls of windows. The colorful leaves create a canopy, and my soft boots making no noise against the brown polished floors beneath my feet. The building's main entrance is very modern and minimalistic, a wide hallway that spans the length of the building with two main branches splitting off to the left and right, windows flanking each of the hallways to create a glass house held up by large columns.

Straight ahead, the large hallway ends in a massive circular viewing area where the central command center is set. To the left, the intelligence center spreads out, where many warriors and soldiers work together to gather information and strategize. To the right is the dormitories, my destination today. I turn right, hoping to slip in without being noticed right away.

As I walk along the familiar hallways of Central Sector, bittersweet memories flood my mind. This was my home away from home for so long that I have a sense of nostalgia at being back.

The hallways turn from glass to wooden panels as I reach the dormitory section of the building, creating some privacy. I go to my old door, press my ring against the stone plate, and enter. It has been a year since I was in this room, but it smells fresh, like the cleaning crew stopped by earlier today. Thank you, Bren.

I softly close the door behind me, dropping my luggage and the long weapons carrier I brought with me. I cross the room and sit on the bed, absorbed in my thoughts. I look around at the utilitarian room, a bed, dresser, closet, and a small desk and chair. Very few personal possessions are scattered around. One of the items is a picture of my parents, Bren, Leona, and I. A black and white photo taken about one hundred years ago is in a frame on my desk. I pick it up and stare, brushing my thumb over Leona's image.

My eyes drift toward my own smiling face, I don't even recognize the person in the photo anymore. I set it down gently and wipe a tear that slides down my cheek without even realizing it. I stand up, cross over to the small window, and push the curtain aside to look out at the forest.

A sharp rap sounds at the door, followed by a gruff voice. "Soph, you in there?"

I should have guessed Ian would know the minute I got here. So much for some privacy. I cross over to the door and open it. He is standing in front of my doorway with a small smile on his lips.

"Hey, stranger," he says. He reaches forward and wraps me in a hug. I enjoy the homecoming feeling. He pats me on the back. "How are you doing?"

"I'm OK," I reply as I release him and step back into the room. Noticing his furrowed brow, I feel like he is trying to read my mind, even though that is not one of his talents. "Come on in." He ducks under the threshold. Being over six feet means a lot of ducking.

He comes into the small room, finds the desk chair, and takes a seat. He places a heavy tome on the desk. I close the door and turn to look at him.

Ian is an elder, one of the original generals of the Great Queen's army over a thousand years ago, even if he looks to be only thirty in human years. He is also my childhood hero, mentor, and champion. He was good friends with my parents before they passed away and is the closest thing to a father I have left.

He spreads his long legs out in front of him and crosses his large, heavily muscled arms across his chest. He keeps his blond hair cut short. His light-blue eyes settle on me. He's waiting for me to start.

I swallow. "Guess Bren told you I was going to be coming back." I lean against the door jamb and tap my finger on my thigh, a nervous habit.

"Yeah, he mentioned it," he says. "I wanted to welcome you home and check on you. I know it must be difficult being back here for the first time since Leona."

I nod. "It's hard but feels good." I pause. "Good" was not the right word. "It feels right."

He continues, "You did great work rounding up all of those artifacts. It's a relief to know those items are back with us."

I ask what has been on my mind since last night, "Ian, I want back on rotation. Bren briefed me what has been happening. I know I am most useful out in the field." I look him in the eyes. "I am ready."

He sighs and looks down. That is not a good sign that I'm getting what I want today.

I ask, "What is it? I know I've been gone for a year, but I feel ready now. I have been working on the artifact-recovery project, but that's child's play. I need to find out what really happened to Leona. With what Bren told me yesterday, it is not a coincidence that she died in a similar accident. It must be tied to these new murders." I push off the door jamb and start to pace.

He puts his elbows on his knees and looks up at me. "Yes, we are including Leona with the other suspicious deaths. I have put together a dedicated task force to start investigating the connections of the murders to the factions."

"Okay, put me on that team."

He looks at me and shakes his head. "I have another job I want you to fill first. You are uniquely qualified, and I don't trust anyone else to handle this task."

I look at him in astonishment, "What is more important than solving these murders?" I ask in outrage.

Ian runs his hands through his hair. "It has something to do with the visitor you had in the woods this morning."

"Brenen told you about the intruder and the box?"

His face hardens, and he looks at the tome on the table. "There's a girl, one who turned twenty and is participating in the Selection Day today. She should get through the tests. Gael Monroe." He looks up at me. "I want you to take a teaching post at one of the sectors and mentor her during the next six-month course."

I glare at him. "Why on Earth is this a priority over the murders?"

"She's a special case." He taps his finger lightly on the tome. "She a firewielder, the first in three hundred years."

This is significant, not only because it is a rare gift but also because I remember it was the power of the Great Queen.

Ian continues, "The last firewielder burnt out."

When a Fae uses his or her powers to the limit, the power will pull from their own essence, their soul. Once they reach a point of no return, the power will burn them from the inside out.

"Larkin, the firewielder who died, was a recluse. He kept to himself, living deep in the forest and rarely coming into town. We think mentally he was not able to control his powers, and they burned him out when he tried to use them. Fire is particularly difficult to wield, difficult to know when you are on the edge of burnout. It tends to consume the users. The only reason we found him at all is because a patrol unit came upon his body in the forest."

He leans forward, elbows on his knees. "There are two theories on what happened to Larkin. The first is he fought off the dark creatures, causing him to burn out. The second theory is he burnt out first, causing the fissures, cracks in the barrier itself. The only fact we are sure of is that the dark creatures and Larkin burning out occurred at the same time. Before Larkin was found dead, there were no cracks in the barrier."

I walked toward the window, needing a moment to digest this information. I was told, along with most Fae, that the fissures in the barrier were due to the general length of time since it was sealed.

I ask, "Who knows about Larkin?"

"Only the council. We did not see the need to cause panic, especially since there were no other firewielders alive at the time. Since fire wielding was the Great Queen's power, the council believes that any firewielder will have the power to reseal the gates." He looks up at me. "Or the power to break them wide open."

I stare at him, the idea of the gates falling completely sent a shiver up my spine.

He sighs. "Ideally, of course, we hope she can close the cracks in the gate. She needs help in managing her powers. They are temperamental, and since you have a knack for auras, I want you to take a look and see what we can do to help her."

I give him a nod in understanding, still trying to adjust to the idea that one firewielder held in the palm of her hand the ability to alter the course of our history here on Earth.

He scoots the chair forward and opens the tome to a page already marked. The pages are yellow with age, the handwriting faded, appearing in the ancient Fae language. The page Ian opened showed a drawing of the box Brenen and I saw in the clearing. A stone box, intricately engraved, blue light illuminating from within.

I gasp quietly and move closer to the page. "This is the box we saw today."

"Yes, I believe so. It's one of the founding relics. Each of the original Fae houses had one. Earth, air, water, fire." He looks pointedly at me. "And time, or Chronos as they called themselves." Ian points at the page. "This is the fire relic.

"You know we derive our powers from Faerie, but they do not teach in our history books the structure of our old society. When we were trapped here on Earth, a new republic was formed. The separation of houses was not feasible, as there were so few survivors. We banded together, one united race, the Fae. The way of the past was stripped from our history books."

I wrap my head around this new piece of information.

Ian continues, "Each house, or court, derived their power from a founding relic. This relic is as old as our people. No one knows for sure how long ago they were created. The common belief is the original Fae found the relics, and this is where the source of our power comes from. Alternatively, some believe the original Fae infused their power into the relics, which grew over time. Either way, the relics became the source of each house's power for a millennium. The power is now embedded in the very essences of each descendant.

"While our power here on Earth is substantial compared to the humans, it is nothing compared to the strength we had in Faerie, specifically when our power was combined with our relics."

He turns the page, and I look at the book. It has drawings of the five relics, each with a unique symbol engraved upon it. I had not noticed the engravings on the box we saw earlier today. I lean closer and can see the flames form the lines of a triangle.

Each stone box relic has its own symbol representing the element. Water has three wave lines enclosed in an upside-down triangle, water spilling from the engravings. Air is an orb, wind swirling, lighting cracking with a symbol of opposing swirls of air encompassed by a triangle with a line. Earth is a jade obelisk engraved with the tree of life encompassed by an upside-down triangle with a line. The last one, time, has the all-seeing eye, representing our past, present, future. Light encircles the eye within a triangle.

I ask, "So I would be in the House of Chronos? I can't believe the council wiped this from our history."

He replied, "There are many who have forgotten or were not born before the Great Queen sacrificed herself, many who were not born before the fissures in the barrier appeared three hundred years ago."

Often, I forget how old he really is. I wonder if he ever feels the weight of his past, of the memories he carries with him.

I ask, "I assume it is not a coincidence that the fire house's relic is spotted at the same time a firewielder comes of age? The fire relic would amplify the girl's powers."

"It is possible the birth of a new firewielder drew the relic forward from its resting place."

I look at him with a raised brow. "Drew it forward?"

Ian sighs and runs his fingers through his short hair. "Since the cracks in the barrier started, dark creatures are not the only things slipping through. We have found many relics that were not originally brought to Earth during the transition. Some of these relics, ancient and very powerful, tend to have minds of their own.

"That is the best theory I have. We do not know much about how the founding relics operate. Many of the elders who would know all perished in the Great War. There is the Oracle. I have sent a message to her, but granted audiences are few and far between."

He closes the tome. "It is clear that the lines between Faerie and Earth are further deteriorating, and we do not know how long the barriers will hold."

I sit on the bed. "Tell me about the girl."

"Gael's gifts were kept secret until recently, when she enrolled in the selection. I spoke briefly with her guardian this week, and he explained it was her choice to participate in selection and to reveal her powers so that she could be part of the Warrior Alliance and protect the gates.

The only problem is that Gael needs help unlocking her gifts. When she practices, her powers are erratic. I believe you can help her. If she tries to reseal the gate before she can control her powers, they could fail, or she could burn out and the opposite effect will happen."

Ian doesn't to say aloud what the opposite effect would be. The cracks in the barrier could worsen or even crumble if she lost control.

I start to say something then shake my head. Ian is still sitting in the chair, fingers interlaced, waiting patiently.

I say, "I will take the teaching post and help the girl, but I want to be kept apprised of the murder investigation. I want to assist in my off hours, be involved when I can. Who do you have working on the case?"

Ian responds, "I am keeping it close, only a few trusted people on the task force. Ethen Graham is leading a group of four other trusted members. Noreen Archer is focusing on the witch angle, Rhea Armstrong is working the intelligence angle from her home office, and we are bringing on a human who was close to the last murder victim, Kyle Armstrong. Of course, Bren as well."

I remember hearing the name Ethen Graham mentioned in stories from the other gate in North America but have never met him. Rhea is a connection I am not surprised by either, given fate leading me to save her life. Noreen is a legend in the Witch Academy and is a highly valued asset.

Ian sighs and stands up. "I will make sure you are on the task force. Thank you for helping where we need you. I think you may be the one person who can help Gael reach her full potential." I nod distractedly, my mind still reeling from the revelations.

He continues, "Gael's up for her physical strength, agility, and alertness test." He looks at his watch. "Scheduled for eleven. Let's see how she does."

I nod and head for the door. As we walk down the dormitory hallway toward central command, we settle into a comfortable silence, thoughts swirling through my mind. We emerge into the viewing platform, the tops of the trees visible from our vantage point. The cliff and the river spread out below us. We find an open spot at the glass-paneled platform and settle in to watch.

With my exceptional sight, I can zero in a half mile away and see five recruits across the river, down below the trees getting into start positions. One individual of the group is slight in stature, blonde hair wrapped tight to her head, grit and determination clear on her face.

I look at Ian. "That's her?"

"She's tough. She will make it."

I reply, "I hope she's tough enough."

TWELVE

Gael—Test 1

t's five minutes to eleven as we walk out of the atrium and see the commanders standing outside the large ornate glass doors, down at the bottom of the stairs. I know from Bennett that there are five identical courses spread out over a half acre, not that we can see them with the dense foliage surrounding them. The courses are woven into the trees, the natural obstacles of the forest part of the test. This is a timed, weighted event. If you don't finish the course, your time is zero, which will drag your overall score below the minimum threshold.

The unavoidable truth is that if you don't pass the physical obstacle course, you don't get in the program.

As we descend the large concrete staircase that leads up to the atrium doors, we approach the commanders. I rack my memory trying to place the names. I believe they are Angus Brando and Ethen Graham, along with three other lieutenants we have not met yet. They look up at us as we walk toward them.

Commander Graham asks, "Names?"

"Adriana Blane and Gael Monroe."

Commander Graham checks his handheld device, looks up, and says, "Please put these on." He hands a black leather strap that looks like a necklace to Ari and me. I look at him a little confused. He elaborates, "The neckless prevents any magic from being used that would otherwise help you through the physical portion of the test."

We fasten the plain black bands around our necks. There is little to no give in the fabric. It is tight against my neck.

Graham continues to Ari and I, "Please stand by the starting lines. We are waiting for one more." Ari and I look over to the gravel that is the start of the course to our right. There are five logs indicating the five starting points to each course lined up in a semicircle. From there, you can see the start of each of the courses spread out through the canopy of trees, the foliage dense and hard to see beyond the first tree line. There are five instructors, so they can monitor each person's separate progress.

I see two other males standing by the first start line. As we approach, one with light-brown hair and chocolate-brown eyes looks up and gives us a devastatingly charming smile. His companion sits up on the rock he was lounging on, elbows behind him, blond hair and green eyes assessing us as we come forward.

"Hi, I am Gael Monroe, and this is Ari, sorry, Adriana Blane. We are in Group 12."

The brown-haired male steps forward, extends his hand, and says with a smile exuding charm, "I'm Caden Emery." I can't help but smile back and shake his hand. He has an easy allure that makes me like him immediately. Caden turns that same devastating smile on Ari.

The blond stands and extends his hand, saying, "Gavin Pierce." We shake hands and nod to one another. Ari steps forward and shakes his hand.

I notice Ari has her eyes locked on Gavin and is slightly staring. Wanting to help her out, I see someone approaching out of the corner of my eye. I clear my throat and say, "Hey, I think the fifth member of our team is here." As I hoped, this distraction allows Ari a moment to collect herself. She smiles at me gratefully.

We all turn as a unit. A male with jet-black hair that is collar length, slicked back from his forehead, dark eyes, and a dark expression is waking toward us. "Logan Barlowe," he says gruffly and then stands to the side, leaning against a large boulder on the edge of the space. He crosses his arms against his chest. I get the impression he wants nothing to do with us. I nod in his direction and then turn to focus on the two commanders and three lieutenants joining us.

Showtime.

They stop before our group, Commander Graham begins, "This is the strength, agility, and alertness test. You are Group 12, and all members are present. This is an individual timed course. All times will be weighted at the end of the day, and you will receive your score at that time. You must complete each section of the test. There are three obstacles to overcome. If you do not finish the course, you will be dismissed from the rest of the competition. Any questions?"

This is followed by shaking of our heads and a grunt from Mr. Stoic, AKA Logan, in the back.

Commander Graham continues, "Alright, let's get started. Each of you must line up on the course starting line. When we blow the horn, that is your start time." I walk over to the next open start line, take out a pair of fingerless gloves from my back pocket, and slip them on, squeezing my fingers into the soft, well-worn leather. I bend my knees in a slight squat, blow out my breath in a steady stream, ready to get this show on the road.

My earlier nervousness is gone as the moment arises. I take a deep breath of the crisp autumn air, in through my nose, out through my mouth, eyes closed to concentrate. I've practiced the obstacle course behind my house a thousand times. I am prepared and ready. I glance to my left, see Logan staring straight ahead in a ready position, and to my right I see Ari. I nod at her, and she nods back.

The horn blares, and my feet are moving of their own accord.

I run forward twenty feet, and glance to my left and right. Logan and Ari are already out of view, hidden by the dense forest. The first obstacle spreads out in front of me. There are several downed trees, scattered throughout the grove. The logs are on their sides like fallen soldiers. Some of them, moss covered, look unstable. I had stopped right at the edge of the light-colored sand covering the forest floor, my boots touching the edge.

Throughout the sand are dark spots. I look at the closest one and see the sand moving, swirling into a vortex moving in a downward spiral.

I pick up a rock about the size of my fist and toss it in the vortex. The rock sinks, and vapor explodes out of the vortex, hot enough that I shield my eyes from the burn. I shake my head slightly as the vapor dissipates then pick up a second rock, bouncing it slightly in my hand. I toss it at the seemingly normal light-brown sand. I brace myself with my forearm over my eyes. In a very anticlimactic event, the stone simply is sucked down under the sand.

Well, now I know.

I continue my assessment, squinting up at the tree canopy. I see hanging logs the size of the fallen trees, tied and suspended by thick ropes pulled tight to the right and left of the grove, creating a tube about twenty feet above our heads. My eyes track the ropes down to the ground then see a sequence of thinner ropes crisscrossing over the entirety of the grove we must cross. They are almost invisible when looked at from an angle. I take a stick and lightly pull up on the closest thin rope, about an inch off the nearest log. I hear a click, drop the stick, and take a step backward. One of the battering rams is released, swinging in a direct path, lengthwise. This would surely knock anyone over in that twenty-foot section.

I chew slightly on my bottom lip as I consider the entirety of the test. I visualize my path, right, left, left, right, left, then at the edge of my sight I see the end of the trap and the forest beyond.

Balancing the balls of my feet, I take off to the right, swiftly dodging the intricate web of thin ropes on the fallen trees. I hop onto the first fallen log, making quick work, then jump to the end of the second tree, repeating the balancing act of missing the ropes and avoiding any rotted areas of the tree trunks.

Then I come up to the third fallen tree, which is slightly out of reach. I pause, back up two steps, and jump as far as I can. My first foot lands, my second foot slips, and I see the end of the rotted-out trunk fall into the sand. Quickly, it sinks underneath the surface. My slip pulled one of the ropes, and I flatten myself to the side of the tree trunk. The log released swings over me in a whoosh of air. I breathe for a moment, gripping the sides of the fallen log with my arms and thighs like my life depended on it.

As the swinging battering ram slows its pendulum, I leverage my leg up and over the flat log, pulling myself onto the top. I crouch down to rebalance my weight. The battering ram of a log has slowed to a stop, and I place my hand on the side of it to balance as I continue my path. This time, I am a little more cautious, looking for more rotten sections, careful to avoid the ropes. I jump lightly to the next fallen tree, and my foot goes straight through. I feel sand beneath my foot and drag my limb up through the hole. I look down. Thankfully, no ropes were touched. I cautiously creep across the fallen tree. A few places bend with a creak and a groan, but I keep moving.

I come up to the last tree, take a deep breath, and jump. Thankfully, the tree is solid. I look forward and can see the end of the course and the forest beyond. If I have any hope of missing the quicksand and landing safely on the forest floor, I will need to take it at a run. Light footed, I cross the thirty-foot tree and take the last jump as close to a run as possible. I throw myself to the edge of the normal forest floor, as far and fast as I can manage. I land hard on my shoulder and roll, ending in a crouch. Eyes scan for any further danger.

I look up into the unblinking, non-expressive face of one of the lieutenants. He types something on his handheld device, unimpressed.

Ignoring him, I am up and running the next second. I click the side of my watch, hear the beep, and see my time. Five minutes and fourteen seconds through the first obstacle. I am on track, but there is not a second to spare.

I come to a sheer cliff. There is no left or right to get around. I must go up. My eyes track upward and see the footholds that will bring me to the top. I am grateful for all the grueling hours spent on the course climbing ropes, clinging from my fingertips. I will need that strength for this next test. I read the cliff, looking for any traps like the quicksand. I see some protruding metal stakes at different intervals. I grimace in distaste, sure they are not designed to be helpful.

It's hard to see on the ground, but I make my best assessment about the most efficient way up the cliff. I see a pocket above my head about six feet. I jump and place my hand in the small area, swinging my body so that my left hand can be placed on a small ledge that only holds my fingertips. I brace my feet in a wedge of the rock and start the grueling climb to the top. I get halfway up, repeating my pocket, ledge, and wedge maneuvers. I get to a point where there is a smooth expanse of granite, no pockets or ledges to rely on. About ten feet away is another ledge I can continue upward with.

To get there, I need to use the metal stake protruding from the blank wall.

I lean my head against the cool stone, closing my eyes for a second. I know as soon as I grab that stake some sort of trap will be released. I take a deep breath. I grab the stake and hop as quickly as possible to the next ledge. As I move, I hear a rumble and flatten myself against the crevasse in the granite. A waterfall of rocks and debris start raining down, missing me by inches. As the debris stops falling, I peer up the cliff and see the top. I swiftly start to climb, one foothold to the next, until I see the ledge. I heave myself over the top of the cliff and relax there for a moment, my breathing labored. I push the button on the watch, five minutes and fifty seconds. The second lieutenant looms above me with his handheld device, marking off my assent.

I lost time on the climb. Fifteen minutes total for the course was my goal. I jump up and see the Aurora River that runs through Tarrin. On the opposite side of the river is one of the commanders, Ethen Graham.

I know the last obstacle is to get to the other side of the river and rack my brain trying to remember anything I ever learned about the Aurora. This was one obstacle we never trained for. I reach the edge of the bank and pause to check for any traps. All I see is the rushing water of the river spanning about twenty feet, swiftly moving. I have no idea how deep it is. I put my fingers to the edge of the river and immediately feel an icy burn. I realize there are no traps for this test. Only brute strength and grit will get me across the river.

I know the water will sweep under my feet, and I will be down river before I can blink. I look to my right and see a large branch on the ground about two inches around and as tall as me. I grab it and break off the small protruding branches, making a walking stick.

I take my first step into the icy water. Immediately, my feet go numb. My teeth start to chatter as the water goes up my thighs. My focus is solely on getting across the river. I repeat my mantra in my head.

I will not fail.

Now waist deep, I plunge the walking stick deep into the riverbed and pull myself a step forward, plant my feet, and then take the stick and reposition another foot ahead. Slow and steady.

The water is now above my breasts. I continue, one foot in front of the other. By the time I get to the other side of the riverbank, my teeth are chattering and my lips must be blue. I drag myself onto the bank and collapse there for a moment. I reach my watch with my fingers shaking and click the button. Four minutes and thirty seconds. Just under my goal. Shivers wrack my frame uncontrollably, and I tuck my arms into my body. As I look up at Commander Graham, I see him mark my completion on his device. I drop my head on the wet ground and breathe a sigh of relief.

I made it through my first challenge.

THIRTEEN

Caleb—Central Sector

As the road drops down into the valley on the final switchback turn, I stare at the overwhelming beauty of the city. Everywhere I turn, homes, businesses, and shops are built around the lush foliage of the natural forest. Great care was taken not to disturb the existing grove, trees uninterrupted by the city built around it. I stare in amazement at buildings intermingled with nature.

On the ground level, the rolling hills in this valley showcase homes built into the sides of the terrain. As I look up, I see houses are perched up in the trees. There are interconnected pathways crossing the tree branches, allowing walkways in the canopy. As I drive on, there is only one wide paved road that winds through the center of the city. Smaller outlets are here and there, which must branch out into the surrounding neighborhoods.

Unlike a normal city with checkered streets in straight lines, all the streets here flow seamlessly with the existing nature of the land. I see multiple bridges spanning a beautiful river, each one intricately carved out of stone. What I do not see are any other vehicles.

The road is paved, so I ask Rhea, "Are there many cars in Idyll?"

Rhea smiles. "Yes, we need transportation outside of Tarrin and use it regularly. However, once you are here in our capital, you can travel through the runestones to any destination within the bounds of our magic. Tarrin spans 840 miles, all of which are accessible by our runestones. Most cars are parked below the residences in underground garages."

She points to an incoming vehicle that turns down a side street. I put the brakes on to watch. A door opens on the side of a home, and the car drives down underground. The door closes and is not visible from the street anymore. I shake my head as I continue my drive through the beautiful city.

Ahead, on my right, I see a large glass building that dominates the grove. Rhea sits up and asks, "Can you make a right into the underground garage? It's right there. See the stone?" A similar stone to the one we saw up on the vista peak is visible, and I turn right. Rhea hands me the ring. "Place this on the stone. It is what grants access to the car park."

I roll down my window, place the ring on the stone, and feel warmth and slight vibration spread through me. The ground opens directly in front of us, creating a downward drive leading to a garage. I glance over at Rhea, who gives me a nod, and I proceed, suddenly feeling as if I have reached the point of no return.

I park, and we start making our way toward the elevator. As we walk through the full garage, we pass multiple high-end vehicles. A Lamborghini Urus is parked right next to the elevator, and I let out a low whistle.

Rhea looks at the vehicle with a slight tilt of her head. "I'm not sure who drives that." She shrugs and pushes the call button.

The glass building is straight above us now. We get in the lift and up we go. The elevator opens into a massive hallway, glass on all sides looking out into the forest. The windows give the feeling we are sitting in a canopy of trees high above the forest floor. I scan the space, noting the massive circular room straight ahead that has a viewing platform busy with people. I look right and wonder briefly where that other hallway leads to.

Rhea motions, and we make a left turn. I keep up with my guide, keeping the questions to myself in favor of taking in my surroundings.

She leads me to a large circular room. There are comfortable group stations scattered throughout. Some stations are set up for larger groups with long tables and multiple computer screens. Other nooks are set up with cushioned chairs and desk spaces. Large windows surround the circular room, letting in the late morning light. Currently, the room is empty. All this space and not a soul occupies it.

I ask Rhea, "Where is everyone?"

"Today is Selection Day. Every year, Fae who have come of age can voluntarily nominate themselves to be evaluated for the Warrior Alliance. All non-essential personnel are off for the day. Sort of like a national holiday."

As she meanders through the room, she continues, "This is Central Sector. This sector is responsible for the city of Idyll and the surrounding areas. There are five other sectors in Tarrin territory. While each sector is responsible for their own monitoring and patrolling, they report back to the Central Sector daily. This is the information hub for all of Tarrin."

She walks toward the large windows. "At any given time, we have approximately one hundred Fae warriors or human soldiers in rotation in each sector, rotating in shifts on their patrols. Many of them are assigned to the dormitories on site to use in between shifts to rest. We also have an infirmary on site where our healers help warriors or soldiers who need medical attention."

She gestures through a large archway, and we walk through. I look up and up and up. Three stories tall, the room is lined with books on all sides. This is the largest library I have ever been in. Where the rest of the building has a wooden planked roof, this one has a stained-glass ceiling letting the late morning sunshine in. On all sides of this massive room are bookshelves with rolling ladders to reach the taller shelves. In the middle are long tables with reading lamps stationed at intervals. The side alcoves are set up with sofas or oversized chairs situated around coffee tables.

Rhea leads me back through the middle of the library and turns right. We pass by small rooms that have whiteboards, desks, and chairs occupying them. She motions to these rooms and says, "Private rooms for group meetings." I nod and looked around.

She asks, "Do you want to see the command center?" I nod, and she continues, "Today is Selection Day, so we may be able to see some of the recruits go through their obstacle courses. The command center has a large viewing area." She continues her tour, leading me to the end of the library and through a huge set of wooden arched doors. "This is the back entrance to the command center. The main entrance is through the large hallway we started in."

I'm pretty much speechless about everything I'm seeing.

We walk into a large viewing area, where several people already standing at the edge of the glass. I can see that it overlooks a huge expanse of open land, undeveloped. The rugged terrain has a river running through it with a large stone cliff overhang ending in a canopy of trees. I take a closer look and see people climbing up the side of the sheer cliff, free handed as far as I can tell. I squint and see five bodies clinging tight.

As I watch, they maneuver up the side, and then suddenly rocks and debris drop down on their heads. I look at Rhea in concern, but she waves it off. "It's part of the test." My brow furrows, and I nod as I turn back to the view, hoping they make it to the top.

Rhea motions to the room behind us and says, "Let's keep going."

We moved to the main thoroughfare of the command center, passing various screens and monitoring equipment as we reached the main hallway. Individuals are busy at work with coms in their ears, dedication evident in their serious faces. Clearly, not everyone is taking the day off.

We walk down the massive hallway toward the main entrance to the building. Rhea stops. "I'm sure you have a lot of questions."

"I do but don't know what they are yet."

She laughs, "You are free to wander around the sector or go into town. That will give you some time to get acclimated. I believe we should have a task force meeting set in the next twenty-four hours."

I say, "I think I will stay close. In case I leave, can I have a talisman to get back?"

She smiles at me. "I took the liberty to request one before speaking with you yesterday." She holds up a talisman, and it glints in the light. "It is keyed to one of the dormitories here at Compound #103, in case you decide to stay."

She continues, "Tonight, the annual Selection Day ball is thrown in honor of all recruits who are invited into the program." She points out the windows to a neighboring building, saying, "It's next door at the Capital Center. If you are interested, dinner is at six, formal attire. I asked housekeeping to bring suitable clothes to your room."

I ask, "Will you be there?"

She looks away for a moment. "Yes, I am obligated to attend as one of the collective members." She starts to turn away and then shifts back to me. "I had hoped you would take the job. I am glad I was right."

Rhea leaves me in the middle of the hallway.

The talisman in hand, I look down at the ring. Running my fingers over the face in the circle, I inspect the insignia. Etched into the surface are three connected mountains with a gate in the foreground, beams of sunlight stretching above the mountains.

This is the same insignia on the collection coin left on Kyle's casket at the funeral. I look up and peer out the glass windows into the new world I have been thrust into. Making the decision to stay, I pocket the talisman and stroll out the front doors.

FOURTEEN

Sophia—Traversing Solo

an and I watch the girl complete her first test. I turn to face him. "I'm going to get some air."

He nods and squeezes my shoulder. "Come by the arena for the final test at two."

"Alright, I'll be there."

I walk across the command center main hallway and spot Manus, one of the most gifted reconnaissance team members in our alliance. Busy at his desk, I walk toward him. He glances up, and a wide grin splits his face as he catches sight of me.

"Haya, Soph. It's good to see you back."

I give him a smile and say genuinely, "It's good to be back. I'm not sure yet where I will be stationed, but we will catch up soon."

He nods, and I can tell he is distracted by someone speaking to him through his earpiece. He puts his hand to his ear and says, "Copy that." Manus gives me an apologetic smile.

I wave and mouth, "See you soon."

Once out of the command center, I realize it really is good to be back.

My soft boots make no noise on the polished floors as I head to the dormitory section of the facility. The need to get out into nature is gnawing at the back of my mind. It has been too long since I've roamed the forest floor. It's been too long since I've been home.

Back in my dorm, I call housekeeping. The staff here in the Central Sector is top notch. They have a Fae who has been here forever, the best at what she does.

"Hi, this is Sophia Beaumont, room 250." I wait for a moment as they pulled my file.

"Ah, Ms. Beaumont, welcome back. What can we do for you to today?"

I respond, "I realize it's short notice, but I need a gown for tonight. Do you still have my measurements?"

Over the phone, I hear a rustling of paperwork. "Yes, Ms. Beaumont, it shouldn't be a problem. Do you have a preference of color?"

I am rummaging through my bag and spotting something shiny at the bottom. I pull out the ruby necklace, and it shines in the sunlight. I tell housekeeping, "Red, jewel tone." I hang the necklace from the lamp next to the bed.

"Yes, Ma'am, it will be ready by five. We will deposit it in your room."

As I stare at the necklace, I reply distractedly, "Fantastic, thank you."

The craftsman tailor Daphne was the best of all Idyll. A true master, she supplies all the sectors' needs. Anything from ball gowns to fighting leathers. The fighting wardrobe she created for me, as with most of the warriors, was interwoven with magical defensive properties. The leather would repel magical potions and deflect any punctures from bullets or other sharp objects.

Daphne's workshop always has a collection of random new inventions that she is working on. Last time I was there, she showed me a leather vest that was designed to repeal Gila venom. Last year, there was a large influx of Gila creatures that spit venom and would sting with its poisonous breath. I wonder what new inventions she has in her shop this year and make a mental note to visit soon.

I glance down, and right on top of my bag is the fighting leather uniform I have not worn in a year. I bite my bottom lip as I look at the uniform then glance out the window. I run my fingers over the worn leather, my fingers tracing the warrior motto imprinted on the back neck of the uniform.

This symbol was used long before humans branded it their own. Before the gates were closed. Three semicircles inter-connected, representing courage, honor, and strength. This was the old motto of the Queen's Guard, now adopted for the Citadel Warrior Alliance. It is a match to the tattoo on the inside, soft part of my wrist, received the day I passed qualifications testing three hundred years ago.

With that memory fresh in my mind, I pull out the leathers and decide it's time.

I quickly change out of the soft brown leggings and ankle boots and into the leather uniform that still fits like a glove. I add a soft layer of cotton that fits perfectly under the leather top, protecting my skin from the heat of the leather. Next were the brown leather pants and a snug long-sleeve leather top that cinches in the back, scooping down in the front, showing a hint of cleavage.

I slip on my shoulder holster sheath then slide in my sword. Next are my two thigh sheaths that hold daggers and one 9mm. I lace up my soft-soled leather boots and left the braid in my hair. The tip of my locks brushes the small of my back. Red highlights glint in the sun.

I look at my reflection in the mirror, my weapons shining, and I smile. A girl can never be too careful.

I quickly make my way out of the compound and up the side of the ridge. I hear nothing but the melody of songbirds, insects chirping, and the wind blowing through the trees. My feet move swiftly and silently through the forest floor, skipping over branches and dodging rocks without thinking. In moments, I am crossing over the bridge that spans the lower section of the Aurora. I pause to take in my surroundings. This beautiful bridge has been here for a thousand years. I look up and see the Aurora River winding in the distance starting from the waterfall, and I know my destination.

Right after the waterfall, there is a quiet section of the river that is my favorite spot in all of Tarrin. Starting the journey, I know it is about a fifteen-minute run at full speed, and I am in the mood to let my feet carry me as fast as they can. I speed through the forest, jumping, dodging, and moving so fluidly, you might only see a blur of movement if you were standing still. I relish the freedom, the wind in my face and the joy of feeling the forest beneath my feet.

As I approach my destination, my feet slow and I come up to the edge of the river. I can hear the thunder of the water crashing down in the distance. A long, flat stone protrudes out into the riverbed, and I can see the magnificent waterfall beyond the bend in the river. I used to spend many relaxing afternoons here with Bren and Ian when I was younger. This place holds a special place in my heart.

I take a moment to enjoy the peacefulness of this place. I walk out onto the stone and close my eyes. I release my mind and spread out my senses as far as they can reach. Not picking up any other energy in the area, aside from the normal aminals of the forest, I relax my mind and sigh to myself. My heart is at peace here in Tarrin.

A small smile plays on my lips, and I walk to the edge of the water. There is a small but very deep pool of water beyond the flat stone. This space warmed by the Earth, the temperature of the water holds a year-round comfortable temperature. The autumn sun beats down on my head, tempting me to jump in as I feel sweat trickle down my back.

I take off the weaponry and leather uniform, placing them carefully on the flat stone right at the edge of the water. I dip my bare feet into the cool water, breaking the calm surface. Deciding to take the plunge, I jump in with a beautiful dive to cool off. My head breaks the surface, and I lazily paddle for a moment. The ice-cold water is a welcome relief to the heat.

The peacefulness is interrupted by a rustling in the leaves. My sensitive ears pick up movement at the edge of the forest. I move slowly in the water, languorously, so as not to alert my intruder. I force myself to appear calm, unaware.

Once my weapons are in reach, I pause and extend my senses one more time. I have the sense of being hunted, but this is no animal. This predator is Fae.

Partly covered by the stone, I take one breath, then I am in motion. I reach up in an arc and have my dagger in my left hand and gun pointed at the edge of the forest on my right. A split second passes, and I pause, breathing heavily.

Someone calls out, "Don't shoot. I'm a friendly."

I tilt my head to the side, gaging if I recognize the voice. I say, "Come on out of the forest." There is no verbal reply, but I see a large shape come to the edge of the forest line, then a male is walking toward me out into the sunlight. My breath catches as I drink in the sight in front of me. Tall, well over six feet, olive skin, dark eyes, and dark hair falling over his brow. He has a roguish grin on his face, as if he enjoys being held at gunpoint.

I say, "Who are you, and what are you doing out here?" My gun is still pointing at his large, broad chest.

His smile intensifies as if he really is enjoying the moment.

"I could ask the same thing about you. Hasn't anyone told you there is a ban on solo traversing the sector?" He walks over to a tree on the edge of the forest and leans against it, striking a relaxed pose. He crosses one powerful leg over the other and drapes muscular arms over his chest. I can see the shrewdness in his sharp eyes and know the predator is lurking beneath the surface. The calm relaxed pose is intent on disarming me.

I look at him and say, "It's been a while since I've been here. I haven't heard about any restrictions."

He looks at me sharply. "It's not safe in the forest." He pauses for a moment before adding, "Alone."

He looks at me in an appreciative way, his eyes drifting down the length of my body, right above the waterline and back up. With that look, I feel heat flooding my cheeks, and my blood pressure rises.

"I can take care of myself. I was enjoying the solitude." I look up at him, pointedly saying, "Until you interrupted."

He lets loose a loud laugh, amusement lining his handsome face. Sobering slightly, he says, "The new restrictions require us to travel in pairs or not at all."

I placed my weapons on the rock ledge, since it seems he is not intent on killing me.

For the moment anyway.

I glare at him. "This is my first day back in almost a year. I haven't heard of the restrictions before now." I drink in the sight of him leaning against the tree and feel an immediate fascination that drew me toward him. His allure is irresistible.

I walk up the bank, knowing the thin loose shirt I am wearing is clinging to my wet skin. I can feel my taut nipples clearly imprinted on the thin fabric, and I have a moment of not caring in the slightest. He was the one intruding.

I raise my gaze to his eyes and again feel pulled by his dark and rugged demeanor. My hips sway as I climb out of the river. I see his eyes darken, sweeping over me as I walk toward him. His gaze rakes over me, lingering on the swell of my hips and the peaks of my breasts clearly visible under the shirt. His gaze finally lifts to my eyes when I am within touching distance.

I tilt my head and say, "You never answered my question. Who are you, and why do you care if I am out here alone?"

The stranger starts to speak when suddenly our attention is pulled toward the forest by a stampeding sound in the distance. He does not have a chance to respond before my head whips around. An influx of coyotes streams out of the forest, winding through the brush, heading straight toward the river. As I look closer, I see them jumping and scrambling over each other to get to the water. They splash into the depths and start to paddle across to the other side. What on Earth? I turn to the stranger next to me, who has drawn his broadsword.

That is all the information I need.

I spin and reach for my weapons. Sword in hand, I ready myself for an attack. The noise stops as the coyotes scramble out of sight. In the deafening silence, the hair on the back of my arm stands up. My eyes scan the perimeter, looking for anything out of the normal. Eerily quiet, it's the calm before the storm.

Deep in the shadows, I see a glint of yellow and squint trying to get a better idea of what it was. As I make out the yellow eyes and features of the creature, the eyes blink, and I raise my sword in preparation.

The beast jumps directly at me.

Mid jump, the features of the creature are revealed, elongated head, pointed ears covered in shaggy fur. Its razor-sharp claws are heading right for my face. I swing my sword up at the beast's outstretched belly.

I realized I'm too late.

Claws are inches from my neck. My sword blade will kill the beast, but not before the talons slice my body. Instinctually, I release my power, and time stops. I take a deep breath. Everything around me is frozen. I look to my right and see the male, name still unknown, leaping forward as if he would knock the massive creature away from me.

Then the strangest occurrence happens. I see his form quiver in the stillness. My head tilts to the side as I look at him in confusion. I see his arms break free, then my time warp is shattered.

Before I can utter the curse on the tip of my tongue, I swing a few inches to the right. Time resumes, and my blade slices the beast's belly open, but not before those claws sink into my turned shoulder. I grunt in pain.

The male crashes into the creature, knocking it to the side while wrapping his arms around me in a tuck and roll that leaves his large body on top of mine. My labored breaths rise and fall, my chin tucked into his shoulder, his legs intertwined with my own. I breathe deep, and his scent is intoxicating. A rich blend of warm spices and citrus tantalizing my senses. I look up into his eyes and see golden flecks glittering in the sunlight. I suck in a breath, this time because of the proximity of our bodies rather than any risk to our lives.

What is it about this male that engulfs me into his aura?

He looks at me. "You okay?"

"Yes, I think he got me in the shoulder, but I'll be okay."

He brings me to a seated position as he examines the wounds, three gashes down my shoulder, one down my hip. "You are lucky. It could have been worse." I look down at my shoulder and see the skin already knitting back together. It is a relief to heal so fast.

It has been a long time since I have seen a dire wolf. The legendary beast was much larger than any normal wolf. Its head would brush my collarbone when standing. I look over at the body of the majestic creature, the length at least twenty feet from nose to tail. It is lying off to the side on the shore, its long shaggy hair matted with blood, razor-sharp teeth exposed, reminding me how close a call it was. A shiver runs down my spine.

Sightings of the dire wolves started after the gates started to crack open, and since then they have been hunted for sport. I ask him, "I thought they were hunted to extinction. Have there been sightings recently?"

He nods grimly. "Dire wolves, dark creatures, and various other nasties have been sighted regularly."

"Uh-huh," I murmur under my breath as I tuck that piece of knowledge away for research later. "How did you break through my time warp? I have never met anyone who could do that before."

He smiles at me, seemingly pleased at having bested my ability. "I have super speed, even for a Fae. I was able to push my way through at max speed." His confident grin leaves me with mixed emotions. Hundreds of years of having an unbeatable gift are gone, and I'm a little disgruntled.

Miffed that he broke my unbreakable time warp, I cock my head at him. "The only reason the beast got to me was because you broke through my time warp. Next time, don't do me any favors." I push off him and stand up, smarting on my right leg, pain shooting from my side down my leg, I can feel the secondary wound knitting together. In a few more minutes, there will be no indication that I was ever injured.

The stranger is up the next moment, looking down at me with a sense of male machismo and a slightly crooked grin. "I like that there's going to be a next time. You would be dead if I did not intervene."

I look at him in distain and roll my eyes. "You would like to think so."

I turn to retrieve my leather uniform and weapons. He grabs my arm and spins me back. I am only inches away from him once again, all too aware of my lack of attire. I look up, and he continues like I had not walked away. "You never told me your name."

His voice pours over me like honey, his eyes boring into mine. I feel entrapped by his gaze, as if I could never pull myself away. Why would I even want to? Captivated, my body involuntarily leans into his warmth, as I silence the small nagging voice at the back of my mind.

Suddenly, darkness overcomes the sun, and a shiver runs down my spine, breaking the enchantment. Instead of the warmth of the sun that brought me here, all I feel now is the cold dampness of beguilement. I shake my head lightly and pull out of his grasp. Confused at the encounter, I turn and start walking toward my leathers at the edge of the stones.

"What's it to you?"

The male, oblivious to the darkness I witnessed and my reaction, says across the clearing in a cocky tone, "Not to worry, Red. I will find out on my own."

My head swivels around at the comment. I know he meant it to be lighthearted, but suddenly it seems like a threat. As my eyes sweep the forest, the mystery male has disappeared as quickly as he arrived.

I look up into the bright sun and remember the warning my instincts gave me.

I whisper into the silence, "Good luck."

FIFTEEN

Gael—Test 2

Throughout my scalding hot shower, I listen to Ari gush over Gavin Pierce. We emerge from the showers and move on to getting dressed, when she stops to look at me.

"Gael, did you see him after the test? He looked like he got burnt by one of those vortexes with steam. The side of his uniform was black." Ari chews the side of her nail before pulling the uniform over her head. "It looked like he healed. Oh, I hope that means he will still do well in the next test."

She pauses in front of her locker, staring at the duffle bag we were issued, clearly still focused on her newfound infatuation.

I roll my eyes and smile at her. She has it bad. "He looked fine to me. We heal fast." That is all I say. "You ready?"

Ari sighs and closes her locker. "Yup. Don't forget your item for the magic test." She raises her fighting stick, and I show her my lighter. I don't need a lighter to create the fire, but it does help when I am focusing. Every recruit has the option to bring one item with them to the magic test for demonstration only. As we leave the locker room, I am thankful we are on our way to lunch. My hunger pangs are getting harder to squash as the day wears on.

We emerge through the glass doors of the cafeteria, trays in hand, when Ari stops in her tracks. The man on her mind is seated straight ahead of us at a round table with Caden.

Ari says out of the corner of her mouth, "We should get to know them, you know, strictly so we can perform better during the group event."

I glance over at her and roll my eyes. "Sure, what better time than lunch?"

She looks sideways at me and grins. "Research purposes only."

I smile at her. *Riiiiight.*

As we approach the table, I ask, "You guys mind if we join you?"

Caden lifts one corner of his lips in a charming smile. "Would love the company." His flirtatious reply has my cheeks warming, and I sit down across from the two guys. Gavin stands, pushes an extra chair toward Ari, and settles in next to her. I can't help but grin at the chivalry. I am happy for her.

Gavin says, "Glad to see you ladies made it through the first test. You ready for the second?"

Ari gives him a megawatt smile. "Yeah, I'm as ready as I'm going to be."

Gavin glances at her "What are your gifts?"

"I have a camouflage gift. I can hide myself and objects I touch as well."

Gavin's brow furrows. Knowing Ari will be demonstrating, I push the tray slightly toward her as I take a bite of my sandwich.

Ari reaches across the table and touches the tray of food, I feel a small amount of energy, and the tray completely disappears. Gavin looks impressed. "Wow, you will earn high marks for that."

I see a blush on her cheeks. She lets go of the tray, and it becomes visible again. "What's your gift?"

He replies with satisfaction, "I am an earth mover."

Ari's eyes widen, and she nods while looking smitten.

Liam walks by as Gavin was speaking, and says to him, "Hope your talents are good enough to carry her dead weight." He hooks his thumb in my direction and then laughs as I compress my lips into a tight line. Gavin turns curious eyes toward me, and I feel the table follow suit.

My cheeks redden as I look up at Liam, saying, "Don't make the mistake of underestimating me. We will see today how the judges mark our powers." I stand abruptly, not liking having him tower over the table.

A loud bell vibrates through the cafeteria, and I glance at my watch. Lunch is over, and we wasted most of it warming up after our trek through the icy water. Other groups start to gather their things and leave the cafeteria. Liam and his crew saunter off, and I sigh as I look at his retreating back.

Ari grips my hand and whispers, "Don't let them rattle you. Today is the day you can show them all."

I give her a quick squeeze and look over at our small group. "Time to go."

Caden and Gavin still are looking at us quizzically but thankfully don't push it as we collectively get up and put our trash in the bins by the door and head to our next test.

In the gymnasium, there are five sections of runestones set up for each participant in our group. To the side are two of the commanders, Ava O'Hara and Gabriella Ventura, along with three of their lieutenants. We approach the instructors, and from the other side of the gym I see our fifth member, Logan Barlowe, approaching from the other side. The instructors note our names on their devices, the same procedure as the first test.

Gabriella walks forward and addresses the group with a stoic demeanor. She is taller than I thought during the introduction. I notice as she crosses her arms in front of her chest how muscular she is.

"Welcome to the magic portion of the testing today. You are given fifteen minutes to display your magical abilities within each of the runestone structures. You are allowed one item of your choosing for demonstration purposes only."

I flick the lid to the lighter back and forth, a nervous habit. I glance at our other teammates and see Gavin has a small rock in his hand. I am curious how he would show his earth-moving abilities with that. Caden brought a jug of water, which would make sense if he had a water affinity. Lastly in our group, Logan pulls a flashlight from his pocket. I am puzzled trying to figure out what Logan's power is.

Gabriella brings my attention back to her. "Each of you, please go to your individual rings."

The rings are set up in a semicircle. We take our places. I look next to me where Ari is stationed and give her a thumbs up, and I see Caden past Ari. He nods to me in encouragement. I give him a nod back. The whistle blows, and we begin.

With a quick flick of the wrist, the flame from my lighter comes to life. I set it down on the ground in front of me. Closing my eyes, I reach deep inside myself where my power comes from. I envision fanning the small flame, imagine it taking on a life of its own. I pull the flame from the lighter and hold it in my cupped hands, sheltering the flame and feeling its warmth rush through my body.

I take a deep breath and focus my energy as I push a trickle of power through the flame. It pushes upward, curving around my body. With a whisper of a breeze, the flame fans. I heard an exclamation from one of the coaches. I'm not sure which one or even if it was about me, but I don't dare take my focus away from what I am doing.

I work the flame into ribbons of fire that reach to the top of the rune-stone structure. The flame is wrapped around me like an elaborate scroll, dipping and diving until I am surrounded by fiery ropes of flame.

Time for the second phase of my demonstration. This is the sticky part. I need to demonstrate how I can make the flame a weapon. I pull on the ribbons of flame and make them into spears, swords, and daggers surrounding me like a fiery army.

My army is holding strong, so I open my eyes and look around the small area, stunned by our team. My focus snared, I observed Gavin displaying his abilities in an expert way. The simple rock has been pulverized into sand, sitting in the palm of his hand as it forms a small cyclone. As I watch, he pushes power into the cyclone, and the sand rises around him. I can barely see Gavin standing in the eye of the storm. Impressive.

I chance a glance past Ari who was killing it with her camouflage skill, and see Caden at work. He took the jug of water and was able to form a solid wall of water, concealing him from view. Suddenly, he separates the water into bullet-sized drops of water, shooting them at the barriers. I see one of the judges flinch and make a note on his tablet.

Beyond Caden, Logan places the flashlight on the ground behind him. In front of him is his shadow. As I watch, he takes his shadow and is manipulating it to make it larger than him. He stretches and pulls the shadow to wrap around him, covering himself in darkness. When Logan disappears into the shadows, I feel my concentration falter, hear a small pop, and watch my magic disappear.

Shoot, when I get distracted, my concentration fails. As I scramble to get it back, I curse to myself.

I close my eyes and focus on gently fanning the flame back to life. This is my major problem. I have trouble holding my concentration, then my magic is gone in a blink of an eye. Very bad if you are in a combat situation. It is very dangerous to rely on faulty magic.

I feel the fiery ropes around me once more, and I rebuild my arsenal from memory. Swords, daggers, and spears. My eyes open, and I channel my energy into maneuvering my weapons into a fighting dance.

I close my eyes and breathe for a moment, repeating my mantra. I've got this.

I pick up a spear and start executing my well-practiced routine. I dip and dive and execute the fighting pattern I have been working on with Bennett. The rest of the flames swoop and dive around me. I get through the set and then hold all the flames still for a moment. I resume the fluid fighting routine, utilizing the flame weapons I have created.

Before I know it, the whistle blows and the test time is over. I pull the flames to my body and extinguish them in one breath. As my eyes open, I look up and see the instructors typing on their devices.

I glanced over at Ari, our eyes locked. I hope our scores are good enough.

SIXTEEN

Caleb—All the Gin Joints

turn my head toward downtown as I descend the massive steps leading from the compound. This new reality is churning in my mind,
making it hard to focus on any one of the magnificent things I have
learned today.

To the right, I see winding, curving walking paths out in front of me.
Unlike a normal city center, there is not one straight road to be found.
Restaurants and boutiques line winding tracks intercepted by trees,
rolling hills, and lush foliage as far as I can see.

The area is quiet, only a few people here and there. I squint. In the
distance is a corner building, two stories tall, dominating the street. I
see patrons opening the door to go in and am reasonably sure it is a bar.
Thinking I could use a drink right now, I head down the winding cobblestone walkway, peering into the shops lining the road as I pass.
Most of the stores are closed, I think, because of the holiday. However,
their window displays give me a good sense of what they sell.

The shop on the right catches my eye. The sign above the storefront
reads, "The Forge: Fine Crafted Metalwork." I stand at the front window admiring the beautifully crafted swords, daggers, and spears displayed in the window among a large variety of weapons that I do not

have names for. I can identify axes, scythes, and various shields that look like they are from medieval times. The rest are wicked-looking blades in various shapes and sizes. I wouldn't want to be on the receiving end of any of them.

Beyond the weapons, I peer into the depths of the shop to see chests, goblets, decorative plates, and figurines that glint in the light. Each item is intricately carved, beautifully crafted.

I keep walking, the next shop is Gwyneth's Genuine Elixirs and Salves. The display in the front glass windows looks like some sort of high-end bath boutique. The bright yellow and white building looks cheerful. The front display promotes soaps and bath salts next to neatly lined glass bottles. I look closer, and the sign below them reads, "Enduring Elixir—Energizing restoration in a bottle." A similar neatly lined row next to it has a sign that reads, "Sleeping Elixir—For a deep therapeutic sleep." On the small shelf next to the bottles, I see short round jars of what look like cream. The sign reads, "Cedarwood magical healing salve—Treat fissures, abscesses, boils, and general wound care."

I wonder how effective the healing elixirs and salves may be in Idyll. I am sure they are better than anything over the counter at my local pharmacy.

Next door, the second shop is inter-connected. This one the opposite of the bright and cheery elixirs and salve shop. The dark wooden shop has a black trim and a wooden sign overhead reading in white, "K's Knockout Potions and Poisons." Curious. I look at the front circular displays of small containers in a variety of colors. The first display I see reads, "Amore—World's strongest love potion." The next reads, "Beautification—Be the best version of yourself."

I give a slight shake of my head and keep walking when the next sign catches my eye. "Offensive Potions and Poisons." Intrigued, I look closer. Below each of the neatly filed rows are labels. "Exploding-destruction grenade." Next on the shelf was "Fortify—Amplifying potion for any power." Next to that is "Stun Potion—Temporarily stun enemies." On the display, I see poisons separated by type: corrosive, irritant, and neurotic. Shaking my head, I may need Rhea to walk me through the best options. I am out of my element.

I turn and look across the street to the restaurant. Dragon Delight Diner is brightly displaying a luminescent green dragon over the building, not a soul inside the glass windows. Next to that is Phoebe's Enchanted Edibles Eatery, which has a closed sign out front.

The corner building sign reads, "Nine Spirits." An open sign is in the window. This was my original destination before I got thoroughly distracted.

I walk across the street and look up at the sign outside of the bar. I shrug at the unusual name and walk into the establishment. Almost like an old cowboy movie, heads turn in my direction, and the doors swing behind me. There's a collective moment of silence, and then the din resumes, people continue their conversations, and the clink of glasses follow.

As I head forward into the bar, I look around at the space. It is a lot bigger inside than it looks on the outside. I imagined it to be a small single room establishment. Instead, the front door opens into a large open space with multiple levels. To the right is an alcove next to a window facing the street. Four or five tables take up space, a few of them occupied by patrons.

My eyes sweep the room up one step. There is a line of round booths against the far wall extending back into the depths of the bar. To the left, two rounded booths are set up, and then the bar top comes into view. A long mahogany counter, intricately engraved, spans the rest of the room.

Beyond the bar is a set of stairs, and a mezzanine is visible with a rod iron rail overlooking the rest of the room. Ornate wallpaper and paintings cover the walls, low lighting hanging above each of the booths to create a warm, vibrant vibe. Jazz music plays in the background. While I have never been a fan of the genre, it suits the atmosphere.

I approach the bar. The wall behind has glass mirrors displaying rows and rows of high-end liquor. Some of the bottles I recognize, and some of them I've never seen before. Do they have different Fae liquor?

A bartender approaches. He wears a long-sleeve shirt and a vest with a bow tie. A white apron is wrapped around his waist, a very old-fashioned ensemble. He has straight shoulder-length dark hair that is tied back. He gives me a friendly smile. "What'll it be?"

I glance at the wall behind him and spot a rye whiskey on the shelf. "Can I get an old fashioned?" The bartender nods and begins making the drink, and I let out a sigh of relief. The rules may have changed all around me, but at least my drink order has not.

He places the drink in front of me, and I reach for my wallet, pulling the ring along with it. The gold flashes in the low light. I pause and consider what kind of money they use.

Before I can ask, he motions to my ring and continues, "In honor of Selection Day, the drink is on the house."

I look at him a little bewildered. "Okay, thank you." I replace my wallet in my back pocket as he gives me a nod and walks toward a couple who approached the bar.

I take my drink to an empty booth across the room with a good vantage point from the front of the bar to the back. I bring the glass to my lips and inhale the sweet burnt-orange fragrance as I take a sip. As the liquid gold pours down my throat, I almost groan with how good it tastes. I have no idea what type of whisky that was, but it is nothing I've ever tasted before.

I glance up and do a double-take as I see a woman walk through the same doors I entered earlier. My head swivels, and I lock eyes with her. She has long blonde hair waving loosely down her back and bright blue eyes. I can see her eyes from across the room, mainly because they are focused on me.

She comes directly toward my booth, no hesitation. Tall and curvaceous, she's wearing a black square-neck dress that wraps around her curves like a second skin. The fabric stops above her knees, long legs walking confidently toward me with her heels clicking on the stone floor. I hold my breath as she approaches. I glance to my left and right, and there is no one around my booth that she could be heading toward but me.

She slips into my booth, and I stare at her slack jawed until she speaks. She glances up at the bartender who has appeared out of thin air. "Hey, Vince, can I get my usual?" she asks.

"Yes, ma'am, coming right up." She smiles at him, a full-blown dazzling smile, and he grins like a fool in love as he turns toward the bar.

She turns her blue eyes on me. "You are Caleb Moretti, the new human replacement hunting Kyle's killer?" She is so a matter-of-fact that it takes me a moment to comprehend the question.

"Yes, Kyle was my brother in arms before he transferred here."

"My name is Noreen Archer. Evan Armstrong works under me at the Witch Academy."

My mind whirls, and I blurt out the first thing I can think of. "So you are a witch?"

She gives me a grin and a flirtatious wink as Vince the bartender brings her drink and deposits it on the table in front of her. He says, "Let me know if you need anything else, Noreen." He looks hopeful that she will ask for something. Anything.

She smiles her thanks, and he walks back to the bar, shooting glances our way periodically.

Noreen picks up the martini glass, two olives, and takes a sip. "Oh, that's good." She looks over at me. "Vince is a god when it comes to drinks. But careful what you order. Some of Vince's work is for Fae or witches. Usually, he adapts to each customer, but it is always good to specify."

"Is that a talent or power of his?"

"Yes, Vince is the best Drykkja in Idyll. Drykkja is a subclass of hospitality Fae who have a variety of powers. They can either make you the most delicious meal, tailor your clothes, or give you the best drink of your life." She raises her half empty glass in emphasis.

"Thanks for the tip." I clear my throat. "So you work with Evan, and he's a warlock because Kyle was human and Rhea a Fae?"

She smiles. "Yup, that's how it works."

I nod and continue despite the sarcastic reply, "So that means the same for you?"

She leans in like she is telling me a secret. "Except my story started long ago." I look at her a little quizzically and she adds, "Evan's started a little while ago."

She settles back in her seat and takes a sip. "I am one of the oldest witches in the academy. I was born well over three hundred years ago." My eyes widen, and before I say anything, she interrupts, "To get this out of the way, I don't fly around on a broom, nor have anything to do with Halloween. I don't mix up magic in a caldron, and I absolutely do not have green skin and a wart." She smiles as if enjoying all the stereotypes.

"So what kind of magic do you use?"

She looks at me and indulges, setting her glass down before answering, "Witches gain some of their powers from their Fae parentage. Typically the type of magic the parent has, the witch will gain to some degree. Witches are connected to the Earth, more so than any Fae due to our human parentage. Most of our magic will pull from the Earth, and we can create a connection between the two that Fae cannot. This allows us to make the runestones and the rings." She motions toward me. "Like the one I see upon your finger."

I nod. "So if you don't mind me asking, what is the gift you gained from your Fae parentage?"

"My mom is Josephine Archer, one of the original Fae trapped on this side of the barrier. She fell in love with a human man, Wyatt Archer, and they had me." She shrugs as if this was a story told time and time again. "My mom is the Great Seer. Her gifts allow her to see the past if she touches a person or object. She has visions of the future that help the council make important decisions. I have received a slice of her abilities. Usually they come in flashes, not whole pictures."

I look at her with sharp eyes. "Do not take this as I'm not appreciative of the information, because I am, but why are you here in this booth with me right now answering my questions?"

She looks down and then up into my eyes. "I have seen your face in this particular booth at this particular time over and over the past three days. When Rhea asked me to make a new ring for a new alliance member, a human and a friend of Kyle Armstrong, I had a vision of this meeting. This vision has been playing in a loop in my mind over the last two days. I was up in the viewing area of the arena watching the selection contestants perform their tests when I felt the pull to the bar." She looked at me over the rim of her glass. "I knew you would be here."

I ask, "So what does that mean?"

She sighs, "I wish I could say with certainty, but unfortunately the visions are not always helpful. I saw this meeting but really have no other indication why it is significant. I knew I needed to meet you, and since I have already been assisting the task force investigating the murders, I am assuming our fates are intertwined by solving them.

"I have found over the years that visions always have a purpose. They interconnect people and places. Eventually, we will see the greater good be served." She pauses as if reliving a bad memory. "I have learned from past mistakes that to ignore the visions is a mistake. Fate is a fickle beast, and you never want to piss it off."

I nod as if this were a normal conversation and I understood everything she was telling me. "This world may be new to me, and I can use all the help I can get understanding all the differences, but I can tell you this. I have been a detective hunting down the worst sorts of criminals for the past decade. I will find out why these murders are happening and avenge the victims."

She smiles at me a little viciously. "Once we find them, we will rip them to shreds."

SEVENTEEN

Sophia—The Arena

By the time I make it back to Central Sector, I am able to grab a bite from the cafeteria, and then it is time for the magic portion of Gael's test. The little adventure in the forest took less than an hour, despite the revelations about the creatures and the intensity of meeting the mystery man in the woods. As I remember, my skin crawls, and I wonder if he will keep his promise to find me. I shiver in the warmth of the gym, remembering the sudden chill in the air, the menacing vibe.

I push the escaping strands of my damp hair off my forehead and blow out a puff of air in aggravation. I should not still be thinking about him. He is long gone and not a threat, I remind myself. He did nothing, said nothing wrong, other than be a slightly annoying male. There is no reason for my unrest.

I straighten my leathers, tucking a piece of the shift stained with my blood under the collar. I push off the thoughts of him and focus on Gael, my new trainee.

She's tall and athletic, blonde hair wrapped like a crown around her head. She is standing with another girl, dark to her light, slightly shorter but very pretty. I appraise Gael and think about what Ian told me. She may hold the power to reseal the gates, if I can help her tap into her full potential.

Two commanders I recognize, Ava O'Hara and Gabriella Ventura, step forward along with three other lieutenants. Gabriella and I go way back, and Ava has been here at Tarrin for a spell. She transferred from a European gate at least one hundred years ago. I focus on the commanders as they start to instruct the next group in the magic portion of the test. Each of the team members goes to their separate circular runestones, and then the whistle blows.

I focus my attention on Gael, who begins strong. I see the instructors marking her powers. She is powerful and able to manipulate the fire well. I appreciate the control it takes to precisely wield the fiery ropes. I hear a murmur from the commanders, who are impressed by her power.

I glance over at the other observers who have come to view the magic demonstration. Gael has attracted a crowd. Typically, this is a closed event, open only to specific instructors, teachers, and the staff hosting the event. Beyond the normal personnel, there are Collective and council members present along with various other Fae observing from the sidelines, me included.

I recognize Kingsley Abbott in attendance, an elder and council member. Kingsley is responsible for overseeing the Warrior Qualifications Training. He has always shown interest in Fae with particularly strong powers. His eyes are glued to Gael, and I wonder if he is one of the elders with the theory that she can help close the gates. He sees me looking at him and averts his eyes quickly toward the other participants.

I return my focus to Gael. I see her open her eyes, and then her magic disappears like it was never there. I stand up a little straighter, someone with such strong and unique power should not falter, let alone completely drop the magic. She starts again and rebuilds the flames. I puzzle why her control is so faulty. It is almost like she must focus her entire energy on generating power, instead of the magic fluidly flowing through her. What would cause magic to be forced?

Normally, magic is an innate gift, something that is almost effortless. In Gael's case, it seems as if she is forcing it to manifest. Gael continues to rebuild what she lost. I can tell it is taking every ounce of her concentration. Then she wraps up the test, finishing strong. Even with her blunder, I know the grade will be a pass. The first firewielder in three hundred years is a shoo-in.

In the past three hundred years, more and more powerful gifts have been popping up. The theory is, since there are cracks in the barrier, we are more connected to Faerie than we have been since the gates closed. This has allowed greater powers to manifest, to evolve.

I watch Gael's team of five move toward the double doors of the gymnasium. They are headed to the tunnels that lead under the arena for their final test. I head out of the opposite set of doors. I don't think Gael even knew I was watching and evaluating her.

I continue through the atrium, out the back doors, and toward the towering main entrance archway to the arena that dominates the skyline. Once inside, I make my way to the right where there is an entrance reserved for Collective members, council members, commanders, lieutenants, and various staff.

As I approach, I recognize Emma, one of the Central Sector lieutenants at the rope. Emma and I went through our Selection Day many years ago. She pulls me into a half hug and says, "When did you get back?"

I smile at her and reply, "Today. I wanted to check out the new talent." I don't want to reveal my true focus until it becomes public knowledge.

She smiles. "Ian and Bren are already in the viewing area. I'm sure they can give you all the stats." I smile and squeeze her shoulder. "Once I get settled, we should catch up over a drink at Nines."

I walk past the ropes and move upward on the ramp toward the massive viewing box specifically reserved for VIP guests. I walk through the large, ornately crafted double doors and onto a glass-walled platform that overlooks the arena. Currently, there is glamor in place to make the arena appear to be densely forested, completely at odds with the sleek interior I am walking through now.

Around me, the Fae are intermingling. Champagne is being carried on black trays throughout the room. I forgot how big a deal they make Selection Day. It has been a few years since I've attended. At least I do not feel too out of place. I look around at the attire. Some are wearing suit jackets, others cocktail dresses and five-inch heels, all intermingling with combat boots and leathers. The social event of the season, debutantes mixing with warriors, could have no other dress code.

I grab a glass of champagne from a nearby server and take up space at the edge of the viewing platform. I look out and see a group competing in their test. Gael's group is up next. Two of the current team members are down, and the rest look like they are struggling.

In the stands, a crowd is cheering them on. I glance around the room. Many on the viewing platform are not even looking at the arena. They are here to rub shoulders with the council members and to mingle with the Collective.

As I look up, I see my brother and Ian standing close together, dark to blond, their heads tilted in deep discussion. I take one step forward, intent on joining them, until I see out of the corner of my eye the mystery man from the forest walk up to the two men. I swiftly turn my head, my thoughts racing. Who is he, and why is he speaking with my family?

I turn away and head over to the food table. I am semi hidden behind an ice sculpture and turn slightly to look casually over my shoulder, trying to be as nonchalant as possible.

I'm too far away to hear anything. I furrow my brow and try to discern what they are talking about. They seem to know each other well and are casual with each other. Suddenly, the man from the forest raises his eyes and looks directly at me. He flashes a wicked smile that freezes my insides, and he winks as if he knows something I don't know. My breath catches, and I wonder again why I am so repelled by his presence.

I look away and then refocus on the group. Only then do I realize all three of the men have turned and are looking in my direction. Bren is looking between the mystery man and me in speculation, Ian with slight curiosity. Bren raises his hand and motions me over. My eyes travel over the trio as I try to unravel the mystery man's secret. Clearly, he has won over my brother and mentor, no easy feat.

I square my shoulders and put on my most confident expression I can muster and head across the room. During my walk, I feel his eyes fix intently on me, imploring me to look at him. I resist by sheer grit and determination, focusing instead on Ian and Bren.

As I approach, Bren reaches out and gives me a hug. Ian leans forward and kisses me on my cheek. I finally, reluctantly, turn and raise my eyes to meet the third of the trio.

"I don't think I caught your name," I say to him, slightly hostile.

The corners of his full lips turn up in amusement. "I am Ethen Graham, Commander of Domain Sector." He looks between Bren and I. "You are Sophia Beaumont, sister to Brenen Beaumont." He leans forward and kisses me on the cheek. Skin burns where his lips brush, and a fire burns through my veins. I breathe in deep and catch his tantalizing citrus and warm spice scent. He whispers in my ear, "I told you I would find you, Red, but I did not anticipate it being so soon."

I shiver in an involuntary response to his nearness. I step back and look up and up. He is taller than I remember at the river, but we were a little preoccupied at the time. The rest of his looks are imprinted on my mind, olive skin, dark hair still sweeping over his brow, and dark eyes with flecks of honey appearing in the light. While recognizing his sinfully handsome presence, I cannot shake the unease I feel being near him.

Bren clears his throat. "So you two met already?"

I look at him and nod. "Yes, I went on a walk this afternoon, and he helped me out of a sticky spot with a dire wolf."

Bren's eyes widen. "You went out alone?"

I look at him and roll my eyes. "I had it under control until he broke my time warp."

Ethen takes one step closer, his finger coming to the low collar of my leather top, brushing it over the bloody shift that has worked its way free and was visible. "It was too close a call to say you had it under control."

Ian says, "I should have told you about going out alone,"

Bren adds, "You broke her time warp?"

I scoff, "Don't get too excited. I think I could have held it if I knew he was going to fight the hold."

Ethen chuckles. "You would like to think so," he says, repeating my words from earlier that afternoon.

Pulling myself from the lighthearted banter, I ask, "So how do you know each other?"

Bren says, "Ethen was transferred six months ago from our Sierra Nevada gate." He lowers his voice so only I can hear. "He has been a tremendous help to our task force investigating the murders."

Ian breaks in, "Sophia, we are placing Gael at the Domain Sector, which will be your headquarters for her six-month training. That way, you can keep informed of the investigations through Ethen while you train Gael." Ian gives Ethen a look, and Ethen nods in understanding.

As I look them over, I sigh to myself. This is going to be a long six months.

EIGHTEEN

Gael—Test 3

No free time between tests this time, Ari and I walk from the magic test and head to our third group test in the arena. The arena is on the far side of the complex, and recruits are ushered through the underground tunnels leading to the amphitheater.

Caden matches his stride to mine as our feet echo in the darkness. He asks casually, "So, Fire Ability?"

I turn and grin. "Yeah."

He lets loose a breath and gives me a wide smile. "You sure fooled everyone. Especially Liam. He has been bragging about how he would get top marks. Bet you pushed him out of the running."

"Serves him right."

Caden's eyes crinkle ever so slightly at the corners. "Yup, serves him right."

We fall into a collective quiet as our small group continues to our third test, each of us engrossed in our own thoughts. The team's nervous energy flows as we make the trek across the campus, our feet a muffled echo in the semi-lit tunnel.

I ask Ari, "What do you think the group test will be?"

She shrugs and looks down, unlike her normal chipper self.

"Not sure. Every year, the scenario is different. Terrain and objectives vary."

I nod grimly as we emerge to the underground entrance to the arena. There is an entire facility under the arena, as we pass by, I see conference rooms, locker rooms, offices, and a huge gym. We get ushered into one of the conference rooms, and a lieutenant asks that we wait for our time slot. The group in front of us has started, and we can hear the cheers from the stands above our heads.

In years past, I have attended the event in the main viewing platform, sitting along with Gwyneth, Kay, and Bennett. Selection Day energy hyping up the crowd. The arena is always transformed into different scenarios, the recruits having to complete their objective, points assigned for swiftness, efficiency, and creativity. Points deducted based on injuries sustained or death to a member. Remembering the excitement of being a spectator, my stomach turns. To be on the other side of the arena is more daunting than I ever imagined.

I sit down and put my elbows on my knees, and I focus on my breath. In two counts, out two counts. Ari has anxiously started to bounce her foot, and the other members are in various states of nervousness. All except for Logan, who is calmly leaning back in his chair, seemingly unaffected by our upcoming test.

Ten minutes pass. The same lieutenant is back and leading us to the edge of the amphitheater. A ramp will take us the rest of the way to the main stage. This is where we are addressed by Commander Damaris Allard.

"In this final test, you will demonstrate how you work together as a team. There is no singular objective in the field. You must always remember the most important objective is to protect the person to the left and right of you." We glance at each other and nod in understanding.

He continues, "The scenario for this test is set in Vista Sector, high in the peaks. A patrol is overrun and has called for reinforcements. Your team is dispatched to help. They are pinned down and fighting multiple creatures on the forest floor. Your team must kill the creatures and save the patrol in distress. You must do this as a team. If any of your teammates are injured, points will be reduced. If any of your team are fatally wounded, then your overall score will be reduced by twenty percent."

Damaris holds up a broadsword in demonstration. "You will be immersed in the simulation, the glamor making the scene look and feel real in every sense. Smell. Sight. Sound. Even the coppery taste of blood from a wound will feel real. If you are injured in the simulation, you will feel it." He motions to the broadsword. "These training swords will be provided, although you are encouraged to use any and all magical powers for your defense.

"Protect one another, and save the team in distress. The simulation is designed to test your ability to work together. Do so honorably. Remember, courage, honor, strength."

We nod in understanding and are issued our broadswords. We stand together at the edge of the arena. I nervously bounce from one ball of my foot to the other. I glance over at Ari and see her chin set. I focus on the gates in front of me and square my shoulders. Suddenly, the horn blares, and the gates open letting in the brilliant sunlight.

At the edge of the arena, we pause to assess the situation. It feels as if I had been transported to Vista Sector. Mountain peaks are visible in the background, and I gaze up at the canopy above us in momentary fascination. I have been a spectator before on other Selection Days, but seeing the glamor from inside the arena immerses me in the setting. We hear cries for help. The warriors are hidden from view in the lush foliage.

We fan out and approach cautiously, looking for any creatures who may ambush us. On my right is Ari then Gavin. I see movement in the brush about ten feet in the air. Suddenly, a dark creature comes crashing down from above. Ari swings her sword up, but I can tell it will be too late. As time slows, I see Gavin out of my peripherals. His hands raise. A massive boulder comes down upon the creature from above. As the creature emits a last high-pitched shriek, it disappears into smoke.

Ari gives Gavin a small smile, and I can't help but roll my eyes. I count in my head, one down.

We continue forward and come to a clearing. Caden motions for the group to gather. He whispers, "We need to utilize our powers. Ari, Logan, you both can conceal yourselves. Flank them from behind undetected." He looks at me. "Gael, Gavin and I can approach from the front for an offensive attack." His eyes meet the rest of our group, and there is a collective nod of agreement. Ari disappears into the forest to the right. Logan transforms into smoke and vanishes to the left.

The three of us remain. There are five creatures attacking a patrol squad of four, the fifth member lying on the ground presumed dead or injured. We continue forward and see a flurry of movement, the creatures and patrol members fighting earnestly. The test is designed to make you engage in hand-to-hand combat. The creatures are winning, and the patrol we are supposed to save is barely hanging on.

I motion to Caden and Gavin to take the ones closest to them. They nod in agreement as we spread out. I sneak up from behind the dark creature closest to me, my sword raised, and I prepare to take him by surprise. I get a foot away, and the creature turns, black scales covering the face and neck, ending in its razor-sharp beak. As it unfurled its wings, I take a step back as I catch sight of black leathery skin covering the appendages. They stand about the height of a man, with a wide wingspan.

I squat down into a low crouch, sword in hand. I thrust the blade forward into the beast's soft underbelly. Before I can make contact, the creature's claw comes down, and I feel a searing pain. I look down and see my forearm has a large gash, blood seeping out onto the ground. Injured but not dead.

I pivot, and the creature is on me. I am ducking and spinning and avoiding contact at all costs. Before I know it, I am moving so fluidly that I am not even thinking about my next move, simply reacting.

The killing dance continues, each of us trying to make a fatal blow. The creature advances, and I sidestep. I push his energy past me, and in his forward momentum, I run my sword along his belly under the wing. The creature lets loose an ear-splitting shriek, blood dripping across his lower body. He crumples and fades into smoke.

I'm breathing heavily. Spinning, I look for my teammates and see Caden and Gavin standing in the clearing. Their creatures have disappeared, and they stand victorious. Ari and Logan are on the far side of the clearing looking triumphant.

Our temporary victorious triumph is short lived, however. Out of the foliage, six more creatures appear. Our teams' eyes meet, and without having to say a word we turn our backs to each other, facing the creatures now encircling us. Sword drawn, I'm ready for an attack.

In a blur of movement, the creatures attack at once. We pivot, dip, and maneuver out of the way. I feel another searing pain on my upper arm and then on my leg. I pull that same energy from before and am moving in continuous fluidity. In a blur of motion, I target the creature right in front of me in the center of its chest, my blow sliding off the creatures' scales. I turn and see Ari fighting two of the creatures. Time seems to slow as I see beyond Ari. The other three members of our team are fighting for their lives.

I take a breath and break into motion. I slide under the creature in front of me and push power from my hands as I move. Fire erupts from my fingertips, scorching the creature next to me, and I push the flames to the one near Ari, who sweeps her sword up the next creature's chest, ending at its neck, almost severing its head. Blood erupts from the wounds, and all three dark creatures disappear into smoke.

I spin and see Caden battling his creature, blood dripping from his arm, shoulder hanging at an awkward angle. Gavin, nearby, raises his sword and decisively sweeps it across the creature in front of him, splitting the neck wide open. In the next moment, he raises his hand, and another boulder crashes on top of the creature in front of Caden. Both dark creatures disappear into smoke. I swing my head around and see Logan breathing heavy, his abilities transcend throughout the clearing, his form barely visible as he battles the last dark creature. Every movement ends in the creature diving into shadows. Finally, there is a pause. Logan manifests directly behind the creature, and he swipes his blade across its neck. The last creature evaporates into nothingness.

Blood splatters across the grove. Our team looks around. All twelve creatures are defeated.

I ask, "Anyone fatally marked?" Our eyes meet, and I get negative answers from the group. All members have made it through without a fatal wound.

The horn blares, and that is the end of our third test.

I rest my hands on my knees, which feel as if they are about to give way. Over the loudspeaker, a deep timber voice announces, "Team 12, all members have completed selection. Caden Emery, Gavin Pierce, Logan Barlowe, Gael Monroe, Adriana Blane.

I wrap my arms around Ari, and we laugh and cry at the same time, out of breath but exuberant. A lieutenant ushers our team off the arena floor. The lieutenants lead us back through the underground tunnel toward where we entered.

At the end of the tunnel, the lieutenant pauses and says, "If you want to shower and change in the locker rooms, the announcement ceremony will be at 4 p.m. Your team did well. Most of the other teams had members not make it through. They had to be combined for their final tests. Good job to all of you."

She turns and heads back to the arena for the final testing teams.

I look at Ari, and a grin splits my face. I cannot contain how excited I am that we passed. I grab her around the neck, and we swing back in forth with excitement as we return to the locker rooms.

Our energy high, Logan walks past us, grumbling, "Okay, don't get so worked up. We still have six months of training."

I do a little skip and link my fingers with Ari. "Don't listen to him. We were amazing!" My smile cannot be contained, and we continue forward.

The rest of the afternoon passes in a blur. Clean uniforms are provided, we change, and then are led back to the arena for the announcement ceremony.

As I look around at the recruits who passed, there is a considerable number of students missing. This group is much smaller than the group we started with this morning. Pushing that thought to the back of my mind, I focus on our team as we are led to the arena floor.

The announcement blazes over the loudspeaker in the arena. "Please join us in welcoming the recruits who have passed Selection Day!" There is a rumble of cheers above our heads, and we get to make our victory lap with thundering cheers from the crowds.

I look up into the viewing platform and spot Gwyneth and Kay waving frantically to get my attention. I look up and wave back with a big smile. Beyond them, I see Bennett. We lock eyes, and he gives me a wide grin and a thumbs up.

I want to bottle the essence of this moment and keep it forever.

NINETEEN

Sophia—Gut Feeling

As I watch Gael's passing announcement from the arena viewing platform, I look around. This was my cue to get outta dodge.

I swiftly say my goodbyes to Ian and Bren and duck out of the room. My first encounter with Ethen has my guard up, the strange gut feeling continually running on a loop in my mind. I keep coming up with the same answer. My instincts are telling me not to trust him.

Now, this will make an awkward six months ahead of me.

Somehow, Ethen has managed to win over my two closest family members. Not to mention, it seems Ethen has set his sights on me being his next conquest. Strands of hair have come loose. Irritated, I push them out of my face. My braid is in shambles due to the eventful dip in the water and fight to the death with a dire wolf.

It looks like I will be working with Ethen for the foreseeable future, so I need to get my head straight.

I walk toward the underground tunnel that leads to the rear exit, away from the competitors. My mind is reeling in the quiet of the tunnel. Wrapped in my thoughts, I am suddenly not alone anymore. I turn, instinctively raising my blade until I recognize Ethen in front of me, his hands up in surrender. I reluctantly relax.

"Good way to get yourself killed," I mutter before re-sheathing the weapon.

Ethen tugs on my hand and pulls me in close to him into the alcove of the tunnel. He says in a low voice, "I wanted to make sure I would see you tonight."

I look up in the dimly lit tunnel. His dark eyes are smoldering.

I push away from him, the shiver of warning pouring through my veins. "Look, Ethen, I think maybe you got the wrong idea. We are going to be working together. I don't think anything romantic is a good idea."

Before I can say anything else, he leans down and whispers in my ear, "Don't shut it down before it even begins." His breath is warm on my cheek. I can feel his lips at my earlobe, and I shiver involuntarily. "I promise you won't regret it."

My mind and body war with each other. Something certainly is not right. A light pops on in my mind, and I realize Ethen's latent power must be beguilement. A natural ability to use charm, allure, and enchantment to sway or manipulate others, essentially captivating them with an irresistible influence.

"Sophia!"

I hear a screech from down the hallway, yank my hand out of Ethen's grip, and spin in time to see my best friend Alexandria Chambers running down the hallway toward me. Her straight dark hair flows behind her in streams. I don't think she even sees Ethen against the wall as she comes at a full run and wraps her arms around my neck.

"Soph, how could you not call me the minute you got back? I ran into Ian, and he told me you were here."

I laugh, "It's been a crazy day, believe me. If I had a moment to breathe, I would have tracked you down."

Alex realizes we are not alone. She lets out a squeak and looks between Ethen and me. I motion to him, "Alex, meet Ethen Graham, Commander of the Domain Sector. Ethen, meet Alexandria Chambers, Lieutenant at Central Sector."

They shake hands. Alex's eyes are round and look at me with the unspoken question that I'm not about to go into right now. I add, "Ethen and I will be working together at Domain Sector." A hard look is all the explanation I'm prepared to go into at the moment.

I look at Ethen. "I've got to go, I'll see you around." His gaze heats up as he looks at me and nods. "See you tonight," he purrs. He turns to Alex and says, "Nice to meet you." A moment passes, and he disappears. I can't even track his movement.

Alex turns to me, her mouth hanging open. "What was that?" she exclaims. "You are back less than a day and have Ethen Graham, the most eligible bachelor in all of Tarrin, on your radar?"

She snorts and loops her arm through mine, continuing as we walk down the tunnel. "Six months of females throwing themselves at him, and you snag him in a few hours." She sighs heavily. "Okay, you have to dish."

I roll my eyes. "It's simple. I must be the only female who has ever turned him down, which makes me interesting."

We start walking toward the dorms, and I tell her about the incident in the woods. How Ethen helped me with the dire wolf and then about the viewing platform with Ian, Bren, and Ethen. By the time I am done with the story, we are back at the dormitories.

Alex grabs my hands and looks at me, concern etched in her face. "If you have a bad feeling about Ethen, you should let your brother know. You always have good instincts, Soph. Don't be afraid to act on them."

I somberly say, "Yeah, maybe I will mention it to Brenen tonight." I reach forward and give Alex a huge hug. "I have missed you so much. When was the last time we got to go to a ball together?"

Alex gives me a grin, and excitement courses through me. She says, "I bet Daphne has created you a stunner dress tonight."

I fling open my door, and sure enough a ruby-red dress is hanging from a hook on the back of the bathroom door. "Yes!" I exclaim, and I go to look at Daphne's design. It's covered in clear protective plastic that I rip off in a moment. I hold up the creation and look in awe. Daphne really is a genius. The color is perfect, a deep ruby red to match the necklace. The cut daring. Fabric satin. I look at Alex.

"I can't wait to try this on!"

"Go ahead." She gives me a motion to proceed. I look down at my dirty fighting leathers and blood stained shift while I pick a leaf out of my hair. Maybe I need to clean up.

"I think I need a nice long bath."

"Okay. Let's meet back here about six and walk together."

"Sounds good." I give her a big hug, saying again, "I am so happy to be back. I missed you." I squeeze her one last time, and she smiles and gives a little wave before disappearing to her own room.

I start the water in the bathroom, rummage through the shelves, and find fragrant bath salts I had purchased before I left. I open the container and get a whiff of jasmine and roses. Perfect. I put a generous helping in the steaming water. As I wait, I scrub my face and see dirt smudged high on my cheekbone.

I wonder briefly why no one told me I looked like a hot mess.

Finally, the tub is filled, and I slip into warm bliss. I settle back and allow my hair to submerge in the scented water and feel my muscles finally relax. I stay in the bath until the water turns lukewarm. I sigh and finally get out.

I wrap myself in a robe and tackle my long locks. I have wavy hair that can become unruly if not treated properly. I apply my favorite products and blow dry my locks flawlessly. I have been debating how to wear my hair with the dress and decide on pulling it up in a sleek ponytail, letting the length flow down my back. The tips of my hair almost reach my bottom.

This will show off the dress and my body to perfection. I swipe some gold on my eyelids, bronzer on my cheeks. Ruby-red lipstick completes my makeup, and I am ready to get dressed.

I slip into the satin dress, the fabric whispering across my skin. The front has a deep plunge, showing the edges of my breasts on either side. Thin straps wrap up and around in a crisscross shape toward the base of my low back, where they begin an intricate corset at the base of my spine. A wide satin sash defines my waist, and the fabric falls to the floor. Two slits on either side go up to the hip, showing an ample amount of leg with every movement. I admire myself in the mirror. This dress is amazing. It has been a long time since I had an occasion to dress up.

I look around the room. Shoes, they must have brought shoes. I see them tucked next to the dresser, gold strappy heels with a slight platform. Straps tie up my legs, matching the ties at my back. I see a box on the dresser and open it. Inside are a pair of ruby earrings that match the necklace. There is a note in Daphne's writing, "I saw the necklace and created these to match. Come and see me this week to catch up." I smile and put on the earrings and the necklace.

I hear a knock, and Alex is ready, perfect timing. I open the door.

"Hot damn, you look good. Every male's eye will be trained on you."

I grin and give her an appreciative look, "You look amazing yourself." Alex's forest-green eyes pop with color against the black creation of Daphne's. A low sweetheart neckline sweeps up to small cap sleeves. As she twirls, the back is completely open down to the base of her back. One slit on the side up to her hip, silver strappy shoes, and diamond earrings complete the ensemble. I let out a low whistle. I link my arm with hers, and we start down the hallway toward the exit of the dormitory.

As we walk into the atrium foyer, I hear the announcement of the new recruits. My eyes sweep the area that is full of dark suits, tuxedos, and every shade of gown you can imagine. Across the room, I lock eyes with the one person I was hoping to avoid. Ethen straightens. His eyes pierce mine. He starts to prowl across the room like I am his prey.

It would serve him well to remember I am no one's prey.

TWENTY

Caleb—Introductions

sip the second old fashioned that Vince brought me after Noreen left. I think he knew I needed a small respite after the whirlwind of Noreen. Damn, if she is not the most beautiful woman—witch, I correct myself—that I had ever seen. Besides the drop-dead-gorgeous package, inside is a keen intelligence and wit that traps me like a snare.

I shake my head. Noreen approached me to solve a murder, not to become enamored. Kyle's murder is where my focus should be.

I finish my drink, the best liquid nectar I have ever tasted. Vince really is a god when it came to drinks. Today by far was the strangest day of my life. Even so, I cannot fathom leaving this mysterious place to return to the normal mundane human life I left this morning.

I give a slight wave to Vince as I walk out of the bar, realizing it is now late afternoon. I look at the ring on my finger and turn my feet toward the compound. I make my way back to the entrance and place my ring on the stone. The doors silently slide open, and I enter the Central Sector once again. As I walk through the beautiful corridor lined in windows, I approach the two branches we saw earlier. Instead of going left toward the intelligence section and library, I head to the right toward the dormitories.

Rhea told me this ring was keyed to room number 103. The hallways turn from glass to wood panels, and I find bronze number plates next to each of the rooms. I follow them in numeric order and stop in front of the door labeled 103. I press my ring to the stone next to the door, and the latch clicks open. Inside is a utilitarian space, a queen bed, dresser, small table, and what looks like the bathroom beyond the connecting door. I walk over to the window and look out to see the forest canopy in a brilliant display of color.

On the bed is a garment bag. I unzip and find a tux. I look at the label and see it's in my size. Rhea said she had "housekeeping" arrange clothing. I add this to the extensive list of incomprehension today.

I walk into the bathroom to find it fully stocked with a variety of toiletries, male and female. I open the dresser drawers in the bedroom and find generic gray sweatshirts, pants, and various undergarments that lead me to believe this is a unisex room used as needed. I wonder how often they have surprise guests and when those guests may need a tuxedo. I get ready for the evening.

I shower and shave my five o'clock shadow. Then I make my way to the garment bag. It's been ten years since the last time I wore a tux. At that time, I needed alterations for my height. I top out at about six feet, broad through the shoulders. Not to worry this time. It is tailored perfectly, like they had my measurements.

I wonder again about the mystery housekeeping services on site.

White-collared shirt, vest, slacks, jacket, dress shoes. There's even a pocket square that matches the dark-gray bowtie provided. I get dressed and look at myself in the mirror. I don't know much about labels, but I am sure the one I'm wearing is premium, the jacket fitting like a glove.

My Italian heritage is particularly dark against the white shirt collar. My hair is slightly longer than I normally keep it, but the dark eyes and rugged jaw line are the same as they have always been. Small crows' feet at the corners of my eyes are the only indication I am not in my twenties anymore. I work out regularly, run, and keep fit.

I glance at my watch, five minutes to six. I reach down and adjust my ankle holster that holds my S&W airweight, my backup weapon. The 9mm is secured in my left shoulder holster, ready for a right-handed draw. Knowing I am walking into an unknown world, I wish I had an arsenal at my back.

I hear the door click as it closes softly behind me. I walk down the hallway. As I get to the end of the dormitories, I see a large guy coming out of his room in a tuxedo as well. He turns, and I recognize him from the funeral. Black hair and blue eyes. He turns his laser focus on me as I approach. "You're Caleb Moretti, Kyle's friend who will be working on the task force."

I nod, a little put off that this is the second introduction where the other person knows exactly who I am when I have no idea who they are.

"Yes, that is right. I saw you at the funeral. Did you know Kyle?"

He nods. "My name is Brenen Beaumont, and Kyle worked under my command at Vista Sector." He looks down for a moment, the loss of a team member still fresh. "He was a good man, a good warrior. We will find out who is behind these attacks."

I nod, saying, "I look forward to bringing them to justice."

His eyes sharpen, and he gives me a small smile. "That depends on your version of justice."

I furrow my brow, having a good idea what he meant by that statement. Before I can say anything, Brenen asks, "You headed to the ball?" I nod, and we start walking toward the Capital Center. Brenen says, "We can grab a drink at the bar while we wait for the tables to be ready. Usually there is a cocktail hour before dinner."

We stride toward the glass atrium. The building is huge. At least three normal stories high, the sides and roof of the building are made entirely of glass. As we walk up the stairs and go through the large arched front entrance, I see marble columns holding the building up, matching marble floors as far as I could see. In the center of the space, a massive curving planter is home to trees, flowering vines, and bushes that are lit up from the ground with small area lights shining up into their branches. Immaculate hedges and bushes line the planter, a wide curving stone bench surrounding the outside. We walk straight through the atrium and enter what must be the grand ballroom.

Four huge chandeliers hang in the foyer of the ballroom, metal brackets holding them from the intersections in the glass ceiling. When

I look up, I can see the twilight starting to take over the sky and know this view will be amazing once the moon and stars come out. To the left is a massive bar that has various males and females occupying the stools and small sitting areas sprinkled throughout the expansive room. Every person is dressed in formal attire.

A huge fireplace dominates the entire right wall, three stories tall. Straight in front of us is a massive staircase that leads up to a second-story mezzanine surrounding the foyer we are in. The second floor has a balcony that wraps around and flows down the stairs. I can see rooms off on the right and left on the second level.

I follow Brenen Beaumont over to the massive bar, and we mill around until we are able to squeeze into a space to order. He looks at me. "Any requests?"

I wonder if he will get one of those special Fae drinks. I reply, "Old fashioned."

He smiles and looks at the bartender, Vince, who gives me a nod. "Two rye old fashioneds."

Vince starts on our order as my eyes scrutinize the room, cataloging every detail, trying to commit each face to memory. There are two sets of double doors on either side of the room.

Brenen motions to the door closest to us. "The dining will be in this room, followed by dancing in the second room."

As I scan the room, I wonder if I will see Noreen tonight.

Vince gives us our drinks, and we head to a recently vacated cocktail table to perch and wait for dinner. I glance at Brenen and mention, "I met Noreen earlier today. She mentioned she is part of the task force as well."

Brenen nods. "Yes, she is helping us from a witch angle, tracking unusual purchases and trying to identify key faction members. Once we can identify them, we can start our reconnaissance. Despite the wards, somehow they are maneuvering the runestones without notice."

That was an interesting bit of information Noreen did not mention earlier. I respond, "Umm. you think she will be here tonight?" I try to sound nonchalant, but I do not think it worked. He looks over and grins.

"Yeah, she's a Collective member, so she is obligated to show up."

Yet another tidbit she did not tell me about earlier. I take a sip of my drink.

I recognize the large Nordic male from the funeral accompanied by another male I have not seen yet approach from the bar, drinks in hand. The large male from the funeral, well over six feet tall and a head taller than me, clasps Brenen on the back and gives him the normal half hug of brothers.

He looks over at me. "I am Ian Cadell, council member that advises the military branch of Tarrin." He extends his hand, and I shake it.

"I'm Caleb Moretti."

Ian says, "I look forward to seeing your thoughts and ideas on the case."

"It's an honor."

He motions to his left. "This is Commander Ethen Graham of the Domain Sector. He will also be on the task force." I shake his hand, glad to meet the task force before the first day.

A bell rings, and a hush falls through the crowded foyer. I glance around looking for Noreen again with no luck.

A large male stands up midway on the stairs with a microphone in his hands. He has a tuxedo on, slicked back dark hair, and a wide smile. "Good evening, and welcome to the Selection Day celebration ball. We are here today to celebrate all the brave recruits who have passed their tests and will start on their six-month course in each of their respective sectors. We know the next six months will push their limits, hone their strengths, and demonstrate their resolve to protect and defend Tarrin."

Polite applause follows the introduction.

"Tonight, we also celebrate the active warriors who put their lives on the line each day. They work tirelessly to keep our homes, families, and businesses safe. Thank you."

The applause is a little louder with the second remarks.

"I would like to invite the recruits who have passed their initial test to step forward to the top four rows of stairs."

I look up at the width of the stairs and see at least twenty-five people can fit across each row. I ask Brenen, "Is this the normal amount of recruits each year?"

He leans over slightly. "Yes, we typically get 125-175 recruits and roughly two-thirds pass the first-day evaluations. This year we had 147 recruits, and only 98 made it through the first day of testing. Over the next six months, they are evaluated monthly and if they do not pass, then they are out of the program."

I wonder what kind of tests they were put through.

As we are talking, the announcer continues with his speech, and we see the selection recruits start descending the large staircase.

Next to me, Ethen Graham becomes still. I think something must have caught his interest across the room. My eyes track to see what he is looking at. He mummers, "I will see you guys later."

He starts prowling across the room toward a lovely woman with black hair and blue eyes. I look over at Brenen and recognize the familiar features. I ask, "Is she a relation of yours?"

Brenen replies through a clenched jaw, "She's my sister."

I let out a low whistle, pat him on the shoulder, and offer, "I'll go get the next round of drinks."

TWENTY-ONE

Noreen—Here It Goes

slip in a side door of the ballroom and head to the large wrap-around bar. An open seat magically opens itself for me, and I slip in. I look over, and Vince is bartending, not a surprise. He spots me across the bar and beelines toward me. It is always a good thing to be friendly with the bartender. I smile as he approaches.

He says, "What can I get you, Noreen?"

"The usual, please." He grabs a shaker with a slight smile.

"You got it."

I glance around the grand foyer at the main ballrooms and sigh to myself. I really cannot stand these events anymore. I used to look forward to these social events to schmooze and push my grand plans for the Witches Academy. Now all I see are the same faces I have seen every year for the last hundred years. I contemplate that it may be time for me to move on to a different role. I feel satisfied with the work I have done and feel the need to set my sights elsewhere.

As I contemplate my life decisions, I perch on the edge of the stool at the bar top, my sapphire-blue dress stunningly matching my eyes. I wear my long blonde hair loose down my back tonight, and I push it to the side as I glance around the room.

When I first was elected as a Collective member, witches' rights were nearly nonexistent. Witches not being Fae and not wholly human, had a hard time fitting to the new reality of our world here on Earth. The Fae tended to have superiority and demanded our services, most of the time through guilt and obligation to our Fae parentage.

As the cracks in the wall spread and many of our Fae parents passed away, we were left defenseless and in some severe cases forced to work for the Fae through intimidation and force. Before new reforms were in place, many witches fled to intermingle and hide with the humans. This was a dark time for witches. Hiding within the human population resulted in a campaign of human fear against the witches that ran bone deep and spread like wildfire across the globe.

We had to fight for our equal rights, demand respect and equality at the collective table. Slowly, we made progress.

When it became safe for the witches to return to the Fae societies, many of the witches returned to run lucrative business. There is now a flourishing mutual respect between the three of our races. Hard fought and won by blood, sweat, and tears. A long, tough battle, but we have made huge strides at the Witch Academy, determined to never be taken advantage of again.

Vincent rouses me from my thoughts and places a martini glass down on a cocktail napkin in front of me. "Let me know if you need anything else."

I take the drink in hand to make my social rounds. "Thanks, Vincent. I'll come back by for a second round in a little bit." I sip the sweet nectar of his drink and savor it for a moment on my tongue. "Wonderful, as always." He is smiling as he turns to the next customer.

In a practiced move, my genuine grin toward Vincent turns into my game face. My smile turns wide, warm, and welcoming. I can feel my eyes sparkling as I turn and face the room. Here it goes.

There is Gwyneth and Bennett Monroe looking at the recruits walking down the stairs. I remember their adoptive daughter was planning to participate in Selection Day. Based on their beaming expressions, she must have passed. I walk up and give them my congratulations. Gwyneth and Bennett kiss my cheek, then Kay, their eldest daughter and witch, turns and gives me a hug. I have mentored Kay for the last two years on her craft. She recently opened a highly successful business downtown, right next to her mother's shop.

As I squeeze her shoulders, I ask Kay in a hushed tone, "How's the storeroom coming along?"

Kay beams at me. "All good. The space is ready for you. I put the key under the register's counter in that little jar you gave me last year."

I give her a wide smile. "Thank you so much for letting me use the space. I will pay you of course."

Kay scoffs, "Don't be ridiculous. My business wouldn't exist without your help. As far as I'm concerned, you can use it for as long as you need it."

I give her another hug. "Thank you so much."

K's Knockout Potions and Poisons has a storeroom in the back of her shop. Conveniently located through the secret entrance, down in a basement, it was previously used by the prior tenant for illegal operations. When the task force decided to switch our location for more privacy, I contacted Kay. Although slightly curious, Kay agreed.

At that moment Gael, the Monroes' second daughter, walks up and is greeted by her family enthusiastically. I take that opportunity to excuse myself. It seems this should be a private celebration amongst her family.

As I turn and face across the room, I see Kingsley Abbott and Faben Schaeffer standing together. Kingsley is a council member, and Faben is his loyal pet. Kingsley Abbott was one of my fiercest adversaries in creating equal rights for witches. Currently, his eyes are trained on Gael, until he feels my gaze upon him. His eyes snap up, as if he's been caught doing something he shouldn't. My eyes narrow as I focus on him. He arrogantly looks away without acknowledgement. Snorting in my drink, I realize nothing is new with Abbott. They turn to a fellow Collective member and strike up a conversation.

As I turn my attention to the rest of the room, I hope to grab the attention of a few guests tonight, particularly that new human again. Suddenly, I feel a presence at my side. Before I glance over, I already know who it is. I say, "Mother."

She says in her perfectly cultured voice, "Is that any way to greet me? Come now, give me a hug."

I roll my eyes and turn and embrace her, wondering what she needs from me this time. Josephine Archer, council member, and long-time tribunal leader to our justice system is one of the most influential people in Tarrin. Josephine is a long-time pupil of Sybil, the Oracle, who has trained her to use her seer gifts over the past eight centuries.

The little chats we have always end with a task she needs from me. I turn fully and take in her appearance, golden hair wrapped up in chignon, bright-blue eyes, and red lips that are a spitting image of what I look at in the mirror every morning. Her black dress hugs her curves. I suppose the apple did not fall far from the tree.

I ask, "What can I do for you tonight?"

She purses her lips and says, "Can't I simply want to say hello to my only daughter?" I give her a pointed look. She sighs. "Well, there was one itsy-bitsy thing I wanted to tell you."

I arch my brow and say, "Go on then."

She pulls a small compact out of her sleeve and hands it to me. "Sybil has asked me to give this to you. She said that when you need her to use it."

I look at the compact. "When I need her?"

Josephine simply shrugs, saying, "You know Sybil. Never can get a straight answer until it suits her."

I remember lessons from years ago. Sybil was one of the original twelve seers of antiquity. She took up residence in Tarrin once the gates closed. Her dwelling was close to the gate, and no one ever visited unless summoned.

I take the compact and slip it into my sheath at my thigh. "Fine."

My mother looks across the room and sees another council member waving our way. She waves back and says, "Have a wonderful evening. I must make my rounds." She embraces me for a moment, her perfume engulfing me, and then she is gone.

I sigh and glance around the room, wanting this night to be over already. I glance to my right and see Ian, Brenen, and Caleb standing at a small round cocktail table. Perfect timing, I can relay the new meeting spot. I stride over and see Caleb's dark eyes lift to mine. That human has been on my mind. First the visions, and now his good looks have drawn my attention over and over.

I smile as I walk toward the group, a little extra sway to my hips. I can feel Caleb's attention on every inch of me as his eyes drift down the length of my body. I approach and say, "Gentlemen, so good to see you tonight." In greeting, I embrace each male, kissing each on the cheek. Lastly, I turn to Caleb. I lean forward and brush my lips against his cheek and cannot help but pause for a moment, breathing deep, taking in his scent. A deep, woodsy pine fills my senses, and I enjoy it more than I should.

I pull away and focus my attention on the room in front of us. I take a sip of my cocktail and say, "Another Selection Day, same old faces." I glance at Caleb. "Except for our one new addition to the group." I smile slightly at him. He looks a little uncomfortable, but who wouldn't, walking into this lion's den for the first time?

I tell the group, "I have acquired our new meeting place." I am looking out at the foyer, but feel I have the attention of the three males. "There is a secret back room to one of the shops downtown, K's knockout Potions and Poisons. I am a mentor to the shop owner, who is a close friend. She has agreed to allow our use to the shop, and I am confident she will be discrete."

Ian nods and looks at Brenen. "I will make sure to tell Ethen and Sophia." Brenen nods and glances over to Ethen and Sophia across the room. His eyes tell a story, and my head tilts to the side. I look at the two again in a different light. Umm, interesting. Bren is not happy about his sister's new love interest. Hopefully they can push their personal complication away and focus on the business at hand. Lives depend on our success.

"Let us meet at 10 a.m. tomorrow, before the group splits into their different sectors. We will come up with our game plan." I give the group a brilliant smile that I have practiced so many times I conjure it without thought. "Enjoy your evening."

I feel Caleb's eyes on me as I depart. As I walk away, a secret smile plays across my lips.

TWENTY-TWO

Gael—First Encounter

look down at the grand ballroom foyer from the balcony above. The last two hours have been a whirlwind.

After our victory lap, we were ushered to the capitol building atrium where we were allowed to meet with our families briefly. Images flash through my mind of the mayhem that followed the announcement.

Gwyneth, tears streaming down her face, hugs me tightly. Bennett picks me up and twirls me around like I'm six years old again. He says, "I knew you would do great." I give him a wide smile, tears trickling down my cheeks.

I look over and see Ari hugging her family. Her father looks so proud. His eyes lift, and he turns and hugs me as well. "Congratulations," he says. "I never doubted either of you girls." I look at Ari and smile. Ari's father, Henry Blane, is good friends with Bennett. Our families have been intertwined for years.

I hear a magnified voice over the din in the atrium. "Recruits, please make your way toward the locker rooms."

I turn to my family, give them all a rib-squeezing hug, saying, "I've got to go. I love you all." I pause and look up at Bennett. "Thank you for everything." I can see moisture in his eyes.

Gwyneth wipes the tears from my cheek. "We don't have too much time. You must go get ready for the ball." She pulls a garment bag that was on the bench and hands it to me. "Shoes and other necessities are in the bottom of the bag." I gave her a watery smile. Earlier that month, Ari, Gwyneth, and I went on a shopping trip to find the perfect gowns for this very occasion.

I turn and link my arms with Ari's, and we head to the locker rooms. The far wall is home to a massive counter that is currently hosting at least thirty-five girls in various stages of getting ready. All imaginable toiletries are lined up along the mirrors, various hairstyling, and makeup.

I look at Ari and say, "Let's get out of here as fast as possible." She laughs, and we walk past the chaos to shower and slip into our formal attire.

I am happy to get out of the madness of the locker room as we head out to the main entrance in record time. There is a lieutenant stationed outside the locker room doors who says, "Please make your way up to the upstairs lobby to wait. Your announcement will be at six."

I look at my watch. We have a little bit of time.

We pause at the foot of the rear stairs, and I look over at Ari. Her floor-length copper satin dress looks stunning. Gold-colored shoes peek out from under the folds of cloth. I say, "Ari, you look amazing."

She gives me a bright smile, looks up with her big blue eyes and dark fringe of bangs, and says, "You look pretty great yourself."

I look down at my champagne-colored floor-length gown and sigh. I love this dress. One shoulder of the dress wraps around, leaving the other bare. Tight around the waist and slightly flaring out at my hips, the material falls in folds straight down to the floor.

I say, "I cannot believe this is really happening. I have been looking forward to this for so long, and now we are living it." I lean in and give her a hug. She smiles, and we walk up the back stairs to mingle before the announcement.

As we arrive on the platform, the foyer of the ballroom below comes into view. A handful of recruits are already milling around. We walk to the balcony edge and peek over. There is a grand staircase that starts wide at the top and then slightly narrows and then widens again leading down to a foyer on the ground floor. The staircase is beautifully carved, the chandeliers glistening in the early evening sky that is visible through the glass ceiling.

As I look over the balcony to the below scene, I am in awe of the mix of the elite. My eyes are drawn to a pair of Fae who are currently standing at the edge of the crowd. I recognize one of them as a council member. He seems to be looking for something. As his eyes scan the balcony, our gazes lock.

A shiver wracks through my body, and the hair on the back of my arms stands up. The expression on his face is that of a predator who found its mark. As quickly as the look passes between us, it is gone. The two Fae have turned their attention to visit with their neighbors, and I am left with an uncomfortable feeling down deep in my gut.

Something is not right.

I look at Ari who has her back facing the balcony, missing the strange look that I may or may not have seen. Ari spots Gavin and grabs my arm. She says excitedly, "Oh, Gavin and Caden are coming over!"

I smile at Ari and shake off the strange feeling, rubbing the chill bumps from my arms.

Hearing the announcer begin his speech, I put my head back into the celebration, shrugging off the distant feeling of alarm.

TWENTY-THREE

Shadow Liberation

look around the room at the smiling faces. Some genuine, some fake, and I feel the weight of my years pressing down on me. This event marks the 977th year I have been attending these festivities celebrating the annual growth of the Warrior's Alliance. 977 years of protecting the gates to keep evil from this realm.

I sigh as the familiar rage boils up in me at the thought of how much time has passed. Long years that I have been forced to protect the gates that separate me from my family. Years that I have had to mourn the loss of my wife and child who were abandoned on the other side.

There are very few of us left, the originals who were forced to flee our homeland. Many here tonight have no memory of Faerie, no memory of the power we left behind. Unknowing or uncaring that there could very well be survivors forever trapped in our beautiful land, sacrificed to the dark creatures. That our *loving Great Queen* sacrificed many to save a few. So many years have passed that many have forgotten how powerful we were, how powerful we can be again. If we are able to get back to Faerie, our power would increase tenfold.

Three hundred years ago, I found a way to break the seal Great Queen Morrigan placed on the gates. I am so close to releasing the seal and being reunited with my family, the very people others have written off as lost to the darkness. The vessel burnt out too soon, his life force drained away. If only he had a bit more to give, I would be home with my family right now.

It almost worked.

I look up at the balcony and see the young, beautiful woman who is the first firewielder I have found in three hundred years.

She will be the key to unlocking the gates.

She will reunite my family after these long years.

TWENTY-FOUR

Caleb—Noreen's Reasons

I am in full reconnaissance mode. Leaning casually against a pillar, I try and differentiate the Fae, witches, and humans present. I study the room, its inhabitants, and their expressions, trying to take in every detail. Dinner has wrapped up, an elaborate affair, and we are now ushered into the ballroom. The swell of classical music is now coming from an orchestra set up on the main stage. Various people have started swaying around the dance floor, dance moves I have never acquired.

I have tracked Noreen's presence around the room. She has filtered from one group to the next, effortlessly leaving every group smiling in her wake. I notice she has had no dance partners yet, not that it is any of my business.

Aside from Noreen filtering between groups, I have spotted Brenen, Ian, Ethen, and Sophia co-habituating in a section of the room that appears to be primarily Fae. Now that I know them to be of Fae ancestry, I can look at the group and see similarities. They are all unnaturally beautiful, men and women alike. They all have uncommon heights and strong builds.

I try to put my finger on what else makes them stand out. It is their

145

eyes. I suspect their eyes hold the weight of years lived, experiences felt that normal Humans do not.

I continue my surveillance across the room and see the military group of men I saw at the funeral. I believe them to be the human unit that Kyle worked with. Speaking with them is on the agenda before the night is over.

Intermingling between these two groups seems to be the witches and warlocks. Primarily women, some men, they have a glow about them that is unique.

I am about to head toward the group of human soldiers when Rhea and her son, Evan Armstrong, approach from the right. I had not seen them at dinner and wondered if she would show tonight, despite her saying she was obligated to attend. I give Evan a bro hug, looking at him and Rhea in a new light. Warlock. Fae. As I look into his eyes, I see he is the same smart kid I've known for ten years.

I ask, "How are you holding up?"

Evan replies, "Managing."

I look at Rhea. "It's been one hell of a day."

She smiles slightly. "I'm glad you stuck around."

At that moment, Noreen glides up to our group and gives Rhea a kiss on the cheek, next is Evan. She says to Rhea, "I know you feel obligated to be here, but no one would say a word if you cut out."

Rhea cringes. "We wanted to make an appearance, speak to a few people, and then say our goodbyes. I wanted to make sure Caleb met the team and was set up for tomorrow."

Noreen nods. "I think Caleb already met the group. Somehow when I arrived, he was already in conversation with Ian, Ethen, and Brenen."

Rhea looks at me quizzically. "Bringing you on board was the right choice. You hit the ground running."

I nod. "I'm ready to start."

Noreen interjects, "Why don't I steal Caleb here for a dance while I go over the details of tomorrow's meeting." She looks at Rhea and Evan and says in a serious tone, "Know that we will do everything in our power to avenge Kyle's death."

Rhea and Evan thank us and slip out a side door.

Noreen turns to me, standing close enough that her dress brushes my shoes as the music swells in tune to some sort of waltz. I look at her a little sheepishly. "The last dance lesson I had was in eighth grade. I'm afraid I may stomp on your toes if we try to dance."

She smiles easily at me. "Why don't we get some air on the balcony? I've made my rounds already." She winks at me. I grin and follow her out to the massive balcony that overlooks the dark forest.

She walks to the edge and leans against the concrete pillars. She looks spectacular in her form-fitting blue dress, and suddenly my voice won't work. Instead of speaking, I lean against the concrete next to her, looking out at the woods.

She says unexpectedly, "I really hate these events. If we were not investigating these murders, I would have turned in my resignation already."

Not sure how to respond, I ask, "Why is that?"

Shoulder to shoulder, Noreen turns and looks at me. "I was getting ready to turn in my resignation last year. Then suddenly my business partner and mentor, Emma died." Noreen sighs. "I had worked with Emma for the last three hundred years. We grew our business together, tackled the collective and witches' rights together. She was out gathering supplies for our store in the forest, same routine she had for years, close to the city, little risk of any danger. She was attacked by dark creatures and killed.

"The council declared it a tragedy, saying she was in the wrong place at the wrong time." She scoffs, "I never bought that it was merely a coincidence.

"Then Kyle came around, asking questions that were burning in my mind." She glances at me. "I will do whatever it takes to find the ones responsible for these deaths and bring them to justice."

I ask, "So, after we bring them to justice, you are moving on?"

She sighs, "I've accomplished the task I set my mind to many years ago regarding my role in the Collective. I guess I'm restless, ready for a change."

"What will you do next?"

She shakes her head, "Not sure yet, but I feel the tides turning." She stands up straight and clears her throat. "Well, I will see you tomorrow at 10. There is a back entrance to K's on Main St. right across from

Nines, where we met. Walk around to the back entrance, and one of us will let you in."

Noreen squeezes my shoulder in passing as she sways back into the ballroom.

As I stare at her retreating back, I realize how far in I am over my head.

TWENTY-FIVE

Sophia—The Amulet

When I walk into the ballroom foyer, Ethen's gaze sweeps from the crown of my head down to my feet, and I can feel the heat across the room. He starts walking toward me with a predatory glint in his eye.

Instead of feeling the same anticipation I see sprawled across his face, my mind spirals into knowing something is not right. Alex murmurs, "Are you sure you won't change your mind? There is a line of ladies who are staring at you in envy right now."

I glance over and see that she is right.

I roll my eyes at Alex. "Yes, I'm sure. Something is not right with him."

To my left, I hear a deceptively charming, very different, male voice. Kingsley Abbott says smoothly, "Sophia, it's so nice to see you again. It's been far too quiet without you around."

If I did not know what kind of beast lurked beneath the charming façade, I may have fallen for it.

Last year, before Leona died and I left Tarrin, I worked with Kingsley Abbott at Vista Sector. His honey-coated voice always hid an ulterior motive. Charlatan for the council, Abbott always seems particularly interested in my powers, interested in any powerful Fae.

Abbott is responsible for overseeing the Warrior Qualification Training and all new recruits. He would visit each sector and observe and analyze the new recruits' powers. Over the years, there have been a handful of unsuspecting recruits who find themselves ensnared in Abbotts web of lies, pulled from training, never to be seen again. The suspicions surrounding these disappearances were investigated by the council. The investigations somehow always found Abbott free of guilt.

Maybe the council never saw Abbott look at the new recruits like they were fresh meat. Or maybe they were involved.

I reluctantly turn and face Abbott. I force a smile and say, "It's good to be back."

Abbott smoothly, "I hear you will be teaching at Domain Sector this year. They will be lucky to have such an experienced warrior to learn from." Abbott says all the right words, but I still feel a cold shiver up my spine.

"You are too kind, I am sure all the teachers are exceptional."

I glance up as Ethen appears and says, "Yes, we are lucky to have Sophia at the Domain Sector." The two males lock eyes, and Ethen grins. "Nice to see you Kingsley." Ethen reaches forward and shakes his hand.

Abbott smiles graciously, glances at me, and says, "Sophia, I would love to introduce you to your fellow instructors this year."

"Sure, it would be great to meet them." I look over at Alex and smile. "I'll catch up with you after dinner." My gaze settles on Ethen. "See you around."

It took all my efforts not to roll my eyes, but I managed, barely. The next hour and a half wasted, mindlessly spent with Abbott guiding me around, chatting with the other instructors. Even when dinner is announced, Abbott seats me with one of the Grove Sector instructors for the long dinner procession. As soon as the last plate clears, I excuse myself from the table with the pretense of going to the lady's room.

Enough is enough. I need a breath of fresh air.

I walk toward the main ballroom and spot Alex, who was with Gabriella Ventura, Commander of Mystgate Sector. I veer toward the ladies. Gabriella, Alex, and I all went through our recruitment in the

same year. Even though we all went in different directions after gradu‐
ation, we have stayed close ever since.

I give Gabriella a fierce hug and say, "I missed you!"

Her wavy long dark hair is free down her back, and she looks like an
Amazon goddess in a tight white dress. Gabriella says with a smile, "It's
so good to see you!"

I see Alex making eyes at one of her fellow soldiers in her sector,
Garrett Caldwell. I nudge her. "Hey, why don't you go talk to him?"

She looks at me for a moment. "Are you sure?"

"Go, enjoy the dance floor."

She gives me a brilliant smile and a quick hug. "I'll come and visit
you at the Domain Sector next week."

"Talk to you soon."

Alex walks over to the handsome soldier across the room near the
refreshment table. I can see them immediately hitting it off.

As I look at Alex's relaxed, happy smile, I realize I have been stuck
outside of life for too long.

Suddenly, there is someone at my back. I breathe in deep and am
engulfed in the warm citrus spice of Ethen. He leans in close to my ear
and whispers, "Have I told you how amazing you look in that dress?"

A shiver runs down my spine, and I turn toward him with a raised
eyebrow. "I don't think you have."

He gives me his half smile that feels rehearsed, playfulness shining
through his tough exterior. He looks at Gabriella. "Hey, mind if I steal
Sophia for a dance?"

She smiles. "Go right ahead." As Gabriella walks behind Ethen's
back, she gives me a thumbs-up and a wide smile. Not knowing how to
get out of the dance tactfully, I give Ethen a tight smile.

He holds out his hand in an old-fashioned way. I slip my fingers on
top of his, and he leads me to the dance floor. As the music cues, he
turns to me then sweeps me into the crowd, effortlessly leading me
across the floor. I look up into his eyes, and he says, "I've been waiting
for this dance all night." I am aware of Ethen's hand at my hip, where
our bodies brush together as we move to the music.

I purposefully guide his hand a few inches higher, and Ethen sighs.
I look him in the eyes. "Look, Ethen, I don't know you." I glance

around the room. "You have Brenen and Ian convinced, but I don't know anything about you."

We circle the dance floor in silence, and then he looks down at me and says, "I know why you came home. Brenen told me about your sister."

My eyes dart away from him and then back. Ethen continues in a low voice, "The reason I transferred to this gate six months ago is that one of the murder cases was a childhood friend of mine, Duncan Mackinley. When I heard of his death..." Ethen leans in closer. "When I heard of his *murder*, I asked for a transfer." His face is drawn into harsh lines, seemingly genuinely saddened, and my heart softens slightly. This is a version of Ethen that seems authentic.

He looks into my eyes. "We will find them Sophia, I promise you that."

That hits home, and I wipe a tear that escaped down my cheek. I say, "I need to get some air." I turn and exit the dance floor. Feeling Ethen following, I ignore his presence as I head for the rear doors.

As I reach for the exterior door, I look up and see Ian strolling across the room. As he approach, I wipe the tears from my eyes, hoping he would not witness them.

Ian says, "Sophia, I'm glad I found you. I was looking for you earlier, but you were stolen away by Kingsley most of the night."

I roll my eyes, and Ian smiles at my rueful look. He glances around to make sure there are no prying eyes then says in a low voice, "The task force is meeting tomorrow at ten at the poison shop on Main Street. There's a back entrance."

Ian leans back, saying in a normal voice, "Well, I'm going to call it a night."

Ian embraces me in farewell. We are cheek to cheek when suddenly he wrenches back as though burned. I look at him in confusion. He reaches for my necklace, as though it is something dangerous.

"Sophia, where did you get that necklace?"

I glance away for a moment, not wanting to confess to lifting the relic from the horde he asked me to find. I look back at him and see Ian cross his arms in front of his chest, patiently waiting for my response.

I shift my weight. "Fine, it was one of the artifacts I gathered. I figured it would collect dust somewhere on a shelf, so instead I decided to wear it tonight."

Ian's eyes have grown big. Rarely have I ever seen him shocked by anything. "I did not feel its power until I brushed against it. I believe it to be one of the Great Queen's relics."

I rock back on my heels to get a better look at his face. "Are you sure?" I lick my lips and glance over at Ethen, who is standing close enough to hear. "I don't feel anything other than the normal hum of power most relics have."

"Yes, I am sure. There is no mistaking that power."

Ian gives me a hard look. "That amulet around your neck is perhaps one of the most powerful in Tarrin."

I look at him in confusion. "What do you know about it?"

He glances toward the ballroom before eyeing me and Ethen. "Let's go to the vault, and I will explain."

I nod, and the three of us head out of the ballroom and through the atrium to the far side of the complex. I let my fingers lightly run over the rubies at my neck as I consider whether the beauty of the necklace is not what drew me to the piece, rather the magic behind it.

The vault is a wing of the capitol building where the most valuable relics from Faerie are kept. Protected by wards, the vault is off limits to all except for council members. I know where it is located but have never stepped foot inside.

Ian leads us through a set of wide-arched double doors, which are secured by a runestone check point. Down a long-carpeted hallway that leads to a set of ornately carved doors that look to be time worn and primeval.

I ask, "Are the doors part of the relic collection?"

Ian nods. "Yes, these doors were Tarrin's original gateway to Faerie, before the queen closed the barriers. The historic preservation of the gateway was put into place after the barrier was sealed. The doors were moved here to our capital building."

I take in the massive, arched wooden doors to the vault. They are beautifully carved, figurines displaying different scenes, chiseled perfectly into sections that appear to tell a story. I hover my hand over the gate and feel ancient energy leaking out, almost tangible.

"What do the carvings depict?"

He turns, pausing for a moment and looking at the doors as if he saw them so often that he forgot to be impressed.

"The carvings tell the story of how the passage between our realms was originally found and the story of the first Fae who discovered this passage to Earth."

Ian approaches the carved doors and motions to the first scene. "The first Fae who found the passageway created the doors to identify and mark the location so that he could find it and return. This is an old fable, told and retold so many times over that we do not even know if it is true."

He crossed his arms over his broad chest. "The old fable begins with the original Fae who found the passageway and explored the Earth realm for many years. He fell in love with a human woman on one of his travels and brought her to Faerie." He points to one of the carvings. "They lived together in peace for many years, until the time when she decided she wanted to return to Earth to see her family."

Ian sighs heavily. "Time moves differently in Faerie. They discovered that when she lived with him in his homeland, she did not age like a human, rather the same as a Fae. Upon her to return to Earth, she was devastated to learn her family had died many years before.

"She was so distressed by the loss of her family that she refused to go back to Faerie. Years passed, and the woman started to age again. The Fae was desperate and pleaded with her to return, that there was nothing left for her on Earth. He finally convinced her to return to Faerie, and then in an act of desperation he infused the gate with magic to only allow him to control the gate, thus ensuring that she could never leave him again."

Ian starts to walk away. I stopped him by placing a hand on his arm, asking, "So what happened to them?"

He shrugs. "No one knows for sure. That is the end of the story that is carved on the gate." He shakes his head slightly and places his ring on the runestone.

I can feel as the magic ripples and excitement sparks through me. I have always wanted to see inside the vault, giddy at the rare look inside.

Ian looks at us pointedly. "If anyone other than one of the elders attempted to use their rings on this stone, there would be an alarm."

I nod, knowing we are seeing beyond the veil tonight.

Ian asks, "When you found the necklace, was there anything else in the collection?"

I think back to the museum where I found the necklace at. It was in Charlotte. "No, I think this was the only item I found at that particular museum."

We walk through the doors. Ethen, who has been quiet for most of our walk to the vault, lets out an appreciative whistle.

A long hallway spreads out in front of us, resembling a museum. Glass boxes display suits of armor, and all manners of weapons are on the walls. I recognize some of the items that I retrieved from my searches of the natural history museums in the area.

I ask Ian, "Were you looking for the amulet? Is that why you sent me on the mission to find the relics?"

He looks over at me. "Yes and no. We knew relics were popping up after being hidden for a thousand years. I wanted to see what else was out there and ensure they ended up back here in the capital." He pauses and looks at the necklace. "I did not know what we would find."

Ian turns and starts down the long hallway. Ethen and I keep stride. He says, "About six months ago, a warrior here at Vista Sector found the Sword of Light."

I remember the story of the Sword of Light from an old history class. "The Great Queen's sword?

"The sword was rumored to be destroyed or lost to Faerie during the closing of the gates. Luckily for us, the warrior who found it had a habit of going to high-end auctions. He saw it and knew it must be a Fae relic. He won it at auction and brought it back with him to Idyll."

Ian is looking at Ethen, whose face had turned pale. Ethen whispers, "Was it Duncan Mackinley?"

"Yes, it was Duncan."

I reach down and squeeze Ethen's hand.

We reach the end of the hallway, which ends in a large circular room, displaying jewelry, sculptures, and artwork that lines the walls. Ian is standing in front of a glass case. When I get closer, I can see it is empty. I look at Ian quizzically, and he points at the placard that is below the case. "Sword of light" is etched on a title card.

I glance over and see Ethen's grim expression. He asks, "Where is the Sword of Light now?"

Ian shakes his head. "Duncan was on his way to the capital, bringing the sword with him when he was ambushed. We found Duncan's body, but the Sword of Light was gone."

We pause and stare at the empty case. I say, "Duncan was targeted because he found the sword?"

"If Duncan's death was not connected, that would be a hell of a coincidence."

In the very center of this circular room is a wide-open space that is marked by a circle on the marble floors. In the center of the floor is a mosaic of Tarrin's emblem, three mountain peaks, with the gate in the foreground. Sunbeams rising behind the mountains. There is a small table set in the middle but no other furniture.

I ask, "What is the circle for?"

Ian responds, "Most of the protections in the vault keep outsiders from trying to get in. The circle in front of you is protected from something getting out." He gives me a pointed look. "This is where we evaluate relics, determine their power. If the power is extreme, we want to safely examine them." He touches a panel in the corner, and the once invisible runes shine brightly on the floor in golden lines. Intricately woven, the gold bands must have taken a whole coven of witches months to prepare.

I kneel and run my fingertips over the top of the closest rune. I feel the power humming from the surface.

I look up. "You want to evaluate the necklace?"

Ian gives me a silent tilt of his head. I reach behind my neck and try to unclasp the necklace. It would not budge. I try again, this time putting in some effort. I look up at Ian and Ethen. "I think it's stuck." Ethen slides up behind me and tries with no success. I look at Ian, in slight panic. He is looking at me in silent contemplation.

I say, "You knew it would not come off." I swallow nervously. "Why?"

Ian walks forward and holds his hand over the necklace. "The last time I felt the power of this amulet, it was around the Great Queen's neck." I suck in a breath, knowing my eyes must have widened. Ian backs away but continues, "The amulet looked different at that time, but I believe that is because the amulet transfigures to the needs and desires of the owner. Morrigan never took it off. It was believed to be destroyed when she was closing the gates."

I mull over this information. "What do you mean, 'transfigures?'"

"I observed once during a battle that the amulet transformed into a full body shield. This shield protected her from any spell or weapon turned against her. It absorbed the power used and pushed it back against her enemies in a great surge of amplified power unlike any I had ever seen before." He glances over his shoulder. "I asked her after the battle how she acquired the amulet. She told me it found her in her time of need, and she could never take it off."

I breathed deep at this piece of news, the beautiful necklace around my neck now seeming like a weight I could not get rid of.

Ian went on, "I want you to go into the circle and try to use your power on the amulet. See how it reacts. I do not believe you will be in any danger. The amulet chose you. I am sure it will protect you the same as it did with the queen."

I step to the circle inlay on the marble floor. I wave my fingers over the runes and take a deep breath as I cross the threshold. I feel the ward snap into place. Any magic made in this circle would stay in this circle and not damage anything or anyone around me.

I pull on the innate magic deep inside me and feel it pooling in the bottom of my invisible reservoir. I feel a slight wind start to stir through the circle, created from the power of my magic. My hair starts to trickle around me, creating an electricity I can feel from the crown of my head down to my feet. I gently, slowly, ease power into the necklace around my neck. I feel its pulse and know in that moment what Ian told me is true. I feel a connection to the amulet, as if it would do whatever I asked.

My eyes are closed in concentration. "What do I do now?"

He replies, "Try to make a shield."

I push the energy up and around me and hear a small intake of breath from Ethen, and I open my eyes. I have created an almost invisible barrier that encompasses my body. The necklace is not visible anywhere else, truly transforming to my will.

I grin at Ian and Ethen. "I can't wait to use this."

Ian smirks. "Release the shield, envision how you want it to look, and see if it will manifest."

As the power releases around me, I look down and see a simple leather band with a silver disc, the Tarrin insignia engraved on it. I rub my thumb over the emblem, the same token given to each warrior when they graduate from the academy. This will blend in seamlessly.

Ian cuts through my excitement. "I am glad the amulet will protect you. But be careful. We do not know the origin of this magic."

My brow furrows. "What does that mean?"

Ian pushes off the pillar he is leaning on. "When infusing magic in an object, there is always a cost. Use the amulet in moderation, only if you need it."

With that dire warning, I look down at the amulet. A shiver of foreboding washes through me. What would the cost be?

TWENTY-SIX

Gael—New Best Friend

The sun has yet to rise, but this is my favorite time to run. Seeing the sun crest over the mountain valleys of Tarrin is the best view and my goodbye to Idyll for the next six months. Back at the Monroe house, my bags are packed, and at 8 a.m. I will be heading to the Domain Sector. Each recruit received their training program itinerary yesterday evening. Domain Sector will be my new home while I go through the rest of my training.

I pause at the top of the mountain, breathe the crisp early morning air. I push back a lock of blonde hair from my forehead, where it has escaped my ponytail. Straight ahead is a flat rock that is my customary perch. This is where I normally wait for the sun to pierce the veil of blue smoke these valleys are known for. This has been my morning routine since I started training for the Citadel Warrior Alliance.

While I am excited beyond anything I have ever experienced for the next six months of Q training, now that Selection Day is over, I will miss this routine.

Catching my breath, my heart rate slows, and I feel the semi darkness of dense forest that surrounds me on all sides. The hair on my arm stands at attention. Normally I can hear the birds chirping, animal life scurrying and active this time of morning. Today, there is a strange silence. I stand up and peer into the forest, alert for danger that I can feel is imminent.

My hand lowers to my boot, where I keep a dagger that Bennett gave me when he found out I liked to run in the mornings. Nothing fancy, with a sturdy, wickedly sharp blade, it will do some damage.

I hear a low growl from the forest. It vibrates the ground, deep and menacing. My eyes focus on that spot in the forest where I hear the growling. I back up one space then another into the small clearing. Suddenly, I feel a presence directly behind me. I whip around, my hair flying behind me. A large, dark creature with leathery black wings and scales covering its bird-like face rears back and lets out a monstrous shriek.

No time for conscious decisions, no time to react. I turn and run into the forest before I can rationalize my plan. I can feel the dark creature closing in behind me, hot breath on my neck. Then, as suddenly as it appeared, it is gone. I am still running full speed into the deep forest, tree branches and brush tearing at my skin. Hearing the silence, I stop, knife still raised. I turn in a circle. My breathing heavy and labored. Eyes darting around, looking for the creature.

The same low growl from before vibrates the earth, followed by the dark creature's high shriek. I creep toward the battle noises coming from beyond the path I cut through the forest. As I get closer, I can see the creature attacking an animal that looks like it is caught in a bear trap. One powerful hind leg trapped, but the animal's massive canines tear into the creature's throat. The creature falls back, injured but still able to mount a return offensive.

As it starts to descend on the animal for the second time, I reach behind the creature's back and slit the throat. Black blood sprays as the creature spins around, attempting to take me out with a claw. I jump backward, and it falls face down on the forest floor, unmoving. I creep forward, the edge of my boot knocking into the creature's back. It doesn't move.

As I sigh in relief, I look over at the animal that is still stuck in the trap. As I took in the appearance for the first time, I realize the animal is really an oversized dog. Paws the size of my palm, body height that would reach my hip when standing. The dog whines in pain, and I jump over the dead dark creature to observe the trap and figure out how to disengage. There were many traps I knew the Warrior Alliance had placed throughout the forest, primarily trying to trap the dangerous dire wolves.

I raise my hands in submission as I approach, trying to convey I am here to help and not harm the animal. He lets out another low growl that shakes the ground beneath my feet. I wonder if he is mixed with some magical animal I have not learned of yet. His size and girth do not match any earthly beings I had ever seen.

I pull my fingers into a fist and inch closer, letting him smell the scent on the back of my hand. His growl turns into a low whine, and I brush my knuckles down the side of his massive face. He turns his face into my hand, and I run my palm over his broad head and over his ear. I look into his eyes and try to convey that I am here to help. His gaze seems to reach down into my soul, and then, as if he accepts me, he looks down at his hind leg trapped by the sharp edges and whines again.

Confident now that he would not eat me, I crouch down and look at the trap. I see two springs, one on each side that push upward, clamping the two jaws closed. I push both springs down at the same time, and the trap releases.

I look at him in the eyes, and say softly, "I'm going to pull this out, and it will hurt. Please do not bite me."

The animal seems to understand. I gently pull his paw from the teeth of the trap. Finally free, the large canine pushes up and away from the trap in a rush, limping slightly.

My knees give way, and I collapse down on the damp earth. My hands are shaking uncontrollably from the adrenaline. I look up at the sky, see the sun peaking over the trees, and feel a tear slide down my cheek.

Suddenly, I feel hot breath on my face, and a wet tongue is lapping up my tears. I look over at the large boxy head of the canine. His jaw looks like it could take my head off in one bite. I let out a shaky laugh and rub his ears. I think I made a new best friend.

I stand on shaky legs. Me and my new sidekick limp back to the

Monroe house in a slow but steady walk. As my home comes into view, I see Bennett on the porch. His double-take of the animal would be comical if I were not still in shock. He approaches, taking in my black blood-stained leggings and shirt, along with the limping dog.

"What happened?" he asks calmly.

I relay the events in the forest. The attack and killing of the dark creature, saving the dog. Bennett looks at me with a pleased smile. "Good job with the dark creature. I'm glad you were able to defend yourself."

He looks down at the dog. "I do not believe that is a normal earthly dog. In Faerie, we had an animal similar to this. The breed was Molossus, a dog derived from Hecate." Bennett's full attention is now on the animal.

I ask, "Do you think he came through the cracks in the wall, same as the dark creatures?"

Bennett hums. "It is certainly possible. There used to be quite a few here in Tarrin. Many Fae brought over their animals with them when we were evacuated. Over the years, they have died out, not enough of them to continue their pureblood breeding. Many Molossus interbreed with earthly dogs, resulting in smaller species. Molossus were known for their fierceness and the loyalty they show to their masters."

I smile. "I think he likes me." I look down at the Molossus and rub his ears. He has been patiently sitting at my side as if he could under-stand our conversation. Bennett reaches out to the animal, allowing him to sniff his fingers. Then he runs his palm down the animal's large head.

Bennett says, "He may have bonded with you."

I turn wide eyed to face him fully. "What does that mean?"

"He may have chosen you as his master." He pauses. "We will have to monitor his behavior, but I see no reason you shouldn't be able to take him with you to your training. If you want to keep him?"

I nod earnestly, and pet his head. "He was amazing, even when he was injured."

"I like the idea of you having him to protect you in the forest, espe-cially if you keep running alone." He gives me a hard look.

The Molossus barks and wags his tail, like he agrees. Bennett says, "I will talk with Ethen, the Domain Sector commander. If the animal is kept out of the way, it should not interfere with your normal training."

I crouch down and give some love to the dog. I have never had a pet before, but it feels right to keep him.

I look up with a wide smile. "I'll take care of him."

TWENTY-SEVEN

Caleb—Forewarned Is Forearmed

sit in a cafeteria that adjoins the Central Sector and the capitol building. I have been here since daybreak, looking for the human soldier team that worked with Kyle. Last night, after speaking with Noreen on the balcony, I returned to the ballroom to find the team was gone. I figure there is no better way to track them down than through their stomachs.

I sip on my third cup of coffee as I wait and contemplate this new world I find myself in.

Sprawled out on the hard plastic chair, my long legs push out in front of me, stretching my stiff back. Jeans, a black t-shirt, and a lightweight jacket that covers my shoulder holster and 9mm, which I never leave home without. When I returned to my room last evening, I found a week's worth of new clothes in my dresser. Jeans, cargo pants, t-shirts all freshly folded, all in my size, waiting for me. Still baffled as to the clothes process here, I am slightly amazed and impressed at the mysterious housekeeping service that runs the hospitality at Central Sector.

Although the amazement of housekeeping had nothing on my last three hours here at the cafeteria, witnessing a variety of activities. It seems that this is the hub for the many individuals who work either in the capital or in the Central Sector. Suits intermingled with casually dressed beings, humans, witches, and Fae all headed either to the capital or Central Sector. Not to mention the Fae warriors, which I identified from their leather fighting uniforms and weaponry that looked medieval.

Interestingly, I see groups of women all dressed in a uniform of sorts. They all have the same glow that I noticed about the witches at the ball last night. I conclude they must be part of the Witches Academy Noreen spoke about. A group of them walk by all wearing white long-sleeve blouses tucked into skirts reaching their knees with matching gray vests. They all have a spark of the illuminance that radiated from Noreen.

Twenty-four hours ago, I was completely unaware, kept in the dark. Now that the blindfold, so to speak, has been ripped from my eyes, I can never go back. The fascination of my new surroundings continues in the background of my mind, while Kyle moves to the forefront. I am getting antsy sitting here for so long. I tap my fingers on the coffee cup in my hands and try to calm my impatience. I sit forward and drop my elbows to the table. I need to speak with his team and get firsthand knowledge of what occurred the day he died.

Finally, at 9:30 a.m., I spot two of the team members walking through the cafeteria doors. I take a sip of my coffee and watch the soldiers order their food and sit down a few tables over. I get up and stride across the room. At their table, I flash a friendly smile and ask, "Mind if I join you this morning?"

The team members look up at me. I can see recognition light their eyes. One of them with light-brown hair and eyes stands up and extends his hand. "You must be Caleb Moretti. I recognize you from Kyle's funeral."

I nod. "You were part of his team?"

The second soldier stands up. "Yes, I'm Garrett Caldwell, and this is Aden Aldridge." We shake hands, and then Garrett gestures to sit.

I scoot in the chair and take out a small notebook I keep in the side panel of my lightweight jacket. "I had a few questions about the day Kyle died."

Garrett says, "I was told you would be investigating his murder."

I continue, "Could you walk me through the op and your history with Kyle?"

Garrett sighs and pushes his plate away.

I suppose I could have waited for them to eat before coming over, but I have an appointment at ten.

Garrett rubs his hands over his face. "Kyle was on our team for a year, we patrolled together, and then he brought us into his side investigation." Garrett looks around, confident no one is within ear shot. "Kyle was looking into strange creature habits that resulted in two deaths and an outpost sector being destroyed last year.

"Kyle was poking around, looking into the areas where the attacks took place. He set up cameras and was able to get footage of unknown suspects transporting dark creatures in Tarrin."

This is the same information Rhea provided the first night we discussed Kyle's death. I most likely would have started with the location cameras too. I make a scribble only I can decipher.

Garrett says, "Then a week later, the cameras were found destroyed. The placement of these cameras was well hidden. It is not likely they were found by accident. At that time, we suspected somehow the faction members were tipped off. It seems unlikely they would have found the cameras on their own. We should have taken better precautions, should have dived into the search for a leak."

I nod. Hindsight is always twenty-twenty.

Garrett continues, "Soon after the cameras were destroyed, Kyle was approached by someone close to the faction leaders. He kept the identity of the informant a secret. This person fed information to him over the next few months. We acted on it a few times, but every meeting we tried to intercept, we were one step behind the targets. Kyle's source swore that the meeting location kept getting moved, all the way up until the final hours of the meet.

"The day Kyle died, he got a tip a few hours before the planned meeting. We jumped on it, thinking we could get ahead of the faction members with such a tight timeline. We should have sent in drones instead of going ourselves.

"We got to the meeting site, started our approach down a cliff. We walked right into a trap. Explosives were set in the mountain side. The faction member looked me square in the eyes and smiled before detonating the bomb. They knew we would be there and how to take us out."

Garrett pushes back his chair and puts his elbows on his knees. He looks up at me. "When you find this son of a bitch, I want to be there for the takedown."

I ask, "Do you have any ideas who Kyle's source was?"

He shakes his head. "No, he was adamant about keeping it secret. I believe his informant was primarily stationed at Central Sector. Every time Kyle met with them in person, it was here."

That is the first bit of new information I have to start my search. I tuck the small notepad inside my jacket. "If there is anything else you remember, please reach out." I hand him my card as I rise from the chair. The two soldiers stand, and we shake hands.

I turn and leave the cafeteria, appreciating the perfect timing as I anticipate the upcoming meeting.

I stroll toward the Central Sector entrance, down the wide steps, and out into the bustling downtown area. Yesterday, it was a ghost town. Today, there is a wide variety of activities, all the shops open for business and people milling about. I pause and take in the lively activity, relatively normal except for the warriors mixed in with witches and humans. Now that I can spot the difference, the obviousness makes me wonder how I never noticed before. It makes me wonder how much I never noticed in the real world.

I make my way down the main street, passing by the shops I looked in yesterday. I pass by K's and glance at the sign, "Open by appointment only." I keep walking, glancing around to see if anyone is watching me. Satisfied I am alone and not being watched, a block up I duck into a side alley. I take a quick look around to make sure no one is following. Then I circle around to the back entrance of the shop. I glance at my watch. I'm a little early. I knock on the door and hear a slight shuffle of movement, and then Noreen swings the door wide with a smile.

"Come on in," she says. I duck down slightly. The door frame is shorter than the standard frames. As I walk into the back of a small shop, a sharp smell assaults my nostrils, tangy. I can't identify what it is. There is a long workbench with a variety of ingredients sprawled out to the right of the shop. Ahead is a cashier desk and beyond that rows of bottled brightly glowing vials.

I look at the worktable and say, "So these are potions?"

Noreen leans her hip against the cashier table and crosses her arms. "Yes, these are potions. What witches lack in natural immunity and strength, we make up for in spells, wards, and potions. Only a witch can feel the Earth's energy and manipulate it. Only a witch can chant a spell into the wards." She starts to walk toward me. "Only a witch can push the Earth's energy into a simple herb mixture and make a potion."

I ask, "What sorts of potions do you make here?"

A slight smile plays on her lips. "All sorts." As she turns and starts walking down an aisle, she continues, "If you are to be part of our team, you will need some defenses." She picks up a long duster coat off a rack in the corner and starts to make her way down the first aisle, picking up a few vials and slipping them in the coat.

"What are those?"

She holds up a vial, unscrews the lid, and slides a bright-green orb in her palm. "Each of these vials holds a potion crafted for different purposes. There are two main ways of delivery. Some will have a casing." She rolls the orb in her hand. "This allows for distance launch that will explode upon impact and immerse the target in the potion. The second is kept as a liquid, meant to be ingested."

I ask, "What is that one for?"

"The green ones are immobilization. It will stop a target for a limited amount of time, hopefully enough to give you a chance to get away."

I raise my eyebrows. "Hopefully?"

Noreen slides the green orb back into the metal vial and screws the lid back on. As she slips it back into the duster, she says, "Yes, hopefully. Effectiveness depends on your target. The more powerful the target, the less effective it will be." She glances back at me as she continues down the second aisle. "If you use them on a dark creature, it should hold for ten minutes."

She holds up a red orb. "This one is an explosive, similar to a grenade." She slides a few into the coat. She holds up a yellow potion that is in a hard cylinder with a small opening at the top. "This one you drink. It is for healing and strengthening. Depending on the severity of injuries, it should heal fully or at the very least heal enough to travel to a true healer at one of the sectors."

She walks toward the back of the store and approaches the floor-to-ceiling locked cabinet. She opens with a key, and I see a wide range of ammunition stacked in neat rows. Noreen says, "Some of this we don't sell to the public, but if you are hunting Fae, you will need to be armed." She rummages through the cabinet looking for something specific. "Their speed and strength alone will put you at a disadvantage. If you ever are in a life and death situation against a Fae, shoot first. You won't get a second chance."

I shift my weight as I take her advice.

She pulls a single box from the back of the cabinet and gently blows the dust from the top of the box. She wipes it down with a soft cloth and then opens it to reveal what looks like sabot ammo. I have seen this type of ammo in shotguns, but this is in miniature form that will fit a 9mm, like the ones in my holster right now.

Noreen holds up one bullet. "This is a specialized bullet that will stop a Fae. The only substance that will hurt a Fae long-term is iron. If the Fae get injured with any other type of weapon, blade, or claws, their natural healing abilities will heal within moments. If they get injured with iron, the cuts will heal as slow as a human. If they get shot with iron, it will poison them, and if not removed immediately, it will kill them."

"Is this common knowledge?"

She shrugs. "Yes, it is known that iron will kill a Fae, similar to how you know a bullet to the heart will kill you." She gestures for my gun, and I hand it to her. Her fingers make quick work of the magazine as she empties it and starts to replace the regular bullets with the specialized iron ones from the case.

She says, "You may know that iron is not a very good medium to use as a bullet. It's too hard a metal, and it would destroy your firearm barrels within a few shots." She holds one bullet up and says, "That is why there is a protective casing to protect your weapon. This casing dissolves upon discharge, leaving only the center iron bullet to penetrate your target."

She finishes loading the magazine and hands me the reloaded 9mm. I tuck it into my holster as she slips the remaining ammo in the box into a side pocket of the duster and comes around the edge of the counter.

She strides closely and pushes the long duster coat in my hands. I look down and wrap my fingers around the soft leather. The inside jacket lapels are purposefully designed to hold the vials. All eight slots are full, three immobilization, three explosive, and two healing potions she selected.

"Thank you," I say.

"No problem. I will charge the Citadel Warrior Alliance. That setup alone is a small fortune."

She taps her fingers on the coat with a smile "Always happy to charge the Alliance."

As she walks toward the back of the store again, I slip on the duster and follow her. In the back section of the store, Noreen pauses near a shelf and pulls a book, and the bookcase full of dried ingredients swings silently forward, revealing a staircase that disappears down into the Earth. Noreen flips a switch, and light illuminates the stairs and room below. She motions me to go ahead of her down the stairs, and I start to descend.

Above me, I hear a knock at the door, turn, and look up the stairs to see Noreen letting in Brenen, Ethen, and Brenen's sister.

Here we go.

TWENTY-EIGHT

Sophia—Task Force

As I walk up to the back entrance of the potions shop, I am still reeling from the revelations of last night. My hand goes to my neck, and I touch the amulet again for what must be the hundredth time. The queen's amulet lost for a thousand years, and it is around my neck this morning. Apparently, for good.

My fighting leathers are magically clean and ready for me this morning. Thank you, housekeeping. I will be traveling to Domain Sector today, my new home, for the next six months. I am dressed in my leather uniform and boots, and my hair plait in its customary braid runs down my back. A small wisp of hair has escaped the braid, and its red streaks glint in the morning light as I turn a corner and look behind me to ensure I am not followed.

I feel a whisper of air moving, and I know I am not alone.

Suddenly Bren appears by my side. I let out a little squeak and slap his arm. "Watch it!"

He gives me a notorious grin and says, "Never gets old."

He looks down at me and sweeps a thumb over the necklace. He says, "Remarkable." I still cannot believe the amulet chose me. After we finished in the vault last night, I found Bren in his quarters. I re-layed the trip to the vault and the amulet's history.

I hear a noise approaching from behind and see Ethen strolling to-ward us. I glance over and see Brenen's face. The light drains from his features. I suppose the only thing that would drive a wedge between the two new friends is the fact Ethen is interested in his sister.

Ethen approaches with a smile. "You guys waiting for me?"

I smile neutrally back. "We just got here." I motion to the door, and Brenen knocks. Noreen opens the door and ushers us inside. I had been to this shop many times, only I never made it into the back work area reserved for employees. The sharp bite of magic permeates the air, and I see the workbenches scattered with supplies. Noreen motions to a bookshelf moved to the side, with a staircase winding down below. I start to descend to the basement.

As I reach the bottom, I am surprised at the roomy space. Fully con-verted into a modern workspace, the stairs as we entered are bright white. In an L shape, the right and central wall is painted in deep grays with full sets of floor-to-ceiling shelves with recessed lighting on each shelf. The colors and lighting make the room feel cozy, and the lights almost reflect as a window would. Beneath our feet are ornamental rugs, squishy sofas, and chairs. On the last wall is a gigantic TV that is hooked up to work as a presentation screen. Under the stairs a bar is set up, seating four. To the right of the TV is a desk setup with a com-puter and two chairs.

Already downstairs is a human male I have never met. Bren walks forward and makes introductions. "Caleb Moretti, this is Sophia Beaumont, my sister. Sophia, this is Caleb. Rhea asked him to come on board. Caleb was close with Kyle, the most recent murder victim."

I shake his hand and can see his sharp eyes taking in all the details. Reserving judgment of the newcomer until he has a chance to prove himself, I ask, "So is this the whole group?" I look around at Ethen, Brenen, Noreen, and Caleb.

Brenen pauses and looks at me. "We are waiting for one more."

There is a loud knock outside, audible in the basement. Noreen walks up and brings down the last in the group. As his feet start to descend the stairs, I know who it is. The gait and the mannerisms are unmistakable. I swung wide eyes at Brenen before the new member of our team is even fully downstairs.

"You want to bring on Theon Whitlock?"

Brenen holds up his hands. "Sophia, it was Ian's idea. Theon is the best at what he does, and he has a personal connection to this case." He looks around the group and points his finger at each of us. "This is personal to us all."

I lean against the far wall and fold my arms in front of me. As Theon settles downstairs, he mimics me across the room. He leans against the bar next to the stairs, crossing his large arms over his powerful chest. He looks mostly the same as the last time I saw him with Leona. Dark blond hair worn long past his chin, dark stubble on his face the only difference. His honey-brown eyes are intense as he sweeps the room.

Theon has the good grace not to look me in the eyes. If he showed an ounce of aggression, my glare would be the least of his problems.

Noreen clears her throat and says, "Caleb, this is Theon Whitlock, the best tracker in Tarrin. I think you have met everyone else." She pauses and looks around. "Brenen, do you want to get started?"

He crosses the room to stand on the stairs, collecting his thoughts. "We are all here for the same purpose. We have all lost someone we loved or cared about to these monsters. I can tell you right now, we will avenge our loved ones' deaths.

"I know each of you have a personal stake in this investigation. I am looking at the most dedicated group we could ask for. And because of this, it is more important than in any other case to keep our emotions in check. Keep a clear mind and work together for our common goal. If we allow our emotions to rule, it will only cloud our judgment."

That last comment was meant for me.

Bren continues, "We are keeping this group tight. What we uncover and discuss about the case stays with this group. There will be no more leaks. The faction members are aware of our movements, either through magic or by betrayal. If there is someone at Vista Sector, someone I know, that has leaked information to the faction members, I will find out about it. I have a short list of suspects. Only a limited number of trusted people knew our strategy."

He turns and looks at me. "Sophia, you will be tasked with finding any objects of power the faction members could be using to shield their activities."

I nod and say, "I can search for any drastic increase in powers or unusual incidents in the daily reports."

Bren turns toward Noreen. "I want you to use your contacts to find any illicit activities that could be related to the faction members. Anyone who is asking for specialized potions. Stealth or strength would be ones to put on our suspect list."

She says, "I have a long list of clients that trust my discretion. This leads to their secrets becoming my secrets. I will compile a list and do some digging."

"Theon, I want you to start tracking the faction members' movements in the forests, starting in Vista Sector. You may notice something we missed at the last ambush location. It has been a week since the explosion, but no rain or heavy weather. See what you can find." Brenen looks at the human male. "Caleb, I want you to go with Theon, track the last-known movements of Kyle's team."

Caleb nods, and Brenen continues, "I will have Rhea send over Kyle's notes to be delivered to your dormitory. I want you to run through all his notes and see what you can turn up."

Lastly, Brenen turns toward Ethen, his long legs sprawled out on the couch, tossing his dagger into the air and catching it. Ethen pauses in his antics and looks at Brenen, expertly retrieving his dagger in a flourish. In one fluid motion, he is standing, and the knife is sheathed.

Brenen says, "Ethen, I want you to go to the Dragon Keep. See if Mac can arrange for a meeting. If Draco and the rest of his flight will help us, he would be a strong ally.

"Take Sophia with you to help foster a new relationship with the dragons. They are temperamental. If we can widen their network to include our team, that will be a huge advantage. Start with Sophia, and we will see how it goes." Ethen nods again, and my eyes widen. The list of beings allowed to speak with the dragons is so limited that there is only a handful at each of the gates.

I look over at Ethen and contemplate how he may know the dragons. Draco was the dragonflight leader here in Tarrin. If Ethen is on speaking terms with Draco, he could facilitate an alliance to help our team.

Dragons are known for their excellent reconnaissance and blending into their surroundings. I seem to recall hearing the name Coner MacKinley, or "Mac" as he was affectionately known as, over the years. He must be related to Ethen's friend who died. I ponder this as I make the connection with the surname of his friend Duncan MacKinley.

Brenen wraps up, "Manus gave us a set of untraceable phones for communication." He reaches down to retrieve a bag sitting at his feet. He walks to each of us, handing out a phone as he passes. "Each one is pre-programed with our contact information, the first initial of your name. The group is Umbra. When we have something to discuss, arrange a meeting time through the phones. No one needs to be a hero. You find something, message the group for a meeting. Do not go alone. Any questions?"

All clear on our orders, we start to file out of the room. Theon approaches and in his deep timber asks, "Sophia, can I have a moment?"

I give one sharp nod and hang back from the group. Theon starts and then stops and runs his hands over his face. "Sophia—"

I cut him off not, interested in his apologies. "Look, I will play nice for our team here. We have a common enemy. Other than that, you have nothing to say that I want to hear."

I turn to leave, but Theon grabs my arm. "Please listen for a—"

I pull my arm away and step a foot closer. "If you ever touch me again, you will regret it. Our history began and ended with Leona."

I turn, and Ethen is directly behind me, a large intimidating wall of muscle.

I look at him and say, "I don't need you getting involved." I push past him, and in the blink of an eye I am up the stairs and out of the shop.

Not looking back, I leave the past where it belongs. In the past.

TWENTY-NINE

Caleb—Investigation with Theon Whitlock

As I emerge from the potion shop after our first team meeting, I hear my name called from behind. Theon Whitlock is striding toward me, my newest acquaintance in this strange new world I am living in. The best tracker in all of Idyll says gruffly, "Caleb, the trail grows cold while we sit here in Idyll." He looks toward the forest, and his wavy brown hair falls slightly in his face. Stubble on his cheeks looks to be about a week's worth. His honey-colored eyes raise to meet mine. "We need to get out to the scene as soon as possible. Have you navigated the runestones yet?"

As I shake my head, and he makes a small, disgruntled noise. "You're about to get a crash course." He slaps me on the back while giving me a wide smile, displaying straight white teeth. His golden eyes give off a bright light.

A handsome man emerges beneath the outward rugged appearance, and I am slightly taken aback.

He pauses and then appraises the leather jacket Noreen gave me. "I see Noreen hooked you up. Do you have any other weapons on you?"

I open the leather lapel of the jacket to reveal my 9mm. "I also have a backup Smith and Wesson on my ankle."

Theon nods. "Iron bullets. Those are good for distance battling Fae. How are you with blades?"

My eyes widen slightly. "I have some experience with hand-to-hand, primary combat knives."

Theon nods. "Typically, you don't want to get that close to any dark creature." He pulls a sword from his back sheath in one long pull. He holds the sword out toward me, hilt first. "These creatures' claws are the size of a male's hand. Their height is well over seven feet, and when they extend their wings, their wingspan is at least twice as wide. Those wings are mostly for show. They can only fly short distances. Their scales protect most of their body, which is why bullets don't work well. Some have success with arrows that are heavy enough to penetrate their hide. They are susceptible to fire, but fire is not always readily available."

He gestures toward the sword and takes it into his hands. "That is why the sword, axe, or mace is the preferred method of killing these creatures. The reach of these weapons allows for distance, so you can kill it before it decapitates you." He makes a wide slash in a downward motion of the sword in demonstration then palms the hilt and expertly slides it into a sheath down his back.

He reaches into his leathers and extracts two of the six blades that cross his sides, his leather uniform designed to hold the weaponry. He hands the daggers to me. "If you are in close combat with one, blades are the best defense. Aim for the soft spots, their throat or groin." I take the daggers and sheath them in the fancy duster that has slots for that very purpose.

I nod in acceptance of the gift as he meets my eyes. I get a return nod in approval. I suppose approval that I am not running for the hills.

Theon continues, "For now, if we come across a creature, let me take the lead." He gives me a hard look, no argument from me, and then Theon turns down the back side of Main Street and straight into the forest. "The closest runestone is this way."

I watch Theon's retreating back and pause for a moment. I look down at the ground and know I have already made my choice. I let out a breath, square my shoulders, and follow Theon. The town disappears behind us and the forest envelops the sky.

About a quarter mile into the woods, I see a small clearing ahead. A stone rises from the ground, like the one I saw at mile marker forty-three. Theon touches his ring to the stone, and a wide, translucent map pops up. I remember seeing something similar when Rhea showed me Tarrin on the mountain peak. It was there a moment and then gone. Now I have a chance to view all the markings on the map in detail.

I walk around the transparent map, trying to memorize the layout of Tarrin. "What do these markings mean?"

He turns slightly. "Each rune will take you to a different place on the map. Here at the bottom, this rune will simply release the ward so you can pass." I scan the map. All 120 runestones are arranged in a diamond-shaped pattern, a beautiful and sophisticated net surrounding the area.

I ask, "What is the distance between the runestones?"

"Seven miles apart."

I let out a low whistle. It is a lot of ground to cover. "Where was the attack?"

Theon points to the far west sector of the map, labeled Vista Sector. As I look closer, I see there are fine lines separating the sectors, six in total.

"So we are here." I indicate the red dot in the middle of the Central Sector. "We travel through the runestones to Vista Sector?" I motion to the other side of the map.

"Yes, press your ring to the location you want to go, and you will be transported."

I try to not let my nervousness show. "Transported?"

He smiles widely, as if he is immensely enjoying this conversation. "Yes, transported."

"Do you use these often?"

"I can travel very fast due to my heritage, many miles before I lose my momentum, but it can drain my energy. Depending on how far and the task at hand, I use them as necessary. I will go first, and you can follow."

He presses his ring to the out most western border runestone and then vanishes into thin air, his body fading until he disappears.

Now, standing alone in the forest, I look around.

I extend my hand and pull it back suddenly. I shake my hands slightly, look at the ground, and then let out a breath. I square my shoulders. I reach out a second time and press my ring to the same rune marking Theon did. I feel a strange tugging around my waist, and then it feels like every molecule in my body is coming apart and reforming. A strange sensation, although not painful as I would have expected.

My molecules reform in a vastly different environment than where I left. In Idyll, the terrain was relatively flat and slightly wooded. Here, the trees tower like giants overhead, and the rocky side of a mountain peak is visible through the foliage in the distance. I turn and look for Theon, who is leaning against a tree that is as wide as a car. He has a leather strap in hand and is sharpening one of his daggers. "How many times did it take you before you actually pressed your ring to the map?"

I shake my head. "Only twice."

He points to the right. "This way. About a mile to the shoreline is where the attack was."

He starts through the dense foliage, and I follow. We walk in silence for about twenty minutes. The terrain is rocky, and I wish I had more durable combat boots on. The lake becomes visible in the distance, and the space between trees widens. The coolness of the morning has worn off, and sweat trickles down my back. We arrive at the edge of the forest line, and there is a wide gravel road and then the rocky edge of a massive lake. I scan from left to right. The water spreads out into the distance, an unending sea of blue.

I turn my attention to Theon. He is crouched down on the gravel road. I walk up and kneel next to him. "These must be the tire tracks of the van." Theon nods. He pulls out his phone and snaps a picture. I ask, "Where does this road lead?"

Looking into the distance, Theon says grimly, "To Idyll."

Theon moves toward the edge of the forest floor. I turn back and peer down the road the other way. The landslide that must have killed Kyle is close. I make my way toward it, squinting up the side of the avalanche. It was a miracle that all four of the members of the team were not obliterated. I start to make my way up the side of the mountain, scrambling up the rubble, looking for the explosive Garrett mentioned.

About halfway into the avalanche of boulders, I see dried blood on one of the huge stones. I pause, kneel, and place my hand on the stone, saying a quick prayer for Kyle.

As I pause here, breathing heavy, sweat beads down my back. I scanned the area, looking up toward the tree line. There is a glint of sun reflecting off metal coming from above. I squint and shade my hands over my eyes. Not being able to make it out, I start my climb over boulders as tall as me. Finally finding the source of the light, I see they are pieces of metal, small remnants of the bomb. Grimly holding one of the larger pieces up to the light, I press my lips together in a tight line. This confirms a bomb was placed here intentionally.

I call down to Theon, "Oy!" I waved. One minute he is at the edge of the forest, and then he is standing next to me halfway up the mountain. I look at him in disbelief, "You really do move fast."

He smiles at me. "Not as fast as some." He pauses and looks at the remnants of the bomb in my hands. He grimaces. "Someone planted that bomb and knew a team would be here." Theon pulls out a bag and starts to slip the pieces of evidence in the pack. "We will bag it and take it to Timothy. He is our explosives expert."

He reaches down and picks up the remaining fragments of the bomb scattered amongst the rubble, adding it to the pack. Tucking it in his satchel, he looks around. "Down by the forest floor, I found tracks present leading from the lake into the forest. Most likely dark creatures are using this flat area to access water. If there are creatures close by, the faction members might be hunting them. The hunters become the hunted. If we track the creatures, hopefully we will find the faction members who are hunting and capturing them."

We start down the rocky side of the mountain. Theon says, "Try not to fire your gun. If there are faction members around, we want to identify and follow to the bigger fish. Remember, guns are not the most effective weapon. Best bet is the daggers."

We get to the edge of the forest when Theon pauses and places his hand on my chest to halt my progress. He says in a muffled voice, "You sound like a bull in a China shop stomping through those trees on the way here."

I look up. "How are you so silent?"

"I take it you've never hunted, deer or small game?" I shake my head. He looks down and then continues, surprisingly calm, with no irritation in his voice, saying, "In the fall, we have loads of dry leaves we can't avoid it. The easiest way to creep through the woods is to use wind as cover. Wait for the breeze to blow, and then you use that for your cover sound." He looks ahead. "Okay, let's begin. I will lead the way. I have an idea where the creatures are headed."

I place my feet where he places his, wait for a breeze, and mimic the steps. We continue in this process for about an hour. He holds up his hand in a fist, a universal signal to stay put. I look around, at attention, and hold my breath as I strain my ears for any sound outside what I have been hearing the last hour. I reach for my 9mm instinctually but then swiftly release it into its holster remembering Theon's advice. I draw the daggers instead.

I hear a one, two, three steps over to my left. I swing my eyes and see a deer pause and look directly at me. I don't hear anything except for my heart pounding in my chest. Suddenly, I see a flicker in my peripheral vision, and a dark creature attacks the deer in a single swipe of its claws.

I stand frozen.

The creature is as Theon described. I hear a loud screech as it swipes the death blow. The long beak and talons glint in the sunlight. Black feathers cover the face and neck, ending in its razor-sharp beak. The creature settles its black, leathery wings into place and starts to feast.

My eyes are focused solely on the scene in front of me, leaving me vulnerable.

I hear Theon yell a warning, and then I duck and roll, a maneuver learned so long ago that I am surprised it came from memory. A second creature soars over my head. I turn, and within a moment Theon is battling the creature. He sweeps his longsword from the creature's low belly up through the center. The creature lets out a loud screech and swipes Theon to the ground close to the deer. I see his head hit a fallen tree, and then he is still.

I can see the creature over Theon and know he is moments away from losing his life. I pick up a rock and throw it at the beast's back. It turns to me with a high-pitched roar. I palmed my two daggers Theon gave me. The creature starts to charge, as I walk forward, waiting for the perfect moment. Timing would be everything in this battle.

The first creature appears in front of me, intent on defending its lunch. I jump back and stare at the furious battle between the two animals.

In their loud, rolling death match, the two creatures start to shriek through this small clearing. I back up two more paces, see Theon sit up, and scramble away. He rises to his feet, walking back to me slowly so as not to disturb the creatures. Blood is dripping from his temple, but otherwise he looks like he will live to fight another day. We continue until we found brush tall enough for cover.

Theon motions me to get down, one finger held to his lips in silent warning. I kneel in the brush, eyes darting around looking for the next threat.

Suddenly, I hear male voices carrying on the wind. "NO! What are you idiotic, pea-brained imbeciles doing? The master is going to be pissed." I see two males walk into the clearing. The two creatures have torn each other apart, both heaving what must be their last breaths. Their leathery wings are ripped to shreds, huge gashes in their shiny black scales on their chests. I see black blood splattered across the clearing.

The first male kneels next to one of the creatures, its breath gurgling with blood in its lungs. The male lets loose an aggravated curse and swipes his dagger over the creature's neck, putting it out of its misery.

I see tattoos wrapping around his wrists and on the back of his hands. I squint and look at the second male, and sure enough he has the same tattoos. The second male heads to the last creature, kneels, and swipes his dagger over the creature's neck.

He looks up at his partner as he is kneeling on the ground, saying, "We have to find two more for the fight on Saturday."

The second male shakes his head. He says grimly, "If we don't, it will be our heads that are cut off."

The first male squints at the sun and shades his eyes. "It's midday. Hard to find any at this time. Let's head back to rest and try again at twilight." The second nods in agreement. They head off to the left, and I look at Theon as he gestures silently to follow them.

We follow, tracking them slowly through the forest. My ears on alert,

I follow Theon. My steps follow his specific route. After about ten minutes, the runestone comes into view. We pause at the edge of the clearing to see the faction members disappear.

I look at Theon. "Is there any way to track them from here?"

He smiles at me, showing those straight white teeth. "Not for most people. Lucky for you, I'm not most people."

He places only his hands, not his ring, over the stone, closes his eyes, and the map populates. The two males' shadowy figures emerge. I jump backward in alarm. Theon opens his eyes a crack.

"This is rewinding the past few minutes for our viewing. I don't stop time, but my powers show it to us again. My gifts come in handy often when I am tracking." He closes his eyes again in concentration, and then I can see the tattooed hand reach down and an touch Idyll rune mark with his ring, precisely where we started this morning.

Theon opens his eyes. "Let's go home."

We both placed our rings on Idyll's runestone mark, which instantaneously transports us back to Idyll. I look around the empty forest, wondering if I would ever get used to that form of transportation.

Theon kneels, looking at the path in the leaves. "These tracks are from us earlier." He points to a second set of tracks. "These are from our two friends." We head in the second direction, only a few minutes after our prey.

The trail ends at the edge of the forest line. The city sprawls out in front of us, and we scan the perimeter trying to find the faction members, all while remaining hidden. From our elevated vantage point, we can see the city winding through the grove. We spot them walking down a side street and then see them slip into an alley behind a huge house. They both duck down through an open basement door and then are gone from view.

I turn to Theon, "Now we have to wait until Saturday to see what they were talking about."

He says grimly, "I only know of one type of fighting that involves slaves." I look at him in confusion. Theon points to his wrist. "Did you see their slave bands?"

Perplexed, I ask, "The tattoos?"

"Those specific tattoos are only given when one becomes a slave. I have not seen slave bands in hundreds of years." At my questioning look, he continues, "Long ago, there were many slaves from the Great Wars between gates. The elite would hold fights for upper-class entertainment. Fights to the death."

I lean against a massive tree trunk and look at the building in a new light. It clearly was a private residence. The two slaves sneaked into the building through the back basement door. They did not want to be seen by any pedestrians or by their master. The first male said in the forest, "the master would not be happy," and I now realize how literal that statement was.

Theon looks at me seriously. "I owe you my life. I know what you did to save me in the forest, and I am in your debt." I give him a small smile, lift my shoulder in a no-big-deal sort of way. As I start to turn, Theon places his hand on my shoulder. "A life debt is no small thing." He repeats solemnly, as if taking a vow, "I pledge loyalty to you, until the day I can return favor."

This is a far cry from hotheads blowing off steam, mouthing off, as I was used to after an operation.

I turn to the forest, unused to such seriousness among relative strangers. "We can set up surveillance on that ridge. You can see the back entrance to the residence from there. If we set up cameras, we can be alerted to any movement."

Theon scratches his chin. "I will call Manus to set us up. I trust him to do this off the books."

THIRTY

Gael—First Lesson

thought getting through Selection Day would be the hardest part of getting into the Alliance.

I was wrong.

As I sit in the large lecture hall, I realize the true test is Qualifications Training. My eyes start to droop as the lecture continues, and I force them open. I sit up, reposition myself in the hard chair, and try to focus. The lecture is on how to use the rune stones, origins and best practices. This is day three, and I have never been as exhausted, physically or mentally, as I am right now.

Beyond the waking-hours struggle, my evenings have been spent in an endless, sleepless dream state on a constant loop. As soon as my eyes close, dreams plague me with broken images of an underground room, a winding staircase ending with a portrait of the Great Queen Morrigan. Every morning, I wake up more tired than when I first closed my eyes. Confusion and anxiety create a pounding headache that carries with me throughout the day.

Ari sits next to me. I can see her eyes drooping. I nudge her, and she sits up straight. Thankfully the instructor is wrapping up class, and we will soon be free to go. Professor Logan Trent hands out the next assignment at the front of the class, and it is passed back to me. He says, "Please complete this homework by Monday." I look down at the page and read the header, "Complete a two-page essay on the origin, purpose and benefits of runestones in a soldier's life." The assignment goes on, but I don't finish reading before I shove it into my backpack.

I turn to Ari. "Ready for lunch?" Our daily schedule has been grueling. Wakeup call at 5 a.m., outside by 5:30 for physical fitness for an hour and a half. 7:30 breakfast, followed by lecture for three and a half hours. Lunch is followed by two hours of small arms marksmanship training, then two hours of combat training. Homework every night leaves little room for anything other than falling into bed exhausted. Only to get up and go again the next morning. Despite the exhaustion, sleep eludes me.

I stifle a yawn as I give Ari a questioning look.

She says, "You bet. I asked Gavin to join us once he is done with his class." I nod, happy that Ari and Gavin seem to have hit it off. As we head to the great hall, my muscles groan in protest as we walk up the hill. Bruises scattered across my body are a testament to combat training. Despite my quick healing from my Fae heritage, the bruises persist.

I ask Ari, "How are you feeling."

She grimaces. "Sore. Tired. Hungry. You?"

I smile. "Same."

We enter the great hall, and my eyes light up. This is my favorite room in the castle. The Domain Sector is the only sector with a castle, a leftover offering to the Great Queen Morrigan. Originally created as Queen Morrigan's lands, the castle was a shining tribute to her. The dark wooden truss beams arch overhead, easing down the walls ending in elaborate wooden carvings.

Each of the carvings depict a different creature of Faerie. I spent the first day looking at each one in depth. Drylands, a wood nymph that could morph into the trees surrounding them. Griffon, half lion and half eagle, perched on a cliff. Crypids, a serpentine lake monster resembling a water horse with small fins and a long neck. Firebirds, their beautiful wings and plumes at the base of their tails, a legendary force of nature. At the head of the entry, mighty dragons flank the room, the one great creature that made it through the gates a thousand years ago.

Large arched windows break between the trusses letting the early afternoon light spill into the great hall. Great trestle tables span the considerable length of the hall on either side of the main stone walkway. The great hall is already halfway filled with warriors, recruits, and other administrative staff digging into their meals.

Smelling the delicious aroma of the buffet at the end of the walkway, I make a beeline for it. The highlight of my days during qualifications training is the food. Starting at the succulent meat-carving station followed by trays of fluffy rice and potatoes in a variety of preparations. Freshly baked rolls and vegetables in savory sauces. Fruits and light desserts wrap up our overflowing plates. The kitchen must feed a small army here in the Domain Sector, and they have it down to perfection. My appetite has doubled since I arrived.

We sit and dive in. I take a fresh bakery roll and slide the thinly sliced meat to make a sandwich. I dip in the savory au jus, take a bite, and let out a low groan. I say to Ari, "This food almost makes up for the combat training." Pure heaven. Ari smiles at me, and we eat in silence, devouring our plates.

The rear door opens, and a female walks into the great hall. I don't recognize her, but she is beautiful. Tall, at least six feet, curvaceous in all the right places with black hair in a heavy braid down her back. She is dressed in full warrior leathers with multiple weapons tucked into the folds of her uniform. As she spots me across the room, she starts to walk toward our table.

Heads start to swivel around the hall. I nervously look around, wondering where she is headed. Certainly, she would have no business with me. As she gets closer, I see her striking features more clearly, porcelain skin, bright electric-blue eyes. Her hair plaited down her back has red highlights, shining in the sunlight streaming through the windows. Deep full-red lips that have nothing to do with lipstick smile at me. Dumfounded, I stare up at her until I realize she spoke and I have no idea what she said.

"What?" I ask unceremoniously.

She says again, "You are Gael Monroe, right?"

I look at her in confusion. "Yes?"

"Can I sit down?" She pulls out the bench across from Ari and me.

As she sits, I look over at Ari, who shrugs.

The woman begins, "I am Sophia Beaumont. Ian Cadell asked me to help you with your training. I believe Ian and Bennett agreed that you need extra help developing your powers." I look at her and then reach deep down in my memory to recall Bennett mentioned this right before selection, which felt like a lifetime ago. He had arranged for someone to help me with my powers.

"Yes, Bennett mentioned it briefly."

The name Sophia Beaumont rings a bell. The Beaumont family is legendary in the Citadel Warrior Alliance. Bennett mentioned the name over the years, and I know there is a male Beaumont who is a section commander.

Sophia brightens up. "I would like to start as soon as possible, but we need to be discreet. I do not want our training to be common knowledge. It may appear as if I am giving you an added advantage during qualifications training, even though your testing has nothing to do with the magic we are unlocking."

My confusion must show on my face, because she looks away for a moment and then clarifies, "Magic is a tool we use, not to be mistaken for aptitude in the field. You can have all the magic in the world and still not be fit to be in the Warrior Alliance."

I am eager to see if she can help me. "I'm ready when you are."

Sophia's lips turn up into a small smile. "Let's meet after your last class today. We can meet twice a week for an hour of magic training." She scoots her chair out. "I am going to be the tactical knowledge and analysis instructor, classes two times a week, starting today. After this class, we can have our private sessions." My eyes grow. Not only private lessons but also a new instructor. Ari looks over at me with excitement.

Sophia gives me a grin, saying, "See you in class."

I nod, and then she is gone.

Ari says, "Do you know who that was? Sophia Beaumont is a legend."

I nervously tap my finger on the edge of the table. "Yeah, but what if she can't help me either?"

Ari grabs my hand. "You are going to do great." I give her a weak smile of gratitude, Ari is the best. I see her spot Gavin across the hall and wave to him. We head out of the great hall to our small arms marksmanship training class as a group.

As we walk, I say to Ari, "Good news, we have two days a week off from combat training." I show her and Gavin a wide smile. "Today is a good day."

The next class passes quickly. I am eager to see what tactical knowledge and analysis will be about. There are sixteen of us in this sector's course. We show up to the indoor training facility, a wide-open room on the east side of the castle that has been our combat training location for the past few days. Large windows let in natural light, and the floors are covered in practice mats.

Sophia is already there. She stands at the front of the room and starts her presentation precisely on time. The talking amongst classmates immediately quiets, and she commands the full attention of the room.

"Two times a week, here in the east training facility, we will practice our tactical knowledge and analysis. By the end of this course, you will be able to evaluate group formations, respond to opposition movement, and utilize terrain to your advantage. You will be able to distinguish the important decisions from the unimportant, recognize signals in situations, and give appropriate tactical responses to each situation presented."

Sophia waves, and a forest scene presents itself behind her. It looks like the glamor used in the arena during Selection Day. There is a small gasp from one of the other students, and we all observe the scene in front of us. Although glamor is a minor talent, the scene in front of us is extraordinary in its detail. There is a group of four soldiers on patrol in a wedge formation below a ridge. At the top of the ridge is a dark creature ready to pounce on the soldiers.

She asks the class, "Can anyone give me an example of a tactical response to this situation?"

Caden responds, "They can shoot it down from a distance, bow or gun, to get the beast on the same level."

Sophia nods then asks the class, "What else?"

Gavin says, "Launch a grenade at the creature."

I respond, "Two members can distract the creature, and the other two sneak up from behind and kill it."

Sophia's brow furrows, and she nods with approval.

She says, "Remember, the dark creatures' scales create an impenetrable layer that is hard to pierce with bullets or explosions to the chest or back. To disable the creature, you must attack its vulnerable areas. Attack its neck, groin, or head, which can be difficult at a distance."

She continues, "That is why the primary weapon of choice for warriors is the double-edged broadsword." She sweeps out the sword at her back, a beautifully, intricately embossed sword for demonstration. "Alternatively, many prefer a battle axe such as this double-bladed war axe." She pulls an equally elaborately embossed axe from her back holster to admire briefly. The blades glint in the light streaming through the wide windows. I detect a note of love in her gaze as she re-sheaths the weapons.

"You have given some great tactical responses. If you find yourself in this situation, you want to get the creature on the same level as you then distract it until you can get in close enough to eliminate the threat. What I want to imprint in your mind is that the best tactical solution would be to avoid the situation in the first place." I glance over at Ari, and Sophia continues pointedly to the group. "Rule number one, stay on high ground.

"The best strategy happens when a collective group discusses and weighs the pros and cons of any plan before heading into the field. All need to agree with the objective, route, and tactical approach. That is why we will be primarily working in groups in this class, same as you would in a real-life scenario."

Sophia breaks us into small groups to strategize the next scenario and then one more. This is by far the best class we have had. Real life scenarios, practical learning. Before I know it, the class is over, and we are done for the day.

Well, the rest of the class is done. I still have an hour with Sophia and magic training.

As the rest of the class leaves, I give Ari a little wave, and she heads to the dormitory. I look at Sophia and ask, "So where do you want to practice?"

She replies, "There is an old ruin over the first bridge, made entirely of stone. Probably the best place for a firewielder. Follow me."

We go out of the compound, through the main gates, across the water, and to an abandoned series of stone foundations. The rest of the buildings are long gone.

As I walk around the flat planes of the foundations, I ask, "What was this place?"

"When the gate first closed, the survivors erected a temple for our Great Queen Morrigan. This spot is very close to the Mystgate Sector and the gate itself."

I look around. I have never ventured this far into Tarrin. Sophia continues, "Years passed, and hope was lost that the queen would return. When the last ember of hope dwindled away, they moved the capital to where Idyll is today."

I nod and absorb some of the history of Idyll I never knew before.

Suddenly, the brush beyond the clearing stirs. I glance over at Sophia nervously, as I have a suspicion of who would have followed us. Sophia raises an eyebrow, and out leaps Orian, the name I have affectionately chosen for my new best furry friend. Orian circles excitedly and yelps at me for some love. I reach down and pet his gigantic head, rubbing his ears as his tail wags happily. I look up, and Sophia is staring, slack jawed, at the massive beast.

I say, "Don't worry. He's mine. Bennett said I could keep him if he stayed out of the way."

Sophia inches forward and peers down at Orian as she re-sheathes her broadsword down her back. I am filled with a little envy at the sword and holster. I wonder where I could get one of those.

Sophia says, "Is that a Molossus? I haven't seen one since I was little. Ian had one." She reaches out, palms up and fingers curled in, toward the massive dog. He sniffs and then licks her hand. I see a genuine smile light her eyes, and then she rubs his ears.

I say, "That's what Bennett said. I named him Orian." Hearing his name, Orian bounds around in excitement. He lets loose a low howl and then settles down on an old-foundation slab. I look at Sophia. "Is it OK if he hangs out while we practice?"

She looks at him and then at me. "Sure, not a problem. Molossus were known for being supremely loyal to their owners. You have a good watchdog there."

I smile and say, "He's rather attached, for sure."

Sophia moves to the center of the platform we are standing on and says, "Shall we begin?"

I ask, "How does this work?"

Sophia begins, "If you can raise your magic, I can assess it with my own." I look at her in confusion. All the practices with Bennett, and he never mentioned that was possible. "Typically, this would be done with someone who had the same magical qualities, but in your case, that seems to be in short supply."

Sophia continues, "Our power envelops us like a shield. I have a knack of seeing these shields. Once your power is raised, I can visualize it and in theory should be able to feel your aura with my magic and help guide you toward your objective. Back before the wall, when we lived in Faerie, Fae could thread their magic together into unstoppable forces."

I ask, "Once you assess my magic, what then?"

Sophia smiles. "The goal is to help you be able to control your magic almost effortlessly. Our magic ebbs and flows like water. It should be reached almost without thought. Think of it as part of the very fabric of our being, the magic bending to our will.

"That is the case normally, but I noticed at Selection Day that you had trouble maintaining it." She looked pointedly at me.

"I'm not sure why it is not effortless with me. I have to concentrate fully to manifest it, and holding it is even harder," I say. "What are your powers?"

Sophie replies, "I have the power to stop time." My eyes widen, and when she sees my surprise, she gives me a brief grin. "But only for brief moments, less than a few minutes at a time. It allows me to get out of tricky situations."

She winks, and I can't help but grin in response.

Sophia continues, "I also have a latent power of precognition. Some of our powers are more developed than others, a latent power is one that is early in developing."

I nod and say, "Like my air wielding power."

She goes on, "Our powers are not stagnant. Rather, they grow as we evolve, sometimes transforming as we mature, or developing new traits when a need arises."

Sophia motions with her hands, and we stand about five feet apart. Sophia says, "Please, let's begin." I let out a breath and pull the magic from deep within, and it rises to the surface. My eyes are closed, and I hear Sophia say, "I'm going to run my magic around your aura."

I feel a presence rubbing against the side of my magic. It feels like a cat rubbing against my leg.

Sophia asks, "You, OK?"

I let out a little chuckle. "Yup, good here. It feels weird."

She says, "I'm going to run over the rest of your aura. Hold tight."

I feel the warmth spread until it surrounds me. I open my eyes, desperate to see what it looks like, and am blinded by a brilliant bluish-white light coming from me. I see Sophia standing about five feet away. Her aura is a ruby red, and where we are connected is a rainbow of colors.

I breathe shallowly and ask, "Is this what normally happens?"

Sophia doesn't say anything, her features concentrating. Instead, she nods in affirmation. She runs her hands over a particular area a few times. "Place your hand right here on your aura." I see her outstretched hand and raise mine to meet hers.

Between us is an invisible barrier, our auras separating our hands. I concentrate and run my fingers over the area. I feel what caused her reaction. There is a slightly raised band that feels rough. I squint, hoping I can see anything that may tell me more about this strange sensation. Suddenly, my attention snaps, and the magic disappears along with it. Sophia lets go of her magic with a sigh.

I asked, "What was that?"

"It appears there's a binding of your magic."

My eyes widen, and I look at her in confusion. "Why would I be able to use my powers at all if that was the case?"

Sophia starts to pace back and forth. With her hands moving as she speaks, she says, "Imagine the magic you are currently using being forced through tiny gaps in the binding that have started to crack open."

"Okay, that makes sense, but that does not explain why or how it got there"

She shakes her head. "I seem to remember, back before the gate, when we lived in Faerie, of powers being bound until one came of age." She looks at me and apparently can tell my level of concern. "It was a natural protection, an innate part of our being that shielded us from our powers until we were ready. I have not heard of any bindings since we were exiled on Earth. Our powers here are muted, a fraction of the power they were in Faerie.

"I will speak with Ian and Bennett to see if they can give us some more background. There may be more information in the archives as well that we can look into."

I ask, "Do you think it has something to do with the fire ability?"

This was the first time I have seen Sophia look concerned. She mutters, "I am not sure. It is clear that you hold a lot more magic than you even realize."

THIRTY-ONE

Noreen—Side Hustle

t has been a grueling week. My client list is extensive, and I am in high demand on a normal basis. This week, I have filled my calendar with clients and turned no one away in hopes of meeting with as many as possible. We need to find a connection. If any of my clients have ties to the faction members, I will find them.

The witch covenant put into place three hundred years ago stipulated that any special requests from either the humans or Fae were to be negotiated for extra payment direct to the witch or warlock. This is how I have amassed great wealth in a relatively short amount of time, comparative to the long lives of the Fae.

I drive up the long, winding private driveway of my last client of the day. One very influential aspiring Collective member. I bury my revulsion deep to maintain the cool professionalism I am known for. I step out of my white Porsche Panamera, my high heels softly clicking on the cobblestone as I unwind from the vehicle. My tight black skirt hugged my curves, and my long blonde hair sweeps loosely down my back. I learned at a young age that images are almost as important as what you are selling.

I walk up the stairs to the grand entrance to the estate, hips swaying.

I am being watched closely. I knew Donovan Barlowe was watching the moment I arrived. He has always had a thing for me, and I have always used that to my advantage, despite my hatred for his mentor, Kingsley Abbott.

I ring the bell, and the door is opened by his butler, dressed in a finely tailored suit with impeccable manners. I will give Donovan this, he is good to his employees. The benefit to being a good boss is that it buys loyalty.

I give Grady a brilliant smile. "Good evening, Grady. Donovan should be expecting me." Grady graciously motions me into the grand foyer and leads me down around the corner to the parlor where we normally conduct our business. Donovan is already in the room, standing at a long-antique bar next to the massive leaded glass windows that overlook the sweeping driveway. I know he was at that window moments ago.

Donovan sweeps across the room and greets me like a long-lost friend, kissing me on each cheek. "Noreen, so nice to see you." I breathe deep and smell stale smoke and bourbon on his breath. I do not flinch; I am used to feeling disdain near him and push it down to the depths of my mind. I focus on the task at hand. He releases my arms.

I give him a wide smile and say, "Donovan, I was so glad to hear from you this week. I have brought your normal orders and a few added items you might be interested in seeing."

Donovan smiles. He is a handsome man in a classical way, dark slightly wavy hair, light-blue eyes, tall and slightly muscular, impeccably dressed as always. He is used to females falling over themselves to get to him and his connections. To his everlasting frustration, I have never been one of those females.

He says, "Sit, relax. Business can wait a minute." He walks over to the bar. "Can I get you anything?" He holds up a decanter.

"Sure, whatever you are having." I settle into the plush settee and cross my legs in a way that shows them off to my advantage. My skirt slits raise to mid-thigh, and I know he notices as he brings my bourbon over and settles in the seat across from me.

Donovan says, "I missed you at the ball. I had hoped you would save me a dance." His sharp eyes drill into me. I remember seeing him after dinner and promptly engaged with Council Member Wyatt until Donovan was far enough away for me to make my escape.

While inwardly I cringe, I smile and say with a wave, "Oh, you know how those events go, endless chatter. I barely even made it around the room."

He smiles and leans forward slightly, "Perhaps we can have a more intimate dinner, you and I?"

Without pause, I say, "I do not socialize with clients outside of our normal agreed-upon meetings. I believe we have had this discussion before."

His brow furrows, and I can see the moment of rage that passes over his features. In a split second, it is gone. If I had not been looking so closely, I may have missed it.

His brow releases, and his lips turn up into a practiced smile. He says in a light tone, "If you were not the best potion master in all of Idyll, I might be tempted to cancel service for that date." He winks at me in a casual flirtatious way that is so at odds with the rage I saw.

Donovan motions toward the case at my feet. "Shall we?"

I smile as I uncross my legs and wrap them next to the couch, saying, "We shall." I place the heavy case on the low table in front of me and swing it open. On top is Donovan's normal order. I point at the vials packed tight in the individual tubes within the case. "On top we have four exhaustion relief vials, four focus vials, four truth serum vials, four mild healing vials."

I pause and remove the first layer of the vials tucked in foam and place them gently on the table next to the case. "Next are some items you have ordered on occasion. Sleeping tonic, healing ointment, headache tonic. Are you still having the headaches?"

Donovan looks away and then asks as he takes a sip of his drink, "Do you remember every order I have made?"

I smile and say, "I would not be good at my job if I didn't, now would I?" A dark look comes over his face. He does not like to admit the weakness.

I pull out the second layer of vials and peek in the bottom where there is one final layer. I quickly put the second layer back in its place, covering up the bottom contents. I look up and give Donovan a wide smile, covering the quick slip he was not supposed to see.

As expected, he takes the bait. This is the lure, the carrot I've been dangling in front of each client in the hopes someone might bite.

He leans back in his chair, swirling the last of his bourbon in his short glass. He rises after taking the last sip, taking my empty glass with him. "Another?" I smile and nod.

As he returns to the sitting area, he hands me my glass. "You have quite the reputation of discretion regarding your clients."

"Of course, my top priority is providing excellent products with utmost discretion." I take a sip.

"That is why you would never reveal whose order is at the bottom of that case, right?"

I respond with a tight smile, "Yes, that is correct. I have one more stop after you tonight." I can feel the tonic he put into my glass sweep through my system. I know it lasts for two minutes and leaves the person under the effect slightly confused and not clearly remembering those two minutes. It is a very handy tonic you can slip in someone's drink and not have them even notice they were under its influence.

He asks, "Who is your next client?"

I quickly say, "I have the Citadel Warrior Alliance on my rotation today. I usually end there since it's close to my house." I look around as if I said something I should not have.

Donovan smiles in victory. "Is that right?" he purrs. I nod, my eyes darting to the exit, when he continues, "Is there anything in there that may interest me?" I look around frantically and stand up to leave. I walk toward the doorway, and Donovan is right behind me. He presses me against the wall and leans his head down to my ear. The stale smell of smoke and bourbon are overwhelming, and my push to get him off is real. He does not budge an inch.

He breathes in deep at the soft side of my neck and says, "What is in the bottom of the case?"

I let out a quick shaking breath, "Concealment tonic," I pause and force out, "Death Powder."

Donovan releases me abruptly, and says in triumph, "I will take the vials you have on my order tonight." He goes back to the seating area and pulls the bottom layer of vials and walks across the room to tuck them under the bar top. As he walks back across the room empty-handed, he says, planting a suggestion in my head, "You must have forgotten their order at your shop, and you will bring it to the citadel tomorrow."

He replaces the second layer of vials back to their original location and sits back down. He gestures for me to join him. I do, and as the two-minute mark rolls around, my eyes clear, and I smile at him as if the last two minutes did not even occur.

"So what will it be today?" I ask.

Donovan smiles comfortably. "I will take my normal order and some of the ointment. I'm running low." I graciously place the contents he requested on the table and close my case.

I say as I stand, "I will bill the house, as normal. Thank you for your business, Donovan."

He wraps his hands around mine and says with a small smile, "The pleasure is always mine."

I nod and walk out of the room, down the front steps, and over to my car on steady legs. I rev the engine and then am down the driveway and out the gates. Only then do I allow myself the satisfaction of letting my smile slip in the dark car interior.

Each potion I have ever made has my essence, my magic interwoven into the fabric of the ingredients. This gives me immunity to any of the effects. A fact that Donovan clearly has never learned. By necessity, it is a well-kept secret of witches.

I have been providing his potions for well over one hundred years. This is the first time he has ever tried to alter my mind. The bitter taste of truth serum is still on my lips, with no effect.

I tap my fingernail on the steering wheel and ponder the last moments. As Donavan had me pressed against the wall, I attached a tracking device to his coat lapel.

Now, I have a suspect and a means to track him to the rest of the faction members.

I pull into my driveway and flip open the burner phone Brenen gave us. I start to ask for a meeting, but then I close the phone, tapping my fingers nervously on the smooth edge of the plastic. I want more than my suspicions when I bring it to the task force.

I hear a beep on the monitoring device and open it. I see the green dot on the screen sitting in Donovan's house start to move. He is leaving. I allow a small smile to play on my lips. Greedily, I look at the screen, oh how I love the hunt.

I pull out of my driveway and start to head in the direction of the green dot. A few turns here and there, and I start to get into an older part of Idyll. This section of town is an area that has been all but abandoned. I pull up to an old textile manufacturing building and see the green dot flashing right in the middle of the building.

I look around. No cars or activity are visible. If I did not have this device, I would think it truly abandoned. I pull off to the side of the road and park out of the way behind a large tree and some bushes. I slip off my heels and slide my tennis shoes on. I always keep a pair in the back seat of my car. Once out of the vehicle, I toss a concealment potion over the vehicle, and it vanishes from view. I take the last little bit of the potion and swallow it. I look at my watch and set a timer for half an hour. After that, the potion wears off.

As I creep toward the abandoned building, the faded sign hangs on by a thread. It reads, "Olivers Textiles and Designs." I walk around back, invisible to any casual observers. I see a shimmer in the ground, illuminated by a full moon. Suddenly, four males emerge from out of thin air.

I cover my mouth and duck behind the edge of the building. Peeking around the corner, I see I have no need to worry. The four males are inebriated. Engrossed in their drunken singing, they do not notice anything amiss. My concealment potion seems to be working. They walk past the stretch of wall I am hiding against without seeing me. As they pass, a whiff of Faerie wine reaches me, and I see one of the males carrying a bottle. Very expensive stuff, only the upper elite can afford the liquor infused with a magic elixir specifically made for the Fae.

Then they are gone, stumbling drunkenly and singing into the forest. I let out a long sigh and turn toward where they emerged from thin air. I see the shimmer of light and reach toward the shimmer, and the glamor fades away as if I pulled a string, unraveling the spell.

The empty, desolate parking lot and abandoned buildings are ripped away. A kaleidoscope of colors, noises, and smells enthrall my senses, and I stare wide-eyed in front of me.

To the left, hundreds of Fae are milling around, drink and food vendors spread amongst the large lot. Loud laughter and mingling pierce the quiet night. The entrance to the building is huge, and within it I can see crowds of people surrounding an open pit. Temporary stadium seating is set up in a circular arena. I hear loud screeching and the roar of a crowd coming from the stands. I edge forward, making sure not to touch a single person, my concealment potion still working. I maneuver to a spot under the stands where I can peer through the slats to get a good view.

My mouth drops as I see the ring spread out before me. A lone Fae and a dark creature are battling. Slave bands on the male's wrists and hands clearly visible. I place my hand over my mouth to prevent a gasp. Slave bands have been illegal for three hundred years.

Slaves were a byproduct of captured Fae during the Great Wars between the gates. Between 500-800 AD, there was feuding over resources. Some gates had superior natural resources than others, which allowed some gates to flourish, and others to struggle. There was mass exodus from less desirable locations, and the desirable locations put up defenses to keep the foreigners at bay. This resulted in three hundred years of conflict. Any captured prisoners of war eventually were sold into slavery.

Enslaved Fae had no rights, and their very lives were bound to their master's will.

It was such an archaic practice, outlawed so long ago, that it is hard to imagine anyone practicing it in these modern times. I have not personally seen a person with the marks in hundreds of years.

I look out at the arena, and blood is trickling down the brow of the male, and he has a sword in his grip. The creature slashes down, and I see crimson blood seeping through his leathers, leaking onto the dirt beneath his feet. The male's knees hit the ground as he grasps his side, blood trickling between his fingers.

There is a collective intake of breath, and I see the crowd turn toward a viewing platform across the arena. There is a thumbs-down from the box. Then I see the creature slash its large claws one more time. The male's head is swiftly removed from his body, and it rolls to the side.

A massive explosion of noise, some in excitement, others in dismay. Money is transferred between betting parties, and the crowd starts to dissipate.

I turn and vomit at the edge of the stadium until the contents of my stomach are purged. Tears flow freely down my face as I look up through red-rimmed eyes, wiping my chin with my sleeve.

The cleaning crew emerges from the edges of the arena, dragging away the body. The head is scooped up into a bag, preparing the arena for the next contestants. In the distance, I see another slave sitting on the sidelines, face blanching as his predecessor is dragged out of the arena. Knowing he may be next.

The crew engulfs the dark creature with a fine powder, and immediately the creature calms. They shackle the neck and lead it toward giant metal plates that have opened in the middle of the arena.

As they lead the beast into the depths of the earth, my mind cannot grasp the brutality I witnessed.

THIRTY-TWO

Gael—Secret Passages

I follow Sophia back from the ruins, my head in a tailspin. I push a few strands of my hair out of my face as we walk back toward Mystfort. My magic is bound, causing all the issues I had during selections, all the issues I have had since my magic came alive.

The constant battle of pushing my powers to manifest, all because of the binding.

Not really paying attention to where we are going, I look up in slight surprise to see Sophia leading us off to the side of the main entrance. Beyond our view, the main gate is stationed, protecting the island fortress from intruders. Tightly secured with normal heavy foot traffic.

Instead of heading toward the main road, we've veered off to one side of the beach, out of view. The waves lap quietly, and the bustle from the main road is a low din. I look at Sophia in confusion.

She smiles and says, "You think there's only one way in and out of the castle?" I look at her quizzically. "There's a second main entrance, the warrior's entrance, which bypasses the normal security at the gate. The guards monitor more closely the individuals who are entering the grounds vs exiting. I would like to avoid their scrutiny since our sessions should be kept mostly between us."

She gives me a pointed look.

"This side entrance can only be accessed by a warrior's runestones, given upon graduation." She pulls out her necklace, and her runestone ring shines in the sunlight. With a wave of her hand, the once-empty beach is now full of small two-seater boats.

We climb into one, and I ask, "No one can see us when we approach in the boats?"

She flicks her wrist, and the boat starts to make its way toward the island at a quick pace. "No, this section of water and the boats are heavily warded."

I look up at the massive island. The sheer cliffs and drop-offs look impenetrable, even with a secret boat.

When it seems we will ride straight into the side of the cliff, a narrow entrance presents itself, and we slip inside, gliding between two sheer stone walls. We continue for a few moments, and the pitch-black of the passage is eerie. I can hear the waves lapping against the boat, water dripping down the walls, into the passage, creating an echo in the darkness.

Finally, a light appears ahead, and we emerge from the narrow passage into a small cavern, illuminated by lights placed in the cavernous ceiling. We arrive at a small beach that must be directly under the fortress. We tie the boat off on one of the pillars and climb out onto the soft sand. I look around in amazement. The beauty of the cavern is inspiring.

I turn, and Sophia is already walking toward a set of stone steps rising into the side of the cave. They end at the blank expanse of a stone wall. I turn and look at Sophia in confusion. She applies her ring to the runes. A rounded doorway illuminates brightly in the low light. Golden runes mark the edges and create a beautiful doorway.

She looks at me, saying, "If you ever try and open this door with someone else's ring, you will be trapped in the runestone." She shakes her head slightly as if remembering some prior incident then grasps the door handle, and we find ourselves in a dark dungeon.

The dampness in the air, dirt floors, and walls covered in chains send a shiver up my spine. I look around, thankful none of the chains are currently in use. I follow Sophia to a winding staircase that requires a third runestone check at the top. Through that door, finally we are in the main castle. I rub my hands over my arms trying to keep the dampness away.

Sophia says, "This is where I leave you. I have a few things to work on in the west wing. If you head straight down this corridor, you will reach the main entry leading to the great hall."

After I say thank you, Sophia is gone the next moment.

I glance down the hallway where Sophia disappeared then turn toward the corridor and main entrance. I open the door a crack and peer around the empty hall. Seeing the coast is clear, I slip through the doorway silently, closing the heavy door behind me.

I start to make my way to the great hall when I feel a prickling sensation on my neck. I swing around. The hallway is empty.

I turn and start again toward the great hall when I hear a voice. "Tsk, tsk, tsk, sneaking around in places you shouldn't be? That's my job."

Surprised, I snap my head around, and Logan is leaning against the far wall right where I exited the west wing. He has arms crossed over his chest and one foot across the other, looking like he does not have a care in the world.

I have not spoken to Logan since our selection test. At that time, he was so aloof it seemed as if he wanted nothing to do with us. Since we have arrived at Mystfort, he has kept his distance from everyone in the program, by choice. Ari and I made a point to steer clear.

I square my shoulders and look him in the eye. "What's it to you?" I turn back to the hallway, gripping my bag, determined to ignore him. Suddenly, shadows form directly in front of me, I screech to a halt, not wanting to run right through them. Eww.

Logan appears from the shadows, my surprise turning to anger, and I cock my head to the side, saying, "Neat trick. Want me to show you mine?"

I hold my palm up, and flames flicker and dance despite the sunshine streaming through the windows.

Logan holds up his hands in surrender, a slight grin on his face. "Hey, look, sorry if that came off as an asshole move. You don't have to tell me why you're sneaking around the castle. I haven't seen anyone else bold enough yet."

I look at him quizzically. "So you've wandered around the entire castle?"

He blows out a breath. "I've seen most of it, but the door you came out of is protected from entry. Even my shadows haven't been able to make it through." He runs his fingers through his dark hair, as if discouraged that there is someplace, somewhere, he can't get into. "I've been waiting around this door in between classes, off and on, for the last few days to see if someone ever came out. Thinking maybe I could slip through. Then you emerged, surprised me, and I lost my opportunity." He loops his fingers through his jean pockets and looks a little sheepish.

I let out a sigh and roll my eyes. "Don't worry about it, but I would appreciate it if you kept my wandering to yourself. I'm not supposed to tell anyone why I was in there, and I could get in trouble."

I see Logan's eyes light up like it was Christmas. "So you are *allowed* to be back there?"

I start to make my way toward the great hall. Logan follows, asking, "What would a recruit do to gain access to the west wing?" I shrug, ignoring the question. He continues, "Hey, give me a small idea of what's over there, and I'll leave you alone."

I turn. "Let's make a deal. You don't tell anyone I was coming out of the west wing, and I won't tell anyone you wander all over the castle like it's your own private playground."

He smiles at me and holds out his hand. "Deal." I place my slender hand in his, feeling the roughness of skin from hours of training.

I say, "Deal."

Logan continues, leaning close, "That doesn't mean I can't figure out what you're doing back there on my own. You know, I can follow you anywhere else."

"If you want to follow me now, I am starving. You don't even have to go all spooky. I'm headed to the super-secret great hall."

Logan gives me a wide grin. "Now that you mention it, I am famished."

Once in the great hall, we grab our trays and head toward an unoccupied table. I look around, and sure enough I see Ari coming through the back entrance to the hall. I wave over at her. She does a double-take at my dinner partner and beelines over to us. She sits, eyeballing me as she says to our new guest, a little unsure, "Hi, Logan."

Ari gives me a long look, clearly looking at me for an explanation, eyes darting between me and the newcomer. She raises an eyebrow, and I sigh. While Logan eats, I tell Ari, "Logan and I met earlier. We ran into each other and were both headed for the great hall."

She looks at me in alarm, saying, "Didn't you come from Soph—"

Logan looks up quickly, on high alert.

I shush Ari and say in a low voice, "Logan found me after my *meeting* coming out of the command side of the castle. We made a deal to not rat each other out to anyone else."

Ari says, "You might as well tell him the whole story. It's not like he won't follow your every move from now on and find out on his own." I look over at Logan, and he shrugs as he takes another bite.

Ari continues, "He's probably been through this entire castle." I can feel my cheeks warming. It had crossed my mind that the master of shadows would not be swayed away from the truth.

Logan says, "Hey, if you could go anywhere, and no one would realize, do you think you would stay quietly in your room when there are all kinds of activities going on in this castle?" He looks around, as if someone else is listening. "You won't believe what I've heard." He pauses as he takes another bite. "Of course, I have been all through the rooms, all except that one blasted door." His brow furrows in frustration.

Logan and I share a smile. I finally relented and say, "Fine. I've private lessons set up with Sophia Beaumont. She is helping me with my magic." At Logan's questioning look, I add, "I've had trouble controlling my magic. Sophia is good with auras and is helping me to control it."

Then I turn to Ari, who is bouncing up and down in excitement, telling her, "The first lesson went OK. She tested my aura and found something." I look down at my tray of untouched food, not really wanting to share.

Ari nudges me, saying, "Whatever it is, we will fix it."

I smile and say, "Sophia found the remnants of a binding. She said it most likely was a natural protection that shielded me from my powers until I was ready."

There is silence at the table, me avoiding two stares. Finally, I say, "She's going to check with her mentor, Ian. They are going to see how they can remove it safely."

Ari turns and gives me a hug. "It's going to be fine." A little louder, she continues the conversation, "Guess that means you are going to be super powerful. Hope you don't get a big ego."

She winks at Logan and bats her eyes. I laugh, and the tension breaks.

Logan, seeing the mood change, pushes back his chair and says, "Let's get some fresh air."

We head out to the front lawn where some outside tables are set up, facing the setting sun that has disappeared from the horizon. There is a slight chill in the air, and I pull my thin sweater closer to me. I say, "It's peaceful out here." Ari nods, and we sit in silence for a moment.

Suddenly, the doors to our left fly open. Loud laughter breaks the peaceful moment. A small group of warriors walk out the front entrance, clearly heading out for a drink at the local pub.

A few cups in, they are already enjoying the night. We are on the edge of the main entrance to the castle, tucked close to the stones, hidden from their view. One last comrade runs up to the group as they are leaving and taps one of the burly warriors on the shoulder.

He says, "Hey, wanted to let you know since you were close to Conner, he left today, did not say why."

The tall burly warrior frowns and says, "Thanks, I will reach out."

The other male leaves the group, the vibe turning somber. A second member says, "That's the fifth warrior gone in the last six months. What is going on?"

The burly warrior to his right says, "I'm not sure, but I will track down Conner and get some answers."

The soldiers depart, leaving Ari, Logan, and I in the quiet darkness of early evening, contemplating what we overheard.

THIRTY-THREE

Caleb—Fight Club

t has been three days of surveillance, and I am itching for some action. Theon and I manned our makeshift stakeout blind in shifts the past three days. The blind was set up by Theon on the Idyll Forest tree line, right before it drops into the city. My shift is about over. I stretch out my long legs, my combat boots scraping over the dry leaves beneath my feet.

I upgraded my footwear on the first trip back to my room. My clothes have become a standard black utility pants, a black t-shirt, and shit kickers, as Theon affectionately refers to them. My shoulder holster with the 9mm is strapped to my back, and the duster Noreen gave me is currently slung over one of the chairs set up in the blind.

The blind seamlessly blends into the foliage. Not being a hunter, I am impressed with the coverage, the blind almost invisible when walking through the woods. Thankfully, the autumn weather is agreeable, no rain or freezing temperatures. Theon assured me that this area was not heavily patrolled by soldiers due to its proximity to Idyll. A quiet nook in the woods, too far away from the runestones to be noticed, and on the outskirts of the city.

The surveillance setup that Manus brought is meticulous. If there is any movement at the front or back entrance of the residence, we are alerted. The suspects, slaves, left two times to run errands for the homeowner in town, and once we tracked them back into the forest searching for the two creatures they needed for Saturday's event.

When we followed them into the forest, we observed them use some sort of powder that they were able to launch at the creatures, causing them to calm and become disoriented. The slaves were able to place the dark creatures in restraints and lead them back to Idyll where they met with comrades at the edge of the forest. They placed them in crates and drove off.

Theon, with his exceptional speed, was able to follow them to an abandoned part of town.

Somehow, he lost them at that point. Visible one minute and then gone the next. Theon's theory is that there must be heavy glamor surrounding the area. He advised that there is probably security watching the perimeter looking for breaches. Our plan is to use the timing of the slave's entrance tonight to slip in undetected.

I tracked down the homeowner of the residence, the master, Faben Scheffer. The file I compiled is sitting on the folding desk set up in the corner. As masters go, the information I had dug up on him is disturbing. Elite, entitled, and loyal to a fault to his mentor Kingsley Abbott, who is also a gem of corruption. He has ties to the underground slave trade he ran for the past three hundred years. Once slavery was outlawed, he nurtured the underground trade in secret. It seems the elders of this society have turned a blind eye to Abbott's extracurricular activities, out of sight, out of mind.

I yawn, and my jaw cracks. I stand up and stretch my arms overhead. I glance down and see the sword Theon presented to me three days ago as a gesture of gratitude for the incident in the woods. I am coming to realize that honor and loyalty run deep with the Fae. At least with Theon. He has been practicing swordsmanship with me for a few hours every day, giving me a crash course on how to survive this new world I have been thrust into.

Going back into the forest has a new meaning to me after our first encounter with the dark creatures.

I pick up the sword and feel the weight in my hand. It is beautiful.

The blade is finely honed and balanced. It has a comfortable black leather grip, ornately carved guard ending in a beautifully engraved pommel with the insignia I am coming to recognize easily as Tarrin.

I roll my shoulders, which are aching from the continued practice. I snort to myself. Sore muscles will be the least of my problems if I am not prepared the next time we face a dark creature. I rotate my shoulders and stretch my back as I walk out of the blind, starting my ten-minute warm-up routine.

Starting in an even stance, I sweep the beautiful blade diagonally and then cut with straight arms at the height of my shoulders. I continue with the diagonal cuts, starting low and sweeping high in a wide circle. Then I switch the movement from upward to downward strokes. I add in the foot work, forward and backward, forward and backward. I pause, slightly winded, and feel a presence to the right of me. I swivel, sword raised, and Theon comes out of the forest with hands outstretched.

I lower my sword to the ground and give him a grin, saying, "Getting some practice in when I can."

As I sheath the sword into the back holster that Theon gave me, I smile with satisfaction. The weight of the sword hilt at the base of my neck is starting to feel natural. It feels good to see the improvement in the past days. I can already feel more strength and mobility during my swordplay practice than when I started.

Hopefully, it will be enough for our next trip into the forest.

I reach forward and shake his hand. Theon asks, "No activity yet?" I shake my head. I take a long drink from my canteen as sweat trickles down my brow. This is Saturday, the supposed day of the event. It's late afternoon.

I say, "It should be any time now."

He sits on a fallen tree stump, pulls out his leather strap, and starts to sharpen his daggers again. I am coming to find this is a habit of his. Those must be the sharpest blades in all of Tarrin.

From his stoop, Theon says, "Soon you will be ready for sword practice with a partner. I have some wooden practice swords from when I was a Q trainer." He pauses as he gazes out into the forest. "We can work on that next week."

We fall back into a comfortable silence.

I ask the question that I have been mulling about in my mind the last few days. "So what is the story with Sophia and you?"

Theon's hand stills the blade on the leather, then he resumes sharpening, not looking up. "Sophia's sister Leona and I shared our lives for many years." He sweeps his blade a few more times. "Leona and I had a mate bond, a rare bond for a Fae. If one is lucky enough to find a mate bond, it is lifelong." He scrunches up his brow as if he is reaching deep into his memories. "I think humans call it soulmates."

He sighs, "The human word for it does not fully explain that the mate bond is a tangible thing. A Fae pair that is mated have a direct link that allows thoughts and emotions to connect them." He looks down at his blade. "If they are both alive."

Not wanting to press the issue, I shift my weight and start to turn, thinking that is all he's going to share. Then Theon surprises me by placing his dagger on his thigh and facing me. I sheath the sword and lean on a tree.

He says, "The day of the outpost attack, Leona and Sophia were out on patrol when the compound was attacked. We lost so many lives in that first burst of power. I was relieved Leona was not there when the initial attack occurred. The creatures swarmed the compound, destroying a structural wall. This caused the collapse of part of the compound.

"Leona, Sophia and the rest of the survivors cleared the area. Then we heard the cries of the trapped soldiers inside. She told me to go, that she would cover outside. Right as I turned, a creature approached. She waved me off, told me go, said she had it covered."

He hangs his head, his hair obscuring his features. "That was the last thing she ever told me. I returned to the crumbling building and helped out two trapped soldiers. I was the sector commander. It was my responsibility to make sure the rest of the soldiers got to safety."

He swallows. "I felt when she was struck and raced outside. It was too late." He raises his head and is visibly shaken from the memories. He resumes the sharpening of his blades. "Sophia has not forgiven me. I will never forgive myself."

There is a moment of quiet. Sometimes there are no words to make the hurt lessen.

The surveillance equipment beeps, and I feel a vibration on my phone. I turn and walk into the blind to view the screens. I pick up the binoculars and see the two slaves leaving the house, headed toward the abandoned part of town we tracked them to a few days ago.

I say, "Let's move."

I sling the duster over my shoulders. Then we are on the hunt. In moments, we are winding through the streets of Idyll. The upscale part of town becomes steadily shabby as we progress into the dilapidated, abandoned section of the old manufacturing district. We see the suspects approach the same location Theon lost them two days ago. They pause, look around, and then walk through the invisible barrier and vanish from view.

We paused for a moment, backs against a brick building. Theon motions, and we make our way around to the edge of the building, out of sight of where the suspects disappeared. Theon motions me to stay put as he assesses the glamor. He places his hands midair and seems to be feeling the invisible barrier. He steps through and disappears. He pops his head through and gestures all clear. I take a deep breath and walk through the invisible barricade. It feels like walking through cold mist, and then suddenly the air is warm again.

I look around and am engulfed in the bright lights and vibrant smells of a festival. Hundreds of Fae are milling around enjoying the food, drink, and company. The energy is high, and in the distance I can see an arena with portable stands set up, packed with people viewing the event.

I lock eyes with Theon and nod. We start our path toward the arena, weaving through the crowd trying not to attract any attention. Theon pays for two pints of what most of the Fae are drinking, a dark-red color that I assume is wine of some type. The event must have been going on for a while. Many of the Fae are stumblingly intoxicated.

We turn from the vendor, and I bump into a big burley male a foot taller and wider than me, reddish-gold beard down his chest. He turns and holds me by the shoulders. His face splits into a wide grin, and he clasps me on my shoulder. I give him a smile and drink from the pint glass Theon handed me. The warm nectar runs down my throat, and I realize too late that this is no normal human drink. Theon smiles and nods to the burley male and takes me by the elbow, and we continue our path. He mutters out of the corner of his mouth, "Don't drink the wine."

I already feel the warmth spread from my head down to my toes from one sip.

By the time we make it to the edge of the arena, I'm seeing double, and the early evening sky is swirling. Theon leans me against the metal pillars holding up the stands. I look up and see the feet of hundreds of people over my head, cheers vibrating the ground. Theon crouches down and shakes me. My eyes drift toward him, and I can feel a smile forming.

"I haven't been this drunk since..." I focus behind Theon's broad shoulders.

Materializing out of thin air is Noreen. I feel my jaw drop, and I stare at the woman who has been running through my mind these past days. She is exactly as I remember, a black dress wrapped around her luscious curves, blonde hair falling down her back. I frown slightly, confused at my daydream, as I reach her feet clad in tennis shoes. That did not match up with my memory.

"What happened to him?" the apparition of my daydream asks.

Theon mutters, "Faerie Wine." I see Noreen's disgruntled face turn toward me, and she rolls her eyes. She sweeps back the front panel of her dress, which reveals a creamy expanse of thigh. My heart pounds in my chest as she plucks a vial from her dress and approaches. She kneels. I get an ample view of her cleavage as she leans close. She pours a little bit of the powder in her palm and raises it to her lips. She gently blows the powder in my face, and it disappears into thin air. I breathe in the sweet-smelling power and feel the cobwebs start to fade away.

Noreen rises. I reach for her arm to stop her. She halts and spins slightly on her heels with a raised brow. I say the only thing that I can think of, "You are so beautiful." She smiles and stands. She offers her hand to help me up. I stumble slightly but regain my footing. I am close enough to inhale her sweet citrus scent as I stare into her vibrant blue eyes.

We stay like that for a moment too long.

Theon asks, "What are you doing here, Noreen?"

She shakes her head and takes a step back. "I followed one of my clients here." She pulls a tracking screen from her hip. "I placed a tracking device on him once he tried to drug me to steal concealment tonic and death powder."

I look at her slack-jawed. "What do you mean, did he get it, are you *okayyy*?" I'm slurring, blinking my eyes and trying to clear the rest of the fog from my mind.

She shakes her head and gives me a hard look. "Don't be absurd. I would never be so careless." She flips her hair away from her face. "It was simply a lure to find any of my clients that may be up to no good." She throws a slight grin. "And don't worry about my safety. I know what I am doing. How did you guys end up here?"

Theon fills her in with our tracking through the forest, the creatures we found, ending with following the slaves to this hidden arena. She nods grimly. "They have resumed the death fighting practice, only this time they have pitted creatures against slaves."

Theon lets out a huff. "That has been outlawed for eight hundred years."

"Apparently, they have taken back the sport, underground hidden right here in the middle of Idyll."

Theon looks at her. "What would make them so bold? If they were caught, it would be a death sentence."

She nods grimly and points to the arena. "I think we are about to find out." I turn and see a platform extended from the edge of the arena nearly to the middle. A well-dressed male approaches from the side entrance.

He arrives at the podium, and the crowd starts to quiet. Tall and lengthy in frame, black hair slicked back from a widow peak, he creates an intangible aura of confidence that echoes through the stands.

"A gracious thank you to all of our members and partners for making these events possible." He gestures toward the edge of the arena that holds a group of finely dressed males. "More importantly, a thank you to all our participants today enjoying the festivities. All proceeds and bets collected tonight will go to our cause."

He makes a wide sweeping gesture toward the rest of the arena with a grin. "Without you, this movement would not be possible. We have worked tirelessly to unify and prepare our followers across all gates. We are Shadow Liberation. Working in shadows, sworn to liberate Faerie." He adds with a dramatic flair, "Soon, we will be in the shadows no more! We will unify Faerie and Earth once again!"

This is met with loud cheering from the crowd. He waits until the crowd's roar starts to diminish. "I know you are all anxious to hear from our fearless leader. Without further ado, please join me in welcoming our grandmaster."

He makes a wide sweeping gesture to the sidelines where, presumably, the grandmaster will emerge to make his entrance. The crowd erupts into applause so loud that the arena floor vibrates. As one unit, the crowd edges forward, everyone straining to get a better look at the grandmaster.

I set my mouth in a grim line as I see Kingsley Abbott move to the center of the arena. He waves in acknowledgment, motions for silence with one sweeping flourish of his hand. "To those of you who do not know me, I am Kingsley Abbott. I was one of the original Fae who settled on Earth, the place we now call home, almost one thousand years ago. We have lived amongst the humans on Earth, far longer than any of us originals ever thought we would. Far longer than is healthy. Far longer than is necessary.

"As we have idled away here in this realm, protecting the very gates that keep us from our homeland, we have seen our powers start to diminish. Our blood becoming so diluted some descendants haven't a drop of Fae blood left in them."

He scowls. "Our heritage is being decimated before our very eyes." Jeers erupt across the stands. "Who knows how long it will be before our very heritage is wiped away as if it never was?"

Abbott motions with his arms for quiet. "The Fae who lived in Faerie can tell you how powerful we were, the power we have now, only a fraction of what we were born to possess." He pauses there to a rise of applause. "Faerie is the source of our power, and like a river cut from its source, only a trickle of our power remains." More jeers from the crowd.

"If you were not born before the gates closed, I will enlighten you.

Not all Fae were 'lucky' enough to remain in Earth's sanctuary. The public believes only a handful of Fae were left in Faerie. A perfectly crafted tale to keep the peace. I am here to tell you they feed you lies!"

There's a loud burst of applause.

"On that day a thousand years ago, our families were ripped apart. Fae who disagreed with the queen tried to destroy the barrier then. Sadly, our supporters were quickly silenced."

"Now, the stories that have been passed down to the generations are known as truth." He pauses there and smiles slightly. "Amusing, if you tell a lie often enough, you can start to believe it."

Kingsley continues, "Our decisions at that time were based on fear. A great fear of the darkness. The dark creatures haunt our children's bedtime stories. We teach our children to fear and our children's children to fear.

"If only we could forget what we have been programmed to fear, if we could remember how powerful a race we truly are, our homeland can be ours again." This is met with loud cheers and wild energy that floods through the arena.

I look over at Noreen and Theon with wide eyes and then focus again on the performance.

He starts again with a somber face. "As you partake in the festivities tonight, I want you to remember why we are here. I want you to remember our ancestors abandoned on the other side of the gate. I want you to remember the families that were torn apart. Families that can be reunited once more."

He looks down. "We have been forced to pretend that the gate must be held at all costs. We have been programmed by other members of the council who say it was a blessing that the queen created the barriers and closed access to Faerie."

Loud jeers and boos are heard across the stadium.

"I say to them, your fear overwhelms your sense of family, your fear overwhelms your loyalty to your people. Your fear threatens our heritage.

"There are generations who have never stepped foot on our homeland. This is an egregious, intentional violation of our rights." This is met with more loud cheers.

He smiles. "I say to you tonight, you need not fear the darkness. The reign of the queen is over. We get to choose our destinies. Tonight, join us, and we will reclaim our heritage!"

He sweeps his hands out and is surrounded by dark creatures that seem to follow his hands. They fly in a semi circle and lightly touch down. There is a collective breath heard across the stadium, and all the creatures, starting from the one farthest away to the one closest, kneel and bow to him. He raises his hands, and the creatures sweep up into the air and start flapping those magnificent wings to circle the arena.

He says in a booming voice, "We can end the centuries of fear. We can finally be reunited with Faerie."

There is a large explosion of applause, and the fans are enthusiastically chanting, "Abbott, Abbott, Abbott."

I turn toward Noreen and Theon in shock. "Have you ever heard of this Shadow Liberation?"

I get two shaking heads, and Theon says, "We need to get out of here undetected. Let's try to sneak out with the crowd that's leaving through the front entrance."

Noreen says, "I am the most noticeable person, Theon. I wouldn't have known it was you unless you knocked on my door, and no one knows Caleb." She pulls a vial from her pouch and drinks it. There is a shimmering of light, and she is transformed into a brown-haired, brown-eyed female who smiles at me. "Lead the way."

My mouth drops open, and I stare at her retreating back. I see her pause, turn, and motion, saying, "Let's move."

Shaking my head slightly, I follow, and we start to wind our way through the crowds. Careful not to be noticed. Careful to travel not too fast or too slow. As we steadily made progress, we see security stationed at the front entrance.

I motion to Theon and point to the back entrance we used earlier in the evening. He gives me a nod, and we head to the back entrance. I can see the shimmering edge of glamor on the other side of a tent. We slip through and sigh in relief. We make it past the edge of the glamor and to the other side.

Unfortunately, my relief is was short lived.

As I look forward, a group of males come out of the shadows, converging into the center of the street. I pause in my progress, assessing, evaluating the odds.

One of the males steps forward and smiles menacingly, saying, "We've been waiting for you."

THIRTY-FOUR

Sophia—Mystfort

The first few days at the Domain Sector fly by in a whirlwind of tasks that most new teachers handle weeks or months before the term starts. Thankfully, my first class was days into the semester, giving me a brief reprieve to wrap my head around teaching again. It has been many years since my last course, I have to wipe the cobwebs off my long-forgotten lesson plans and reach deep into my memory.

I look out the window of my appointed office and tap my finger on the pencil I have clutched in my hand. Otherwise still, I stare out the iron plated window at the enchanting view below. Emerald Lake, the massive lake at the heart of Tarrin, spreads out in front of me. Rising out of the massive cove is an island formed of jagged mountain peaks and sheer cliffs densely populated with mature maple and birch trees. Perched on the very top of the mountainous island is Mystfort, the original castle built for Queen Morrigan, built when there was hope she would return.

On cool mornings when the sun peeks over the horizon and hits the water, mist surrounds the island, creating the illusion of the castle floating in the air.

Mystfort is where we are holding classes for this sector. Most of the central interior of the castle is maintained as it was built for historical purposes. The beautifully created tapestries line the walls, the great hall the same as it was a thousand years ago, a true step back in time.

The east and west wings, however, were updated and converted for more practical use. In the eastern wing, the original training facilities were updated, new locker rooms were added, plumbing and lighting installed. The west wing of the castle was converted to function as the command center, modern updates to provide the central command operations and dormitories. On average, there are roughly one hundred residents, warriors, teachers, and staff fluctuating slightly during each season, residing in Mystfort. Across the draw bridge, on the mainland, is a small village of residents that make Mystvillage their home year around.

This afternoon was my first class, after which I had my first training session with Gael. I contemplate what we discovered today. The magical binding of her powers was unexpected. Only hearing secondhand stories about the old country, I have never personally seen a binding of powers. I sent a message to Ian after the session was over and am still waiting to hear back from him.

As I look across my desk, I am thankful my class schedule is only two days a week, giving me ample time to track down objects of power that may be in use by the faction members. Papers are spread out and stacked in the corners of the large desk I was given. A side chair is pulled up and I have a set of discarded incident reports that I have already reviewed. Two hours in, I realize I may have underestimated Manus's thoroughness. At this rate, it will be Christmas before I can go through them all.

Manus hand delivered the files the first day I arrived at Mystfort, nervous that a digital trail would lead the faction members directly to us. While I appreciate his diligence, rifling through the mounds of paper on my desk is not how I envisioned my search going.

Despite the means, the information is crucial. Manus has sorted the files by location and then by incident. That man is a genius at what he does, and I am grateful to have him as an ally. Each incident report is meticulously written, showing any activity that demonstrated unusual powers in the past year. Incidents including Fae who used any extreme power, change in habits, or any unusual creature activity.

The sun is now low in the sky, and my eyes are strained as I close them and press my thumb to the bridge of my nose. I stretch my back and pull my arms over my head, hearing the groaning, creaking joints as they pop into place. A movement out the window catches my eye, and I focus on the outdoor bailey training grounds. Archers and outdoor shooting practice is in progress toward the outer walls. Directly below, I see the stables and an outdoor training circle with a crowd starting to form around it. I can make out two males, circling, swords drawn, and I hear the dull thuds of impact, followed by cheers from the crowd.

As they turn, I see one male face turns toward his opponent, giving me a clear glimpse of his face. It is Ian. As he turns, sun glints on his short blond hair, and the second male comes into view, Ethen. I sit back from my desk slightly. It has been three days since I have seen him. Shortly after my arrival at the Domain Sector, Ethen was pulled away with urgent sector business, and I was wrapped up in setting up the new course. We agreed to meet the day after my first class to make the trek to Dragon Keep, a four-hour trip one way.

We are set to leave at first light. Most people are not allowed in the Dragon Lands due to the accord that was placed into effect long ago. A small part of me is excited to be one of the few beings to interact with the dragons. I have never been near a dragon in my lifetime. I am sure the number of people who have is limited. Dragons have a long history of distrust and are very territorial.

I tap my pencil on my desk and contemplate our trip. We will be meeting with Draco, the flight leader, and Conor MacKinley, his bonded rider. I was surprised to learn that there were still bonded riders alive and living with the dragons. I only know of them from old legends. Conor's son Duncan MacKinley was Ethen's childhood friend who was killed. Conor raised Ethen as his own from an early age after he was orphaned.

Ethen provided the CliffNotes version before we split ways a few days ago. Ethen and Duncan grew up together in the Sierra Nevada gate. Draco took command of the Tarrin dragonflight around one hundred years ago, moving his family with him to Tarrin. Ethen stayed behind. He had received a promotion to commander in the Sierra Nevadas.

I push the paper away, needing to stretch my legs and breathe some fresh air. I re-sheathed my weapons and run a quick glamor over my desk to ensure the documents are not visible if someone is to pop into my office while I was out. If someone stumbles into the protection, the glamor is designed to revert to a forcefield deterrent and alert me. In theory, it should give me enough time to return to my office to find the intruder. At the very least, it should deter any snooping. A quick flick of the key and my office door is locked, and I am headed down the twisting interior stone circular staircase that leads from the east turret I was occupying.

Heading out the rear entrance of the castle toward the training areas, I pause and breathe deep the crisp autumn air. As I approach the fighting ring, Ethen and Ian are wrapping up their practice. Both winded, shirts discarded, and sweat trickling down their backs. Muscles rippling and testosterone almost visibly vibrating the air. It is no surprise they have acquired quite a crowd, many of them females, lining the ring to watch.

I lean against the railing, hoping to catch Ian before he disappears. I need to update him on the Gael situation. The males finish in a flourish almost too quick to track. The crowd erupts in cheers and catcalls as Ian and Ethen bow low to each other and then to the crowd. Clearly enjoying the spectacle, Ian and Ethen give the crowd one last grin and wave as they head to a discarded pile of clothes and weapons at the edge of the ring.

Ian slaps Ethen on the back as he picks up his discarded shirt and wipes his brow. Spotting me in the crowd, Ian walks toward me as I motion to him. Ethen follows, and we meet at the fencing as the crowd dissipates, many disappointed eyes tracking the shirts being put back on and weapons holstered.

I say, "You guys sure know how to put on a show." Ethen winks at me as he holsters his daggers at his ribs. I ignore the flirtation and turn toward Ian, asking, "Did you get my message?" He nods and looks around. The crowd has all but disappeared, and the three of us are alone at the edge of the fighting ring.

Ian asks, "What happened?"

I say, "I tested her magic. I have never seen it before, but I believe her magic is bound." I describe the sensation of Gael's binding, how it appears as if her magic is being pushed through the cracks of the barrier.

Ian looks at me in silent contemplation. "What you are describing certainly seems like a magical binding, although I have not seen one since we lived in Faerie."

Ethen and I look at Ian intently, hoping for more information than that.

He sets his jaw and looks away. "Natural bindings commonly occurred in Faerie, manifesting when one's natural abilities proved a threat to the body they inhabited. Each house's relics helped control these bindings, by absorbing the power of each descendant, and redistributing these powers amongst the living. It is no surprise that the fire relic has made its appearance at the same time a young firewielder is coming of age. We need to find the relic. It will help regulate Gael's power."

I give Ian a nod and ask, "The real question is why a Tomte was looking for it and how to get it back from him."

"I don't know why the Tomte was looking for it, but I think it's safe to say he won't be able to hold on to it for long. The ancient relics are not bound to any one person. They are pure magic and have a spirit of their own. My guess, the relic is drawn to the young firewielder, and no matter how hard our Tomte tries to keep it in its grasp, the relic cannot be controlled."

Leaning against the corral fence, I push a few wayward wisps of hair out of my eyes as Ian says, "While I am here, I want to meet with a few others before heading back to Central Sector."

He looks at Ethen and gives him a grin and another brotherly clap on the back. "It was good to get in a session with you while I was here." Another male goodbye, and Ian heads back to the keep.

At the top of the rear stairs to the castle, a large male dressed in full warrior leathers motions down to Ethen, his ebony skin beautiful in the early evening light, muscles rippling. He has close-cropped black hair and dark eyes that currently look intense.

Ethen turns to me. "I am wrapping up the issues I was dealing with the last few days. That is Kane, my second in command, with an update."

He looks down at me with a wicked smile. "I'm looking forward to tomorrow, an entire day of uninterrupted time with you." I swallow and feel a slight flush on my cheeks.

Ethen gives me a wink, and as he walks away, says over his shoulder, "See you at sunrise, Red. Pack a saddlebag. We may have to stay overnight."

THIRTY-FIVE

Gael—Library and Blueprints

stare down a long hallway, torches lighting the path on either side. Intercepting each torch, elaborate stained glass windows are visible but blocked by stone. It appears as if a beautiful room is completely sealed with stone on all sides.

I am walking down the long hallway. At the end, a golden throne appears. It is raised on a slight platform, beautifully and elaborately engraved. Despite the beauty of the room itself, my gaze is transfixed by the long table in the center, a beautifully engraved box illuminating the room with a blue-white light.

Beyond the throne, a winding staircase is visible. Up, up, up I follow it, until it emerges into a grand castle. I turn and see the painting of Great Queen Morrigan, a crown upon her head, a sword in her right hand, and the fire box on the left. A high-pitched scream vibrates the walls as if it is shrieking to get out.

My eyes pop open, and I sit straight up in bed. Sweat trickles down my brow, and my long blonde hair is damp with perspiration. My breathing labored, my eyes darting around the empty room. Deep breaths in and out, I close my eyes while trying to regulate my heartbeat. I was in my room, in the dormitory section of the domain. A wet nose nudges my hand, and I glance down at Orian. The giant Molossus's eyes are fixed on me. He lets out a low whimper, as if concerned.

I rub his ears and say softly, "It was a bad dream." He jumps up on the bed and circles once, twice, and snuggles into the folds of the blankets.

These dreams since I arrived at Mystfort have plagued me every night. Always the same dream, the closed-off throne room, the beautiful box, the hidden staircase ending with that dreaded painting. I have scoured the eastern training side of the castle, from each turret to each basement, and have not found that painting. Strangely, I have not seen any paintings of Great Queen Morrigan, despite searching every nook and cranny. If this castle was built for her, why are there no paintings?

I throw off the covers and walk barefoot to the window that overlooks Emerald Lake, inky black in the darkness. The only light visible is the heavy full moon that hangs low in the sky, casting a shimmering glow over the water. I throw open the window and breathe in the fresh air. I glance at the clock, an hour before my alarm is set to go off. I splash cold water on my face and decide to start the day early. This is my first full day off since arriving at Mystfort, and I am excited to explore the village with Ari.

We have only been to the village once before but found a lovely coffee shop with outdoor seating we loved. We are scheduled to meet for coffee later this morning. Since I am up so early, I have time for a quick run before the day starts. I put on leggings, a loose top, and my jogging shoes. I plait my hair down my back and then am out of the room with Orian on my heels.

Down the rear steps, we circle around toward the edge of the outer stone walls. I wave to others I see each morning, now becoming routine. Orian and I follow the wall to the main gate, over the bridge, veering off into the mainland forest. Finding a rhythm, we approach the ruins Sophia Beaumont took me to for testing. I pause there and take in the landscape. I lace my fingers behind my head and breathe in the early morning air, enjoying the solitude as I pace back and forth. My mind reels from the dream, wondering where that painting is.

As I stand on the ruins of the temple, I can see the island in the distance. The western side of the castle is visible at this angle, glinting in the early morning sun. I look down at Orian and say, "I think we need to look on the western side of the castle." All I got was Orian's whine in return. He does not look impressed with my search for the underground throne room. I rub his ears and say, "Come on, boy." We head back to the way we came, the castle not too far. I am lost in thought, running through all the possibilities of where the underground throne room could be and why they would have closed it off.

On autopilot, I return to my room, shower, and change quickly, inspired by my idea on the temple grounds. I head directly to the library to see if I can find any information on the original building of the castle. This is my first exploration of the massive library. I've only glanced by as I hurried to and from classes this week.

As I walk through the beautiful carved entrance that spans two floors, I realize what I have been missing. Three stories high, the library is at the back of the original main keep of the castle, beyond the great hall. It fills the entire northern turret facing the lake. On one side of the massive circular room, wide-arched windows currently let in brilliant morning sunlight. These windows are intersected by elaborately carved stone archways. Massive pillars holding the weight. The rest of the space is floor-to-ceiling books, rolling ladders on each floor. I see six comfortable small sitting areas on the ground floor, each one with its own fireplace. Squishy chairs and lamps invite one to cozy up with a good book. Right in the center is the librarian's desk, the host to such a beautiful place of knowledge.

I approach the desk and look around. This early on a Saturday, I am not surprised it is empty. Not knowing where to start, I see a map stationed to the right, broken out by genre. Some of these are familiar, and some are surprising. Familiar genres that are expected, adventure, fantasy, mystery, biography, nonfiction, fiction. Followed by some that must be unique to a training facility. Magical realism, potions, runestones, history of the gates, Faerie, creatures, human lore, and lastly Morrigan, who has her own section. I ponder the long list of subjects and decide if there are building plans that they would be in the nonfiction section. Second floor, section B.

I head up the beautiful, curved staircase to the second floor, my fingers trailing on the polished wood, admiring the beautiful space.

Walking down the short hall, I stop to read the labels until I get to BN, Nonfiction. I pull a book from the shelf and read its call number on the spine, BN,4427, B855,1829 and then look at the cover. This one is a self-help book on weapon care. I sigh as I return the book to the shelf and look at the rows and rows of books, slightly discouraged. There must be thousands of books in this section alone. I need a catalogue to find anything I am looking for. I start to randomly look at a few books here and there, not finding anything close to what I am looking for.

Suddenly, over my shoulder, I feel a tap, and I swung around in alarm. I had not heard anyone approach. I blink my eyes, trying to clear them, but I stare through the transparent form of a burly male, the staircase behind him visible. Jumping back slightly in alarm, I realized he must be a ghost.

A large male, wide through the shoulders, is slightly rounded in the middle, dressed in old-fashioned attire that went out of fashion hundreds of years ago. He grunts, "You did not check in at the desk. Permission must be granted."

I swallow nervously. "Sorry, I did not see anyone at the desk."

I see his eyes bulge in offense. "So that means you get to wander into someone else's dwelling?" I hear the outrage in his voice.

I blink a few more times. He continues, "Umm, I will let it pass since this is your first time in the library. I never forget a face. What are you looking for?"

I stare for a moment and then remind myself how to speak. I mumble, "Castle blueprints."

"That's right. You're close. Over here..." He starts to float toward the end of a row, to a large cabinet that has pull-out drawers. As he starts to rifle through them, I creep up behind him, peering at his face. He turns, slowly. "What ya looking at?"

I back up, shake my head, and squeak out, "Sorry, you're a ghost!"

He glowers at me. "Well, of course I am a ghost." He slams the drawer closed and shoves the blueprints into my hands.

I stutter a little, the coldness of his hands shocking when they brushed mine. "But..."

I don't get anything else out before he cuts me off, saying, almost to himself, "I have been here since this library was built," He places his hands on his hips, looks around the room in appreciation. "I was the one who designed this library. It was my life's dream." A shadow crosses over his face. "Unfortunately, I died before I saw it complete. I was directing the workers on the construction when out of nowhere one of those blasted stones fell on me. Well, I was not going to let death come between me and this library."

He looks over as if realizing I am still here. He gives me a sly smile, as if telling me a secret, "To tell you the truth, I love being a ghost." I blink my eyes again, not knowing how to respond to any part of this conversation.

Suddenly, he starts to grow and morph into a huge apparition, many times his normal height. My heart starts to beat fast, blood rushing toward my head. The temperature drops and the lights flicker.

"Welcome to my treasure without fee, where queens and villains shared wisdom is key. Before you flee, return what you take, or suffering will be. Mahahahaah." The ghost starts to dissipate into mist, saying in farewell, "Enjoy your companyyyyyy." A soft chuckle follows as the mist drifts off down the stairs.

The temperature returns to normal. The lights brighten the space once again. A final shiver racks my body. Perplexed, I look down at the drawings in my hands and then back up to the now empty hall.

Shaking off the chill in the warm room, I head to a long table that is in the middle of the aisle and spread out the blueprints. There are several layers, the original stone foundation, the updated east wing with the training facilities, and then the updated west wing that houses the command section for operations. I scan the pages hoping to see any evidence of an abandoned part of the castle.

As I am rifling through the pages, I feel a prickly sensation on the back of my neck. I turn abruptly, swinging around, looking in the shadows. It feels as if someone is looking over my shoulder. Maybe I am a little jumpy after the encounter with the librarian. I shrug off the sensation and resume my search.

In the west wing, I see the dungeons Sophia and I walked through and the passage that exits into the hidden cave. Directly above is the administration section of the command center. On the north-western section, I see a section of the map that was blocked off as if it was an empty space. It appears to have a tunnel that disappears off the drawings. I tap my finger on that empty space on the map, thinking if there is an abandoned throne room. It might have originally been connected to the temple built on the mainland.

I sigh and stretch my arms over my head. The west wing of the castle is off limits to non-warriors. Lucky for me, I made friends with the one person who may be able to sneak in undetected. I feel that familiar compulsion to find the mysterious throne room that keeps haunting my dreams.

Quickly looking around to see if anyone is around, I roll up the prints and tuck them into my satchel.

"Tsk, tsk, tsk. Not again, Gael."

I swing around and see Logan leaning against one of the marble pillars, one leg crossed over the other, in his relaxed pose. My heart rate jumps for a moment and then evens out. He continues, "Caught redhanded, twice in two days. Not a good track record." He pushes off the pillar. "I better stick with you. You make a very bad criminal."

I glare at him over the top of the blueprints. "I'm borrowing them and will return them when I am done."

I start forward, and suddenly Logan is in front of me. I look up into his eyes, crinkled in amusement, noticing how handsome he really is up close. I say in aggravation, "Are you following me?"

He replies, "Only because you end up in the strangest places, doing the strangest things."

I roll my eyes and sidestep him. I make it to the start of the stairs when I hear him say nonchalantly, "All documents in the library are tagged. If you leave with anything, it will alert the librarian, who is particularly possessive of all things in his domain. He can be downright scary if you steal something from the library. There are wards in place that are not for the weak of heart."

I remember the ghost's parting rhyme, wondering what kind of "suffering" he meant.

I sigh and trudge back to Logan, who took the vacated seat at the desk. I plop down in the chair across from him. I say, "I've been having these recurring dreams about a throne room. I think it's somewhere in the castle, and I feel compelled to find it."

Logan crosses his arms across his chest and ponders what I said. "Did you find a location on the blueprints?"

I roll out the pages. "Look, here on the northwestern edge of the island. It appears there is an empty space, not used at all, simply marked out. There's a tunnel that leads away from the room. I think they connected the temple on the mainland to the throne room."

Logan peers at the blueprints, saying, "So you want my help in finding this abandoned room?"

"Well, I thought I might mention it to you, since you wanted to sneak in anyway... Come on, maybe if you found an entrance, we can figure out a way to sneak in together."

Logan grins and says, "You are right. I wanted to scout that section of the castle anyway."

He turns serious and looks at me intently. I feel like there is a "but" coming.

He says, "Your magical affinity is fire. The last descendant of the Great Queen died three hundred years ago, also a firewielder. Tell me, are you a lost descendant of Morrigan?"

I look at him and confess, "I'm not sure."

THIRTY-SIX

Caleb—Fight or Flight...I Would Always Choose Fight.

"Can I shoot them?" I mutter out of the corner of my mouth to Theon.

He gives me a nod. "Absolutely."

I draw my weapon, and there is an explosion of movement. I see Noreen move in a flourish, throwing down a vial that has shadows erupt and wind up the sides of the buildings, creeping and crawling up the walls and over the street, engulfing us in a shadowy tunnel.

I see her draw two blades from under her dress and attack the faction member on the far right. Theon takes the two in the middle, and the two faction members on the left start to move toward me.

I aim, pull the trigger in quick succession, and two rounds hit their targets. Recognized for my shooting skills in the academy, my marksmanship badge pays off. One Fae is quick enough to dodge slightly and gets a slug in his shoulder. I get the other squarely in the chest. I hope these bullets are as effective as Noreen told me. I am not sure I will be getting a second chance.

They fall back behind a vehicle parked on the street. The one hit in the shoulder drags his comrade to safety. I look over at Theon and Noreen. Theon has his sword drawn and is making quick work of the two members in the center of the street. Noreen is weaving and ducking all blows in such a fluid blur of motion that I can barely see her. The next moment, I see Noreen removing a blade from her opponent's side. Crimson starts to show on his white button-down shirt. He holds his side and raises his bloody fingers, looking confused. He drops to his knees and collapses on the ground. Noreen gives him a smirk and whirls toward the rest of the fighting.

She shouts, "Behind you!"

Out of the corner of my eye, I see motion coming toward me.

The Fae I got in the shoulder is charging toward me, and he looks furious. Maybe his comrade didn't make it. I raise my gun, but not in time. In seconds, he has spanned the distance between us, and my gun clatters to the ground as he knocks into my arm. I stumble back and pull my daggers and sweep one at him, too late. His speed and strength are apparent. One moment, I see him reach for his blades, and then they are ready. He gives me a sinister grin.

We start to dance.

His shoulder wound is the major weakness I want to exploit. Without this advantage, his speed and dexterity will outweigh my hand-to-hand skills. He sweeps forward, and I block, deflecting his blade away at the last moment, and I move in to strike. I dig my fingers into his shoulder wound as deep as I can. I swipe low over his thigh with the dagger in my other hand. He screams in pure rage. I fall back, and Noreen comes into view. She tosses me a dagger as she passes. "Use this one."

Then she is off to help Theon. I grip the handle of Noreen's blade as the rage-filled Fae comes at me, slightly limping, murder in his eyes. I know if he gets a hold of me, it will surely be a slow death.

I fall back in my stance, and we circle for a moment. Blood is dripping down his thigh and his shoulder where I shot him, but he looks rather determined. I wait for the attack that is imminent. He lunges, and I parry to the side, sweeping the blade deep into his belly, a lucky shot taken when he is slightly off balance. My blade is deep, and I push upward with all my strength, hoping to hit a vital organ. His shocked eyes look down at the wound. He collapses to his knees and then falls to his side. I look down at the blade Noreen gave me. It must have some special properties.

There is a break in the commotion, and we are all breathing heavily, ready for the next threat as we survey our surroundings. The faction member Theon was battling is on the ground, various wounds visible, unmoving.

I ask, "Where is the fifth one?"

From the shadows, the last member of their team is behind Norreen, one arm holding her around the waist, the second pressing a blade to her throat. The metal flashes in the streetlamp as he says, "You three will come with me." He gives a sinister grin. "If you want this one to live."

A calmness overtakes me. I set down the blades and show him my hands. "We will do what you want. Don't hurt her."

I see the Fae's eyes dart to Theon, who has taken a step forward.

He yells, "Stay back!" Theon inches forward one more time. The Fae, agitated, starts to scream again.

Time slows down. I lock eyes with Noreen and give her a small nod. She nods back and then suddenly kneels, leaving an open target. In that split second, I draw my backup gun at my waist and shoot instinctually. The Fae freezes and looks down at his chest in confusion before looking back up at me. He stumbles backward, falling to the ground.

Noreen runs toward us. I grip her by her arms and ask, "Are you OK?" She nods into my chest, and I look over her head at Theon, who gives me an affirmative nod.

Noreen turns to look at the wreckage, saying, "Five bodies will be hard to cover up here on the street."

I look at her. "They won't heal?" She shakes her head slowly. "The blades I use are dipped in a death potion, and the bullets iron." She looks around. Her shadows are slowly dissipating, removing our cover. "We need to get these bodies out of sight."

I nod in agreement and look down the empty street. "Whatever we decide to do, we should do it quick. If they were assigned to watch this street, someone knows there was a breach and will come looking for them."

Noreen's gaze is fixed on the manhole cut into the center of the street. "I have an idea." She motions to the grate in front of her. "I think they are using the old tunnels underground to move the creatures from location to location. I saw them ushering the creatures underground after the last fight. This entrance probably connects."

Theon looks toward where we were and looks back at the grate in the ground, appraising the distance. "Let's get them underground. We are sitting ducks here." He pries open the grate and dumps in the five bodies as if he were throwing sacks of flour. "You stay here out of sight for a minute. I want a quick look in the tunnel. It will most likely be heavily surveilled after they find this lot." He motions to the bodies heaped under the manhole.

"I want to see where it connects. These tunnels were abandoned ages ago. I don't know if anyone remembers the layout." He pauses and then says wickedly, "We may be lucky enough to feed the monsters tonight." With a grin, he disappears. Noreen and I sweep behind the corner, out of sight of the street, the grate still in view.

I look at Noreen and see a scrape across her temple, red blood dried on her face. I raise my hand to her temple and ask, "Are you okay?"

She is holding her side as if it is bruised, and she has a swollen line from a blade across her upper arm. As if she feels my stare, she glances down at the wound and lifts her skirt again. This time, I can clearly see the small arsenal of vials and blades strapped to her thighs. She chooses a vial and drinks long and deep, the color a bright yellow. I remember in her shop this one was for healing. As she swallows the last drop, I see the scrape above her eye starts to mend and then disappear. She stands up straighter, letting go of her side. Her ribs must be healed as well.

I stare at the blade wound on her arm, which does not disappear. She grimaces and says, "I'm not surprised that their blades were also dipped in poison. Their poison is not as good as mine." She smiles at me a little. "I personally trained most of the witches in this town. With every potion master I ever taught, I have taken precautions."

She looks directly at me. "It's bad business to be taken out by your own potions, which was the first lesson I was given by my mentor." She smiles ruefully. "So I created an antidote of sorts that will make me immune to any poison I have ever brewed or taught to any of my proteges. I take it regularly, and it makes me immune to most potions and poisons." She glances down at her arm. "This wound will heal more slowly than others, but it won't kill me."

She looks me up and down. "Are you injured?"

I shake my head. "No, I think I was lucky. I shot two and stabbed the last one with your blade." I hand the dagger back to Noreen, hilt first. "Thank you."

She gently lays her hand over the blade and guides it back to its holster in my jacket. "You need this more than me. I have a supply back home anyways."

Theon scrambles out of the manhole. As he emerges, a loud screeching howl permeates the quiet night air. He pushes the manhole cover back, and the sound silences. He comes toward us at a run with a large grin splitting his face. "Let's move. I fed our enemies to the very beasts that have hunted us. There will be nothing left but bones in the next hour." He seems quite pleased with his idea of poetic justice.

Noreen nods. "We can take my car. It's parked over on the east side of the building."

We make haste across the empty streets, my eyes darting to all the side streets waiting for any further trouble. Thankfully, all is quiet, and we get to Noreen's vehicle without issue. We slip into the dark interior as silently as possible, the lights extinguished. Noreen starts the engine and doesn't flip on the lights until we are well away from the event.

As we pull away silently, I contemplate the revelations that have unfolded in the past few days. I glance over at my two new comrades, and each has the same grim expression. Our foe is greater than we envisioned, more organized, and has more followers than we ever imagined.

A rebellion is underfoot. The faction members not only have a cause to believe in but a charismatic leader who has managed to keep his uprising a secret for years, inspiring loyalty and righteousness among his people. Values that will be hard to sway for any of the members. Not to mention the promise of increased powers and abilities. Greed and vengeance interwoven in the rebellion's cause will be difficult to dismantle without massive bloodshed.

I need to set my sights on finding the informant who was helping Kyle before he died. There is at least one person who is against the movement. One person tried on multiple occasions to help stop the organization. This person is the key to understanding and dismantling Shadow Liberation.

I look over at Theon in the front seat. "We need to set a meeting with the group." He gives me one silent nod I can barely detect in the darkness.

Just because our enemy is now known to us does not make our task easier.

THIRTY-SEVEN

Sophia—Dragons and Bonds

When I step foot out of Mystfort's back entrance, the sun is cresting over the horizon. True to its name, mist has started to form around the island fortress. Sounds from the stables seem to echo in the weak morning light. Dressed in my customary fighting leathers, hair in a simple braid down my back, I walk comfortably, my soft soled boots silent. I have added a beautifully engraved double-edge axe to my weapons ensemble today, complementing my normal sword, daggers, and one 9mm. I throw my packed saddlebag over my shoulder and make my way to the stables. The trek today will be about fifteen miles through grueling mountainous terrain taking roughly four hours on horseback.

Dragonkeep is in the middle of thirty square untouched miles of land set aside per the original Dragon Accord with Tarrin's dragon-flight. There are no runestones for transportation. There are no modern roads, no evidence of Fae, human, or witch existence. This is because no one is allowed on the Dragon Lands except for the small, trusted group granted access by Draco himself. To enter this hostile territory without permission is a death sentence.

As I approach the stables, I hear a shuffling movement. I round the corner and spot Ethen saddling a beautiful stallion, well-built, strong legs, taller than most horses. With handsome, bright eyes, a long, graceful neck, and pointed ears, he looks like he belongs on the show floor. As I approach the duo, the black stallion turns toward me in a curious way. I pull a carrot snagged from the kitchen and offer it to him. Immediately, we became friends.

I rub my fingers down his ebony mane as he chews on the carrots. Ethen murmurs, "You already won him over." I lift my eyes from the stallion and give Ethen a side glance and a small smile.

"What can I say? It's a gift." I look around the rest of the stables. "It's been a while since I've ridden."

Ethen motions over to the next stall, which houses a similar breed, this one a mare, a soft gray, almost white color. I ask, "Tennessee Walkers?"

His eyes widen slightly. "Yes, that's right. Her name's Pearl."

I walk over to the next stall and pull out another carrot. I make my next best friend as she munches on the carrot happily, and I rub her ears. I say to Ethen, "At my old outpost I had one."

"Did it get away after the attack?"

A shadow crosses over my peaceful mood. "I never saw her again after that day." I look up at him. "I like to think she is happy in the forest somewhere."

The stable doors swing open, and I see Kane stroll toward us, his powerful frame outlined by the golden sun, now fully risen. I tilt my head and ask Ethen, "Who else is going on this trip to the Dragon Lands?"

He says, "The three of us. Kane and I are the only ones in Domain Sector who have been given access." Kane walks toward another occupied stall and greets his horse. "Kane, this is Sophia. Sophia, Kane." We lock eyes. He gives me a nod and heads to the tack room for his saddle. Not much of a talker.

I look at Ethen and ask, "What did you have to do to get permission for me to enter the Dragon lands?"

He gives me a smile and wink. "That was easy. Anyone can request access to enter." I look at him quizzically with one of my eyebrows raised. He looks down at the horse as he brushes the stallion's gleaming coat.

His demeanor a bit more somber than before. "Only by proving yourself will you be granted access to leave."

With that bit of cheery news, Ethen strolls toward the tack room, and returns with a saddle. I say to his retreating back, "That would have been good information to know before petitioning Draco."

Ethen shrugs. "Same rules apply to everyone. Ian thought you would have the best shot at winning Draco over. It is your gift after all."

My words from earlier now sound hollow. A cold shiver runs down my spine.

I push the whisper of fear away, remembering why I am here, to uncover the mystery surrounding my sister's death. I am here to avenge not only hers but four other connected murders. I contemplate my sanity for making the trek to the forbidden territory as I run through the familiar but rusty routine in preparing the gray mare for our journey.

Ten minutes later, the three of us are mounted and moving to the front of the castle. We travel through the gatehouse and across the bridge, which takes us to the mainland. The bridge leads us right through the main street of Mystvillage. This remote village reminds me of towns hundreds of years ago. No motorized vehicles, no modern human technology. At this early hour, there is bustling activity on the street. Various vendors are setting up their shops.

As we make our way down the center road, citizens stop their various tasks and take a moment to look at our small group. The older generation halt their movements, staring at us without faltering. The young children hide behind skirts, wondering why the adults look so somber. Surely, they are wondering if they will see us return or if the beasts in the mountains will eat us.

As we get toward the end of the small town, our journey into the mountainous terrain begins. As I start climbing up the hillside, I dig deep into my memories, remembering the history lesson of dragons. Most children are told their magical stories from a young age.

The epic history of Fae and dragons started millennia ago, among the first of our kind who settled in Faerie. It was discovered that if a Fae and a dragon bonded, it created an amplification of power. Dragons derive their magic from the elements. When partnered with Fae magic, the power creates such an amplified ultimate force that no one is able to challenge it. Kingdoms were created and held based on these bonded relationships.

In Faerie, the sacred bond between Fae and Dragon was a lifelong ritualistic vow. This bond resulted in a sharing of life force, a constant ebb and flow of power from one partner to another. Dragons only allowed this bond to Fae if they were deemed worthy. If a bonding was attempted and the Fae not strong enough to hold the power, tragically it would end in their death.

The most popular children's bedtime story is one where Great Queen Morrigan flies into battle with Titus, her bonded dragon, during one of the old territorial battles in Faerie. The Great Queen's arsenal at its peak comprised of fifty mature dragons and bonded riders. The queen protected and nurtured her dragonflight, providing safe grounds for them to live and raise their young in peace, free from any hunters. In turn, the dragons were loyal to the queen, providing protection from any foe.

This symbiotic, harmonious relationship was shattered during the last battle. The queen held the dark forces at bay with the strength of her dragonflight. While the dragonflight was occupied on the southern front, the enemy set an inextinguishable magical fire to the northern forest where the younglings' sanctuary was. The blue inferno burnt the forest to ash, all dragons, young and old, who dwelled within perished, unable to escape. As the battle waged on, the queen sent the last remaining dragons through the gates in hopes of saving the ones she could.

Devastation and loss of so many of the dragons in battle, compounded with the loss of their families in the inferno fire, created a vast chasm between dragons and Fae. In their grief, dragons refused any relationship to Fae once the gate was sealed. The accord was forged during the first hundred years of the gate closing, and the dragons carved out a section of terrain they approved of. This land is now called the Dragon Lands, where they have remained, secluded for a thousand years.

The dragons in Tarrin numbered less than twenty when the gates closed. Dragon's reproduction was so low that there have only been three fertility cycles since trapped on Earth. This resulted in approximately thirty new offspring, the most recent happening about sixty years ago. I contemplate the numbers and estimate the dragon-flight to be roughly fifty mature dragons and ten younglings in Tarrin's Dragon Lands today.

The accord held the local dragonflight to the boundaries of the Dragon Lands within Tarrin. In turn, this vast area is off limits to any Fae, human, or witch not approved by Draco, the leader of Tarrin's dragonflight. Dragons are allowed to hunt outside of Tarrin, but they are bound by the accord to hold a strict secrecy of our culture. If drag-ons leave, they are not to be visible to humans. This is becoming more and more difficult, with human technology improving. In the past fifty years, strict guidelines have been put into place. Due to the growth of the flight and difficulties in maintaining strong hunting grounds, there has been talk of expansion of the Dragon Lands. Negations are contin-uously in the works.

The Fae relentlessly tried to use the dragon's request for more land as leverage to facilitate more bonded riders. Efforts to cultivate bonded relationships over the past years were met with resistance. The deeply broken trust of the dragons has kept them sheltered, away from most Fae.

I have heard rumors, at other gates, that strides have been made, and more dragons have bonded with Fae. I have heard there are a handful of Fae who have chosen to live at the Tarrin Dragon Keep in hopes of being nominated. If the dragons find a nominated Fae worthy, they can hope to bond one day, despite the thousand-year vacancy.

Duncan and Ethen grew up with the dragons in the Sierra Nevada Gate. Duncan was the son of Conor MacKinley, who was bonded to Draco. Ethen's father died when he was only ten. Conor took Ethen in as his own, and Ethen spent most of his childhood with the Sierra Nevada dragonflight, becoming part of the MacKinley family. When Draco and the MacKinleys moved to Tarrin, Ethen stayed behind be-cause he had been promoted to commander. A few months ago, when Duncan was killed, Ethen requested a transfer to be closer to Conor.

I ask Ethen, "How many are living at the Dragonkeep?"

He turns and looks at me. "Last time I was up here, there were twenty poor souls hoping for a bond. In the latest round of land negotiations,

Draco expanded his hunting grounds twenty miles into Domain Sector, granting access to the lake. In turn, the dragons must consider new nominations for the bonding ritual that the council provides. There are twenty nominees sent by the council. They are staying at the Dragonkeep until the first snowfall." Ethen smiles a little. "Draco will never force any of his flight to bond with a Fae. The consideration will never be real until the dragons decide they want it to be real."

I consider what Ethen said and ask, "Have you ever wanted to be considered for a bond?" I glance over to Ethen and then Kane, who has come up next to us on the widening path.

Ethen looks up toward the early morning light and says, "Of course, when I was a young lad, I had Conner and his bonded dragon Draco to look up to. Centuries spent with the dragonflight made me realize how fanciful those dreams were. The distrust and animosity run deep. I believe some wounds may never mend."

He looks over at Kane, who surprisingly chimes in, a slight smile curving his lips showing straight white teeth. "It's a young man's dream."

I ask Kane, "How is it that you have been granted access to the Dragonlands?"

He replies, "When I was also young, I was one of the hopeful bucks looking to get noticed by the dragons. At that time, dragons were even less hospitable than they are now. After a year at the keep, I proved myself worthy. There was one dragon I believe would have bonded with me." Kane looks down at the horse beneath him and stokes the mane. "However, all that effort was in vain. Yaz became flight leader and imposed a strict ban on bonding." I see Kane's jaw harden with the memory.

"That must have been disappointing. How long was Yaz in charge?"

Kane glances at me. "Yaz reigned for five hundred years. A hundred years ago, Draco challenged him for the territory and won. Draco has held the title of flight leader since then."

I give him a sympathetic smile and say, "Are you going to try again to be considered for a bond, now that there's been a change in leadership?"

Kane shakes his head. "The dragon I was close with died right before the transition of power. Dragons live very, very long lifespans even compared with the Fae." Kane lets out a heavy sigh. "Even though dragons live long lifespans, they are still susceptible to eventual old age and sickness. Adalinda, the dragon I was close with, died of natural causes."

"I am so sorry you were cheated out of a true partnership."

He gives me a single nod and looks straight ahead, ending any further conversation, the hurt still palpable. The three of us continue for a while in companionable silence.

The early morning light turns to mid-morning. The terrain becomes more jagged, forcing our small group into a single row as we wind up the hillsides. For a few hours, we continue, dodging obstacles. We arrive at the edge of a wide mountain river, the mountain peaks soaring high above creating a picturesque image that sparks my imagination.

I pause to breathe in deep and enjoy the surroundings for a moment. Kane says, "We are close to Dragon Keep. It is a good idea to rest for a moment before we head inside the walls."

We lead the horses to water. Ethen turns toward me and asks, "How's your research going? Any luck?"

I say, "The amount of paperwork Manus dropped will take me a while to wade through." I swipe my brow. The morning has turned warm, and I fill up my canteen.

I recall the stack of papers on my desk and say, "I started with the most recent activity, looking for any unusual behaviors, powers, or traits. Actually, there was one file that was under your command, a soldier named David Elwood. He's gone missing, last seen after David and his partner came back from rotation a month ago. Seems strange."

Ethen glances over and says, "We have been searching for him. This is part of the issues Kane, and I were working on through the past few days. David was part of the third squad that decided to leave the Domain Sector in the past year. We tracked down David's squad partner, who also has mysteriously gone to another gate and was unreachable. The area they were last patrolling boarders the Dragon Lands."

I raise an eyebrow. "That is suspicious."

Ethen nods. "On our return trip today, we will follow David's patrol coordinates to see if anything stands out."

Suddenly, Ethen's attention is piqued, and he turns toward Kane. Silently, they exchange a look that puts me on guard. I place my hand on the hilt of my sword and expand my senses. I hear the rustling of leaves in the breeze but otherwise do not hear or see anything out of normal.

Ethen turns toward the forest and says, "I know you are there Ryker, Marduk. Come on out to speak to us."

A low growl is felt vibrating the Earth. I see a shimmering light as the glamor is released. Once hidden from my senses, now I can visualize massive claws as they come into view. Two dragons, larger than I ever imagined, push through the trees into the clearing. They stand approximately twenty feet tall. My head barely reaches the tops of their legs.

Beautiful, iridescent scales shimmer in the morning light. The one on the right is a deep maroon color, the left a vibrant green. The scales I see starting about their knees wind up their massive torso to their short necks and elongated faces. I see wings tucked tight to their backs that connect to the upper shoulders. Long, massive tails disappear into the forest beyond.

Their bright, deep-set eyes appraise us, and the slightly larger emerald-green dragon on the left says, "You've become bold, Ethen and Kane, bringing a stranger into our midst. You know the accord. Anyone who wanders into our territory is fair game for our brothers and sisters' enjoyment."

Ryker appraises me intently, his long neck bringing his face close to mine. He deeply inhales my scent and then turns his attention to Marduk, the second large maroon dragon.

Ryker and Marduk seemingly have a non-verbal conversation, communicating telepathically. I glance at Ethen and Kane, hoping this is a normal occurrence. I see Ethen and Kane are wary. I tighten my grip on my sword hilt. I can feel the tension in the air. I recall from deep in my memory that dragons have the ability to communicate over large distances.

Ryker and Marduk's silent communication is followed by a low hissing sound from both beasts in anticipation. Both dragons regard me as if I would be a tasty meal. It takes all my mental fortitude to stand my ground. I know instinctually giving an inch would be like waving a red flag at a bull.

Ethen interrupts the hissing, saying loudly, "I sent word ahead to Draco. He is aware we are coming. Kane, Sophia, and I should have a clear passage to the keep. If she is harmed, it is your head that will roll."

Ryker responds, "The accord is clear. The only Citadel Warriors allowed are Kane and you." He scoffs, and a large plume of smoke streams out his nostrils. "It has been over one hundred years since any other warriors have been allowed on our lands." He pauses and then lets out a dark gruff laugh. "That is, any warrior who has been allowed to leave."

Ethen's jaw sets in a grim line. He shifts his weight and appraises Ryker. "There is a common enemy we have found. It is building strength. We are in negotiations to combine forces and defeat the ones who threaten this world."

Ryker turns those illuminance green eyes toward Ethen and says calmly, "Funny, Draco never mentioned that to me." The last words come out in a hiss directly at Ethen's face. It seems there may be some unsettled business between this Ryker and Ethen.

Ethen responds with a cruel smile. "Maybe Draco does not tell you everything."

There is a huff of smoke that billows out of Ryker's snout. "You dare challenge my authority?"

Not being an expert in dragon-Fae interactions, I refrain from comment despite my opinion that antagonizing a dragon would be bad for your health.

Ethen shrugs nonchalantly. "If the shoe fits." Ryker lets loose a roar that vibrates the ground violently. I look at Ethen and whisper out of the corner of my mouth, "What is wrong with you?"

Kane gives Ethen a similar look. "Ethen, poking the beast is probably not a good idea." I can see Kane positioning himself defensively. I grip the handles of my sword and axe as Kane says, "Do you forget, brother, the dragons are even quicker than you."

In a flurry of movements, Ryker attacks Ethen. His massive tail swinging around, I roll, and the tail misses me by an inch. I see Kane pull his broadsword back and duck out of the way of Marduk's massive tail. A moment too late. The barbed end of the appendage knocks Kane into a wide tree.

Out of the corner of my eye, I see Ethen's massive crossbow is in hand as he aims for Ryker, but he is too late. The arrow whizzes by, lost to the forest.

Rising from a low crouch, I extend my sword in one hand, axe in another. I run and slide under the beast and sweep long and deep into Ryker's hind legs in the crease behind the knee. The dragon lets out a loud bellow as I see blue blood start to roll down his leg from the wound. I hear a whistle through the air as a massive arrow is shot, and I see it penetrate his scales on the opposite-side shoulder.

Ryker turns his murderous eyes from me to Ethen and pauses for a moment, as if deciding which of us he wants to eat first. I can see the moment his decision is made. He charges at Ethen.

I move quickly, sweeping the axe back into its holster. I advance at a run, dancing up the left hind leg, the size of a tree truck. I reach the lower back of the beast, grip the scales with one hand, and catwalk across the enormous back of the dragon. I am at the middle of Ryker's back before he recognizes the threat and tries to rake his razor-sharp claws over me. I flatten down flush and dig my heels into his scales to gain a footing, his claws not reaching. He starts to thrash violently back and forth, while I hold on for dear life. I spider crawl the remaining few feet to situate myself at the base of his neck, grunting at the effort. I know I cannot hold this position for long.

During one of his downward motions, I sweep my sword at the base of his neck, finding that soft spot between the scales. I feel the beast freeze. His gigantic breaths lift me up and down. I can feel his rage barely contained.

I scream down, "What are we doing here, Ethen?"

He looks up at me and the dragon. "Ryker, it's up to you. Are we having peace this trip, or will you be losing your long, miserable life today?"

I feel a visceral response in the vibrations under me. A low growling noise begins and then echoes through the clearing. This is followed by a long pause and then a grumbled response. "Peace."

Ethen nods, still aiming the enormous crossbow directly at Rykers's head. I see Kane has regained his fighting stance, crossbow aimed at Marduk. Blood is dripping down Kane's temple and the right side of his body. He must have been stuck good with the barbed end of Marduk's tail. Despite the blood, his stance is strong, and he has a grim expression. A glint in his eye tells me he would prefer it if the latter choice is taken and I slit Ryker's throat.

Ethen says, "Sophia, why don't you remove your blade slowly and come on down?"

I let my sword drop and slide down the massive front leg. I back up to appraise the two dragons one more time. Ethen says, "Let's try this—"

Ryker lets out a massive roar, and fire erupts from his mouth in a long trail heading straight for Ethen. I put up my hands, pull deep, and use my magic. The world freezes, the flames about a foot away, the two dragons frozen.

I look over at Ethen and have a moment when I want to let those flames torch him. This male and his ego almost got us eaten by dragons. I sigh heavily and touch Ethen on the shoulder. He is released from my time warp. I hold the rest of the clearing in their frozen status.

I say, "I can only hold them for a few minutes. What's the plan here? Antagonizing them is not helping our cause."

Ethen appears as if he still wants to fight, looks at my face, and grudgingly responds, "Sadly, if we kill them, any negotiations with Draco will be over."

I hear a loud, deep chuckle from the forest and freeze.

I turn my head, and materializing out of thin air is the largest dragon I have met so far. Pure black with the same iridescent scales as the other two, a massive dragon most likely topping twenty-five feet is standing at the edge of the clearing.

Ethen says steadily, with an edge in his voice indicating his rage, "Draco, was this a test?"

I keep the two dragons held in stasis while watching the conversation out of the corner of my eye.

Draco scoffs, "Not entirely." He moves into the clearing, looking at his two frozen dragons intently.

He turns and then surveys me.

I am still holding the clearing still, my hands outstretched. Draco leans in close to me. I can feel the hot breath on my cheek as the dragon breathes my scent in deep. Draco says, "Ryker and Marduk told me of your presence when you were detected within our boundaries. I arrived after the first skirmish erupted.

"I wanted to see how this newcomer faired with my hot-headed commander." He finally turns and looks at Ethen. "Opportunity presented itself. Blending into the shadows gave me time to contemplate the alliance you suggested."

Ethen says, "You are lucky Ryker is breathing. We have had *two opportunities* to end his life."

Draco turns abruptly. "Do not forget where you are, *teaghlach*, or the terms of our accord. It is within my rights to give permission for this land and to take that permission away. Ethen Graham, Kane Abara, you have been given permission. Do not test me, or I will revoke it."

Draco swivels his head to look at me, calming. "I would be remiss if I did not point out that the newcomer is the one who has had two opportunities to end Ryker's life, not you, Ethen." I glance over at Ethen and see a snarl appear. His arrogance and pride are taking a hit.

I am still holding the frozen two dragons in place and mutter to Ethen, "I am about to lose the time warp."

I feel the cracking of the magic around me, and then my powers retract. Time unfreezes in the clearing. The flames from Ryker's mouth burn the empty space in front of him, and he looks around the clearing. Ryker spots Draco, and immediately his demeanor changes, his killing rage turns to confusion and then to acknowledgement.

The huge beast turns and kneels before his king. Marduk quickly follows, Kane falling in behind Ethen and me.

Draco approaches the two dragons, and they start to communicate again. Silence greets us. I see the emotions cross the three dragons' faces. Clearly Draco was not happy with his two commanders. Ryker lets out a loud screech in protest at whatever Draco said. This is met with Draco's menacing low growl. Ryker and Marduk quickly turn toward us, and then the silent internal conversions were over.

Draco starts, "I have decided to allow Sophia access to the Dragon Lands on a temporary basis, due to her skills in besting my commander while still showing respect for our lands and not ending his life."

The giant green dragon lets loose a puff of smoke, clearly disgruntled.

Draco turns to me and says, "You spared Ryker's life twice in a fair fight. This creates a debt between you and Ryker." He turns to look at Ryker. "You are to pay the life debt to Sophia by granting her a mark."

Ryker turns toward me and huffs out a second plume of smoke. I try to gauge the reaction of the massive green dragon before me. Then, surprising me, he lowers his enormous head in a low bow.

I quickly look at Ethen for clarification and am surprised to see his face full of disbelief, quickly followed by anger as he stares at Draco. Ethen's eyes dart to me. The anger fades as he focuses on me, and he clears his throat. I can still see the simmering rage beneath the calm exterior, and I wonder what this mark was and why it would cause Ethen's wrath.

Ethen says, "I haven't heard of someone receiving a mark in hundreds of years. From what I remember, if you accept the mark, you can call Ryker in a time of need. He will be bound to save your life, as you have spared his life."

Awe-struck, I ask, "What exactly do you mean?"

Ethen responds, looking at Draco, "You might be better at explaining. I have never experienced it myself." It clicks that maybe a mark has something to do with bonding.

I swing toward Draco, who says very matter-of-factly, "The practicality of the ritual is that Ryker will mark your wrist. The blood and magic will bind your agreement." My eyes dart between Ethen and Ryker and then back to Draco, sure there was something else. Draco sees my look and continues, "Only if the recipient is worthy will the mark be accepted." I hear another loud huff and feel the hot breath of the dragon, Ryker, once more. Clearly, he is annoyed that I am not falling over myself to get this mark.

I ask Draco in a low voice, "What's the catch?" I have the impression that Draco smiles in amusement, if a dragon can smile.

He says, "No catch, you spared Ryker's life in a fair fight. He is honor bound to save yours. This magical agreement keeps him honest."

I look over at Ethen, whose expression has turned to stone.

I ask Ethen, "What is it?"

Ethen clears his throat and says, "I believe if you take the mark, it is the first stage in the bonding process, the preliminary test for compatibility." I swallow, remembering from our history lessons potential Fae who were not worthy did not survive the bonding ritual.

Time hangs in that moment. A split second, instinctual decision that may alter the course of my life. I look at Ryker and decide. Deep in my gut, I know this pivotal moment is meant to happen. One of those gut instincts that keep me on this winding path of my life. It has never steered me wrong before. I send out a prayer that it holds true this time.

I inch closer to Ryker and extend my arm. There is a murmuring from Ryker in a language not heard for a thousand years, then a swipe of a claw across my wrist, leaving a bright-red line of blood. He takes a drop of his own blue blood from his own open wound and holds it over my wrist.

A single droplet falls into the wound. Tingling magic washes through me, and the wound heals, leaving a beautiful iridescent green dragon tattooed on my wrist, directly above my Warrior Alliance tattoo. The image is half curved, the wings creating the outer part of the circle. I look at it curiously. It appears as if half the image is missing. The iridescent glow is bright even in the sunlight, beautifully depicting an exact drawing of Ryker.

I look up at Draco, who looks down at me, saying, "The mark is done, the debt to be settled at the time of your choosing. At your time of need, press on the mark and say his name. That will summon him to your side." I gulp and remove my hand from the claw slowly, backing up a few paces, not entirely sure if I could trust this hot-headed dragon to do anything to help me. Especially in my time of need.

Draco says, "Now that this is wrapped up, come and join me at the keep, and we will discuss this mutual problem of ours."

I glance at Ethen and Kane who turn to retrieve our horses, still tied up by the bank of the river. Ethen's emotions are locked down, but I will never forget the moment of rage that filled his face. He moves toward Pearl, and we mount, following the massive dragons heading toward their keep.

As we leave the bank of the Aurora River, my thumb passes over the shimmering tattoo at my wrist. I look around the small clearing and feel a shift in my fate. Our lives are made up of pivotal moments. Whether you agree or not, your destiny will change your direction.

A shiver runs through me, and I recognize the fiery winds of fate leading me.

Shaking off the inter-turmoil, I pull my leather sleeve down to cover the mark and follow our group into the forest.

THIRTY-EIGHT

Gael—Warnings and Tunnels

reach down and pat Orian's massive head, rubbing his ears the way he likes. I get a slobbery lick on my hand and smile. "Thanks, Orian."

We are outside on a small patio in Mystfort Village, the street vibrantly alive with activity. An elaborately carved sign is proudly displayed out front, reading, "Phoebe's Enchanted Eatery: Coffee, Tearoom, and Bakery." This is just one of many shops and boutiques on the main street in Mystvillage. Each one as unique as their owners.

Phoebe Boucher, the owner of this establishment, has come around twice now asking if I needed anything. I smile at her and say, "Thank you, I'm good with just coffee."

She winks at me, her curry red hair as lively as her personality, and slips a small pastry on the table, saying, "Try it." She touches my shoulder and gives it a slight squeeze. With a small smile, she sashays away.

I shout after her retreating form, "Thank you!"

She returns to a table on the other side of the patio. I take a bite of the sweet treat, and it melts in my mouth. Well, I surely will be a patron for life now.

I look down at my watch. Ari is late, of course. I finally see her walking up and motion her over with a wide smile.

Suddenly, a shadow crosses the table. Orian lets out a low warning growl. I squint up into the bright sun as a large male form appears. Seeing only the outline, I tense as he says in a thick voice, "Hi, Gael, I'm Ian Cadell. Sophia asked that I investigate a few things for her. Mind if I sit and tell you what I found?"

Letting out a breath and the earlier tension, I nod and rub Orian's ears so he knows we are okay. Ian sits at our small table, long legs sprawled out in front of him. His light hair is cropped short, bright-blue eyes shining even in the shade.

Ari stands by, hesitant to interrupt. I motion her over and say to Ian, "Whatever you need to tell me, Ari can hear."

He gives her a nod as Ari sits next to me. Ian says, "Sophia is away for a few days, but I wanted to let you know what I found. Bennett mentioned that you know about your birth parents, or rather the limited information that he had. Your father, a warrior, died in a creature attack before you were born, and your mother died in childbirth."

I look away. I don't really like remembering the details.

Ian continues, "After which, Bennett and Gwyneth Monroe adopted you. I am still tracking down any information I can gather about your birth parents, I believe that will help us in figuring out where your powers came from. But in the meantime, I wanted to share with you my theory."

I look up at him, curiosity brimming. He says, "I believe the binding Sophia found is a natural defense of your body trying to protect you from your powers until you are ready. Now, everyone will mature at different times, but I think it is safe to say you are on the brink of your powers fully manifesting.

"I am concerned about your abilities, concerned that they may cause you to burn out." I look at him in confusion, and he clarifies, "A firewielder is a wonderful, powerful gift, but it must be used in moderation. Fire is particularly difficult to wield, tough to know when you are on the edge of burnout. I want you to be careful using your power. You won't realize when you've gone too far or used too much until your well is empty. The last firewielder burnt out, and he was experienced, living well into his seven hundredth year.

"I'm sure you will be fine, but be careful how long you use your magic. If the magical binding of your powers is ripped away suddenly, you run the risk of being overcome with the sudden influx of power." Ian shifts his weight, looking at me intently. "Most people learn their powers slowly as they age and develop. You will need to learn to master them in one fell swoop."

I mumble, "Understood."

Ian continues, "When I get back to the Central Sector, I will look in the archives to find information on removing the binding safely." He rises from his chair. "Until then, take care of yourself."

Ian gives Ari a nod and turns toward the main thoroughfare that leads to Mystfort, disappearing around a curve in the road.

Ari says, "Wow, if Ian wanted to warn you directly, it must be serious."

I say, "I understand the risks, but I feel like it would be a relief to have this binding, this weight, removed." I sigh and brush my blonde braid over my shoulder.

Ari looks at me sharply. "Gael, you must take this seriously. I overheard something, a conversation between Bennett and my father before selections. They swore me to secrecy, but I think it's important for you to know."

I look at her in curiosity. "What did you hear?"

"I was practicing my invisibility, seeing how long I could hold it for. Each day, I would be able to hold it longer and longer. It was sort of a game. If my dad could find me, he would win. If I was hidden well enough, I would win."

I nudge her shoulder. "Go on, get to the story."

"Okay. I, um, was out behind the house. Bennett had stopped by after dinner. I was excused early so I went out into the garden practicing my concealment—"

"Ari! Spit it out. What did you overhear?"

She looks at me a bit sheepishly. "They headed to the garden and were talking about you. My dad was telling Bennett that you should be warned that your powers could overcome you and you could burn out, like Ian just said right now. Bennett said you would be fine, especially because your powers did not come close to Larken's.

"I did not know who Larken was then, but I looked it up later.

Larkin was a firewielder, a cousin to the Great Queen. So that means you may be a long-lost descendant of the Great Queen too."

I nod and tell her, "It's crossed my mind."

Ari's jaw drops. "Okay, we are going to circle back to the fact you knew this and did not say anything. Anyway, Bennett said Larkin was a degenerative mess, unable to control himself, and that was why he lived in the forest all by himself, eventually burning himself out. My dad disagreed and got angry, saying Larkin was the last of the Great Queen's line and was exceptional. He chose to live in solitude after losing his wife during the Great War."

Ari started wringing her hands. "Bennett and my dad argued. Ultimately, he said Larkin's final burnout is most likely what caused the gates to fissure, creating the cracks that allow in the dark creatures. He said that since a firewielder's power comes from same blood line as the Great Queen, it has the power to force the gates closed or break them open."

This bit of information gets the reaction she originally wanted. I can feel the blood draining from my features. It suddenly makes more sense why Ian, a council member, would bother himself with my powers.

I tell her, "So if I lose control of my powers, I could make the fissures in the gate larger." This horrid image rolls through my mind. The danger that theory presents makes my blood run cold.

Ari continues, "Then I moved slightly, making a noise, and they both saw me. Bennett told me he did not want to worry you about this, because your powers were nowhere near as strong as the last firewielder. He said that if this theory became public knowledge, it would cause many to be wary of you and your powers. He did not want that for you.

"Now we know your power is bound, and once it's released...who knows how that would affect you? Who knows how that may affect the fissures in the gate?"

I say, "You are right. I will be careful with my magic."

Ari squeezes my hand in reassurance. "I wanted to let you know since, since I would want to know."

"Thank you for telling me. While we are truth sharing, I need to tell you about something else."

I look down at my hands, wondering if she will laugh at my crazy dreams. I blow out a breath of air. "I've been having this recurring dream ever since we arrived at Mystfort. Not just any dream, it feels like a premonition, like something is trying to communicate with me. I know it sounds crazy, but I have not slept since we got to Mystfort, and I feel like I am be haunted by this dream."

Ari nods. "With all the other mysterious things going on with your life, this makes total sense." She gives me a grin. "What's the dream about?"

I take a deep breath and grab her hand. "Thank you for believing me. I don't know what I would do without you."

I let go and look around the quiet patio. No one is paying any attention to us. "I'm in a throne room that appears to be buried. It's a large room with stained glass windows, but it appears to be completely covered by stones on the outside, like this room was buried under the castle. There's a long walkway, ending in a golden throne. There are tables set up with old relics, but one item draws me toward the table, and every time I stop directly in front of this illuminated box. Sometimes, in my dream, I reach out to touch it, and then dream shatters like a mirror breaking into a hundred pieces.

"In the last dream I had, I don't touch the box but instead pass by the table, walking up a winding staircase. This eventually exits into the castle. I turn, and there's a painting on the wall. It is Queen Morrigan, a crown on her head, sword in right hand, the box in the left. I know it sounds crazy, but I hear this screaming inside my head, and I feel like she is trapped and only I can release her. I want to track down this throne room for my own sanity."

I look down at the table, gathering my thoughts. "I have a feeling that someone or something is pushing me to find this room. Every night, I dream about it."

Ari says, "If you need to find this room, I will help you, but promise me you won't use your powers."

A tear slips down my cheek. Ari is simply the best.

I brush the wayward tear away. "I looked in the library early this morning and found old blueprints to the castle. I found a section of the map that looked like it may be the room sealed off from use under the west wing. The tricky part is how to get there undetected."

"I think I have an answer to that." Logan materializes in the seat opposite of Ari and I.

I jump and say, "Logan! Stop doing that!" Ari knocks over the chair next to her, and the whole patio silences as her cheeks turn red and she lifts the chair upright once more. We get a sidelong look from the other patrons, and eventually the attention returns to normal.

Logan turns to me, grins. "What fun is there in that? Anyways, don't you want to know what I found?" He leans back on the chair, looking pleased with himself.

I sit up straight, my ears perking. "What?"

Logan beams and says, "I was able to get my shadows through the tunnels under the castle."

"What tunnels?"

"The first few days in Mystfort, I found a series of abandoned tunnels under the castle. They were under the main keep, so I did not think too much about them. They were old servants' passages from the kitchen to the rooms, most of them sealed closed with stones.

"After our conversation earlier today, I went down to see if I missed something, and voila! The servants' passages go to the main keep, but I found one passage that was originally sealed shut, running west. The stones were crumbling with disrepair, so I simply moved a few bricks out of the way. I followed the tunnel and found it led to a whole series of tunnels under the west wing. I checked, and they go to a series of rooms. One is a storage room in the back. We can sneak in that way."

I give him a wide smile and then turn to Ari. "Let's go tonight." I look over at Logan, who gives me a nod, and I grin in anticipation.

Tonight, I will find the room that keeps haunting my dreams.

THIRTY-NINE

Sophia—Dragon Keep

We steadily make progress through the forest, dragons leading the way. Draco, Ryker, and Marduk in front, Ethen, myself, and Kane bringing up the rear. As we crest a mountain top, I see a narrow valley stretching out in front of us, surrounded by sheer cliffs on all sides.

The mountain peaks in the distance still have a dusting of snow from last winter. Our trail ends at the beginning of a massive stone bridge that spans the valley from the ridge where we are standing, ending at the castle gates far in the distance. Pearl edges the stones at our feet, and I hear a low whimper as pebbles roll down the edge and off into the vast chasm below. I agree with her sentiment. I've never been too fond of heights. No way am I happy about crossing the massive valley on the bridge. I close my eyes briefly, remembering why we are here.

The three massive dragons push off the edge of the cliff to soar up into the vast blue sky. Ethen and Kane edge their horses forward, and I take a deep breath.

Here we go.

Pearl eases us onto the stones with her steady hooves, and we start to tentatively make our way across. I glance down to my right then to my left and decide it's best to keep my eyes on the stones directly in front of us. The river is swiftly flowing at the bottom of the ravine, a winding blue line barely visible. The bridge is wide enough for the horses to ride side by side.

The bridge is safe. The bridge is safe. The bridge is safe.

That mantra runs through my mind, steadying my nerves.

Distracting me from the perilous journey, a massive stone castle comes into view, protruding from the depths of the valley. Mountains flank both sides of the castle, the front entrance hundreds of feet above the ground. The only ground access to the castle is by the very bridge we are on that ends at the gate house. I see a dragon land on one of the turrets and then disappear out of sight.

I can make out at least ten other turrets that are visible from our vantage point. Clearly this is the way most of them enter and exit the castle. Since flight is their primary method of travel, why the dragons would even build a bridge at all is at the top of my list of questions.

The castle, heavily fortified in the middle of the wilderness, sounded by nature's own defenses, is virtually impenetrable. If the dragons do not want you there, you are at their mercy.

I shoot a glance up ahead, seeing the three dragons escorting us swooping down under the bridge's high arches, straight toward the raging river. At the last possible second, turning sharply, they shoot straight up to the sky. I marvel at the freedom they must feel, and my heart twinges in envy.

While the dragons show off, I look at Ethen and ask, "Why would dragons need a castle?" Ethen looks over at me with a surprised look, and then I see Kane smirking over Ethen's shoulder. "What?"

He lets out a small chuckle, the only laughter I have seen out of him all day.

Ethen's lips twitch. "You will see soon enough." I can feel my temper rise. I tamp it down and lock it away. Emotions I can deal with later. We ride the rest of the distance in a tense silence, each of us wrapped up in our own mental drama.

We finally approach the lowered drawbridge that leads toward the gate house. The three massive dragons, black, green, and maroon, land spectacularly at the end of the bridge in a flourish, right before the massive entryway. I can see males manning the towers above us. Strangely, no other dragons are around. For such a large castle, I expected to see more activity, but I don't dare ask another question, as Draco, Ryker, and Marduk are now within earshot. We make our way under the ten-foot-wide outer wall and into the inner ward. A large bailey is visible, surrounding the castle, with a wide expanse of grass.

Suddenly, from my right I hear a loud beating of wings, and a massive, dark-green dragon lands on the edge of the outer wall. His claws overhang the edge of the stones, some breaking apart and falling to the ground under his sharp talons. Looking directly at us, he lets out a roar that shakes the ground.

Pushing off the stone ledge in one fluid motion, the dragon drops to the ground at the edge of the bailey. He starts to approach, and I take a defensive stance. As I track his movements, I see a shimmer of light, and the dragon transforms into a large male, roughly seven feet tall, dark hair, and dressed in fighting leathers. His long strides eat up the remaining distance. My head swings toward the three other dragons in the courtyard, who have also transformed into large males. One light-brown coloring, the other with a copper head of hair, the center one pitch-black. My head swings back around, and I look at Ethen and Kane, who are both appraising my shock with amusement.

I abruptly snap my lips closed and cross my arms over my chest. It would have been nice to have a heads up about the transformative nature of the dragons we are to negotiate with. Ethen mutters out of the corner of his mouth, "Apologies, Sophia, dragons are particularly secretive about their Fae form. Only a handful of the original Fae who settled in Idyll still remember, and the ones who do keep quiet in fear invoking their wrath."

I know dragons have transformative gifts, being able to camouflage themselves into their surroundings and hunt in secret. I had no idea that they could transform into our very image. The old stories told how one would never know before a dragon came upon them. The dragon would simply appear, and then it would be too late. This is normally told to children so they won't wander too far into the forests.

The new large male approaching says loudly, "What is the meaning of this?"

He trains hate-filled eyes on me. To our left, the center male steps forward. His commanding demeanor and coloring match his dragon form. I can only guess that it is Draco. Long black hair is braided down his back, chiseled features drawn into a hard set of lines.

Draco responds, "I could ask the same thing to you, Yaz. You know the rules about entering the grounds in your dragon form."

Yaz scoffs at the wall that now has a crumbled edge of stone and ignores Draco's comment. He says accusingly, "Another Fae." He looks at me with a sneer and continues, "Centuries spent keeping our distance all for naught." He looks me up and down in disgust. Turning toward Draco, Yaz says, "In the hundred years since you arrived, you have undone all our safeguards."

He pauses and turns toward me. "Now you are welcoming them with open arms?" He lets out a grunt of outrage.

Yaz, merely a few feet away, is suddenly directly in front of me. He leans in close, closer than I am comfortable with even if he is in Fae form. I place my hand on the hilt of my dagger at my thigh. Ethen, noticing, places his hand over mine to hold me back. My fingers freeze, but my body is humming with the stress of not moving.

I feel Ethen at my back as Yaz slowly breathes deep, as if catching my scent and relishing it. Like Draco in the clearing, it seems as if they are studying me by scent.

Suddenly, Draco cuts through this awkward moment, positioning himself between Yaz and myself. "You no longer are this flight's leader, or have you forgotten the last time you challenged me and lost." He is now right in Yaz's face.

Yaz holds his gaze then turns bright eyes toward me. I square my shoulders and stare back at him. He spits on the ground at my feet, turns, and walks toward the keep, not saying another word.

I look around and see a crowd has gathered around the courtyard, some up on the stone patrol path looking down. Some have emerged from the grand stone entrance to the castle keep. There must have been at least fifty residents, male and female. I wonder how many female dragons live here.

Draco pauses for a moment and lets Yaz walk away. Addressing the crowd, he says, "Show's over, folks. Back to your stations." He looks over at our small group. "Let's talk inside where we have some privacy."

The tension in the air dissipates, and the crowd starts to disperse, some looking disappointed that there is no bloodshed. We collectively nod and follow Draco toward the keep. Ryker and Marduk give Draco a small bow outside the steps and head toward the left wing of the castle.

Draco leads us up the impressive stone entrance and into a great hall. Light streams in from the beautifully arched stained-glass windows. Tapestries depicting dragons in battle line the walls. Before I can take in all the details, Draco motions toward the right wing and leads us down a long hallway into a large library. On one side of the room, an oversized ornately carved desk is positioned with two guest chairs opposite the massive carved throne behind the desk.

On the far wall is a massive stone fireplace elaborately carved on each side with images of dragons spewing fire. The fireplace is flanked by squishy, comfortable-looking armchairs that invite one to cozy up to the fire on a cold winter day. The walls are covered floor to ceiling with leather bound books, a rolling ladder visible in the far corner.

Draco motions toward the fireplace seating area, and we settle into the comfortable wingback chairs. He walks over toward the wet bar on a side table. "A drink for anyone?"

He pours from an elaborate crystal decanter the amber liquor into four glasses. He carries two lowball glasses to Ethen and Kane, returns, and then strolls across the room to hand me a glass with a contemplative expression on his face. I force myself to meet his eyes without looking away, fighting the urge to shift my weight under his steady gaze.

Finally releasing my stare, he turns and looks at Ethen, saying, "Conor was pulled away unexpectedly this morning. I will update him with what we discuss today."

He sits and pulls a glass jar across the table. As he lifts the lid, a smoky, sweet aroma permeates the room. Draco pulls some paper from the jar and starts to roll a cigarette. He lights the end with the lightest of breaths, and a sweet smoke with notes of tobacco, leather, and spices starts to swirl around his head. I recall Ian smoking a similar tobacco mix with my father when I was young. Draco motions an offering of tobacco, which collectively we decline.

Draco leans back in the chair slightly and sprawls out his long legs. "Apologies for Yaz's welcome. He is the slowest to come on board with the re-emerging Fae bonding. He was the leader of this flight for many centuries. When I came and changed some of the old-fashioned narratives, he was not pleased."

I remember Draco's comment from the courtyard about Yaz's challenge toward him and his subsequent loss.

Ethen leans forward. "It's not the first time we have had Yaz's welcome. Although, we should have warned Sophia."

I shift in my seat and send Ethen a glare across the room. I haven't forgotten my earlier angst about being blindsided by dragons' transformative nature. Ethen goes on, "Which brings us to why we are here. There has been an uptick in dark creature activity. We are investigating a string of Fae murders by dark creatures. There is suspected foul play because of the locations and types of kills.

"Last week, we were able to confirm our suspicion via drone footage of their organized movements. The purpose of the transportation of dark creatures is still unknown. However, we believe the murders were to cover up their activities. We believe Duncan's death is connected to four other murders and the attack on one of our outposts a year ago."

Draco's shrewd eyes sharpened at the mention of Duncan. I wonder how close they were. Duncan, the son of Draco's bonded rider Conor. Draco says only one word. "Explain."

Ethen proceeds to lay out what we know so far, the murders, the increased dark creature activity, Duncan's purchase of a relic that has now gone missing. Our theory that he was killed on his way to deposit the Sword of Light into the capital archives. Ethen tells of the compound that was attacked, my sister who died. He tells of the most recent attack of the human squad that was able to capture and send live footage to the command center showing faction members capturing and transporting dark creatures. When Ethen is done debriefing Draco on the events that led us to his door, he sits back and waits for Draco's response.

Draco taps his finger slightly on the edge of his crystal glass while his expression is darkly contemplative. Abruptly, he stands and walks toward the wide arched windows to look outside. "Knowing Duncan from the day he was born, I knew he had a secret the day he died.

Duncan always had a love for antiquities and would attend auctions often." A dark shadow crosses his eyes, and Draco turned toward Ethen. "If Duncan knew the sword was the Great Queen's relic, I am sure he kept it from me and his father in fear of its destruction."

Draco takes a few steps back toward the sitting area, asking Ethen, "What is your plan to avenge Duncan's death?"

Ethen nods. "We have a small but dedicated task force formed of individuals who have been directly affected by these deaths. Most recent events lead us to believe there was an information leak, so we are keeping our group small and vetted. If the dragons would be willing to help with reconnaissance, this will greatly help our team uncover the truth of these deaths." Ethen looks directly at Draco. "We will be able to avenge Duncan's murder, along with the others we lost."

Ethen looks over at me, a moment that Draco catches and takes note of.

Draco gives a slight nod toward Ethen. "Duncan was like a son to me, the son of my bonded Fae. Blood of my blood, flesh of my flesh. If Duncan was murdered, I want his murderer brought before his father Conor for execution.

"We will help with this *task force* you have created." At that moment, Ryker pushes open the heavy wooden doors to the library. He strolls in and looks expectantly at Draco as if he has been summoned. I feel the tattoo on my wrist pulse as if it is drawn to Ryker. I rub my thumb over the mark instinctually. I glance up, feeling Ethen's eyes on me settling on my wrist. I draw my wrist back toward me, hiding the now slightly glowing mark from his view. Ethen's eyes harden with the same look of jealousy I felt back by the river.

Draco continues, "Ryker, I want you to assist Ethen and Sophia's investigation into the murder of Duncan MacKinley. Bring his murderer to our feet to be executed." Ryker swings his light-brown stare toward our small group. I can see surprise and then disdain crosses his features as his eyes pass over Ethen and Kane. His gaze lands on mine, and curiosity settles as our eyes meet.

Draco says almost in passing, "It's not all bad, Ryker. It could be convenient for you to have Sophia close. If she needs to use her mark, you won't have far to travel."

Ryker narrows his eyes at the reminder. I could have sworn I saw a slight smile cross Draco's features as he turned away.

A scary monster with a sense of humor.

As a dismissal, Draco says, "Now, if you will excuse me, I need to tell Conor what really happened to his son." He strides out of the study, leaving me with the four towering males, who look as if they want to murder each other. Lucky me.

Ethen says, "Ryker, you can meet up with us at Mystfort." The large male does not even acknowledge the words, rather turns on his heel and walks out of the study. I look over and see Ethen glowering at Ryker's back as he disappears down the curved hallway to the right.

Ethen says, "We accomplished what we came here to accomplish. Let's head out."

As I walk out the front gates of the dragon keep, my mind reels with the knowledge of how lucky I am to have survived my first encounter with dragons.

There is only one way forward, and I plan on meeting it head-on. We retrieve our horses, cross the bridge, and then turn toward the eastern mountains. David's old patrol route is in this direction, and hopefully we will gain some answers to the patrol's mysterious disappearance on our way back to Mystfort.

Suddenly, appearing from the right is Ryker atop a large brown stallion. I look at him in surprise, unsure when I would see him next after his abrupt exit from the study.

I say, "You're coming with us?" A stiff nod is all I get in response, but Ethan glowers.

I shrug and accept the newest moody male in our group. It may be useful to have a full-fledged dragon on our side during our return to Mystfort. If this dragon holds up to their legendary skills, Ryker may be the key to unlocking the mystery surrounding the murders.

FORTY

Noreen—Wards Are No Match for Explosions

I drop off Caleb and Theon at central command and warily head back to my place of refuge and solitude. As my headlights illuminate the three-story glass-front structure built into the side of a cliff, my normal sense of peace is gone. I drive down into the Earth, place my hands on the steering wheel, and lower my forehead, letting out a deep breath. I usually make weapons for battle. I am not normally the one in the thick of it. I turn off my vehicle and step out of the car still in my business skirt and white tennis shoes. I grab my heels and walk up the stairs to the front door. The lights spill out into the forest beyond my steps.

I look around, feeling as if I am being watched, my senses still on high alert. I gaze around the perimeter. Nothing is moving. I shuffle to the right, finding the black tourmaline stone with my rune mark etched into it from my anchor ritual. I renew often, always wanting to be prepared. I swipe my thumb over the interconnected triangles representing protection. I feel the power vibrating from the stone, close my eyes briefly, and feel the layer of protection over my dwelling. All seems to be operating as normal. I then move to the left, checking the runestones at each corner. Nothing seems to have been tampered with.

Satisfied that my protections are strong, I cross the threshold, feeling the moment I am inside the shield. I let myself into my residence, flip on some lights, and bolt the door behind me for good measure. I slip off my shoes, and head barefoot toward the kitchen, pulling the bottle of vodka out of the fridge, and a glass from the cabinet on my way. I lower myself on a barstool and pour a drink, wincing at the various bruises and scrapes as I sit, the healing potion I took at the scene only getting me patched up enough to make it home.

I let the liquor pool in my belly, sending warmth through my body. Wishing I had the same regenerative healing as the Fae, I stand, gingerly, to rummage through my potions room off the side of the kitchen. Finding the bottle that I need, I make my way through the dark house to the massive bathroom off my bedroom. I run bathwater as cold as I can stand it, pouring in the potion vial at the end. Undressed, I slip inside the icy water, the healing properties of the potion working its magic. The short stool next to the tub holds my thigh sheath and remaining weapons, a good idea to keep those close. I sigh as I rest my head against the tub wall and take another sip from my glass, pondering the events of the evening.

Once the healing potion has worked its magic, I towel off as quickly as I can, dressing in warm leggings and a loose-fitting sweater. As I leave the bedroom, I hear a vibration from the other room. My phone is buzzing. I pad silently into the kitchen, pick up the phone, and see the screen lit up with Donovan Barlowe's name. My throat goes dry. I drop the phone on the counter as if it is on fire.

My thoughts whirl, playing out different scenarios. Does he know I put a tracker on him? Does he know I am the one who is responsible for the five souls down below the rally, given to the dark creatures?

Before I can run through all the options, the phone stops ringing and a voicemail popped up. I click the speaker and hear Donovan's silky voice. "Darling Noreen, I was hoping to catch you. I needed an extra vial of the headache potion. My head is killing me. Please come by at your earliest convenience."

I close my eyes and cross my arms over my chest, wondering if it is a ploy. I rub my arms, wincing when I feel the blade cut across my upper arm. No amount of healing tonics will heal that wound. It will heal as slowly as a human.

I turn my back on the island and open the fridge. Before I can decide what to eat, my phone rings again. I reach for the phone, click the green button and say, "Hello?"

Donovan Barlowe's voice comes through the speaker, sounding more agitated. "Noreen, did you get my message? I am in desperate need of a tonic. Would you mind popping over here?"

I clear my throat, saying, "Donovan, that is not possible. You know not to call me off hours. I can come by your office in town tomorrow, but right now it's five in the morning."

Donovan sighs into the phone, "What if I come to you? It will only be a few minutes." I see a second incoming call from the burner phone sitting on the counter. It vibrates with Caleb's number.

I say, "Sorry Donovan. It's not a good time. I will call you tomorrow." I end the call and let out a breath, picking up the burner phone and flipping it open.

I hear ragged breathing, sounding like someone is running. I say, "Hello?"

Caleb's voice comes over the speaker mid-run, he yells, "They followed us. Theon and I fought one group off, but they probably will be coming for you next. Stay in your house. We are almost there."

Alarmed, I say, "Yes, OK, I got a call from Barlowe, the client I bugged. I think he's on his way over here."

Suddenly, I hear a loud crash, like a wrecking ball hitting the house. I rush forward toward the front door and peek out the curtains to the front driveway where I park my car underground. All I can see is a giant crater in the Earth. The only way through wards is blunt force.

I yell into the phone, "They breached my wards. Hurry!"

Slipping the phone into my pocket, I run toward my closet, pulling on my leather boots and jacket. I reach into the pockets, feeling for the weapons and potion vials I keep loaded.

I take a deep breath, exhaling silently as I walk through the house, heading for the front doorway. I drop one of my shadow vials at the entrance and then head to the back doorway, doing the same. I crouch down under the kitchen island, silent, straining to hear any movement.

A voice comes through the shadows. "Noooooorrrreeeeen... I tried to do this the easy way. I don't want to see you get hurt." I hear

Donovan's smooth drawl filter through the room. I hold my breath, trying to gauge where he is. It sounds like from the bedroom. "My boss wanted you dead. I convinced him you would be an asset if you would hear me out."

I can hear him getting closer to the kitchen. I maneuver myself silently around the island and through the front living room. I flatten myself against the wall, barely breathing.

Donovan continues from the kitchen, "When he found the tracking device in my coat..." He lets out a low chuckle. "That was clever by the way. When he found the tracker, I told him I thought it was you. I told him we've known each other for years, that you would see why this movement is so essential."

I silently walk down the hallway, heading back toward the main entrance, grateful that Barlowe's chatter seems to have dried up, each word making me sick to my stomach. I reach the end of the walkway, and as I am going to make a run for the door, I am yanked backward, a fist in my hair and a knife to my throat. I let out an involuntary gasp as I look up into Barlowe's crazed eyes.

He smiles at me, saying, "I told him we could finally be together, no more excuses." He leans down closer. "Finally, after all this time."

I slowly lift a vial from my jacket, tilting my palm until the powder is released. I press myself into him and whisper back, "Not a chance in hell..." He pulls back, surprise on his face. I raise my palm to my lips and blow the death powder gently into his face. His features go slack, and his body collapses to the ground. Involuntary spasms cause his limbs to twitch, and then the movement finally stops.

I lean against the entrance to my home, my heart pounding. I take one step back and then another, heading toward my front steps and freedom.

I hear footsteps pounding toward me. Caleb and Theon are running up the long driveway. I stagger out of the shadows still blanketing my doorway and wave to them an all-clear.

Theon says, "I will check the perimeter for any others."

I see a four-by-four SUV screeching to a halt. Brenen climbs out. He shouts, as he looks around, "All clear?"

Theon returns from around the back of the house, dried blood on his face, saying, "All clear."

Brenen says, "The calvary is on the way. An explosion this close to the city will attract attention. Caleb, Theon, you head to the safe house. We will meet you there after our interviews with the police. We can pass this off as a gas explosion, isolated to the garage, no casualties. This should be wrapped up in a few hours, and we will meet you at the safe house."

Caleb walks toward the entrance, finding the body of Donovan Barlowe. He says to Brenen, "How do you explain the body?"

Brenen answers with a grin, "I will put him at the bottom of a ravine. No one will ever find him." Brenen picks up the body. As I look at it, my only regret is that he did not suffer more.

Brenen disappears, gone for a moment and then returns, less one Donovan Barlowe. He wipes his hands on his jeans, turns to Caleb and Theon, saying, "You guys need to get outta here."

Caleb turns toward me and asks, "Are you OK?" He looks me up and down in concern.

"I'm fine, a little rattled, but otherwise fine." I sigh and push my hair out of my face. "I wish I could have made him suffer. He wanted me to join his cause." I let the disdain, fear, and anger I feel come through.

Theon says to Caleb, "Remind me to never piss her off." That makes Caleb grin as he looks me over.

He crushes me to his chest, saying in my ear, "I'm glad you are okay."

Caleb turns, and they climb into the SUV. Their tires screech around the corner. As their taillights fade, I see red and white sirens pulling up my driveway.

I look over at Brenen and say, "Get ready for the performance of a lifetime." He gives me one solitary nod, and we face the music.

FORTY-ONE

Sophia—Creature Horde

t's been three grueling hours on horseback through the treacherous terrain. Our horses must have nerves of steel. I know my knees are shaky on the steep declines, but it seems like second nature to them. I reach down and pet Pearl's mane. My mare's name suits her coloring perfectly. I murmur to her softly how good a job she has done as I pull out my last carrot, and she munches on it happily. As we approach the river, I dismount, and she drinks the cool water.

I sigh in relief to be off her back.

This brief repose is needed for the horses and for me. The rest of the group seems like they could keep going forever. I, however, am sore in places I forgot I could be sore in. My thighs are burning, and my back is sore despite my rapid healing. I kneel and fill my canteen in the swiftly moving water. I try to focus on anything but my sore muscles and the male aggressive tension in the air. Three hours and the strained silence is almost my undoing.

At the beginning of our trek through the mountains I tried some light conversation, which was quickly shot down with one-word answers and glowering looks between the males. Ryker and I may have gotten off to a rocky start, but Ethen and Kane seem to have a level of aggression that points toward a history I am in the dark about.

Ryker joins me at the riverbank, filling up his canteen. I seize the opportunity and say, "Do dragons patrol this area?" We are on the very edge of Dragon Lands. If he has any useful information, it could help our search.

I get a glance and another one-word answer. "No." He starts to turn back toward the bank.

I stop him with a hand on his forearm. "Look, if you want to truly help solve the murders, we need to find a way to communicate." I sigh heavily and continue, "I know we had a rocky start. Let's start over." I stand and dust off my leathers. "I am here because my sister was murdered during an attack on our outpost a year ago. I will do anything to catch her murder, to avenge her death."

Ryker's hard glare is upon my face, but I see a flicker of understanding loss. Inspired, I continue, "Even if you were ordered to be here, Duncan was murdered as well. If we work together, we can hope to avenge these deaths." I hold my breath, hoping for a positive reaction.

Ryker stands to his full height, towering over me by at least a foot. He looks down and reaches for my hand, his thumb brushing against the tattoo at my wrist.

My breath catches at the sensation, our eyes connect, and I can't help the small shiver down my spine despite the warmth of the late-afternoon sun. He gives me one nod but not another word. He turns and walks back toward his horse.

I blow out an exasperated breath and turn back to Pearl with a few explicit words mumbled under my breath. Suddenly, I hear a whistle from the edge of the forest. I turn, and Ethen motions toward Ryker, whose attention seemed to be caught. I can see his back retreating into the forest. I quickly follow, wondering what could have tripped Ryker's senses.

Ethen puts his hand on my shoulder. "Maybe you should hold back."

I give him a look that speaks volumes, wrench my arm away, and say, "Don't worry about me. I can take care of myself." I follow Ryker into the deep undergrowth, Ethen and Kane at my heels. I spread out my senses and feel nothing unusual in the surrounding area.

Ryker abruptly stops and stares down a chasm in the mountain side. I inch forward until my arm brushes his side, peer down into the depths of the Earth, and let out a breath I didn't realize I was holding. Deep below is a withering mass of dark creatures. They appeared trapped in the Earth, continually fighting to get out.

As we watch, I see one rise and appear to be struck back down by an invisible force. I back away slightly and motion to the group. There, at the mouth of the crevasse in the mountain, it appears there is an entrance accessible by foot.

I say, "Let's go back for the horses and make our way to the entrance. I want to see the relic up close that is holding the horde hostage."

Ethen shakes his head. "It's not a good idea. We should go back to Mystfort and gather reinforcements."

I turn and look at Ethen, who seems unsurprised by the horde and unwilling to approach. Before I could respond with my concerns, Ryker says, "Why? This is still Dragon Lands. No one else is permitted. We will go and scout it out, and I can give this information to Draco."

The familiar rage passes over Ethen's features, and once again it seems he is having trouble containing his anger.

He finally turns toward the horses and says, "Fine, let's go."

We loop back around and head down the rocky mountainside toward the entrance. Once down on the valley floor, we tie up our horses and approach the cave with caution.

Standing at the flat dirt entrance to the cave, I look to my left and to my right. Towering sheer stones line either side of this narrow passage that bottlenecks before opening into the cave where the horde is corralled. Straight in the center, a lone staff is situated, seemingly protecting the entrance. We approach slowly, cautiously.

Wanting to know what kind of magic protects the horde from not only escaping but from anyone else finding it, I inch one foot in front of the other. Ten feet away, I can make out the details of the beautifully molded golden staff, intricately carved with an emerald the size of my thumb in the center eye. This staff was clearly left in place to guard the entrance. This must have be the source of the dark creature's invisible prison.

Suddenly, I feel magic wash over me. I turn and start to retreat. My feet feel like they are stuck in quicksand. I have a sudden undeniable urge to get as far away from the horde as possible. I shake my head slightly, trying to dispel the magic but unable to break its hold. The best I can do is not move at all. I look to my right. There is Ethen and Kane with the same compulsion. All three of us freeze in a state of mind over magic. Our minds tell us to move forward, the magic pushing us away.

Ryker appraises us in confusion. He turns and looks at the staff that is in the center of the entrance, cocking his head to the side. He slowly walks forward and places his hand about a foot away from the staff, testing its energy. "This is a repelling compulsion, guarding the horde from any who come across it."

I look over at Ethen and remember the groups of patrol units that mysteriously asked for transfers and left the area. This compulsion must have affected them to the point they could not get far enough away.

I mutter, "How do we break this compulsion?"

Before anyone can answer, I hear a loud crack, look over at Ryker, and see he has ripped the staff from the earth. He takes the golden rod and starts to crush it between his hands. One hand on either end of the staff, he pushes them together as if he were crushing a soda can. He scoops his hands and holds on to the golden powder that remains, plucking an emerald from the center. He blows the gold from his fingertips, and it catches in the wind.

My mouth hinges open, and I stare at him. "That was a priceless artifact," I hiss in Ryker's direction, my outrage tempered by the fact that I can now control my body's movements.

I swing toward Ryker. Before I can say another word, I hear a faint rumbling, the ground vibrating. Loose pebbles on the dirt path start to move. My eyes peer into the depths of the cavern, and suddenly the horde is released. I flatten my back against the nearest boulder as the winged creatures spill past us. I see Ethen and Kane on the opposite side of the passage, also seeking refuge against the rocks.

My eyes look for Ryker. There in the sky, his wings furiously beat against the late-afternoon sky. A loud roar is released, and fire scorches the Earth, a line of flames from the beginning of the passage, as far back as the opening allows. The loud screeching from the dark creatures erupts. The smell of burning flesh invades my senses.

Fire only temporarily slowed the massive outpouring. As soon as the flames die out, the flow of creatures simply continues.

I hear a bellow from Ryker above, "When I create the opening, run!" Another line of flames erupt from Ryker's mouth. I turn and force my feet into action.

Ethen, Kane, and I run as fast as the wind. My feet a blur of motion, tree limbs thrashing across my body, I can feel the cuts sting my cheeks and brow.

I veer off to the left, out of the stampede path. I lean against a huge tree trunk, my breathing labored. To my right, the horde keeps running, some of the creatures attempting flight, but their strength is waning. To my left, I hear the crashing waterfall as it drops off a sheer cliff.

Ryker lands next to me in the small clearing, saying hurriedly, "Climb on. I will carry you out."

I look at him and say with short breath, "What about Ethen and Kane?"

He snorts, "You only get the offer because of our mark—"

Dark creatures swarm the small clearing we are in. I sweep out my sword in one hand, the double-edged axe in the other. I strike down one, two, three creatures.

Ryker has made quick work of the rest and turns toward me, "Now, can we—"

My vision doubles, I can see in my foresight two more creatures which flank Ryker, tearing into him. My breath catches. Unaware of what is to come, Ryker is flanked, the creatures only feet away from his back.

Pulling my depleted reserves of power from deep within me, I raise my hands and freeze the clearing. I run directly at Ryker, sword drawn in one hand, axe in the other, knowing my depleted magic will hold for only a moment.

The time warp unfreezes, and Ryker's confused expression at my attack would be humorous in a different situation.

I swing directly over his shoulder, one creature down, then swing right to take out the second creature in one fluid motion. I pivot and sheath the weapons at my back, rather pleased with myself.

I turn, giving Ryker a cocky grin. I am ready to rub in the fact I saved him. Yet again.

My swagger is short lived, however, because the moment our eyes lock, the earth starts to crumble under my feet.

I see him reach for me, then in a split second I tumble down the side of the mountain, the waterfall only a few feet from me. I desperately reach to grab a hold of anything to keep me on the mountainside. My hands find the protruding trunk of a tree that slips out of my grasp.

At the last moment, I reach out and grip a ledge on the side of the mountain, holding on by my fingertips. I can feel my fingers slipping against the loose dirt and water, I glance down at the rugged rocks below and make one final lifesaving maneuver.

Pushing my weight with all my momentum toward the water as my fingers lose their grip. I feel the water as it engulfs me, pulling me down.

I sink deep into the pool at the base of the fall, and then a sharp crack is felt as my head hits the side of a boulder. The last image I have is staring up out of the churning water, seeing the fiercely beating wings of an emerald-green dragon.

The world turns white as a glow engulfs me, and my mind drifts into a peaceful slumber.

FORTY-TWO

Gael—Throne Room, Dark Creatures, and Power

stare out the window, impatiently drumming my fingers on the ledge, looking at my watch for the hundredth time. The little glowing clock face shows one minute has passed. Now it reads 2:53 a.m.

I let out a sigh and roll my neck front and back, side to side, in anticipation. I stretch out my arms, not knowing really what to expect from our upcoming adventure. Sneaking through the school was never on my agenda when I started training.

Black leggings, black long-sleeve hoodie, and black sneakers complete my outfit. My blonde hair is braided. I raise my hood to cover the bright locks that would shine in the dark corridors.

I hear a knock at the door and rush to open it, seeing Logan standing in the hallway. I welcome him into my room, saying in a low voice, "Glad you knocked this time."

I start pacing in nervousness while Logan sprawls out on my bed.

I look over at him and say, "Make yourself at home."

He gives me a grin. "Thanks." He pulls a knife from a sheath at his thigh and starts to toss it in the air, gripping the blade as he catches it on its downward spiral.

"Why do you need a weapon?" Sure, we used weapons during our training, but I have none to my name, aside from the small dagger Bennett gave me.

Logan sits up, unbuckles the thigh sheath, and hands it to me. "It's yours if you want it. I've got a backup." At my blank look, he says, "Never know what you're going to come across when you're sneaking around where you shouldn't be."

I buckle the sheath to my thigh, saying, "Thank you." The knife is well balanced and beautifully crafted. Before I can ask where he got it, I hear a soft knock at the door. I swing it open to see Ari in the hallway. Caden Emery and Gavin Pierce are standing behind her.

My mouth drops open, and I whisper, "What are they doing here?"

Ari gives me a little smile. "Are you going to make me explain in the hall?" I roll my eyes and let the group into my small room.

I cross my arms over my chest. "What happened?"

Ari says, "Gavin was over, and I told him he couldn't spend the night." Ari's cheeks turn red, and I realize I have been so checked out that I never realized Ari and Gavin had become a thing. "Anyways, I'm such a bad liar. He got the truth out of me and insisted that he come, and Caden is his best friend..."

I roll my eyes and say, "Three people were going to be hard to sneak through the castle. Now we have five."

Logan interrupts, "I can conceal five people in shadows if necessary." He has pulled out a second dagger and is doing his throw and catch routine, still on my bed.

Caden looks doubtful. "Now is not the time to overestimate your abilities."

Logan stands, and shadows move from him toward the ceiling, eventually covering the whole room in shadow. I hold out my hand, not able to see it in the darkness. Logan releases the shadows. Light spills in once more.

I look over and say a little shaky, "Only do that if you have to." He gives me a grin, "Sure."

I continue, looking at the group, "Well, now we know we can escape undetected. The plan is to move toward the main keep. There is an entrance into the old servants' tunnels through the kitchen. Once we are in the tunnels, Logan knows how to get to the west wing where we think the abandoned throne room is."

I look at the group before me and say, "Look, I roped Logan and Ari to go with me. Caden and Gavin, you don't have to come."

They look at each other, and then Gavin says, "Ari is going with you whether I like it or not. I'd rather be there if something goes wrong."

He looks at Caden, who says, "Don't look at me. I'm along for the ride."

I nod. "Okay, let's get going." As we leave my room, I hand out flashlights to the group. "Ari, you and Gavin share. Logan and I will share the last one."

We head down toward the great hall, the hallways dead quiet this time of night. Silently, we sneak into the kitchens. Logan leads us to a huge walk-in pantry. He lifts a rug, and beneath it is a hatch that has a set of stairs down into the Earth. He starts down the stairs and clicks on an overhead light. There are old wooden shelves with abandoned jars and crates.

Logan says, "I think they used to use this as a cold storage room." I nod and remember the castle was built long before modern electricity and refrigeration. We walk toward the end of the small underground root cellar.

Gavin says, "There's nothing down here."

Logan smiles as he pulls a shelf to the side, and there is a secret entrance that disappears into darkness. I look over and see Gavin, who looks interested for the first time since our adventure started.

I click on my flashlight and follow Logan into the dark tunnels. I shine the light up and down the walls getting a feel for space. At one point, this must have been lit by torches, metal brackets lined the stone walls. As we walk, the fine dirt beneath our feet billows into a cloud of dust.

I raise my shirt to cover my nose and mouth, saying, "Step carefully so the dust is not so bad."

I am grateful that Logan knows where he is going. I would be lost in a few minutes, winding left and then right and then left again. Finally, we end up on a set of stairs going up into the west wing of the castle. At the top of the stairs, we find ourselves in a utility closet.

Logan says, "From here on, if we get caught, we are most definitely suspended."

Logan cracks the door open and motions that the coast is clear. We walk, hugging the edge of the corridor until we reach a doorway that Logan pauses at. He places his finger to his lips in a universal signal for silence.

This room appears to be a war room. A wide central display map dominates the middle of the space. Idyll is laid out with markers showing where we were, creature movements, and the other sectors. The walls are lined with paintings of Fae, who I only knew by the little golden labels under each of the frames. Mostly generals and commanders who have led this sector over the years since the barrier was put into place.

I take in the surroundings, but my gaze is focused on the painting at the end of the room, drawing me like a moth to a flame. Great Queen Morrigan presides over the room in her sovereign regal appearance, a crown upon her head, an elaborate jeweled necklace at her throat, sword in her right hand. My eyes are drawn to the engraved box on the table next to the queen, the engravings glowing iridescently.

This painting has haunted my dreams for a week.

I approach slowly as if I expected something to come out and grab us. Logan, Ari, Caden, and Gavin hang back as I peer at the Great Queen's face and then focus on the glowing box emanating fire within.

Logan clears his throat. "We better get a move on. The longer we wait here, the better the chance we may be caught." He looks around the room and back to the door we went through.

My gaze snaps to his, and I nod. I reach to the right of the painting, saying, "I think there is an entrance behind..."

As I run my fingers against the back of the frame, I feel a button. I press it down and hear a faint click. The frame moves from the wall as if on a hinge, and a doorway presents itself behind the painting.

Gavin says, "I didn't really believe we would find anything."

I grip my flashlight and click it on, peering inside the room. I see a familiar set of winding stone steps heading down. I glance behind me and ask, "You guys ready?"

We start to descend the winding staircase beneath the castle.

Dampness surrounds us, and I feel a chill that was not there on the main level. I hear the painting click closed, and the light from the war room is snuffed out, pitching us into total blackness.

Near the end of the stairs, the room is a dark inky black. I shine the flashlight on the walls and see a torch, covered in webs. I focus my energy and create a small flicker of fire in my palm and transfer it to a torch.

I light a second torch and hand it to Logan, saying, "Light the others on this wall. I will start over here." The dim flickering throws an eerie light across the space. As each new torch is lit, the room finally comes into focus.

It is exactly as it was shown in my dreams. A long hallway, lined with stained glass windows shining nowhere, the entire room enclosed with stones. Logan asks, "Why would they entomb this place?"

Gavin answers, "Once they knew the queen wasn't returning, they must have sealed her throne room away, out of sight."

I see Ari across the room, looking at a long table strewn with jewels and priceless artifacts. I approach saying, "This must be an offering to her, long forgotten." I pick up a beautiful necklace encrusted with gems. My thumb removes the grime from its surface, revealing the beauty underneath, glinting in the torchlight.

Right in the center of this table is the box I touched in my dream. Strangely, the rest of the items in the room are covered in inches of dust. All except for this box, which shines brightly, not a speck of dirt on its surface.

The box, out of place in this forgotten tomb, seemingly draws me to its power. The rest of the items were left here, forgotten, ages ago.

When I touched the box in my dream, the world splintered into a hundred pieces. My mind spirals, wondering what will happen in real life.

Ari comes and stands at my shoulder. "Is that the box you saw in your dream?"

I simply nod.

She says, "We shouldn't be down here longer than necessary. Why don't you take it with you to unravel its secrets in our nice warm dorm room?"

She turns and walks toward the second table, laden with ancient weapons. I can see jeweled necklaces around her neck and smile slightly.

I take a deep breath and reach for the box, the beautiful blue-white flames illuminating the etchings on the top. My fingers reach one inch, two inches. It feels like I am pushing through molasses. The tips of my fingers brush the very top of the box, and I feel the binding within me break wide open. Brilliant blue-white light shines as the power is released. I feel it vibrating from my toes to the crown of my head. Then as suddenly as it came on, the light dissipates, and I am left in the silence of the tomb.

I look around, and Logan, Gavin, Caden, and Ari look at me as if I grew a second head. Ari rushes up and says, "What was that?"

I look at her with wide eyes, and say, "I'm not sure, but it feels like somehow my binding was broken."

Ari's eyes grow wide, and she goes from excited to worried in a heartbeat. "How—"

There's a low bang from above, we hear shouts, and the alarm starts to wail into the night.

I look at the group and say, "Something is happening."

I scoop up the box and put it in my bag, rush toward the nearest torch and extinguish it, yelling, "Put out the torches. We need to move toward the castle."

We rush up the winding staircase, exiting through the painting, the war room thankfully still empty. We close the secret door, heading toward the main entryway leading to the hall. I open it a crack, only to discover the hallways full of warriors, all of whom are armed to the teeth and rushing toward the main entry leading to the great hall.

I close the door and lean against the wall. "Warriors, armed, running for the front entrance."

Ari says, "Let's get out of here, and once we are in the main castle, we can figure out what is going on."

I nod, and our small group slips out the doorway, blending in with the crowd of people exiting the west wing.

We follow the crowd, running side by side, winding through the hallways toward the front entry to the castle. We turn the corner and suddenly are outside on the main stairs, in the same location Logan and I met only a few days ago.

We emerge on the front steps of the castle. I stop short, staring at the wreckage of the once peaceful grounds. Dark creatures have infiltrated the grounds, warriors running toward the gates trying to secure the breach, shouting commands. Fighting takes place every few feet, the ground littered with dark creatures and warriors alike. I peer beyond the fighting and see Mystvillage in the distance, overrun with darkness.

Suddenly out of the corner of my eye, a dark creature flies directly over us and attacks a warrior to my right. He cuts down the creature with one mighty stroke of his broadsword then runs directly at the main gate that is overflowing with creatures. The entire grounds are in chaos. The loud shrieks of creatures mixed with the shouts of warriors are deafening.

Logan shouts, "We need to get to the armory—"

Two more creatures drop down right in front of us. They widen their leathery wings and let out a shriek that rattles the windows behind us.

Logan says, maybe a little nervously, "Just like old times."

I may have laughed if I wasn't busy trying to rein in my erratic breathing. Collectively, the five of us take a step back. This is almost the exact same situation as our selection test. This time, the threat is most definitely real, and we are ill-prepared, magic our only true defense.

I reach for Logan's arm. "Back up, slowly." Ari, Caden, and Gavin are behind us. As calmly as I can, keeping my body still, I say to the group, "Go, get to the armory. I can distract these two long enough for you to get by."

Ari says, "Not a chance I'm leaving you—"

A third dark creature lands behind us, circling us like prey. I breathe deep. As the dark creatures lets loose loud shrieks that vibrate the ground, I take a step backward, my back now brushing the others. We are trapped.

I reach down and grasp Ari's hand. "We go down fighting." Our eyes meet. I lift my palms, and fire erupts in my hands, I take one step toward the closest creature. Suddenly, Orian is at my side. He lunges directly at the closest beast, capturing it by the throat. Loud snarls are heard as I see him thrashing right and left.

I have no time to focus on Orian as the other two creatures attack. Logan turns into shadows, and I let my power flow out my fingers. Not needing a flame to start, more power than I ever had before free flows from my palms with no hindrance of a binding. I feel an exhilaration I never felt before, knowing this is how my power is supposed to feel, free and unencumbered.

I whip lassos of fire around both creatures, and they dissolve into ash. Pulling the power back toward me, I pause with flames in my palms, looking out over the castle grounds for my next targets. The power within me is so euphoric, and all I can think of is how I want to set it free. Giving the power free rein, I feel it pooling under my feet, swirling, lifting me up off the ground.

With this vantage point, I have a bird's eye view of the dark creatures swarming the castle. I reach out with my mind, targeting the creatures closest to me. I reach deep. Bluish-white light extends from my fingers, pulsing in its brightness. I direct this energy out in tendrils toward each of these dark creatures. In a pulse of light, these creatures are turned to ash. I target the next group of creatures, and in a second pulse of light the next group of creatures turns to ash. I make my way across the Bailey. With each pulse of power, another group of creatures is destroyed.

The light seems to attract the horde. More and more creatures approach, until they are climbing over themselves trying to reach the brilliant bluish-white light that surrounds me.

The horde seems endless, my progress toward the gate halted as I am overcome with their snarling bodies. More and more keep coming, climbing, surrounding me until not an ounce of light is visible. Kneeling down, I dig deep into my power and feel it ebb and flow through my mind like quicksilver. I let the power build, and then I feed the embers with a breath, fanning the flame.

As I exhale, I lift my palms and push the power out, away from me as hard as I can, screaming in the effort. As the power explodes outward, my body crumbles, and I collapse in the aftermath, breathing heavy.

I crack open my eyes and see ash raining down from the sky, blanketing the ground. Not a single dark creature in the vicinity. I peer through the wreckage and spot Ari across the bailey.

Tears trickle down my cheeks. My power is pooling down deep in my belly, joyful at being used, at being free for the first time.

Suddenly I feel the ember's lightning once more, asking for more. More power, more destruction. This wave of power entices me to continue, to burn it all to the ground. It becomes a roar in my veins, wanting to be let loose. Flames erupt again from my palms, and I start to stand.

Suddenly, Ari's face is in front of me. She's talking, but I can't hear her over the roar in my head. Slowly, her voice comes into focus, and she's screaming at me.

"Gael, control the power. Do not let the power control you."

I take a deep breath of air and let the power go, shoving my hands deep into the earth, snuffing the embers, screaming in my disappointment. Tears stream down my face. Ari wraps her arms around me and holds me as I fall to pieces.

Sobs rack my body as I fight off the desperate need to keep the fire burning. Orian comes and sits next to me. He licks my tears one more time, and I hiccup a small laugh as I turn my face toward him.

I say, "Thank you for saving me." I get a wet slobbery kiss in return.

Sitting in the rubble of my own making, I hold out my hands, flipping them over so that the palms face up. The power that was released almost took over, overwhelming me with its sudden influx. I remember the warnings given this past week, and my hands started to shake.

Grasping them together, I start to rock slowly back and forth, terrified of this power within me.

FORTY-THREE

Sophia—Testing Bonds

The first thing I notice as my eyes crack open is the warmth at my back and the smell of burning wood. I sit up abruptly and then promptly lie back where I was. My screaming head pounds as if it has a life of its own. Through the throbbing ache, I squint to get my bearings on where I am.

The last thing I remember is Ryker's large wings beating against the blue sky as I stare up at him through the churning water.

I glance around. I am in a cave, deep in a mountainside. In front of me is a roaring fire keeping the autumn chill out of the air. Behind me is a wall of muscle. I glance back, and sure enough Ryker is looking down at me in slight concern. I breathe deep and am engulfed in his sharp, spicy scent. The intoxicating smell has me leaning in slightly. No one should smell this good after the day we had.

I ask, "What happened? What happened to Ethen and Kane?"

Ryker's amber eyes look down at me, and his light-brown hair falls over his forehead. He says, "You hit your head on a rock. You were unconscious. I pulled you out of the water and brought you to this cave to recover. You were going into shock from the cold." He motions toward the fire in way of explanation. "Your amulet protected you from most of the damage. If it did not, you would still be at the bottom of the waterfall."

I place my hand on the necklace, thankful that it was there when I needed it. That must have been the brilliant white glow I remember right before passing out. I look around the rest of the cave and see Pearl tied up at the edge. It is her saddle blanket covering us.

Seeing where my eyes land, Ryker says, "Pearl found us after I had made the fire. She's a smart and resourceful mare." I see clothes strung up on the edge of the fire and realize I must be naked under the blanket.

Never one to be particularly modest, it was, however, slightly embarrassing due to our tenuous relationship. Ryker says, "Ethen and Kane made it out of the horde and found refuge on the other side of the river."

I ask, "Why did we not meet up with them?"

He lets out a long sigh, "Your immediate needs outweighed tracking down those two. You were going into shock. I had to act quickly."

"How long was I out?"

Ryker looks at the fire. "A few hours."

I look away, unnerved. Being at Ryker's mercy, vulnerable and unconscious for hours while he saved my life, seem like he earned his mark back. I look out the mouth of the cave. Darkness has fallen, and it would be too dangerous to try and make the journey back to Mystfort until sunrise.

I say lightly, "I suppose you earned your mark back. How does that work after the fact?" I feel Ryker shift, and he rises from the folds of the blanket. He strides across the cave as if being naked is as normal as breathing, which for him could very well be.

Feeling the absence of his warmth, I shiver slightly. He himself was the flame when he was at my back. I watched him pull on his breeches and had to squash a little disappointment that flared to life. Going to Pearl's saddlebag, he takes the spare set of clothes I packed that morning, which seems like a lifetime ago. Ryker returns and hands the clothes to me and turns away to tend the fire, giving me a bit of privacy.

I tentatively sit upright and pull on a loose-fitting cotton shirt, hoping my leather uniform will dry overnight. I reach up to my hair, still in its tight braid and still saturated with river water. I undo the braid and run my fingers through my hair. The heat from the fire should dry it quickly. I wrap the blanket around my shoulders and draw my knees up and rest my chin on them, staring at the fire.

I say, "Thank you, Ryker, for saving my life. I guess I have to give you back your mark." I glance down at the beautiful iridescent-green dragon tattooed across my wrist. It seems to glow in the shimmering firelight. It is so lovely. I am surprised at how sad I am to see it go.

A shadow crosses his face, as if the idea of me returning my mark is upsetting. He turns toward me. "Do you want to return it?" Not knowing how to answer, I realize the truth is that I do not want to let go of the warmth I feel every time I passed my thumb over the tattoo.

Ryker adds, "You saved my life again, the second time today, in the clearing. The mark stands, as we have both saved each other this afternoon."

I slowly retract my arm and tuck my hands under the folds of the blanket for warmth. My shivers have returned, and I scoot closer to the fire. Ryker lets out a sigh and moves to settle down behind me. I look at him in confusion.

He says, "I can hear your teeth chattering across the cave. If we are ever going to get some sleep, you need to get warm."

I can feel my cheeks heat in embarrassment. "I'll be fine," I say as I scoot even closer to the fire.

Ryker lets out a snort, "Yeah, I'm sure you would be, but I would lose my mind hearing the chattering all night."

He sits behind me and wraps his arms around my shoulders, my body stiff as a board. "Will you relax? I'm not going to take advantage of you in the middle of a cave, with a head injury and Pearl looking at us so intently."

I laugh and look over at Pearl, who has her eyes fixed on us as if tracking every movement. The tension eases a bit. I relax in his arms, and we end up in the same position I woke up in earlier.

"Tell me something about yourself, Ryker." That request is met with silence. He shifts his weight as if to get up. I stop him with a hand to his arm. "It doesn't have to be some big, bad secret. It could be anything, something small. You could start by telling me about the animosity between you, Ethen, and Kane."

He shifts slightly, tucking me in close as my shivers had returned.

Then, to my surprise, he responds, "I was Yaz's second in command when he was challenged by Draco. When Draco won, Yaz fell into disgrace, and by association so did I. The last hundred years built some, *animosity*, between Kane and I." Ryker looks down at me, the firelight turning his hair a golden hue. "Kane has hated Yaz and me since Yaz banned his bonding mark five hundred years ago.

"Now, of course, Ethen's loyalty is to Draco. Which means Yaz, and by association me, is seen as the enemy. Together, Ethen and Kane's dislike of me has grown over the past months of Ethen arriving." He shrugs slightly, as if it were inevitable and really beneath his concern.

I nod and murmur with a slight smile up at him, "I don't know. It could be your charming demeanor." I get a disgruntled grunt in response, and Ryker falls back into silence.

I look down and realize I have been absentmindedly running my thumb over the small tattoo at the base of my wrist. I halt my motion and glance up at Ryker, who is staring at me, eyes suddenly hooded.

I ask, "Why did you do it?" I clear my throat and clarify, "Why did you allow a mark?"

There is a long pause, and the tension returns. When I think he won't respond, he says, "The main reason I am now loyal to Draco is because I desire a bonded rider." He picks up my wrist and rubs his thumb over the mark. A shiver runs down my spine. "It is rare to find a Fae who would match well with a dragon. Before the gates closed, we were free to let fate take the reins and lead us to our bonded match. Even then, it was difficult to find the one person who would complement each one's powers, to allow them to mold and intertwine into one.

"This bond was highly coveted by dragons and Fae alike." He sighs and releases my arm. I feel the loss of the warmth that has spread through me and have an uncanny urge to return his hand.

"Since the loss and grief after the war, a veil of distrust and hurt blind most to what once was. When Draco took command, I asked him if I served faithfully, if he would allow nominees to be introduced." He looks down and then focuses on the fire. "The nominees that the council sends are Fae who are vastly unqualified. Most have been born into their positions and are so ill equipped that it repels our dragon half. Most, if not all, are ill suited to the bond and shouldn't waste their time."

When he pauses, I look up at him and ask, "So you thought I would be worthy? Why?"

Ryker says simply, "I felt your power, and it drew me to you. I know Draco felt it as well. Even Yaz seemed to notice through his rage."

I think about the few times I thought the dragons were smelling me. Ryker is still staring into the fire. I motion to my tattoo. "So this mark is the first step in the bonding process?"

Ryker looks down at me. "It is a gift, a promise to save a life. Once you have the mark, I will save you no matter the cost." He stares into the fire. "Also, it is a way to test compatibility. Only worthy nominees would be able to accept the mark. Non-worthy nominees would be overcome by the magic and perish."

I shake my head slightly, this conversation confirming my suspicions on how serious the decision I made back on the banks of the river was. My gut instinct was to accept the mark. I am hoping I did not make a mistake.

I ask, "So what is the second stage of the bonding process?"

Ryker picks up my wrist once more, the tattoo glinting in the fire-light. "The second mark is also a gift, a promise from you to save my life, no matter the cost. The third mark binds us together, intertwining our life forces. When one parishes, so does the other."

"This binding, it strengthens each other's power?"

Ryker nods. "Sharing of power is one of the best ways to test how a full binding would affect each party involved." I look back at the fire, wondering what that would be like.

Ryker says, perhaps slightly uncertain, "If you are open to testing the power dynamic, we can, once you are recovered."

"It's a lot to think about."

I tuck the blanket in close to my chin and stare into the fire. I feel my body's fatigue as if it is an actual weight around my neck. I settle into the silence that follows, my thoughts a whirlwind in my mind. Unable to focus on any one revelation, I allow my mind to drift into nothingness. With the crackling fire and the warmth at my back, I can feel my exhaustion as it overtakes me and my heavy eyes close.

Abruptly, I awake and find the masculine pillow at my back is gone. I sit up and look around in alarm, my weapons carelessly strewn by the fire. Ryker is battle ready, looking magnificent in the glowing light of the fire. His breeches low on his hips, his muscles rippling, with a lethal expression on his face. I look toward the entrance and see two shadows approaching. My heart pounds. I calculate how many seconds it would take me to grab my weapons. The figures come into the light, and I can make out Ethen and Kane's features. My tension dissipates in a rush, and I sigh in relief as I sit up fully.

My gaze focuses on Ethen, whose eyes have locked on me. I see disbelief stretch across his features, as he takes in the cozy picture we must make. Ryker and I, both half-undressed, blankets strewn across the small cave, close to the fire. The disbelief on Ethen's face is followed by hurt, and then finally his features settled into hard lines of anger.

Ryker relaxes his stance slightly as Ethen and Kane come closer into the cave. I look outside and see the sky lightening; daybreak is close to hitting the horizon.

Ethen says to me, "I suppose worrying all night was not necessary. You appear to be fine."

I rise to my feet from the folds of the blankets, the sheer soft cotton shirt hitting my upper thighs. This appears to enrage Ethen even further, as his gaze rakes from my unbound hair down to the tips of my toes.

Ethen says in a cold tone he has never used with me before, "We'll wait for you outside. While you dress." He swiftly turns and leaves with Kane.

I let out a heavy sigh and run my fingers through my long hair, which had turned into a tangled mess overnight. I turn toward the fire and reach for my leathers. Thankfully they are dry, and I pull on my leather pants. I glance up and see Ryker appraising me, his arms crossed as he leans against the cave wall.

I snap, "What?"

Ryker shakes his head slightly. "I did not realize you and Ethen were...intimate."

I snort in amusement, "We aren't *intimate*, in the way you think." I shake out my leather top, which thankfully is also dry. I see Ryker still looking at me, so I continue, "There was some attraction, until I realized he was using his beguilement on me."

Ryker raises a brow. "Most don't even know it is happening."

I shrug. "I have a latent power of prophesy. It helps me break any sort of enchantment." I cinch up the laces in the back of my top, trying my best to ignore the conversation.

Ryker moves forward and comes to stand right in front of me. He tilts my chin up with one finger, stopping my movements as I gaze into his golden-brown eyes. I take a sharp inhale breath as his eyes dip down to my lips.

He pauses there for a moment, says to me, "While we still have a moment of privacy, I want to test how our powers would work together."

He leans down and grasps my wrist, sweeping his thumb over the tattoo. "If that's OK with you?"

"How—"

But he presses me against the rough rock wall at my back and leans into my neck. He breathes in deep and runs his lips against my throat, murmuring words I can't decipher. My heartbeat picks up, and I am flooded with his magic that now engulfs us. I can feel it rubbing against my aura, as if asking for permission to enter.

I lower my guard, and his power pours into me. I gasp and clutch his biceps for support, as my legs have turned to jelly. I tilt my head back and lean against the wall as if it is my last lifeline. I let the ebb and flow of the power wash over me in an endless wave of pleasure.

Suddenly, the bliss starts to recede, and in alarm I open my eyes. Where is it going? I strengthen my grip on Ryker and start to pull the power back toward me, wrapping it around me like a blanket I never want to take off. I see Ryker's eye widening in surprise and then turn into dark-green embers that seem to glow from within. The same eyes I have seen staring at me from the form of a dragon.

He crashes his lips down to mine as he presses into me, not an inch of space between us from our lips to our feet. Rational thought long gone, my instinctual response has me running my hands down his chest, my hips rocking into him. His tongue breaks the seal of my lips and brushes against mine. I groan and lean into the kiss, relishing the emotions as they rack my body, the warmth spreading from my fingers down my spine, pooling low in my belly.

Ryker breaks away suddenly. His ragged breath indicates he is as affected by the kiss as I am. He leans his forehead against mine then looks up toward the mouth of the cave. With the slight distance between us, my rational thought returns to my mind, and I focus on the ebb and flow of power I feel coming from a great distance.

Ryker says, "Something is happening."

The power seems to have flooded the landscape, a brilliant light illuminating the sky outside the cave. Our eyes meet, and Ryker releases me, gently holding me upright until my wobbly legs chose to stand on their own.

I bring my fingers to my lips, a slight tremor to my hand. The electricity of that kiss has me forgetting where we are, who is outside waiting for us, and the crazy last twenty-four hours. I shake my head slightly to clear it. I look down at my wrist, and the dragon mark is brightly shimmering, as if it too was affected. Ryker sweeps his thumb over the mark, saying almost to himself, "I have waited so long."

Before I can respond, I hear a loud voice calling our names, "Sophia, there has been an attack! Hurry!"

I push out of the depths of the cave, and we rush to the entrance to see a pure bluish-white glow in the distance, pulsing. In time to the pulses of light, we feel the power rolling through the land. I look over and see Ethen and Kane on their horses, looking in the same direction.

Ethen's haunted eyes meet mine, and I hear him whisper, "Mystfort is under attack."

As suddenly as it began, the magic abruptly ends, the sky returning to the early morning darkness.

Ethen calls, "Meet us at Mystfort." With a flick of his reins, he and Kane disappear into the forest.

Ryker and I hurriedly grabbed our supplies. I slid on my leather knee-high boots, re-sheathed my weapons and looked around to make sure we were not missing anything. Ryker had already snuffed out the fire, and Pearl was loaded up and ready to go. Without a word we walked toward the entrance of the cave.

Right before we reach the edge, Ryker reaches down and lifts my wrist to his lips. Warm breath and the gentle pressure of his lips on the still shimmering tattoo has my heart pounding again.

He leans in close and whispers in my ear, "You will be mine." His gaze drops to my lips, and his eyes return to the dragon's stunning emerald that seems to glow from within. He rubs his thumb over my lips, sighs, and drops his hand.

I mount my horse before saying, "Let's live through the day first."

Ryker mounts, and I nudge Pearl into motion, and we head toward Mystfort as fast as our horses allow on the rugged terrain.

Weak sunlight is breaking over the horizon as my thoughts whirl through my mind. What explosion of power did we see, and was it connected to the horde we accidentally let loose in the mountains? These worries wipe the memories of Ryker's kiss from my mind.

Fear ripples through me as I remember what happened to my sister's outpost, and I nudge Pearl to her limit.

FORTY-FOUR

Caleb—The Informant

Coffee in hand, I stare out the window. Early morning light spills through. I set the cup on the ledge and run my fingers through my dark hair, my features creasing in agitation. I pace the same stretch of wooden floor for at least the hundredth time. It's been three hours since we left Noreen's house. My patience is wearing thin. Theon is perched at the end of the table, leather strap in hand, sharpening his blades in a never-ending pattern.

I keep my eyes on the warn floorboards as images flash through my mind in a constant loop. The rally, Shadow Liberation's speech, slaves fighting to the death, dark creatures being led into the tunnels. Fast forward, images of the ally battle, five Fae dead, fed to the creatures. Ambushed at central command before we made it inside, running through the dark forest, hearing Noreen's voice on the phone, then an explosion. Running up the drive, seeing her house on fire, Donovan Barlowe dead on her threshold.

The final loop has me ending at the window once again, the chair holding my leather duster and sword to my right, my holster still on my back holding my 9mm, loaded with iron bullets. That may have been the only thing that kept me alive the last twelve hours.

Suddenly, the door crashes open. I have my weapon pointed at the door before my eyes even register who it is. I see Brenen holding up his hands, pull my finger off the trigger, and holster the weapon, saying, "Sorry, a little jumpy here."

Brenen nods and pushes the rest of the way into the cabin, dragging a young male in behind him. My approximation would be twenty years old, however, my appraisal of Fae beings is still spotty.

I ask, "Who is that?"

"Meet Kyle's informant. He found me at Noreen's house after the police left. He said he would only talk to you."

The young male looks around the room, eyes wide, and I can feel the tension snap into place in the small cabin. Theon, Brenen, and I surround him as Noreen closes the cabin door softly behind her.

The informant's eyes settle on me. "You're the human who was friends with Kyle?"

I look at him, tilted my head slightly. "Yup." He looks at Brenen and then back at me. I give him one silent nod, cross my arms in front of my chest, and wait for him to continue.

Brenen says to the male, "Tell him your name."

He looks me in the eye. "I'm Logan Barlowe." My gaze flicks to Noreen, who does not seem surprised by the news. I'm sure she knows most of the family descendants in Idyll.

I ask, "So you were looking for me?"

Logan looks down at the ground and then back up at me. "I didn't know who else to go to, but since you knew Kyle..."

I drag him over a chair into the middle of the room and set him down in it. I then pull up a second chair and place it right in front of him, sitting eye to eye.

"What is it that you want to tell me?"

Logan says, "We have to stop my father from getting to a friend of mine. He wants to use her to open the gates." I guess Logan did not know that his father was at the bottom of a ravine as of this morning.

I narrow my eyes at him. "Who is the girl, and how?"

Nervously tapping his foot on the floor, he says, "My father asked me to keep an eye on her, to get to know her, and to feed him information on how her powers were developing. He put me in the same group as her during selections, but we became friends. I never told him a thing about her, Gael Monroe."

At the mention of the name, Brenen's eyes narrow.

Logan then glances around the cabin, adding, "Not that it matters now. Everyone probably knows."

I look at him in confusion and ask, "Knows what?"

"You haven't heard what happened?"

"Why don't you enlighten us?"

Logan looks around the room. "There was a horde attack at Mystfort."

Bremen steps in front of Logan, grasping his shoulders. "What do you mean an attack? When?"

Logan, anxiously looks at Brenen with wide eyes, saying, "Early this morning, 5 a.m., there was a horde of creatures. They overran the village and then Mystfort." Brenen lets go of Logan's shoulders and turns to face the wall, he slams his fist into the post and the walls shake.

I remember from Theon's story that Leona was Theon's mate, Brenen's sister and Sophia's twin, who died in a creature attack a year ago, similar to the attack Logan is describing now.

Logan adds, "But I don't think there were too many casualties. Gael turned them all to ash."

Brenen turns and looks at him. "Explain."

"We came out the front of the castle. Hundreds of dark creatures were swarming the fortress. Two creatures attacked our small group. We had no weapons. Gael said to get back, and then she used her powers. As she moved across the bailey, she burned more and more dark creatures until they started to engulf her. For a moment, we couldn't see her at all. She was completely covered and then...she exploded her power outward in a huge sphere, incinerating the horde on top of her."

I hear Brenen take a deep breath. "She's a true firewielder." He turns toward me. "Sophia was tasked to help her control her powers."

Logan leans forward. "We must protect Gael from my father. He has ways that will force her to help him. He cannot be allowed to take her."

I look grimly at Logan. "Your father is not taking anyone anywhere. He attacked Noreen this morning. It was the last thing he ever did." I look at Noreen over Logan's shoulder and give her a slight nod.

Logan's face freezes for a moment, and then a grim expression took over, settling into acceptance.

Brenen turns into command mode. "Theon, Caleb, Noreen, you three go to the nearest runestone and get to Mystfort. Watch your back. We don't know who we can trust at this point. Once you get there, find the girl and do not let her out of your sight. I will find Sophia. Ethen should be with her. Once we have made sure our team is all in one piece, we can meet to make our plan of attack. Make sure you have your burner phones on you."

The next moment, Brenen disappears into thin air. My jaw drops, and I look at Theon. "Can you do that?"

Theon chuckles, "No, but it would be a pretty neat trick if I could."

Logan says, "When you see me at Mystfort, pretend you don't know me. There are eyes and ears everywhere."

I nod in acknowledgement, then Logan disappears into shadows, suddenly gone. I shake my head and say, "They sure like to show off."

Theon grins and says, "Don't be jealous."

I grab my duster, re-sheath my sword, and then am ready to go. Theon, Noreen, and I jump in the four-by-four, traveling the short distance to the nearest runestone. Moments later, we emerge at Mystfort, a massive island fortress standing tall in the distance. Smoke is billowing from the small streets of the village on the mainland. All is quiet as we silently moved through the street.

We advance toward the castle. The one roadway onto the island is wide open, with no guards to be seen. Destruction is everywhere we turn. Most are dark creatures. Occasionally we see a warrior limping around, checking on a comrade. We walk through the devastation, through the main gates and stop short at the sight of the inner bailey. A massive burnt crater is directly in the center. Ash is still falling from the sky.

Theon says grimly, "This must be where the firewielder made her stand."

We made our way into the keep. Wounded warriors litter the hall, all in some stage of healing.

I look over at Noreen, who is looking directly at a young woman, maybe twenty, long blonde hair covered in ash from her head to her toes. She is sitting at the edge of the hall, her back leaning against a pillar, rocking slowly back and forth.

Noreen motions me over. "That's her."

FORTY-FIVE

Shadow Liberation

t's been three hundred years since I walked through the halls of Scarborough. My feet silently cross the ancient stone motif, the symbol of the house of Hanson.

As I cross the circular room, memories of our failure all those years ago bitterly run through my mind. The furious words, the disappointment that has not been rectified these long years. At that time, we were scattered, only a few pockets of supporters congregating across the globe. Aric Hanson united the movement. Once he located Larkin in Tarrin, the last firewielder, we were overjoyed. The failed attempt almost worked, the vessel burning out before the gates could open.

Now I have been summoned once more, most likely because the news of the new firewielder has reached Aric's ears. He placed me at Mystgate in the hope the next firewielder would emerge. If fates allow this time, the new firewielder will finish the job, started three hundred years ago, and will open the gates once and for all. After all, this firewielder shows the promise of being stronger than Larkin.

Scarborough castle, located on the eastern edge of the Baltic Sea, is downright frigid this time of year. I pull the fur-edged cloak around my shoulders as I ascend upward into the tallest turret, finally emerging in the bright sunlight. Wind whips around me at a furious clip as I approach a small group inside the open-air aviary.

I duck under the low doorway and approach. Ravens, crows, and countless other birds flit around. Aric Abbott Hanson, one of the original Queen's Guards, arguably one of the most gifted of the guards, is bent over tending to his ravens. He has an affinity for animals, a power that allows him to not only to communicate with them but to control them.

A gift that he passed down to me, his son. I was born Kingsley Abbott Hanson. The last name I have forgone since the gates closed and my father sent me to spy on his enemies.

As I stand to my full height, I say, "Father."

Aric releases a raven and rises. The side of his face is visible. A long, ancient scar runs from his temple and disappears down under his collar. I know there are three more scars, the tops of the other two peeking up from the top of his shirt. I know these scars run the length of his shoulder and almost killed him during the Great War for the queen.

He was fighting a dark creature on the edge of the sea. The creature flung him into the salty water before the wounds could heal. That tragedy forever marking him.

He says without looking at me, "There's a new firewielder."

I clear my throat and say, "Yes."

My father's piercing eyes land on me. "Interesting that I heard this from all my other sources but not you."

Silence stretches between us, before I say, "I was compiling the information. I wanted a plan before I brought it to you."

My father lets loose a gruff laugh. "You are the one I put in that station. You are the one who was supposed to alert me the moment another firewielder was found."

My jaw tightens, and I look straight ahead. "Her power was temperamental, still growing in its maturity. I was waiting until her power fully manifested."

Aric grunts, "It has fully manifested now, wouldn't you say?" I gave him a swift nod. He continues, "I sent the tome to find the ancient fire house relic. It seems all that effort was in vain. The relic must have found her."

Aric shakes his head slightly, continuing, "The girl, the firewielder, is now the center of attention. No easy way to get to her now that her tale has spread across the gates."

"I have a plan."

"Hummph," Aric says, "I heard that you've become sloppy, killing Fae out on patrol. I heard about the slaughter of five members of our alliance at a rally last night. There is movement against you. They know who you are now."

My eyes widen in surprise. I can feel the snare closing in on me. I had been able to keep the secret movement quiet for so long. Perhaps I have grown comfortable with dual lifestyles, thinking we are impenetrable. Apparently, my luck has run out.

Aric's arm swiftly pins me against the stone pillar. "What, nothing to say for yourself?"

I shake my head, and he releases me with disgust.

He says, "I'm sending Nyx back to Mystgate with you. She can clean up your mess."

My eyes widen. Nyx has not left my father's side since the gates closed. She is an ancient Fae who can seize your mind with a simple phrase or change in tone of voice. Once she has control of a mind, no one can break free.

You will then do her bidding, willingly or not. Nyx is simply the scariest Fae I have ever met.

FORTY-SIX

Sophia—Aftermath of the Firewielder

The two-hour trip back to Mystfort goes as fast as our horses allow. My mind continually replays the last time I rushed back to a compound in fear of it being taken over by dark creatures. The loss of my sister a year ago at the forefront of my mind.

We drop into Mystvillage, I rein in Pearl, and we get our first bird's eye view of the town. Ryker stops next to me on his stallion. I grip the reins, pushing the panic to the back of my mind. Smoke is billowing from burn piles, the sickly black smoke of burning dark creatures wafting through the air. I see villagers cleaning the streets from rubble, righting benches and repairing damage. I push Pearl forward, trotting down the main street at a fast clip. I approach the nearest shopkeeper, a female with vibrant red hair outside of a coffee shop. I ask, "What happened?"

She turns and pushes a mass of curls away from her face as she looks toward Mystfort, cupping her hand over her eyes, squinting into the morning light. She turns and looks at me saying, "A horde attacked in the wee hours. Every soul was fighting those blasted creatures."

She paused then adds, almost reverently, "Then suddenly from the castle, the illumination from the firewielder appeared, pulsing outward. The light attracted the dark creatures. They were pulled to it like a moth to a flame. They tried to bury her in their darkness, but she turned the horde to ash."

The shopkeeper gives me a wide smile. "A true firewielder has been found."

I raise my eyes to meet hers, asking, "Where is the firewielder now?" She points at the castle.

We move toward the castle grounds. Ryker asks, "You know the firewielder?"

I nod. "Before I left for the Dragonlands, I was teaching her how to control her magic. We discovered her magic was bound. Apparently, her powers have fully manifested now."

Ryker contemplates that. "The last firewielder I have heard about was Queen Morrigan."

Sighing I say, "Yes, there was one other descendant, but he died three hundred years ago."

"At the same time the fissures in the wall started?"

"Yes, we believe the firewielder will have the power to either seal the gates back up or throw them wide open again."

On that grim note, we fall into silence as we continue our way through the village. We cross the main gates and halt our horses when we approach the inner bailey. The earth is scorched, only dirt remaining in a perfect circle, ash still falling from the sky.

Suddenly, on the stairs leading up to the keep, I see Brenen appear out of thin air. We lock our eyes, and then he runs toward me. I dismount Pearl and am immediately engulfed in a giant bear hug. We stay like that for a moment, remembering Leona.

Tears stream down my face, and I pull away slightly. As I wipe the tears from my face, I look into my brother's eyes. I can see shared grief reflected in them. He squeezes my shoulders, and I smile at him.

"I'm so glad to see you."

He says, "Me too." Brenen lets me go and takes one step back to appraise the scorched earth in front of us. "The lessons with Gael went well, I see."

I frown at him. "Something must have broken through Gael's bindings. Before I left for the Dragon Lands, she did not have the power to do this." I gesture to the scorched earth in front of us.

Brenen asks, "How long have you been gone?" His eyes flick toward Ryker, who has given us some space during our reunion. "And who did you bring back with you?"

I sigh and push wayward strands of hair that have escaped my braid out of my eyes. "It's a long story. Brenen, meet Ryker, Draco's dragon commander. Ryker, meet Brenen, my brother." The two males, standing about the same height, appraise each other as they shake hands.

I say, "We need to find Gael and see what happened."

Brenen says, "She is in danger. The faction members want to use her to open the gates. I already sent Noreen, Theon, and Caleb to watch over her. We need to debrief each other on what has transpired while you were away."

I look at him curiously, "Wait, I thought I had the big news. What happened in Idyll?"

Brenen's scans the perimeter and says, "Let's have a meeting. The rest of the team should have arrived already. I will find Ethen and figure out a secure spot."

He rakes his hands through his black hair. "It's been a week."

I nod. "We'll take the horses to the stables and meet you inside."

Ryker and I walk toward the stables, the grounds behind the castle eerily quiet after the pulse of activity at the gates. I open the doors, leading Pearl toward the tack room. We deposit the saddles and bridals and lead our horses to two empty stalls side by side. Using the brush I snagged in the tack room, I start to brush out Pearl's coat.

Breaking the silence, I ask Ryker, "The testing of the bond, is it always like that?"

He looks at his stallion he is brushing. "The beginning part of the ritual can be done various ways." His eyes darken, and he gives me a sizzling look. "Although, I can't think of anything I would have changed."

I blush crimson and ask, "So, it's not always..."

He walks over toward the edge of the stable wall. "Sharing of magic can be intense. How that manifests depends on the two sharing powers. It can be pleasurable." He pauses there for a moment as if reliving our kiss.

As I look up into his eyes, he wraps a wayward strand of hair behind my ear and continues, "It can be adrenaline in a battle. It can be comforting in sadness."

I ask, "So the kiss, after the magic, was because you wanted it? Not because of the bond?"

He tilts my head up before saying, "The kiss was because I have thought of nothing else since you were marked."

My breath catches, and I feel a flush heighten my cheeks.

Ryker pulls back slightly. "However, the timing was purely to piss off your comrades." My jaw slightly drops, and I roll my eyes.

Males and their egos.

At that moment, my phone starts pinging with messages from the group. The task force wants to meet urgently. Directions are given to the conference room in the west wing of the castle. I message back confirming we will be there. We certainly have news to share with the group. Hopefully with our combined efforts, we can form an action plan.

Ryker and I head back toward the keep, through the great hall, looking at the wide array of wounded being cared for by our healers. I can't help but be grateful these warriors have a chance. I wish Leona and I had a firewielder to protect us from the horde.

I gaze around the room, looking for Gael but not seeing her. I hope the rest of the team has tucked her out of sight and out of danger for the time being.

FORTY-SEVEN

Noreen—House of Fire

As I look across the crowded great hall, I see Gael Monroe tucked in a corner, still covered head to toe with ash. I have only met her a few times, my relationship with Kay, her sister, and Gwyneth, her mother, allowing our paths to cross. The last time I saw her was at the Selection Ball. She had looked like a young women excited to see her dreams coming true. Now, she slowly rocked back and forth, shocked eyes not tracking anything in front of her, a shell of her former self.

I glance at Caleb and Theon. "I know Gael's family. She knows who I am. I will try and speak with her first. Hang out and keep an eye on our backs." I get a nod from Caleb and Theon, who take up residence on a bare patch of stone wall near the rear entrance, closest to Gael.

I approach, seeing her friend Ari next to her, with her arm around Gael's fragile-looking shoulders. Logan is leaning against a column. True to my word, I do not acknowledge him in the slightest. Opposite Logan are two other young Fae males who appear to be the same age, strangers to me.

I kneel slowly, until I am eye to eye with Gael. She slowly stops rocking, and her eyes focus on me. Her features are blank. She doesn't acknowledge I am even here. I glance at Ari and say, "Hi Gael, Ari, do you remember me? I work with your mother and sister at the shop in Idyll."

Ari gives me a slow nod of acknowledgement, and I take that as a sign they may accept my help. I ask, "Are you physically OK? Any injuries we need to look at?"

Ari looks at the small group, returning to Gael. "I think we are okay. Gael is in shock." At that, Gael resumes her rocking back and forth.

I say, "Gael, I know you have had a great expenditure of power tonight, that your reserves are depleted. I have with me some of my potions. They may help your body recover faster."

I place my hand on her knee, halting the rocking. Gael's eyes focus on mine for the first time. I pull a bright-yellow vial from my dwindling supply and place it in her palm.

"This will help your body recover." I see her slender fingers wrap around the vial. "Your mind's recovery is up to you."

Gael gives me a slow nod, and opens the stopper, and drains the small vial. I say, "That's good. It should kick in right away."

I glance at Ari, who is looking at Gael in concern, then refocus on Gael. I see color start to return to her lips and cheeks, which are still covered in ash. Her eyes brighten, and the spark of the former person I knew comes back to life. She licks her dry lips.

I ask, "Water?"

I get handed a canteen that I pass to her. She drinks deeply, draining it. Finally satisfied, she hands the canteen back, and I pass it to Logan, who tucks it away. Ari hands Gael a soft cloth, and she wipes her face clean.

I ask, "How are you feeling now? Better?"

She nods and asks, "What are you doing here? I thought you lived in Idyll."

"Yes, but I have heard some disturbing news today that could not wait." I look around our immediate vicinity, and it appears we are alone, although I remember Logan's warning at the cabin.

I say in a low voice that only Gael and Ari could hear, "There was a threat on your life, Gael. It is imperative that we speak in private." Gael's eyes widen in surprise, and Ari's head swivels around.

I back up slightly, continuing in a cheerfully loud voice, "You most definitely need some rest and recovery time. Let's head to your quarters and get you situated." I gently raise Gael to a standing position, and our small group starts to head toward the dormitories. I keep Gael's arm tucked into mine, supporting most of her weight. As we exit the great hall, I see Theon and Caleb tracking our movements and following at a distance.

Once we cross the corridor, the din quiets, and I can hear our footsteps on the stone floor. Gael whispers, "If there's a threat, shouldn't we hide?"

"We are heading toward the dormitories and can use one of the unoccupied rooms."

We reach the end of the hallway. With a flick of my wrist, the door opens, and we walk in, shutting the heavy door behind us. I let out a little sigh of relief. I am seeing shadows around every corner.

The tight space gets even more crowded as Theon and Caleb duck in after us. Eight in a room that was designed to accommodate one.

Gael sits on the edge of the bed, looking up at me in concern. "Tell me what's happening."

I sigh and pull up the lone chair in the room. I sit down and wearily pinch the bridge of my nose. "Well, the shortest version of the story, is that your powers are now out and visible to the world. There are those who would exploit your powers for their own gain." Gael looks at me in confusion, asking, "Why would they want to use my powers?"

I ask Gael, "You know the stories of the ancient firewielders? Well, there were five ancient houses in Faerie, one for each element. Earth, air, fire, water, and time. The ancient firewielders were of the House of Fire. This house was the most powerful and ruled for many years. Their power was sought after and coveted. The Great Queen was one of the last-known survivors of this clan." I try to phrase the next part in a way that does not scare her.

"Most of the firewielders perished over time, the power too much for them to handle. Many burnt out. I don't think that will happen to you, but you must be cautious."

Gael says in a quiet voice, "I understand now, more than I ever did before my power was released."

I go on, "The Great Queen sealed the gates with her fire magic. There are some who believe the same magic the queen used to seal the gates will break them wide open. The last-known firewielder died three hundred years ago in correlation to the fissures in the barrier."

She says, "You think there are people who want to use my powers to open the gate?"

"You would be surprised how many people want that. There is a movement, a group of people who call themselves Shadow Liberation whose sole objective is to open the gates and return to Faerie."

Logan steps forward. "I have a confession to make." He lets out a heavy breath and then turns and looks at Gael. "My father is a member of the Shadow Liberation."

Gael's face pales, and one of the males lets out an explosive curse. He throws Logan against the wall and has him pinned in a moment. Logan does nothing to defend himself.

I jump out of the chair, but Caleb beat me to the pair. He pulls the males apart, saying, "No need for violence. Logan was an informant to my good friend before he died. He came to me after Gael's powers emerged, notifying us of the threat. He is on your side."

The young male yanks himself out of Caleb's grasp and says, "He was sent here to spy for his father. How can we trust him now?"

I look away for a moment and pull a vial from my cloak. I tap my finger on the edge of the vial, contemplating.

I look over at them. "Well, we do have an opportunity to know for sure." I place the vial on the small desk. It glows from within, light blue, casting a shimmer over the wood. "Gael, it's your call."

Her eyes flit between the vial on the desk and Logan, betrayal etched in her eyes. Before she can say a word, Logan picks up the vial and downs the truth serum. I stand up and push the chair forward so Logan can take my place.

I say, "The potion works for two minutes. Anything you ask, he will answer truthfully. Rather, he will answer the truth as he knows it."

Gael looks at Logan. "You were sent here to spy on me?"

Logan's eyes are tortured. He replies through clenched teeth, "Yes."

"What did you tell your father about me?"

"I never told him anything real about you. I made up stuff to keep him satisfied. I told him your powers were weak, that you could not hold a flame beyond minutes at a time. I told him we were friends and that if your powers manifested, I would know."

Gael, with tears in her eyes, asks, "Were you ever really my friend?"

"My father placed me in your selection group, wanted me to get close to you. I tried to stay away, tried not to get involved. Then you started sneaking around, and I knew you would get caught. I started to help you." He paused for a moment. "Yes, we became friends."

I glance at my watch. "That's two minutes."

My phone beeps, and I pull it out. Theon and Caleb's also chime. A team meeting in the west wing. I look at the small group in the room. "We have a team meeting to find a plan forward." I look at Gael. "We will find a way to keep you safe and to ensure that our world is not torn apart by dark creatures." I look at Theon and Caleb. "One of us should stay with Gael to guard her. I can stay, if you both want to go to the meeting. You know what I know. Tell them what we found."

Caleb and Theon take me up on it and leave. The door swinging silently closed behind them.

FORTY-EIGHT

Caleb—Debrief

Theon and I walk toward the west wing of the castle, our boots heavy on the stone floors, any pretense of trying to camouflage our presence unnecessary since the hallways are empty. We arrive at a conference room, a long narrow table, screens mounted on the walls, and a coffee station set up in the corner. I grab a cup of joe, over twenty-four hours without sleep leaving me on fumes.

As my single-serve coffee brews, I look around the room. Brenen, Theon, and I are present, waiting on Sophia and Ethen. My coffee finished, I burn my lips as I gulp the steaming liquid down, not caring in the slightest. If I could get a direct IV, I would.

Ethen arrives, looking harried, his hair disheveled, leathers dirty as if he slept on the ground last night. I suppose that could very well be the case.

Sophia walks through the door, followed by a large male, at least as large as Brenen, hair a golden brown reaching below his ears. He has short stubble and eyes the color of honey. The male has a commanding presence of a general. I am not the only one to take notice. Ethen turns his back on the male and starts a coffee.

Curious.

Brenen says, "Ryker, this is Theon Whitcock, a tracker, and Caleb Moretti a human detective. Theon and Caleb, this is Ryker, the dragon liaison." We shake hands, and I can't help but wonder what he looks like as a dragon.

I say, "Noreen is guarding the firewielder. We will catch her up once we are done."

Sophia and Ryker sit at the table. Theon and I sit on the opposite side. Ethen takes up residence against the wall in the back of the room. Clearly there is something going on between Ethen, Sophia, and Ryker. The hostility is so thick I could cut it with a knife. I sip my coffee and keep an eye on the group, watching their telltale signs.

Brenen sits and gives me a nod. "Let's get started then. I know we all have had a tough twenty-four hours, but we need to debrief each other's teams. It seems a lot has transpired. Caleb, why don't you start?"

I nod. "We started at the explosion site, tracked the movements of the dark creatures through the forest. We came across two faction members and were able to observe them from a distance and then follow them back to Idyll. We followed them to a private residence and then set up surveillance on this residence. We determined that the two members we followed were slaves, owned by Faben Schaeffer, a loyalist to Kingsley Abbott, who is the ringmaster of this circus.

"Last night we followed the slaves to an abandoned part of Idyll. We discovered a glamoured section of town that hid their rallies. We were able to infiltrate the rally and observe the messages. They are growing their ranks, calling themselves Shadow Liberation. They are recruiting Fae to join their cause. They are well organized and well connected.

"Some of the members joined based on their greed for power, promised more power when they get back to Faerie. Although, I do not think that is the most dangerous motive. They convinced their followers that families were torn apart, left for dead on the other side of the barrier. Their cause is to rescue the family members stranded in Faerie and to open the gates. With righteous followers, it is very difficult to convince them to change their minds.

"Then we get to the entertainment portion of the night. They are capturing the dark creatures and bringing them to underground fight clubs, fighting them to the death against slaves. Abbott has the ability to control dark creatures. It was part of his show at the rally."

Brenen leans back in his chair and runs his fingers through his hair.

I continue, "After the rally, we were stopped by five members waiting for us at the exit. We killed them, but not the one who sent them. The one who sent them was a client of Noreen's. She placed a tracker on him and followed him to the rally. He found the tracker, and he sent a kill squad after Theon and me and personally went after Noreen. He is also dead."

Sophia, Ethen, and Ryker look at us in silence, then Sophia whistles, "Wow, you guys have been *bussssy*."

Brenen pushes his chair away from the table and starts to pace back and forth. He looks at our group. "Okay, Sophia, bring us up to date."

She begins, "I was tasked with helping Gael unlock her powers, and I discovered her powers were bound at birth. I spoke with Ian, who was going to help her find a way to safely remove the binding."

Sophia glances at Ethen. "Then Ethen, Kane, and I left for the Dragon Lands. We spoke with Draco. His bonded rider Collin's son, Duncan, was killed six months ago. We believe Duncan was murdered for a relic he had on him at the time of his death. Duncan had acquired the sword of light at an auction, the queen's sword. We believe the faction members killed Duncan and currently have the relic. The dragons have agreed to help us catch the murderers, if we agree to bring Duncan's killer to their feet for judgment."

Sophia lets that little piece of information marinade. I am sure my form of judgment is vastly different than a dragon's.

Sophia continues, "On our way back to Mystfort, we came across a horde of dark creatures. It makes more sense now why they would be hiding the horde away. If Abbott can control them, he may have had a plan for using them."

Ethen spoke up with a snide undertone, "Don't forget to mention why the horde was released."

Sophia looks over at Ethen, and then at Ryker. "There was a relic guarding the horde, a repelling magic that froze us in place. This is how they were managing the horde without anyone knowing about it.

Ryker destroyed the relic, freeing us from the magic, and in turn releasing the horde that attacked Mystfort."

Ryker leans forward, grasping Sophia's wrist. "Well, if I did not destroy the relic, all three of you would have succumbed to its snare." He rhythmically starts sweeping his thumb over her wrist, where I can make out a tattoo. Sophia snatches her hand away as if burned, tucking her hands under the table.

She says, "Thankfully, Gael destroyed the horde, which brings us to our next topic. What is the next threat?"

Brenen sits down and says, "Kyle's informant came forward and told us his father, Donovan Barlowe, asked him to spy on Gael. Donovan, and by association, the Shadow Liberation, believes that Gael can open the gates, because she is a true firewielder."

Brenen looks around the table and says, "This has become far larger than any of us imagined. We need to protect the gate and Gael. I will send a message to Ian to send reinforcements."

Noreen enters the room. She walks purposefully, but I can tell something is off. Her eyes are unfocused, and she stops directly at the far end of the table. "You are too late."

She collapses to the floor, her head banging sharply against the table edge. I reach her first, roll her over, and cradle her head on my lap. I brush the hair from her face as her eyes finally seem to refocus on me. Terror replaces the blankness from before. She looks up at me, eyes wide, horrified.

She twists her hands into my shirt, saying, "We are too late. Nyx is here. She took Gael."

Then all hell breaks loose.

FORTY-NINE

Gael—Forgiveness

look over at Noreen, who stays behind while the other two members of her team leave. My mind is still reeling from Logan's confession, the reach and demand of Shadow Liberation chilling me to my core. I picked at the edge of my comforter, wrapping my mind around the revelations. I remember the dark creatures from the forest, the horde descending upon Mystfort. Those were only the ones that slipped through the cracks. The notion that this group of people wanted to open the gates fully, letting the dark creatures devastate this land, is unthinkable.

I look up and see Logan leaning against the window seal, Ari, Gavin, and Caden congregating near the bathroom door. Having six people in this tight space is getting claustrophobic.

Apparently, Ari thinks so too, saying, "I'm going to go get some food. I'll bring you back a plate, okay?" I gave her a nod, and she wraps me in a tight hug. "We won't let anything happen to you."

She pushes off the bed and heads toward the doorway. Gavin and Caden both volunteer to get food with Ari. They seem to want to get out of the tension-filled room as quickly as possible.

As the door closes, I sigh and lean my back against the wall, curling my feet up and under me. I wrap my arms around my knees and rest my chin. As I replay Logan's confession, I rewind and remember something that Noreen said right before the confession. She mentioned the firewielders as a house and that the Great Queen was the last descendant.

I look up at her and ask, "Noreen, would all firewielders have bindings on their magic until a certain age?" I look at Logan and then back at her saying, "The reason I ask, I found the queen's throne room, and when I touched a relic, my bindings were whipped away, as if some magic held it in place."

Noreen tilts her head slightly. "I don't know much about the firewielders but do recall hearing about magical bindings when the Fae lived in Faerie. The binding could be an inherited protection, an innate part of your essence until you reach maturity. I have heard the relics absorbed the power of each descendant and worked as a medium to control the output to each living member."

At my confused look, she clarifies, "It sounds like, from your story, the relic unlocked your binding. You should speak with the Oracle. She holds the history of Faerie in the palm of her hand. I will work on arranging it."

I turn wide eyes toward her and give her a nod, impressed that she has contact with the Oracle.

Logan shifts his weight, and I raise my eyes toward him. He looks away, almost as if he was worried about what I might say.

I sigh, "Logan, I forgive you." His head swings around as if I surprised him. "Thank you for telling me. Knowing how far this group will go, knowing that you've been fighting against them for so long, means a lot to me. Thank you for not betraying me to your father. I understand why you did what you did."

A slight flush has creeped up Logan's neck, and he shrugs.

Before he can respond, the door flies open on its own accord. A female appears, saying in an icy voice, "You have no idea how far we will go to achieve our objectives."

I register a quick image of long black hair and porcelain skin before my mind goes blank.

FIFTY

Sophia—Visions

stare down at Noreen. There is a moment of silence and then a flurry of activity. Each member of our team has weapons re-holstered and is out the door in seconds. We rush down the corridors, following Theon and Caleb to the room Gael was in. The door gets thrown open. The room is empty. Theon bangs his fist on the doorway in frustration as Ethen pulls open his phone.

I hear a ringing, and Kane's voice on the other side.

Ethen says, "Lock it down. They found the firewielder and took her." There was a muttered response I could not make out, then Ethen says, "Keep me posted." As he slips the phone in his pocket. He turns and asks, "Who the hell is Nyx, and how did she control Noreen?"

Noreen steps forward. "Nyx is an ancient. She has been alive longer than Sybil, my mentor. Her gift is mind control. If she gets within eyesight of you, she can snare your mind. Once she is gone, or once you complete the task she assigned to you, her hold on your mind ends." She raises a shaky hand to the cut on her forehead, as if only now realizing she was bleeding.

Ethen asks, "How the hell do you fight against someone like that?"

Caleb emerges from the bathroom with a wet cloth and presses it against the gash on her forehead.

She says grimly, "You don't."

Noreen stops suddenly in the center of the room. I walk around her and see her features go blank, and her eyes roll back into her head. I catch her this time when she collapses.

Caleb asks, "What's wrong with her this time?"

Theon answers, "I think she is having a vision."

Noreen's eyes snap open, and she sits upright. She looks at Caleb, who is standing directly behind me, her fingers gripping my leathers as if her life depended on it. She says, "I saw Gael, at sunset, destroying the barrier. Dark Creatures swarming from gate, disappearing into the night." Her brow furrows, as if she was trying to remember some detail.

She looks back at me, saying, "Sybil."

I look at her in confusion. "What?"

Her eyes focus on me. "Sybil knew we would need her talismans." She pulls out a small compact and says, almost to herself "Of course she knew. She gave me a way to reach her in our time of need. We all need talismans."

I frown. "Will talismans protect us against Nyx?"

Noreen looks up at the faces staring down at her. "It is our best bet against her. Sybil gave me a way to contact her. She said to contact her in our time of need. Well, I have never had a greater need than right now. We only have until nightfall, which is only a few hours away."

Noreen rises to her feet. "Each talisman must be gifted to each individual person. That means you need to come with me to meet Sybil. Knowing her, she will be expecting us." She walks out to the hallway. "I will contact her now. Her dwelling is close by, close to the gate."

I walk toward the doorway and peer into the corridor. I see Noreen run her fingers over the small compact and flip it open. A mirror is visible, and then a shadowy image of another person appears. They have a short conversation, and then Noreen snaps it closed. She sighs and slips the mirror back into her sheath. Turning toward the room and me in the doorway. She says, "Sybil is waiting for us."

I give her a nod and then hear a noise to my left. Ari, Gavin, and

Caden are returning with trays of food. Ari sees the open doorway and the group inside, and her face turns ashen. The tray falls from her frozen fingers, and she drops to her knees. Tears stream down her face. She knows without words that Gael was taken.

Ethen comes up behind me, seeing the recruits. He grimly looks down at me and says, "We better get to the armory." I give him a nod, and our group follows him from the room, down a long corridor toward the west wing, through the security measures, ending at a large steel safe door, large enough to walk through. Ethen types in the combination, shifts the handle, and the door swings open. Inside lining the walls are every manor of weapon you could think of.

To the right are rows and rows of potions. Noreen heads for the potions, pulls out six yellow vials, and hands them to each of us. "You will need this for the coming hours."

Ethen says, "I will call Ian for reinforcements. Pick whatever you want." He gestures toward the massive vault and turns to walk down the hall to make his phone call.

I turn toward the vault, open the vial, and drink the liquid in one swig. Instantly, the headache that was pulsing behind my eyes eases and I feel as if I had slept for twelve hours. Renewed strength pulses through my veins, and I realize how worn out I was, emotionally and physically.

As I peruse the armory options, I pick up a double-edged sword, double the weight of the one currently on my back. Too heavy. I start to put it down when I feel a presence at my side. I glanced over to see Ryker standing a few inches from me.

I say, "Bet this wasn't what you thought you signed up for."

A slight smile plays at the corner of his mouth. "It's best not to go into these situations with a ridged plan. Too many moving pieces, you will never end up where you think you will at the beginning."

I give him a small smile and say, "Truer words have never been spoken."

I set down the axe, pull armor from the wall, and proceed to strap it over my shoulders. I look at his leathers. "Do you need any armor?" He shakes his head, takes the axe I was looking at, and slices it across his skin. He appears unharmed. "My skin is impenetrable."

I close my jaw and turn away. "That must be useful."

He says, "The same protection my dragon form has, I have in my Fae form. We are still vulnerable in certain areas, the juncture of our joints, where our magic is at its weakest, but you already know that." He smiles. "I don't plan on letting anyone close enough to try."

He reaches down and pulls my hand toward him, gaining my attention once more. He brushes his thumb over the tattoo. A shiver runs down my spine. I pull my wrist back and glare up at him, saying, "Stop doing that."

He says, "It seems I can't help myself." The heat in his eyes has my heart pounding.

Brenen walks up, plucks the double-edged axe I was looking at from my hands, and says, "This is perfect." Brenen effectively breaks the mood, and Ryker pushes off the edge of the wall that he was leaning on to start pulling weapons off the display.

I turned toward Brenen and give him a look, mouthing, "What the hell?"

He looks at me innocently. "What?"

Ryker swaggers across the room. Once he is out of ear shot, Brenen picks up my wrist and says, "Do you know what this means?" I look away for a moment and then meet his eyes. I give him a silent nod. "Are you sure about it?"

I look over at Ryker and say, "No, I'm not sure about much, but I do know that I trust him to protect me."

Ethen walks back into the room, sees Ryker, and heads in the opposite direction with a scowl on his face. He starts to load weapons into an extra sheath hanging from the wall.

Brenen, watching the display, says, "I can't keep up with your love life, Soph."

I let loose a short laugh. "Join the club."

FIFTY-ONE

Noreen—Oracles and Talismans

The forest gets darker the closer we get to the gate. Sybil's dwelling is by the Mystgate. The team is behind me. Silence has fallen on our small group, the direness of our task ahead weighing on our minds. Before we left, Ethen checked in with Ian, who promised he would send resources to Mystfort. However, the fear was, the more people present, the more people Nyx could control. The more people she could ultimately use to her advantage. It was decided that our team, protected by the talismans, would approach the gate and battle Nyx at sundown, the rest of our reinforcements holding back until we gave the all-clear signal.

I see a small clearing up ahead and know we have arrived. The same chill I get every time I approach this place runs up my spine. The Oracle may be the only one who can provide a defense against Nyx, but I know she will exact a cost for each talisman. I prepared the team before leaving, handing them various offerings we could give to her for payment. I warned them that what the oracle demands for payment could be none of what we brought.

She could demand something we may not be willing to part with.

The house was built into a tree as round as a dance floor. The main entrance to the dwelling is a round door nestled under branches that wind up the tree into the canopy. Above the first floor, multiple windows are visible, shining bright lights in the dim forest, a second and third story visible from the ground. A large deck surrounds the entire third level, which I assume is her private residence. I have only ever seen the first floor, which is where she visits with clients.

I look up, noticing the normal birds that filter about, Sybil's treasure trove of feathered friends darting from one branch to another, singing their melodies.

The door swings open, and she emerges, beautiful beyond mortal vision. Even though I expected it, she is still hard to gaze upon. A long white robe that cinches at her waist. Long copper hair winding down her back, free flowing. What makes her so hard to behold are her pure-white eyes that seemed to draw you into their sphere. A goddess of beauty tucked away here in the middle of the forest, only taking callers she is familiar with.

I once asked my mother why Sybil was so private. We don't even know her real name. Sybil or Oracle were general terms for what she can do, not who she is. My mother responded with a question, "If you lived countless lifetimes, wouldn't you want some privacy?"

I hear surprised responses from my team behind me and remember the first time I met Sybil. Her luminous aura shines with wisdom and divine power that can be overwhelming. I bow my head slightly. "Greetings, wise seer, thank you for allowing our audience today."

Next to me, I can see the rest of the group following my lead, Ryker at the end getting nudged into murmuring a greeting. Sybil walks forward, extends her hands wide in greeting, and makes a welcoming gesture.

"Welcome to my home. I am happy to help the daughter of Josephine. I have been expecting you."

"We have brought tokens of our appreciation." I reach down into my satchel, and she stops me with a hand on mine. Electricity runs through my body, and I feel every nerve ending stand at attention. She removes her hand, tucking it away under the folds of her robe.

"No need to show me what you have brought. Leave it by the entry once we are done." She beckons us closer. "Please come inside. I have prepared what you seek."

I glance beside me, and our group walks through the low doorway. As we enter, I look up. The inside of this dwelling is magically enchanted to three times the size that it appears from the outside.

Sybil motions toward the sitting room, chairs surrounding a large hearth. "Please sit. I will bring refreshments." As we settle in, Sybil deposits her customary tray of delectable pastries and tea on a low table.

I grab a powdered treat and motion to the rest of our group. "You're missing out if you don't try these."

I see a few of our group exchange glances, a few brave enough to try the pastries.

I smile to Sybil, "Wonderful, as always."

She beams at me. "My pleasure." I think she secretly has visitors so she has an excuse to eat the treats.

Sybil brings over a small curio box and deposits it on the table. Silence descends on the group, and the weight of what is in the box hung heavily in the air. She says, "Many weeks ago, I foresaw this point in time. I could feel a balance of power shifting, could see the darkness gaining ground. The same darkness that would gladly overrun this world."

She opens the curio box and starts to pull out the items and place them on the table. "I saw the firewielder come into her power, a catalyst to the darkness."

She spreads small circular tokens attached to leather bands on the low table. The tokens, perfect circles, are engraved. The center has three mountains, representing Tarrin, the gate in the center. The outside band of the token is a thin circle band, engraved with runes intersected by triangles forming a sun.

Sybil glances around at the group. "I saw a group of warriors banding together, mixed heritage blending and melding into a perfect vessel to defeat this darkness. These tokens will protect you from the dangers you face, the darkness that wants to overtake this land, if you remain true to your objectives. Follow your heart, and it will guide you to the best path forward."

She stands. "Please rise, and I will present." She begins by approaching Caleb, looking at him directly. "Human." She reaches for Caleb's hand. To his credit, he tries not to jerk his hand away at the electricity he must feel. She places the token in his palm, murmuring over their clasped hands.

She releases him and precedes to me. "Witch." She places a token in my palm, clasps her fingers over mine, murmuring so quietly I could not make out the words. The electricity runs through my body before she releases me.

The Oracle moves systematically on to Sophia, Brenen, Theon, all Fae. She pauses before Ethen and places a token in his hands. She tilts her head to the side. "We all have choices that define us. Choose wisely, and you all will live to see the sun crest the horizon on a new era." She turns from Ethen and ends her presentation with Ryker.

She says, "I did not see you until most recently. I was most pleasantly surprised. The dragon will be a great ally in this war. A word of wisdom, do not fight fate. It compels each of us, willingness only allows the journey to be easier."

She places the token in Ryker's palm and murmured to him. One last token remains on the table, Sybil picks it up and hands it to me, saying, "Noreen, you must give this to Gael when you see her. It was prepared for her in advance. My daughter Phoebe helped me." I wrap my hands around the last talisman. Now, the air feels lighter than when we first arrived.

Collectively, we let out a breath and turn toward Sybil.

I say, "We are deeply grateful for your gifts today. Not to overstep, but I had a vision of the firewielder breaking the gate that is not far from here. I would advise you to vacate the property. I don't want to see you caught in the middle."

Sybil smiles. "I will be gone from this place after you depart. But not for the reasons you think. I have no fear of danger, but I know my role in this battle has come and gone. I am one to see and prophesize, never one to interfere directly. If I act on what I see, it will throw fate out of balance. When I step out of my role, disastrous things tend to happen."

Sybil leads us to the entrance with a flourish. We deposit the offerings at the doorway as requested. As we exit the dwelling, she says from the front steps, "Remember, courage is not the absence of fear but rather the assessment that something else is more important."

She disappears, the door closing with a soft click. The sound of birds chirping vanishes, and the lights go out. The whole area appears to be abandoned.

I look over at the sun low in the sky. "It's time."

FIFTY-TWO

Caleb—Mystgate

As we leave the Oracle's dwelling, I shake myself slightly, clearing my mind for the task ahead. Nothing should surprise me after the week I've had, but that encounter has my skin crawling. I grip the talisman that is around my neck and feel a vibration from the cool metal down my body. Despite lying on my chest, the metal has never warmed my skin, even though it has been around my neck since it was presented to me. Whatever magic is in this talisman, I want it gone as soon as this battle is over.

I look around our group, all faces set in grim lines as we follow Noreen toward the gate. We are all dressed in the same uniform of weapons and artillery provided by Ethen at Mystfort. The sun is low in the sky when we leave the Oracle's dwelling. In the last hundred meters, the temperature has dropped, and clouds cover the sky in an eerie blue glow. The forest looks like a different planet altogether.

I look over at Theon and ask, "What's happening?"

His face is set in grim lines. "Ever since the barrier started to crack and break open, the immediate area surrounding the gate has transformed. The fissures and breaks in the seal have allowed Faerie to bleed into this world." I contemplate what the world would look like covered in this blue glow.

Ethen says, "To seal the gates, the Great Queen used her magic and melded it with the darkness, freezing it in place. That is why the gate is so dark, the bright blueish white of her magic mixed with the darkness."

I nod in understanding, and we continue our journey toward the gate. I try not to be unnerved by the forest, the light making it hard to distinguish the difference between a rock and a tree root. An enemy could creep up on us without us even being aware. I keep my eyes peeled and my itchy finger on the trigger. We emerge into a small clearing, and I get my first glimpse of the gate. True to their words, the eerie blue-black color surrounding us seems to be coming directly from this source.

Standing approximately twenty feet tall, a round circular opening seems to pulse the light outward. As we get closer, I can see it is set up on a platform, blue and black swirls covering the opening, as if the surface of the barrier is liquid metal. The outer edge looks like tree branches welded into place, holding the structure together. I pause with the rest of our group, scanning the clearing, looking for our enemy.

The clearing is empty.

I motion to Theon and Ethen. "We can set up an ambush, surround the clearing—"

I hear a low feminine chuckle from the far end of the clearing. "Now, what's the fun in that?"

A tall, slender female emerges from behind the gate. Abbott emerges directly behind her. Straight black hair down to her hips and porcelain skin makes her look as delicate as a doll. She slowly walks forward, hips swaying, with a slight smile on her red lips.

Nyx says, "This world should never have belonged to the Fae. We need to return to our homeland. Why do you fight it? It is inevitable."

Sophia steps forward. "You have taken from me what was most important. You have taken loved ones from all of us. Lives you threw away like garbage in the street.

"All for what?" Sophia growls, spreading her arms wide. "Death and destruction are all that await you in Faerie. Do not delude yourself into thinking anything different." She points her sword arm directly at Nyx. "If you open that gate, it will mean death for us all, you included."

Nyx sighs, bored, "Your pathetic attempts to stop me are futile. Do you think those talismans will really help you?" She lets loose another low chuckle. "Sophia, you of all people should think outside the box."

She turns toward Abbott. "Let's get on with it. Release the beasts." She gestures with her hands, and Abbot raises his.

I hear a rumbling in the forest.

I look around and see glowing yellow orbs tucked under branches and leaves. The eyes start to move toward the clearing. Hundreds of eyes, waiting, hunting.

Nyx says, "I can't lie to you about your chances..." She looks over our small group and gives a slight smile of anticipation. "You have my sympathies."

Nyx motions toward the gate, and I see the young female firewielder step forward. She approaches the gate and lifts her hands. Bright bluish-white fire pushes into the gates. The blue-black mirror surface starts to ripple. I glance over and see Logan, silently watching, his body motionless, his eyes blank. Clearly Nyx has control of his mind, as she has control of Gael's.

The beasts start to emerge from the forest, one charging directly at us. Mid-jump, feline features of the creature are revealed, elongated head, pointed ears pinned back to his head, covered in shaggy fur. Its razor-sharp claws heading straight for me.

I pull the trigger, and the beast falls at my feet. A second races toward us, and I see Theon sweep his sword up in one long diagonal motion, the beast is sliced in half. I hear Brenen yell, "Sophia, you and Ryker go after Nyx. Everyone else, spread out and tackle the beasts."

Chaos erupts in the clearing, each of us fighting for our lives.

FIFTY-THREE

Sophia—Nyx

give Brenen a nod and feel Ryker at my back. Noreen grasps my hand and places a talisman into my palm, saying, "Put this around Gael's neck."

Then she is gone, battling the next beast to cross the line, a bright-red orb thrown into the beasts followed by a loud explosion. Brenen and the rest of the team spread out, forcing the beasts back into the forest, leaving a path in the middle for Ryker and me to approach the gate. Every few feet, a beast breaks through the line of warriors, only to be struck down by our blades.

Sword in one hand, axe in the other, I glance over at Ryker as he sweeps down a blade, severing the head of another beast. Another attack from the left, and I strike it down with one sweep of my sword.

I look forward and see our objective. Nyx standing to the side, Gael pulsing her power into the gate, turning the smooth surface into liquid metal.

Nyx glances back, sees us, and starts to turn. Before she can respond, I let out a bellow and charge forward, my axe aiming for her neck, my sword to her ankles. She parries out of the way, a delicate touch of feet to the ground, and then she is spinning in my direction, fluidly attacking in such quick movements that I can barely stop them from hitting their intended targets. My amulet glows brightly in the night, and my shield repels all her blows. It starts to absorb her hits and push back at her.

Nyx's eyes narrow, and she starts forward, determined to strike me down. Her attack pushes her directly back with the same force.

I can see out of the corner of my eye that Ethen breaks away from the line we are holding, approaching our small group in the center of the clearing. He turns and stands side by side with Nyx, handing her the Sword of Light.

My eyes widen, and Ethen says, "Sorry, Soph, I really liked you, but you made your choice."

I feel the betrayal to my core, my sixth sense was trying to warn me since I met him. "Why?"

Ethen looks away and then back at me. "I came to Tarrin when Duncan called and told me about the Sword of Light that he happened to score at an auction." He lifts the sword from Nyx's grip, admiring it in the strange blue-white light. "I tried to convince him, turn him to our side, but he refused.

"He was always so stubborn, could not see the true path forward. I had to take it from him. I didn't have a choice."

I set my jaw in a tight line and meet his eyes with a look that shows no mercy. "There is always a choice."

Nyx grabs the sword and starts forward. I study her movements, sure that the sword will cut through the amulet's protections.

Before Nyx makes it down the platform, Ryker appears behind them, sword in hand. As he is about to drop death's final blow, Nyx tilts her head back with a battle scream and faster than I can track sweeps the Sword of Light, cutting him from his shoulder down his body, sinking the blade deep in his belly. My mind freezes in place, as I watch in horror, unable to move.

Ryker's shocked eyes turn and look at me. The blade runs through him easily. His normally impenetrable skin flayed wide open.

I yell, "Ryker!"

As he falls backward, away from Ethen and Nyx, I reach his side and hold pressure on the wound. I see Nyx return her attention to Gael, who stopped her magic when Nyx was not fully concentrated on her.

I drag Ryker over to the edge of the clearing, pulling him behind a boulder. I hold my hand to his chest, blood spilling onto the dirt beneath us. Tears are running down my face, mixed with his blood on my hands.

I look up. My vision doubles.

I look across the clearing and see the team losing ground, the dire wolves pushing forward against the line they formed, which collapses. Our team is overrun by the beasts. I look over at Gael, and the gate's fissures widen and then crumble.

The blue-black mirror surface disintegrates into powder. Dark creatures in every form I could imagine start to creep, fly, and charge out of the gate. I look up into the sky, illuminated by the bright magic below, and see the winged creatures disappearing into the night.

Nyx moves forward and touches the gate, and her hand pushes through to the other side. She turns a triumphant smile toward Ethen and Abbott, who is still controlling the beasts at the edge of the clearing.

She says, "We are done here. Let's take the girl and continue to each of the gates."

I yell through the darkness, "Nooooo!"

Then my vision returns to normal, Gael is starting her magic back up. The dire wolves are still held back by our team. I look down at Ryker and say, "I give you the second mark." Ryker's eyes widen, and he starts to speak. I stop him by saying, "There is no time. Just do it!"

Ryker's eyes meet mine, and he sees the knowledge of our situation.

He slices my wrist and drops my blood onto his open wound at his chest murmuring words into the darkness. I feel the magic well up inside of me and pulse outward. I can feel our combined essences melding into one. I can feel his wound closing. I can feel our power amplified. I look down into his eyes, which have turned into his dragon eyes, pulsing emerald, green, rolling in the power.

He sits up and says, "Let's finish this."

Ryker takes a few steps back into the forest, transforms into his dragon, sweeps me up onto his back, and lets out a magnificent roar that shakes the clearing. He pumps the massive wings behind me, and then we are airborne. One extensive line of fire, and the dire wolves are reduced to ash.

He turns his focus onto Nyx and lets out a long plume of fire. She dodges out of the way. I can hear Ryker in my head, as clearly as if he were speaking normally to me. "Jump down and give Gael the talisman."

Before I can comprehend the fact that he spoke to me telepathically, he dumps me unceremoniously onto the ground. I tuck and roll into a half kneel, focusing my full attention on Gael, then I am in motion. Dodging left, right, dire wolves seemingly only targeting me now. I feel fire at my back and can hear the squeals and smell the burnt flesh of the beasts.

One hundred feet, fifty feet, then I tackle Gael to the ground and forcefully push the talisman around her neck. I am holding her down, until she stops moving. Her eyes blink open, as if coming awake from a trance.

She says, "Sophia?"

I let out a breath and release her. "It's good to see you again."

I hear a loud yell in dismay from the forest, look up and see Nyx through the ring of fire that has protected Gael and me from her, Ethen, and Abbott's wrath. Ryker, attracted to the noise, swivels his massive head and lets out a roar, followed by a line of fire directly at her. I see Nyx raise her hands defensively, and then in moments she is turned to ash. As she disintegrates, I mutter, "Good riddance."

Then, out of the corner of my eye I see Abbott and Ethen. They both mount dire wolves and disappear into the forest.

My eyes return to Gael and follow her gaze to the gate, which has broken wide open. Beasts of every imaginable size, shape and breed flow through the opening, as if they were waiting on the other side. Gael, tears streaming down her face, says, "I'm so sorry."

I scramble over to her, pick up her hand, and say, "You are the only one who can close it back up. This is your time. This is your fated moment."

Her eyes narrow through the tears. She sets her jaw and gives me a solid nod. She stands up, dusting herself off.

I can see Gael pull her power around her, encompassing her in a ball of bluish-white light. Ryker opens a line in the fire, and she approaches the gate, beasts running on either side of her, as if she were a rock in a river.

Gael places her hands directly on the gate, and I can see the very center of the gate melding together into one solid piece. It starts to expand like ice crystals forming, encompassing the gate as it moved toward the edges.

Gael's shoulders start to sag. She looks over her shoulder, eyes a brilliant blueish white, saying, "I don't think I can finish it by myself."

I push forward, touch her shoulder, and pulse my magic into her, combining our strength, amplifying the seal. I can feel Ryker's essence, my essence, and Gael's all forming one unified force. With a great explosion of power, Gael pushes into the gate, and it seals. The final momentum propels Gael backward, sending all three of us flying.

I blink my eyes open, my head lying in the dirt, ears ringing. In front of me, I see a burning trail of fire. Smoke billows in the distance. I feel hot breath on my side and look up to see Ryker in his dragon form. He transforms in front of me, cradling my head in his lap, running his hands through my hair, asking, "Are you alright?"

I look up into his blazing green eyes, and nod, "I think so."

I swing my gaze around the clearing. The gate is sealed, no fissures visible. The blue-black light is gone, and I look up to see stars in the sky.

Suddenly, I raise my head. "Where is Gael?"

Ryker says, "She's right over there. Logan is helping her."

I swing my eyes over to the side of the clearing and see Logan brushing the hair away from her face and murmuring to her softly. I turn toward the rest of the clearing. Brenen and I make eye contact, and I place my hand to my heart, mouthing, "I love you." I turn and see Caleb, Noreen, and Theon. Thank the heavens, we all made it out alive.

I turn toward Ryker, bury my head in his chest, and let out the sobs that accompanied the shaking of my hands.

I stay like that for what seems like eternity.

FIFTY-FOUR

Gael—Firewielder Next Steps

wipe the tears from my face and raise my face from Logan's shoulder.
As my eyes open, I look over his shoulder and see a pile of ash,
something shining in the darkness. I stand, and Logan releases me. I
move toward the ash, Logan saying, "I think that's what's left of Nyx."

I crouch down and scoop up a handful of ash, letting it trickle
through my fingers on the breeze. I say, "She got what she deserved."

I reach down and pick up the Sword of Light. It is luminescent in the
night. This relic may be one of the few remaining items left from the
original firewielders. I intend to keep it in the family, so to speak. I tuck
the hilt into my waistband, thinking I need Sophia's contact to get me
a proper back sheath.

I look out across the clearing and say to Logan, "I feel deep in my
bones that this is only the beginning. The Shadow Liberation will not
stop. If there are more firewielders out there, I need to find them. We
need to come together, fight together." I look up into Logan's handsome face, smeared with soot and blood.

He nods grimly. "I will help you no matter what."

I reach down and grasp his hand, looking into his eyes. I run his
palm against the Sword of light's sharp blade. I ran my own palm

against the other edge, and we mix our blood together in ancient custom, sealing our promise.

Suddenly from the forest, I hear a rustling, I pull my magic, fire pooling into my palms. Orian jumps out of the forest floor, tackling me to the ground. I laugh as he licks my face. His whole-body quivers in happiness that I am alive.

As I wrap my arms around his neck, my heart picks up a beat, and I know I will live to fight another day.

FIFTY-FIVE

Kingsley Abbott Hanson

Tree branches tear at my skin as we flee the forest. I can still hear the dragon's roar rolling through my mind. Nyx burned to ash, the firewielder back in the hands of the enemy. My face curdles. Father will not be happy about losing the firewielder or Nyx, but he will be pleased if we achieved our objective.

My mind focuses on the gate, and I smile in triumph. Dark creatures are spilling out into this world, but that is not an issue for me, as I can control any beast I come across. The gate is open, which means we can go back to Faerie. My smile widens, and I chuckle into the night. Kara and I will finally be reunited. My family will be whole again.

Suddenly, the dire wolf screeches to a halt. Ethen Graham's beast stops next to us. The creatures' wariness means danger is close. Did they come after us? Shouldn't all those dark creatures keep them busy? I swing my head around and then feel the hot breath on my neck. I look up into the sky and see the dragon flapping his long wings over me.

His roar shakes the ground, and he plucks me off the wolf and grips me with my shirt. I glance over and see Ethen gripped in the rear legs. With a few flaps of the dragon's mighty wings, we soar over the hills and mountains of this land. The terrain becomes rockier, sheer cliffs dropping hundreds of feet. We emerge into a long valley, a massive castle looming ahead.

Roars vibrate the valley as I see more and more dragons swooping around us, nipping at our heels. I am dumped into the inner bailey of the castle at the feet of a massive black dragon. Suddenly, the dragon transforms before my eyes, and I am looking at a massive black-haired male with death written on his face.

He kneels, appraising me silently, then turns to stare at Ethen with disgust. He gives Ethen a swift kick in the gut. "You are the ones who stole the Sword of Light."

My eyes wide, I say, "Why would the dragons care if Ethen stole the sword?"

I realize my error the moment I speak. The dragon's lip curls into a snarl. "You will find out soon enough."

He stands and kicks me with a massive boot to the skull. Blackness engulfs me.

FIFTY-SIX

Aric Abbott Hansen

News from Tarrin has reached my ears. It is not good. Reports indicate the gate was briefly opened and then resealed. The council is currently celebrating the firewielder for her heroic acts.

I throw my crystal glass into the fire and scream at the flames.

This will be the last victory of the supporters. They must not be allowed to keep up this façade. The simple truth is that we do not belong in this realm. We need to return to Faerie. The gates must be destroyed.

As I stare into the flames, I vow to finish what we started three hundred years ago. Despite my son's shortcoming, he was the only blood I had left. I will avenge my son's death. I will find the other firewielders in this world.

I have heard rumors that I will follow up on personally. I will be the one coming after them, and there will be no escape.

If you want something done right, sometimes you must do it yourself.

www.ingramcontent.com/pod-product-compliance
Lightning Source LLC
Chambersburg PA
CBHW010513100726
47903CB00009B/2725